"Full of beauty, and hope, and reminders that it's never too late to roll up our sleeves and rise above the mistakes we made. I cheered, I cried, I swooned while reading about Blake and Kat, and their journeys to finding love, to finding themselves, and to becoming the sisters they were always meant to be. Take this book on vacation with you, and let its heart and humor sweep you off your feet!"

—Ali Hazelwood, *New York Times* bestselling author of
The Love Hypothesis

"A unique and fun twist on the enemies-to-lovers trope, *The Beach Trap* features two half sisters who hate each other, but are thrown together one fateful summer to save their family's beach house. It's *The Parent Trap* meets *Flip or Flop* (with not one, but two hot handymen). In other words—the ultimate vacation read."

—Colleen Oakley, *USA Today* bestselling author of
The Invisible Husband of Frick Island

"*The Beach Trap* is both a celebration of sisterhood and an unflinching examination of how where we come from shapes who we become. . . . With an HGTV-worthy plot, heaps of family drama, and a side of romance, *The Beach Trap* hits the nail on the head when it comes to the perfect summer read. Don't forget to pack this one in your beach bag!"

—Sarah Grunder Ruiz, author of *Love, Lists, and Fancy Ships*

"From the deft manner in which the authors shift the narrative between their two protagonists to the dual romances that unfold with just the right dash of snarky wit and sexy sizzle, readers will find *The Beach Trap* to be an absolute delight."

—*Booklist*

"A juicy beach read!"

—Motherly

"Ali Brady . . . hit the ball out of the park with their debut—the story is just so well-done. The writing is vivid, and I felt like I was transported to the beach or living in the beach house. *The Beach Trap* is a sweet and uplifting story that had me cheering for Kat and Blake to resolve their differences and come to terms with their family's sordid past. It will be the perfect book to take to the pool or the beach this summer."

—The Buzz Magazines

"If you're a fool for HGTV and sibling rivalry novels, toss *The Beach Trap* into your bag."

—*The Augusta Chronicle*

THE

Comeback
SUMMER

Ali Brady

Berkley
New York

BERKLEY
An imprint of Penguin Random House LLC
penguinrandomhouse.com

Copyright © 2023 by Alison Hammer and Bradeigh Godfrey
Readers Guide copyright © 2023 by Alison Hammer and Bradeigh Godfrey
Excerpt from *Camp People* by Ali Brady copyright © 2023
by Alison Hammer and Bradeigh Godfrey

Library of Congress Cataloging-in-Publication Data

Names: Brady, Ali, author.
Title: The comeback summer / Ali Brady.
Description: First Edition. | New York: Berkley, 2023.
Identifiers: LCCN 2022054124 (print) | LCCN 2022054125 (ebook) |
ISBN 9780593440179 (trade paperback) | ISBN 9780593440186 (ebook)
Classification: LCC PS3602.R342875 C66 2023 (print) |
LCC PS3602.R342875 (ebook) | DDC 813/.6—dc23
LC record available at https://lccn.loc.gov/2022054124
LC ebook record available at https://lccn.loc.gov/2022054125

First Edition: May 2023

Printed in the United States of America
1st Printing

Book design by Ashley Tucker

To our sisters, Elizabeth and Ellie

We can choose courage, or we can choose comfort,
but we can't have both. Not at the same time.

—BRENÉ BROWN

THE

Comeback
SUMMER

One

LIBBY

I WAS TWO YEARS OLD WHEN MY SISTER, HANNAH, WAS BORN, so in theory I shouldn't remember that day, but I do. Or maybe I've just been told the story so many times that it's cemented itself in my memory. Whatever the reason, I can still see it clearly in my mind:

Walking down the long hall at the hospital, my black patent-leather Mary Janes clicking on the linoleum and my sweaty hand holding tightly to my grandmother's. GiGi led me into the room, where my mom sat on the bed holding a little bundle in her arms. My dad stood next to her, a proud smile on his face as he gazed at his new daughter.

And it hit me: this small person had just replaced me.

But then GiGi helped me hold the baby, and something swelled inside me, warm and bright, as I stared down at her little red face and big brown eyes. My dad said, *What do you think of your new sister?*

And I smiled and said, *I'm gonna take such good care of her.*

Not that I've been doing such a good job of it lately. In fact, I've been struggling to manage all my responsibilities. Take this morning: not only did I sleep through both of my alarms and wake up to find a present on the floor from Mr. Darcy, my cat, but thanks to the lead foot of the 146 bus driver, there's a coffee stain the size of Lake Michigan on my shirt.

Not a good look for the dreaded "we need to talk" video call that I'm supposed to be leading in less than fifteen minutes with Mr. Rooney, CEO of a multimillion-dollar underwear company and one of our last remaining clients.

I wonder what GiGi would do—not that she'd ever be so clumsy as to spill. Although, knowing our grandmother, she probably kept an entire spare wardrobe at the office, "just in case."

The woman was prepared for everything, and I'd give anything to be able to call and ask her for advice. Not about my unfortunate coffee mishap, but about how to save the business she built from the ground up more than fifty years ago.

The Freedman Group was our grandmother's pride and joy. As the first woman to own a PR firm in Chicago, Ruth Freedman didn't just break the glass ceiling—she shattered it, becoming "one of the most in-demand public relations experts in the country," according to the *Chicago Tribune*. But in the last three years since she died suddenly of an aneurism and left the business to my little sister, Hannah, and me, things have gone downhill. Fast.

Which is why we can't lose the UnderRooney business. I glance down at my watch—a vintage Rolex GiGi left me—and I can practically hear her saying, *More is lost from indecision than making the wrong decision, bubeleh.*

Oh, screw it.

I take a quick detour into Bloomingdale's and grab the first scarf I see. The bright floral design is totally not me, but maybe Not Me will have better luck than I'm having today.

My palms and pits are sweaty with stress by the time I rush back outside. The sun is shining, there isn't a single cloud in the clear blue sky, and only a handful of tourists are milling about on Michigan Avenue. It's one of those late-spring days that hold the promise of summer just a few weeks away, which would make me happy if there wasn't doom and gloom waiting for me upstairs.

I push through the revolving doors to our building and hurry over to the elevator bank as my phone dings with an alert: our ten thirty meeting is starting.

I'm officially late—at least Hannah will be upstairs already. My little sister wakes up every day at six o'clock on the dot (with only one alarm) so she can run for an hour before coming into the office. She says it helps her handle her nervous energy—which, I've heard, is a benefit of exercise. If only I was the kind of person who enjoyed breaking a sweat. Sweets are more my thing.

Just before the elevator doors close, a hand slips through the crack, forcing them back open. I glance down at my watch and curse—it's 10:31.

When I look back up, I gasp.

"It's you," I accidentally say as Hot Office Guy steps inside. I've admired him from a distance since the first time we crossed paths in the lobby two months ago. And now he's here, like a gift from the universe, looking like a snack in dark jeans and a fitted blazer. His brown hair is mussed; I wonder if he overslept this morning, too.

"It's you," he says back to me. His voice sounds even sexier than I imagined it in all the conversations we've had in my head. He steps closer, and I can smell wintergreen on his breath.

Hot Office Guy's blue-gray eyes drop down and I try to suck in my stomach. His lips quirk in a half smile as he picks up the tail of my new scarf. I hold my breath as he gives it a yank, pulling me toward him. I brace myself, hands on his broad chest, then slowly tilt my head up.

My heartbeat quickens as his lips find mine. They're full and firm, and he tastes like coffee and vanilla—the real kind, not the sugar-free stuff I drink.

His hands are on the small of my back, pulling me closer as he deepens the kiss. I relish the sensation of his skin, rough with the stubble of a few days' growth, and my mind wanders to how it would feel against other parts of my body . . .

The elevator dings.

"Is this your floor?" he asks, and I look up.

Hot Office Guy is leaning against the other side of the elevator, looking up from his phone with mild annoyance.

"Yeah, sorry," I say, hoping my cheeks don't look as red as they feel.

As I rush out, I scold my overactive imagination. This is what I get for staying up late last night to finish the latest CLo book. Alas, my life is not a romance novel, and I must accept that I'm not meet-cute material. I was born to play the role of the chubby, clever sidekick in someone else's love story—and I'm damn good at it.

"LOOK WHO'S LATE," Scott, our office manager, calls out in a singsong voice. "Your baby sister had to start the call without you."

I shoot him a dirty look as I hurry down the hall to the office Hannah and I share. Scott was the last hire GiGi made before she passed away, and we haven't had the heart to fire him—even though he spends most of the workday shopping online and scrolling social media. That's what you get for hiring a person whose claim to fame is going viral in a YouTube video of himself as a six-year-old.

I'm responsible for at least a dozen of the video's seventeen million views—I can't get enough of tiny Scott standing in a department store dressing room, arms crossed, declaring his mother's outfits either "great!" or "not great!" The video earned him the nickname Great Scott, which we ironically use to tease him, and which he unironically seems to enjoy.

"Bee-tee-dubs—bold move with the scarf. We like," he calls after me, reminding me of one reason we keep him around and, I imagine, the reason GiGi hired him. The man knows how to turn on the charm, and the few clients we have left love him.

Hannah's sitting at her desk, her back stiff with tension. She glances at me briefly; her face is pale and her eyes wide with barely concealed panic.

"Is there anything we can do to change your mind?" she asks Mr. Rooney, focusing on her computer screen.

I catch the tiniest wobble in her voice and feel a rush of guilt for being late. Hannah prefers to stay behind the scenes, while I handle most conversations with our clients. She's going to be an emotional wreck after this, and it's my fault. I shouldn't have left her to face this alone.

"Unfortunately, there's not," Mr. Rooney says. "But I wish you and your sister the best of luck."

My stomach drops twenty-one floors to the Chicago streets, where I'm afraid we might end up, out on our asses.

"Thank you," Hannah says to Mr. Rooney, her voice deceptively strong. She ends the call and slumps forward, head in her hands. "It's over, Libs," she says. "I'm so sorry, I tried—"

"It's not your fault," I say, rushing over to her.

"I just froze," Hannah says, and I curse myself for every detail and decision that kept me from getting here in time to help.

"What else did he say?" I ask, wondering if she reminded him that it was us—Hannah and me, not GiGi—who helped guide UnderRooneys through a nasty public scandal about their factory conditions a few years back.

"You heard most of it. He apologized, said it wasn't personal."

I scoff—it's never personal for them. Most of our former clients are old men, half of whom don't trust their business to two "little girls"—their words, not ours. The other half have retired and been replaced by slightly younger old men who have no sense of loyalty to the firm that helped make their brands household names.

The one thing all our ex-clients seem to have in common is that they're looking for a change. Which is ironic, given how much we've been trying to keep things the same. But we just don't have GiGi's magic, and I hate knowing that everything she worked for might end with us.

So much for *l'dor v'dor*—one of our grandmother's favorite Hebrew sayings. From generation to generation. More like from gold to dust.

"Is it as bad as I think it is?" I ask my sister.

While I bring my creativity and imagination to the table, Hannah is the analytical, business-minded one—she'll know the financial impact of this loss. Knowing her, she probably ran the numbers last night. Hannah always prepares for the worst-case scenarios.

"It's not good," she says, rubbing her temples with her fingertips; one of her headaches must be coming on, and I make a mental note to pick up some Advil for her. "I don't know how to keep us in the black without UnderRooneys."

A flash of panic hits me, and for once, I can't find the words to make things better. Hannah looks up at me with her big brown eyes and asks, "What are we going to do?"

The question takes me back two decades, when she was seven and I was nine. We were sitting on our bedroom floor, both shaken by the news that our parents were getting a divorce. Hannah looked so small in her nightgown, her knees curled into her chest, her eyes red from crying. Even though I was shocked and scared, too, I summoned a smile and said what she needed to hear: that everything would be okay.

It was true then, and it's true now.

"We're Ruth Freedman's granddaughters," I remind her, back in big-sister mode. "Nothing can stop us."

Hannah exhales in relief, and I wish there was someone to reassure *me*. But there isn't. There hasn't been since I was nine years old. So, I sit at my desk and turn away from my sister, hoping to hide the panic that's racing through my veins.

Two

HANNAH

MY DIGITAL CLOCK READS 6:03 A.M. AS I DRESS IN THE SOFT morning light of my bedroom. After the night I had, with one stress dream after another—my teeth fell out; I couldn't find my keys; I ended up in my high school English class buck naked—I need to run. Desperately.

My brain is often a mess of anxious thoughts, like a hundred hyperactive monkeys chattering away, and even more so after our bad news yesterday. Hopefully my morning ritual will quiet them down.

I open my sock drawer, then freeze. It looks like a raccoon has rifled through it, and my compression socks are missing—the ones I special ordered because they improve circulation and help prevent calf cramping.

Libby.

My jaw clenched in frustration, I head across the hall to my sister's bedroom and open the door an inch, peering into the darkness. A Libby-shaped lump is buried under a mountain of blankets on the bed, various tchotchkes crowding the nightstand and dresser. On the floor near the foot of her bed are my socks.

Unfortunately, my sister's demon cat is perched right on top of them, his yellow eyes glinting. Libby named him Mr. Darcy because he's "aloof and proud with a heart of gold." More like vicious and cunning with a heart of malice, if you ask me. And whenever Libby takes my things, her cat guards them fiercely, for no reason other than spite.

I tiptoe into the room, careful not to wake my sister—she needs her sleep to cope with the inevitable stress we'll face today—and creep toward the dark gray cat, reaching carefully toward my socks. We lock eyes, staring at each other like two cowboys in a showdown duel. I don't even dare breathe.

Lightning fast, he swipes out a paw, and I yelp, pulling back in pain.

"Damn you to hell," I whisper.

He hisses.

In her bed, my sister stirs. "What're you doing?"

"Getting my socks, thief," I say. "And your devil cat just scratched me to the bone."

"C'mere, Mr. Darcy," she says, patting her bed. The cat jumps up and curls next to her, gazing at me with a smug expression.

Wincing at the pain in my hand, I straighten up. "Stop stealing my running socks. It's not my fault you haven't done your laundry in three weeks."

Her muffled voice comes from under her covers: "My feet were cold last night."

"Because you put the AC down to sixty-two!" It's true; I woke up shivering in bed.

"I sleep better in cool temperatures."

"Says the woman with six blankets piled on her," I mutter under my breath. "Don't you care about reducing our carbon footprint?"

Libby responds by giving an exaggerated fake snore, a not-so-subtle hint that she wants me to leave.

I roll my eyes and head out, then pause at the door, remembering Libby's devastated expression yesterday when she realized that UnderRooneys had dropped us. Like it was *her* failure, even though it was out of our control. She was a ball of worry after that, but she kept a smile on her face. So *I* wouldn't be worried.

My big sister. She carries so much weight on her shoulders.

"I'll be back in an hour with a sugar-free vanilla latte and a muffin," I say in a quiet voice.

There's a pause. Then, from under the covers: "You're the best." Another pause. "And I'll borrow your regular socks next time."

I smile as I close the door behind me. Yes, she can drive me insane, but I wouldn't want to live with anyone but my sister—and I wouldn't want to run a business with anyone else, either.

I RUN EAST down shaded streets lined with redbrick homes and apartment buildings, appreciating the beauty of our neighborhood. Lakeview is within walking distance of the Lincoln Park Zoo, Wrigley Field, delicious restaurants—and just a short bus ride from our office.

My hair is piled in a fat bun (no ponytails while running; too easy for a murderer to grab) and I'm wearing my bone-conduction headphones so I can listen to a podcast while also hearing what's going on around me (don't want to get flattened by a bus or kidnapped by human traffickers).

Right now, the hosts of my favorite podcast, *Murder on the Mind*, are telling the story of Lori Hacking, a Utah woman whose husband lied about being in med school, then killed her when she discovered the truth. They're getting to the good part, describing the bloodstained knife that Mark Hacking used to cut up their mattress to hide evidence.

Libby thinks my true crime obsession is the cause of my neurotic tendencies. But I like to remind her that correlation is not causation, and I actually feel calmer when I listen to these podcasts. She's tried to get me to read romance like she does, but the endings ruin it for me every time. Too perfect, tied up in a neat little bow.

Real life isn't like that; as children of divorce, we know that all too well. Libby says that's the point: romance novels are comfort reads. No matter how bad things get, there's a guaranteed happy ending. But I like true crime because it *doesn't* always tie up neatly. It's gritty, complicated, and most of all, real.

The street ends and there she is, Lake Michigan, turquoise water stretching as far as the eye can see. I can't help smiling at the beauty. Summer in Chicago is our collective reward for surviving another freezing winter; everyone bursts out of hibernation to fill the beaches, cheer at baseball games, go to street festivals and farmers' markets.

Turning south, I head toward the skyscrapers of downtown. When I catch sight of our office building, all my worries rush back: *How will we pay Scott? How will we pay ourselves? What if we end up homeless and living on the streets, mugged and beaten and left for dead?*

I turn the volume up on my podcast and quicken my pace, until all I'm thinking about is the burning in my lungs and the murder in my ears.

BY THE TIME I get home, I'm sweaty but more relaxed. I walk in to see Libby, sitting bleary-eyed at the kitchen table, her hair a messy tangle. I hand her the iced latte and muffin, as promised.

"Thank you, my sweet sister," she says, and takes a sip.

After that, I take my medication, giving silent thanks to the chemists and pharmaceutical scientists who created the small white tablet that keeps a smile on my face (most days, anyway). Without it—and the coping skills I learned from a couple of years in therapy—I'd probably be curled in a fetal position after the Great UnderRooney Debacle.

Then I sit at the table and wait for Libby to be ready to talk. Caffeine and sugar are to my sister what running and murder are to me.

My eyes drift to the bookshelf, filled with Libby's romance novels interspersed with pictures of our family. There's one of Dad and his girlfriend on his deep-sea fishing boat down in Key West; another of Mom and her husband, George, in front of their cozy cottage on Martha's Vineyard.

Our parents have been living their own lives for so long that they sometimes feel more like distant relatives. Dad left when we were still in single digits to follow his dreams of Florida sunshine, and Mom took off after I graduated from high school. They're not bad people, just a tad self-centered and flighty. Our grandmother was the constant in our lives, the giver of advice, the purveyor of wisdom, the mentor and guide we always turned to.

"I love that picture," Libby says, pointing to one of us with GiGi at the entry to the office, next to the big gold letters that say THE FREEDMAN GROUP. "Remember how she'd always say, 'This will all be yours when you're older, if you want it'?"

"Every single time we visited," I say, nodding.

We must be around twelve and fourteen in the picture, both of us at that awkward braces-and-pimples stage. GiGi looks glamorous, as usual, dressed in slim-cut slacks and a fitted jacket, her gray hair in her signature sleek bob.

My eyes prick with tears. "I miss her so much."

"Same," Libby says, sighing.

The office was busy and bustling back then, filled with professional men and women doing important work. I was always awestruck and tongue-tied when we visited, hanging back while my sister talked to everyone; even as a teenager, she carried herself like she already belonged there.

A wave of sadness comes over me thinking about how different the office is now. We haven't had the funds to renovate it, so it still looks like it's stuck in the early 2000s. We've had to let every employee go except for Scott. And now we've lost almost every client.

GiGi's legacy deserves so much better.

"What are we going to do?" I say, turning to my sister, needing her reassurance. If Libby doesn't know, we're sunk.

"I have some ideas," she says.

I exhale in relief and reach for a notebook. "Great, I'll start a list."

She shakes her head. "Let's get ready and head to the office for a brainstorming session." Her eyes sparkle as she adds, "You can organize it all on the big whiteboard."

And just like that, I know it'll be okay. Our strengths—Libby's creative energy, my analytical mind—balance and complement each other. As long as we're working together, nothing truly awful will happen. This is just a bump in the road. A chance to regroup and rebuild.

You girls are unstoppable, GiGi used to say. And I believe her. I believe in us.

Three

LIBBY

HANNAH LEFT FOR THE OFFICE AN HOUR AGO, BUT I'VE BEEN piddling, mostly staring at the blank page in my notebook and feeling guilty. Sometimes, I wish I was Catholic so I could confess my sins weekly and get on with it. Instead, I have to wait until Yom Kippur to have my karmic slate wiped clean.

I know being late yesterday isn't the biggest offense—it's a lot less awful than murder or infidelity—but I dropped the ball. It was my job to lead that call with Mr. Rooney, and I left Hannah to carry the burden. Falling short on both my business-partner and big-sister responsibilities.

The year our parents got divorced, GiGi took Hannah and me to see a child therapist whose office was next door to an Italian restaurant. I don't remember much about the sessions, but I do remember sitting with GiGi during Hannah's appointment, eating my pasta con broccoli (with no broccoli) while GiGi sipped her red wine. And I clearly remember GiGi saying: *You're the one constant in your sister's life now, bubeleh. She's*

counting on you to be strong and brave and set a good example.
I promised GiGi I would.

And I'm going to do my damnedest to keep that promise.

TWO HOURS LATER, I'm on my third cup of coffee at the office, staring at the still-blank page in my notebook. Usually, I thrive under the pressure of a deadline and a good, juicy problem to solve—but there isn't this much at stake when it's a client's problem.

I open my desk drawer and pull out the small leather-bound journal GiGi always carried with her. Its pages are mostly filled with tidbits her clients dropped about their personal lives, fodder for future conversations. She'd remember to ask if Harvey's grandson had gotten into his dream college, if Betty's daughter found the perfect wedding dress, or if Little LuLu was ready for her bat mitzvah.

Maybe that's where we went wrong. I should've asked Mr. Rooney about his latest colonoscopy results.

Even though I know it's futile, I flip through the pages, hoping a nugget of her brilliance will jump out at me. Over the last five decades, GiGi worked for a portfolio of giants—but it was the Horwitz Hotel chain that put her on the map. She suggested the Jewish-owned hotel chain support the Black community after a rival hotel was in the news when an employee called security, assuming a registered guest was trespassing simply because he was Black.

One of the Freedman Group's founding principles was using public relations to do good in the world. Our grandmother famously turned down a three-million-dollar project for a brand with a reputation for being homophobic. She made an effort to use small-business vendors; she even funded a scholarship for women of color going into public relations.

This business carries more than her name. It's got her heart. Her *neshama*. A lump forms in my throat and I blink away the tears as I tuck the notebook back in the drawer. Hannah is already in the conference room, waiting for me.

Which means I need a list of big ideas, stat.

BY TWO O'CLOCK, the glass walls are covered with colorful Post-it notes, listing every business we have even the slightest connection to. It's like Jewish Geography meets Six Degrees of Separation.

We have no shame in reaching out to the *bubbe* of someone Hannah went to college with who happens to be next-door neighbors with the guy who opened a kosher BBQ place on Broadway, or calling a friend who once hooked up with a guy whose family owns a chain of small grocery stores. Nothing and no one is off-limits.

I spin in my chair, admiring our handiwork. There have to be at least three dozen businesses listed. "I feel better already," I tell my sister.

Hannah sighs, and my confidence crumbles.

"Most of these are small businesses—it would take at least twenty of them to cover the Rooneys' annual scope," she says. "And based on the numbers I crunched last night, we've got enough in the bank to last us three months. Tops."

My stomach sinks. These tiny accounts aren't going to help—we need something big.

"What if we go after Hanes?" I suggest, thinking of Under-Rooneys' biggest competitors. "Or Fruit of the Loom?"

"It's a great idea," Hannah says, though I can sense the "but" coming, "but the contract has a noncompete clause, remember?"

"Fuck," I say, grateful Hannah pays attention to those stacks of pages we sign and initial. We can't represent any direct competitor of a client for two years after the working relationship ends. It's one reason GiGi made an effort to diversify our client roster.

"Let's try searching the *Business Journal* again," my sister suggests. "There's got to be something in there about a company with a scandal brewing. A sexist CEO? Anti-climate policies?"

"If it's in the journal, chances are they already have a PR agency," I say, trying not to sound as defeated as I feel. "And GiGi wouldn't want us to represent a business that doesn't align with our values."

"Hmm." Hannah stands and rubs her neck. I reach for the bottle of Advil I picked up for her yesterday, which is still in my bag. She takes the pills and we both stare at the wall, hoping to see something we may have missed.

It's not until the air conditioner kicks on that I realize how quiet it's gotten in the room. Hannah is the one to break the silence.

"We might have to cut the scholarship," she says.

"No." My voice is sharper than I mean for it to be, but public relations has always been dominated by white men, and our grandmother was committed to diversity and inclusion long before they became buzzwords. "That's a nonnegotiable. I'd sooner close the business than put an end to the scholarship."

Hannah slumps in the leather executive chair next to

mine. I wonder how much we could make selling these to an office furniture resale company.

I'm about to suggest we take a break when the door opens.

A woman walks in, radiating such confidence that I wonder if we were expecting her. But no; we cleared our mostly empty calendars today.

The woman reminds me of Kristin Chenoweth: petite, blond, and perky. Her golden hair looks professionally styled, and her outfit—a pink sleeveless shift dress—looks like it was made just for her. She's smiling with such unbridled excitement it's unsettling.

I'm so taken aback, I momentarily forget that we were in the middle of a very important meeting when she waltzed in.

"Can I help you?" I ask, a tinge of annoyance in my voice.

We told Scott no interruptions. Not even if Taylor Swift got engaged or Britney announced a tour like the last time he barged into a meeting with news of an "emergency."

Hannah kicks me under the table, and I turn to look at her, even more confused.

"I sure hope so," the woman says, a slight Southern drawl in her high-pitched voice. "My name is Lou—"

"Short for Louise, not Loser," Hannah says.

Our visitor laughs and gives Hannah a megawatt smile. "So, you've heard my podcast?"

"And your TED talk," Hannah says, blushing. I look between the two of them, confused. My sister doesn't blush.

"That's actually why I'm here," Lou says, her voice dropping an octave. She places her hand on the back of a chair and looks at me. "May I?"

I nod, still trying to wrap my head around what is happening. And where the hell Scott is.

As if on cue, he walks down the hallway holding two Starbucks cups. He does a double take, his eyes going wide as he watches Lou sit down. Then he slips into the room, heading straight for her, a guilty grin on his face.

"What are you doing in here?" he asks Lou under his breath, his smile never fading.

"You two know each other?" I ask.

"Who doesn't know Lou?" Scott says. "Short for Louise, not Loser."

The three of them laugh like they're on the inside of a joke I'm clearly on the outside of.

"She was supposed to be waiting in the lobby while I grabbed the two of us Blonde Americanos," Scott says, then turns to Lou. "I told you the sisters were in a very important meeting."

"They are now," Lou says. She folds her hands in front of her and looks at Hannah and me, ready for business. "My TED talk, 'Crushing Your Comfort Zone,' is about to reach ten million views."

"Lou's work has revolutionized the self-help industry," Hannah says to me, jumping in. "Her first book was on the *New York Times* bestseller list for, like, a year—"

"Sixty-two weeks, actually," Lou says.

"And her podcast has a massive following!" Hannah looks more excited than I've seen her since she got her double-walled vacuum-sealed water bottle.

"My podcast is just a launchpad for the real work I want to do," Lou says. "I have an entire product line coming out next summer: a new book, a guided journal, exclusive webinars, and a shit ton of merchandise. It has the potential to be big—but only if it's done right. Right?"

"Right," I say uncertainly. Lou's smile confirms that this is the correct answer. "But . . . what exactly is your program?"

"Glad you asked." Lou stands and moves to the head of our table. "Did you know less than two percent of people ever reach their full potential? The vast majority of human beings on this planet are living a sub-potential life. And do you know why?"

I'm about to throw out some ideas (poverty, repressive government regimes, lack of affordable housing) but Lou keeps going.

"Fear," she says, letting the word hang in the air. "We're afraid to grow, because growing requires us to leave behind our small, comfortable lives and step into the unknown."

She continues, describing what she calls a "comfort zone," a metaphorical safe space that stems from early life experiences.

"Everyone talks about stepping outside their comfort zone," Lou says, "and they might do it for a while—dillydally like a tourist seeing the sights—but as soon as something scary happens, they step right back in." She shakes her head sadly before fixing her sparkling brown eyes on me, then Hannah. "That's why it's not enough to simply leave our comfort zones. We have to *crush* them!"

Lou slams her hand on the table, making the rest of us jump. I'm officially under her spell, listening as she describes her proprietary questionnaire that determines exactly what type of comfort zone her client is stuck in. The data is analyzed by a team of experts who develop a personalized twelve-week challenge to crush the client's comfort zone and help them achieve their true potential.

"This could be even bigger than my last book," Lou says,

"which is why I'm looking for a PR firm to help manage everything from the reveal to the rollout. I'd prefer something woman-owned—"

"We're women," I say, hoping this comes across as charming and not desperate. I don't have to understand math to know that this woman's business could be the answer we're looking for.

Lou's smile grows, and for one shining moment, I feel like we have a fighting chance to save the Freedman Group.

"You should be aware that I'm talking to a few other firms," Lou says, and I deflate the tiniest bit. "But I like you ladies. You've got chutzpah. And I'm looking for a team that isn't afraid to bust their asses."

"We're not afraid," I say, even though I am a teeny bit afraid.

"Good, because in addition to the standard proposal materials—my public relations partners must agree to one crucial thing."

I sit up straight in my chair, mimicking Hannah's perfect posture.

"If we're going to work together, y'all will have to walk the walk," Lou says. "It's impossible to truly understand the power of crushing your comfort zone if you haven't crushed your own."

"You want us to crush our comfort zones?" Hannah repeats, sounding skeptical.

"Exactly!" Lou says, her eyes sparkling.

Scott perks up, clearly excited. "You'll give them one of your twelve-week challenges?"

"Damn right," Lou tells him before turning back to us.

Judging by Scott's reaction, these challenges can't be too hard. It could even be fun, challenging myself to do something like learn a new language or read a dozen self-help books.

Lou leans forward. "So, are you in?"

Hannah and I look at each other, utilizing our sisterly power to communicate entire sentences with our eyes. Hers are asking, *What do you think?* And mine are saying, *I think we have to do it.*

Her eyes widen in alarm, but before she can telepathically tell me to slow down and think this through, I turn to Lou and say, "We're in."

Hannah kicks me under the table as Lou whoops with joy.

"I was hoping y'all would be up for the challenge." She pushes her chair back and stands, looking down at us like a proud fairy godmother. Something about her makes me feel all warm inside, like her words have given me a hug and made me believe in myself—in us—again.

"Libby," Hannah whispers. "We need to—"

"Let's talk about next steps," I say to Lou, ignoring my sister.

"I'll send you the questionnaire," Lou says. "Once you complete it, my team will need forty-eight hours, and then I'll assign your challenges."

"And if we do that, you'll hire us to do your PR?" I ask. I want to make it clear that we're doing this in exchange for her business.

Lou shakes her head but softens it with a smile. "You've got to play the game to win the prize, my dear."

"Libs," Hannah whispers again. She looks nervous, but honestly, I'd be worried if she wasn't. It's her job to worry about the details of the deal. It's mine to imagine our future with Lou as a client. I can picture it—the halls bustling, filled with staff. The office looking trendy and chic. Maybe we'll have enough money left over to set up another scholarship in Gi-Gi's name.

"Thank you for considering us for this amazing opportunity," Hannah says, breaking the spell. "But my sister and I would like to talk it over before we commit our resources."

Before we what? I'm about to jump in and tell Lou not to listen to her, that we'll do whatever it takes, when Hannah lays her hand on my knee. She doesn't make eye contact, but the gesture tells me everything I need to know.

My unflappable sister doesn't have an impulsive bone in her body, but once she wraps her head around the logistics, she'll agree with me that this is the best—the only—way to save our family business.

"Fair enough," Lou says, smiling as if she heard every word Hannah and I didn't speak out loud. She turns to Great Scott and takes one of the two cups in his hands. "Thanks for the Americano, doll."

And with that, she's gone.

Four

HANNAH

LOU WALKS OUT, LEAVING THE CONFERENCE ROOM WITH THE eerie calm that follows a thunderstorm, the air infused with electricity.

"She's an absolute legend," Libby says. She sounds like she's seen the face of God. "I am literally obsessed with her."

"You *literally* never heard of her until twenty minutes ago," Great Scott says.

Libby faces him. "Yeah, well, that just goes to show how amazing she is."

I know what my sister means—Lou commands attention, even more so in person than on her podcast. It's why she can go by her first name only, like Beyoncé or Adele.

But now that she's gone, my head is buzzing. I need to work through the details. GiGi taught me to double- and triple-check everything before committing to anything.

Yes, it's flattering that Lou wants to work with us—but that doesn't mean we ought to. It feels a little manipulative, forcing us to prove ourselves by completing her challenge. Our work should stand on its own merits.

Plus, what do we even know about Lou? She seems to be purposefully vague about her background; no one knows much about her except that she rose out of obscurity and became one of the most popular podcasters in the business. Her mystique is part of her appeal, but it's smart to maintain a healthy skepticism.

"It's an amazing concept," Libby says. "Crushing our comfort zones! Yes!"

"Your entire life is a comfort zone," I point out. "Comfort foods, comfort books, comfort movies. You relish your comfort zone."

"And I've been stuck in it! I need to break out so I can flourish to my true potential! *We* need to break out—our business needs to break out!"

"If you say 'break out' one more time, I'm going to lose it," Great Scott says mildly, not looking up from his phone.

I fold my arms, needing to process my thoughts before I can articulate what about this proposal doesn't sit right.

Libby comes over to my side of the table, her forehead wrinkled with worry. "You're not convinced," she says. "I can tell you're not convinced."

"I didn't say that. It's just—"

"Come on, Han!" Libby says, pleading. "This is our chance to really break—" Great Scott cocks an eyebrow, and Libby swallows. "This is a huge opportunity!"

It's easy to be swept away when my sister gets like this. I love her passion and energy, but my role in our partnership is to be levelheaded and rational.

"I know," I say, "but we need to be smart. Let's make a list of pros and cons."

Just saying those words makes me feel calmer. I walk over

to the whiteboard, write PRO on the left side and CON on the right.

"That's a great idea," Libby says, sitting. "Pro: it'll save our business."

"Let's be more specific," I say, then turn to the whiteboard and write as I speak. "Con: we have to spend the entire summer convincing Lou to hire us."

"Why wouldn't she hire us? We're amazing," Libby says.

Great Scott barks a sharp laugh.

Libby whirls around to face him. "What's so funny?"

His feet are up on the table and his eyes are on his phone, his face the picture of innocence. "Something on TikTok. You wouldn't get it."

I roll my eyes and turn back to the whiteboard. "Even if Lou does hire us, we won't get a dime until then—and she won't make that decision for twelve weeks."

I write in large letters: CON: NO $ GUARANTEED.

Libby huffs. "Okay, but no one else is offering us anything at all, so there's at least the *possibility* of being paid. You heard all the things she's looking for—a scope that big would replace what we lost from the Rooneys, right?"

"I'll need to crunch the numbers, but maybe," I say, and write that down: PRO: POSSIBILITY OF $. "But another con is these crazy challenges. Who knows what we might be assigned? You haven't listened to her podcast. One person's challenge was to give up all sugar, alcohol, and caffeine. Another one had to live in his car for twelve weeks!"

Libby blanches. "I'm sure we can handle it. We're strong and capable. Write that down."

"That's not a pro about Lou's business," I say. "It's more a pro about us."

"We have to make a thorough list," Libby insists.

"Fine," I say, and write WE ARE STRONG on the left side of the board. But I also write CRAZY CHALLENGES under the cons.

"Con: that squeaky voice," Great Scott says. "I have a migraine from the high pitch."

I add that to the right column: LOU'S VOICE INDUCES MIGRAINES.

Libby throws up her hands. "Oh, come *on*."

"We have to make a thorough list," I tell her, mimicking her words.

When she sticks her tongue out at me, I grab the eraser and chuck it at her. She ducks and it sails over her head.

"Loving the professionalism," Scott murmurs. "Maybe I should call HR. Oh wait, you let them go . . ."

Libby straightens up, brushing her brown hair away from her face. "Here's a pro: getting Lou's business would put the Freedman Group on the map again!"

I write that down: PUT US ON THE MAP. She's right; Lou is exactly the kind of big, flashy client GiGi would've taken a risk on. "I agree," I say, which is my way of apologizing to my sister for throwing the eraser at her head.

"Thank you," she says, smiling. Which is her way of apologizing for sticking her tongue out at me.

"Shut *up*!" Great Scott gasps. I whirl around to see him gaping at his phone. "I swear to God that woman cannot be fifty-five years old, but Wikipedia says it's true. Put that as a pro."

"That she looks young for her age?" I ask, confused.

"Flawless skin," he says in a firm voice. "Anyone who takes care of their skin can be trusted to take care of everything else. Including their professional life. Write it down."

"Write it! Write it!" Libby chants, clapping her hands.

I know when I'm beaten, so I shrug and write FLAWLESS SKIN under the pro column.

"Yes!" Libby raises her hand toward Scott for a high five. He grunts in return, and Libby drops her arm awkwardly back to her side.

"We also need to consider Lou herself," I say. "She's used to having total control of her brand. Will she listen to us? Will she accept our expertise? She could be difficult to work with."

Scott chimes in again: "She will absolutely be difficult to work with. Mark my words, besties."

DIFFICULT TO WORK WITH goes under the cons.

Libby glares at Scott. "Whose side are you on?"

"I'm neutral," he says. "I'm Switzerland."

"Another potential con," I say, on a roll now, "is if we upset Lou, she could go on her podcast and say negative things about our business. One bad comment times ten million listeners adds up to a bad reputation that there's no recovering from."

MIGHT PUT US ON BLAST, I write on the board. The con section is longer than the pros now, and my heart rate settles.

I continue. "Another con is—"

"Enough!" Libby marches over to the whiteboard and snatches the marker from my hand. Then she writes under the pro column in huge letters, WILL SAVE OUR COMPANY.

"We have no other options!" She waves her hands at the dozens of Post-it notes on the glass walls. "Are any of these people asking us to work with them? No. And none of them are big enough to make a difference anyway."

I press my lips together, knowing she's right.

"Yes, it's a gamble," Libby continues, "but as GiGi used to say, 'if you're going to climb a mountain, make it Masada.'"

Her cheeks are flushed, her eyes bright. Usually, I love it when she gets like this. It means that something big is going to happen, something *exciting*.

But it can also be terrifying, especially when the neurotic voices in my head start chattering: *This isn't going to work. What if she gives us some ridiculous, embarrassing challenge? What if we spend twelve weeks trying to convince her, but in the end she doesn't hire us?*

We could spend our entire summer trying to make a comeback, and it could all be for nothing. And I know from experience that the harder you try to hold something together, the more it hurts when it falls apart.

"We've been stuck in a hole for so long, and it's getting deeper," Libby says, stepping closer. "Lou just dropped down a ladder, Han. I know there are no guarantees, but we're *worth* taking a chance on."

I have reservations. They're right there, at the back of my throat, but I feel myself getting swept along in the current of Libby's passion. I don't want to let her down. Or GiGi.

So I take a deep breath and say, "Yes. Okay. Let's do it. We can at least try."

Scott groans.

Libby cheers.

And I tell myself to be excited, too.

To: Hannah.Freedman@TheFreedmanGroup.com;
Libby.Freedman@TheFreedmanGroup.com
From: Lou@CrushYourComfortZone.com
Subject: The ultimate challenge: crushing your comfort
zone

Congratulations, ladies!

Today, you will take the first step on the journey of a lifetime.

This journey will not be easy. It will force you to grow, which can be painful. But the opposite of growth is stagnation. And there's nothing more painful than being stuck. Trapped.

Remember: a comfortable cage is still a cage.

Luckily, there's a way to break free. To escape the chains that have kept you from realizing your full potential.

I can show you how.

This will require everything you've got—all your determination, vulnerability, and honesty. But I promise that if you take this journey with me, your life will change forever.

We start today.

Are you ready?

Click here to log in and access your introductory questionnaire.

—Lou

Five

LIBBY

HANNAH AND I SPENT THE WEEKEND FILLING OUT OUR QUES-
tionnaires so Lou and her team could analyze them before our
meeting today, when she'll officially assign our challenges.

It took *hours*.

There were hundreds of questions, from practical things
like how many hours of sleep I get a night (seven on average,
but preferably nine), if I remember my dreams (not usually), or
if I'm superstitious (very).

It was like doing an inventory of my life—how I liked to
play as a child (Barbie and Ken, falling in love), how my parents rewarded me back then (cartoons and candy), and how I
reward myself today (buying a new book or a pastry).

I answered questions about my religious beliefs (culturally
Jewish, but more spiritual than religious), how physically active I am on a scale of 0 to 10 (4 for me, probably an 11 for Hannah), and whether I get energy from being around people or
being alone (definitely from people).

The second I hit submit, my stomach was in knots at the
thought of strangers studying my answers. Analyzing my flaws.

It got even worse after Hannah had the not-so-brilliant idea for me to listen to Lou's podcast—her show is not the gimmicky armchair psychology I thought it would be.

Lou—which I'm starting to suspect is short for Lucifer—digs into her guests' lives, asking questions that gave me secondhand discomfort, just listening.

In a live Q & A with listeners, she made six out of seven people cry. And the only reason the seventh didn't cry was because he started yelling at Lou, which is arguably worse.

I should have taken a page from Br'er Rabbit and pretended to love all the things that make me uncomfortable, like conflict, cleaning, exercise, and horizontal stripes. *I should have lied.*

But it's too late now. Hannah and I are in the conference room, sitting opposite Lou, who looks sharp in a pink blazer and matching lipstick.

"Ladies," Lou says, "I've run y'all's answers through my system, and I'm so excited to share the results."

Her eyes twinkle and my stomach tightens. I wonder what happened to Lou in her childhood that made her get such joy out of making people uncomfortable.

"Hannah, should we start with you?" Lou asks.

Hannah sucks in a quick breath, and I feel guilty enjoying this brief stay of execution, but not guilty enough to volunteer to go first.

"Based on your results," Lou tells my sister, "you have great physical strength and endurance. You push yourself physically and aren't afraid to go the extra mile."

Her words are true: my sister never breaks a sweat when we walk back from the grocery store, even when she's carrying both our cases of LaCroix—Pamplemousse for me, Cerise Limón for her.

"You enjoy a good physical challenge, and you excel at mental challenges as well," Lou says. "Your mind has an uncanny ability to analyze data and break it down, seeing patterns and making connections. It's probably why you've got a penchant for true crime—if I had to guess, you solve the mystery before most people."

Again, it's accurate. When we read *Verity* for a book club, Hannah figured out the twist a good forty pages early.

"You tend to see the world in black and white," Lou says, glancing down at her folder. "And shades of gray make you feel out of sorts. You have introverted tendencies—"

I stifle a laugh at the obviousness of this statement, and Hannah shoots me a dirty look.

"You keep your emotions close to your chest," Lou continues. "It takes a lot for new people to get past the walls you put up. It's for your protection, but it also keeps people out."

I look at my sister, who is sitting up straight, her fingers nervously twitching in her lap.

"Since you excel in areas of mental and physical strength, there's room for improvement with the other two categories: social and emotional. It feels safer to avoid connecting with other people, but it's holding you back. Does that sound about right?"

Hannah nods ever so slightly, and Lou offers a sympathetic smile as she says, "To crush that comfort zone, your challenge will focus on interpersonal strength. You're single, correct?"

"She is," I say, answering for Hannah when she doesn't do it fast enough.

"Perfect." Lou rubs her hands together like she can't wait

for what's next. "In this challenge, you will go on twelve first dates over the next twelve weeks."

My face lights up as Hannah's falls. There's nothing I love more than love, and I've been telling Hannah for years that she needs to dive back into the dating pool—although for Hannah, it might feel more like a belly flop.

"You want me to date twelve men?" Hannah asks, dumbfounded.

"Not all at the same time," Lou says, giving a musical laugh. "I'd suggest one date a week."

"But . . ." Hannah says, and I can see her mind spinning as she tries to find the words to get herself out of this pickle. I resist my big-sister urge to save her, because I agree; this could be just what she needs.

"But feminism," Hannah finally says. "A woman doesn't need a man to complete her life."

"I'm all for independent women," Lou says. "But this isn't about the other person, the man—or woman, if that's what floats your boat. It's about opening yourself to new people and possibilities. Knock those walls down, darlin'."

Hannah looks at me, her eyes pleading for me to say something. So I do.

"She's in."

Beneath the table, Hannah tweaks the rolls on my side. I slap her hand away, keeping a smile on my face as Lou tells Hannah the details of her challenge, which isn't so bad.

I know my sister would love to be in a relationship again. But like Lou said, she's built a barricade around herself. Hannah has kept her heart under lock and key ever since that Jackass Who Shall Not Be Named abandoned her five years ago.

She's gone on a handful of dates since then, and there was one guy from her running club who stuck around for a few months, but none of those other men could offer her what she had with her ex: history.

I've tried to tell her a connection like that takes time, but deep down, I know she's afraid to get hurt again.

This could be the push she needs. Her chance to fall in love with someone tall and handsome and kind who treats her the way she deserves.

Six

HANNAH

NO.

No.

No.

It is taking every bit of strength I possess to keep my expression neutral and my body planted in my chair. It feels like a giant bear trap has snapped shut on my torso, crunching my rib cage, collapsing my lungs.

I have to go out with a dozen strangers?

Making small talk with randos is my worst nightmare. I have a recurring dream where I'm forced at knifepoint by a serial killer to go room to room in a massive apartment building and converse with the occupants. I always wake up in a sweat, trembling all over—and not because of the knife-wielding murderer.

Now I have to spend my entire summer essentially living that dream.

Beside me, Libby's grinning like the Cheshire cat, giddy about the prospect of me going on all these dates. Which is hypocritical, given that she hasn't been on a date in years. *She* should have been given this challenge.

I'm one of those pathetic girls who had the same boyfriend all through high school *and* college, assumed we'd be together forever, then got dumped without warning. In the five years since, I've gone out with other men, mostly because my sister tells me I have too much main-character energy (her words, not mine) to become a sad spinster destined to die alone (my words, not hers).

But I've had zero chemistry with the guys I've dated, and the handful of times we made it to the bedroom, it didn't go well. I'm getting queasy thinking about it, the awkwardness of being naked with someone for the first time, the constant worry that he's bored or annoyed or internally critiquing me.

If we weren't in the middle of a meeting with a potential client who could save our business from utter ruin, I would excuse myself to the bathroom. Maybe to vomit. Definitely to cry.

But Lou's already turning to my sister to deliver her challenge.

"Libby," Lou says. "Based on your results, you are socially adventurous. You're adept at conversing with individuals from a wide variety of backgrounds, and at discerning people's true intentions."

Libby lights up, relishing the compliments, which are all true. She inherited GiGi's ability to schmooze potential clients while also sniffing out red flags. But even though she's a confirmed extrovert, Libby doesn't have much of a social life anymore; given the shaky state of our business, it makes sense that she's been focusing on work. But maybe her challenge could be to rekindle some friendships? Or hobbies?

"However," Lou goes on, "the most striking theme of your questionnaire is your fear and avoidance of anything physically uncomfortable. Learning to tolerate physical discomfort, to push not just your mind and spirit but also your body, will be the most crucial element of crushing your comfort zone."

I'm nodding along; I've told Libby this before. I don't expect her to join my ten-mile weekend runs, but she avoids *anything* physical—biking, kayaking, walks longer than a couple of miles. I know she has some insecurities about her body, but I've run marathons with people of all shapes and sizes. Body size doesn't correlate with fitness.

"Your challenge," Lou continues, "will be in the area of physical strength. You'll be required to complete a twelve-week training program, culminating in an organized race or sporting event."

Libby sucks in a gasp. "What exactly do you mean by training?"

"I'd suggest physical activity six days a week, at least thirty minutes a day. And for the event—maybe y'all could compete in a race together!"

"In public?" Libby whispers. She's gone pale.

Lou gives her a quizzical look. "Well, yes, that's implied as part of the organized event."

"I—" Libby's eyes dart toward me in a silent plea. "My sister and I should discuss this in private."

"Oh no," I say, enjoying the way the tables have turned. "You were fine with me being shoved out of *my* comfort zone. If we're doing this, that means *you* are doing this."

Lou gives me an approving smile. "I love that attitude, Hannah. That's exactly what I'm looking for in an agency partner!"

Libby swallows. I can tell she's trying to conceal her rising panic; I felt the same way a few minutes ago. But seeing it from the other side makes me realize that Lou is onto something. Okay, so I hate my challenge. But maybe I have been scared for too long when it comes to social situations. Going on these dates probably won't lead to true love, but it will force me to confront my biggest weakness, which could help me at work, too. I'm still embarrassed by how I froze up on that phone call with Mr. Rooney the other day.

Plus, I would *love* to train for a race with Libby.

And that's when it hits me: I have the perfect event.

"The Down & Dirty!" I say, turning to my sister. "I've been wanting to do it for ages. It's a team event, running interspersed with obstacles. The goal is to finish, not to win. You'll love it."

Libby shoots me a death glare that says, *I am not going to love it and you know that very well and why couldn't you suggest a one-mile fun run at an elementary school or something?*

But Lou beams at me. "That's a fantastic idea, Hannah. A strong support system is key to crushing your comfort zone."

And damn it all if I don't glow at the praise. There's a reason Lou has millions of podcast listeners, why her book sold for a rumored two million dollars in a seven-publisher auction. She inspires people to follow her.

With my phone, I do a quick search for the Chicago Down & Dirty. If we start next week with the challenge, the race will happen after the twelfth week of the program. Almost like it was meant to be.

"Now, listen up, girls," Lou says, turning serious. "I'm going to check with you every few weeks. I expect you to follow my method to the letter—it's crucial that you understand my philosophy if you're going to represent my brand."

"What about the PR plan itself?" I ask.

"I'd like a proposal by the end of the summer," Lou says, tapping a pink fingernail on the table. "I'll see how you do with your challenges, review the proposal, and make a decision."

Libby's eyes widen in panic. "But shouldn't we discuss a contract or—or a letter of intent? If we're doing all this, it would be nice to have some kind of . . ."

"Guarantee?" Lou finishes. Libby and I both nod, but Lou shakes her head. "Sorry, ladies, life doesn't work that way. If you want to win, you gotta play the game, am I right?"

I don't like the sound of that, but before I can say anything, Lou's already moving on. She gives us more details on the program, showing us the Crush Your Comfort Zone journals she developed, with prompts for each day. She reminds us to listen to the exclusive webinars she's developed, and then she's out the door, leaving the office sparking with electricity.

As soon as she's gone, Great Scott peeks in. "So . . . how'd it go?" When he hears about the dates I have to go on, he sucks air through his teeth. "That *will* be a challenge."

"You think that's bad?" Libby bursts in. "Hannah's making me do the Down & Dirty!"

"Oh shit," he says, his jaw falling open. "Isn't that the one where you have to crawl through a mud pit under electrified wires?"

Libby turns to me, eyes wide. "*Hannah!* What the actual f—"

"Look," I say, jabbing a finger in Libby's direction, "you're the one who wanted to work with Lou, remember? Now we're in this together. And as for you." I point to Scott. "We need four people for our Down & Dirty team. Welcome aboard."

He blanches. "Oh no—"

"Oh yes," Libby says, then turns to me. "What about a fourth?"

"I'll ask that running group I used to be in," I tell her. The group fell apart when most of the members got married or had kids, but I'm sure I can convince someone to join us.

With a heavy sigh, Libby collapses into her chair. "It'll be fine, right? What's the worst that could happen?"

I'm about to say, *Being murdered by one of my dates, chopped into pieces, and mailed around the world*, when Scott cuts in.

"Besides being forced to face your deepest fears, delving into the hidden corners of your psyches, and bringing up old wounds that have haunted you both since childhood?" He laughs darkly. "Sounds like a piece of cake."

Seven

LIBBY

LATER THAT AFTERNOON, I'M SITTING ON THE COUCH AT home, cocooning myself in comfort by eating ice cream and planning one of my movie theme nights, which I love and Hannah tolerates. I'm thinking *When Harry Met Sally* for the movie, with pastrami sandwiches (from the "I'll have what she's having" scene) and coconut cake with chocolate sauce (on the side, of course).

I used to throw parties all the time, back when I had a lot of friends—people from college, people from trivia nights at Four Farthings and euchre night at McGee's. But Hannah needed me when she moved back to Chicago, and when you say no to invitations enough times, people stop asking.

My parties back then were epic and always on theme. Like the Passover Is Over party, where I served nothing but dips and leavened bread, and the Yellow Party, where everything from the food (popcorn and banana pudding) to the drinks (spiked lemonade) and people's outfits were all the same hue.

These days, Hannah humors me by participating in my "parties for two," as I call them. Usually, they are just the thing to make me feel better—but the nauseous feeling I've had since Lou dropped her comfort zone bomb on us has only gotten worse.

It's like I'm standing on the edge of a cliff. I could take the leap and be a hero, saving our family business—or I can take a step back like a coward and only save myself. Of course, if I was really a hero, there would be no hesitation.

The front door opens and Hannah walks in, fresh from a casual, just-for-the-fun-of-it five-mile run. Her face is red and wisps of curly brown hair are plastered to her cheeks—but she still looks beautiful.

Our whole lives, Hannah has been the smart one, the pretty one, *and* the fit one. I've been the . . . other one. I know our parents didn't set out to treat us differently, but it was hard to ignore the fact that my mom bought "the family" a treadmill for my thirteenth birthday, while Hannah got a leather jacket for hers. GiGi was the only adult in my life who loved me for who I was and didn't try to change me.

"Hey," Hannah says, flopping onto the couch near my feet. Mr. Darcy hisses and scampers away—there's no love lost between those two. "Feeling any better?"

"No," I say, stabbing the ice cream with my spoon for emphasis.

"Me either. Is this even legal? Forcing someone to go on dates?" Hannah asks.

"No one is forcing you—and all you have to do is let a guy buy you dinner. Easy-peasy!"

"There's so much more to it than that," Hannah says, sinking back into the couch.

"The kissing?" I tease, poking her thigh with my toe.

"Stop," she says, grabbing my foot. "I'm serious."

"Hi, Serious—I'm Libby," I tease, pulling out one of our favorite bad dad jokes.

I expect Hannah to laugh, too, but her face closes up like a flower blooming in reverse and I realize I'm going to have to use a different tactic.

"Look at you," I say. "You're even pretty when you're sweaty. I promise, once you put yourself out there, men will start lining up outside your door."

"This isn't some romance novel, Libs," Hannah says, her voice wavering. "I can't just snap my fingers and get a date—I have to pick the right app, weed out the weirdos, and after I find one that *might* be normal, I'll have to message him and do all that stupid get-to-know-you stuff. *Then*," she says, drawing out the word for emphasis, "I'll have to figure out what to wear, meet him at some crowded bar or restaurant, and make small talk. It'll be torture for me, you know that."

I do know that. Since we were little kids, I've been my sister's voice in social situations. Not because she doesn't have a lot to say—she does, but it takes time for her to warm up and trust people enough to be herself.

"I wish I could go on the dates for you," I tell her. "And you could work out and run the race for me."

Hannah sits up straight and looks at me, and I can see the wheels turning in her mind. She stands and starts to pace in front of the couch—the woman is even active when she thinks.

"It's not a bad idea," she says.

"Han," I say, backtracking, "there's no way. We have to document the whole thing in those journals for Lou, and . . ." I hesitate, trying to find a way to explain that girls like me who have "such a pretty face" have a different dating experience than girls who look like Hannah.

45

"Not the actual dates," Hannah says. She takes the pint of ice cream from my hands, helping herself to a bite. "But we could help each other—do the parts of the challenge that come naturally to each of us."

"Explain."

"You download the app with my picture and profile; you do the swiping and chatting and date planning."

"You'd let me pick the guys you go out with?" I ask, starting to get excited.

"I trust you," Hannah says around a mouthful of Chunky Monkey. "You'll just have to get me up to speed on anything that we—well, that you and the guy—talked about before the date."

"And what will you do for me?"

"I'll set up a training schedule," Hannah says. "And we'll do it together. It'll be fun!"

"You have a warped sense of what that word means," I say, grabbing my ice cream back.

Hannah slides over until she's practically sitting on me. "Picture it. You and me, jogging the lake path, doing burpees—"

"No burpees," I say.

"Okay, no burpees," Hannah says. "Pleeeeeease, seester."

I think back to a quote I saw scribbled in GiGi's notebook the other day: *The idea is not to live forever, but to create something that will.*

We already lost her. We can't lose the company she spent her whole life creating. The company she trusted us with.

"It'll have to be NTNT," I tell Hannah, harkening back to our childhood code for "no tell, no tell"—referring to the sisterly secrets we promised never to tell anyone in authority. Usually benign things like someone (usually me) sneaking something we weren't supposed to (usually treats). "We can't tell Lou that I'm doing all the swiping for you—I don't think she'll like that."

"NTNT," Hannah says solemnly. She extends her hand, pinky out. "Deal?"

"Deal," I say.

A smile spreads across Hannah's face as I wrap my pinky around hers, sealing our fate.

CRUSH YOUR COMFORT ZONE
THE ULTIMATE CHALLENGE COMPANION JOURNAL

BEFORE YOU BEGIN
A NOTE FROM OUR FOUNDER

Welcome to the Program.

By now you have received your Challenge. You may be feeling excited, anxious, overwhelmed, terrified—or all these things at once.

Honor these emotions.

Allow them.

Over the next twelve weeks, you will analyze your belief systems, thoughts, actions, and reactions. Every aspect of your past, present, and future will be open for introspection and interrogation. Nothing is off-limits.

Be aware that this process will be uncomfortable, even painful. Over time, my hope is that you will move beyond enduring this discomfort to a place where you welcome it.

But for today, give yourself space to feel whatever you need to feel.

And tomorrow, let's get to work.

—Lou

Eight

HANNAH

THE NEXT TUESDAY AFTERNOON, WE'RE IN OUR SHARED office. This week is our "prep week"—devoted to getting everything in order before we officially start the challenge. Yesterday, we spent the entire day developing our strategy for securing Lou's business—we both know we need to knock this proposal out of the park. Right now, Libby is at her desk, allegedly doing research on the demographics of Lou's ideal target audience. But her earbuds are in, which means she's listening to a romance novel on audiobook, and based on the glazed look in her eyes, she's in the middle of a sex scene.

Yay for her, I guess. I've spent the past several hours moving funds around to cover our expenses, including the scholarship and Great Scott's salary. If we're careful, we *might* make the budget work for the next twelve weeks. Just barely.

I close my eyes, tired of staring at spreadsheets. All that financial data, right there in black and white, is unsettling.

My mind drifts to the reading I did this morning in Lou's journal. We officially start the challenge next week, but our journal contains a few optional writing prompts to get us warmed up. Last night's was a little odd:

My comfort zone is like _____ (fill in the blank with an object, location, or other entity).

I stared at the question for ten minutes, unsure how to answer. My comfort zone has to do with avoiding social situations in which I feel uncomfortable. What *object*, *location*, or *entity* would that be? I couldn't come up with anything, probably because my brain thinks concretely, not metaphorically.

But now it hits me, as I look at my computer: my comfort zone is like a spreadsheet. I feel best when my world is organized and predictable. My Bullet Journal, my Outlook calendar, and my to-do list are my lifelines. Order and reliability make me feel safe and secure.

All the things I hate—meeting new people, calling them on the phone, making small talk with strangers—are unpredictable. I never know what the other person is going to say, so I can't plan what *I'm* going to say. Plus, I'm constantly fighting intrusive thoughts: *Am I boring? Am I annoying? Am I laughing too loudly or speaking too quickly or using too many big words or saying "like" too much?*

"Hannah, line one!" Great Scott calls from his desk down the hall.

I grimace. Phone calls are the worst—the awkward pauses, the absence of body language. But I'm supposed to be stepping outside my comfort zone.

"Send it through." I hit the button to answer via speakerphone and say, "Hello, this is Hannah Freedman."

"BANANA!"

Shock ricochets through me. This voice. That nickname. I haven't heard either for five years and never expected to again.

I glance at Libby; she's taken one earbud out and is frozen in shock and horror.

"Hang up," she says.

But I can't. An external force takes over my hand as I pick up the phone and put it to my ear, willing my voice not to shake as I say—

"Josh?"

YES, IT'S HIM. Joshua Andrew Jacobson. My high school and college boyfriend. My first kiss, my first *everything*. The boy who promised we'd be together forever, then dumped me without warning, plunging me into a black hole of depression from which I never would've surfaced if not for my sister, my excellent therapist, and the magic of selective serotonin reuptake inhibitors.

One week before the start of our senior year in college, we were moving into our own apartment—the first time we'd officially lived together. I was unpacking boxes in the bedroom when he burst in, a huge grin on his face, and told me he'd been accepted for a semester abroad at the University of Queensland.

I was completely shocked—I hadn't even known he'd *applied*. We were finance majors, set on a well-plotted course we'd both agreed upon: after graduation, I'd join Libby and work for GiGi, and he'd work with his dad, a financial planner. Now, after taking *one* biology class with his roommate, he wanted to study coral reef ecology? It had sounded absurd. I hadn't even expected he would do it.

Until he got on a plane to Australia a week later, leaving me behind.

But that wasn't the worst of it. He didn't break up with me. Not then. We tried to maintain a quasi relationship long-distance but could rarely connect, because he was fifteen hours ahead of me. Without the person who had been my other half for the past eight years, I spent the semester floundering. But I held on, telling myself he'd come back and we'd pick up where we left off.

That's when he dropped the bomb. He was staying for another semester. And we were over.

"How are you? It's been a while," Josh says in my ear, sounding for all the world like he's my long-lost pal and not the guy who dumped me over the phone. From Australia.

Over at her desk, Libby's eyes are blazing. "Tell him to *fuck off*," she whispers fiercely.

I shake my head at her and speak into the phone. "I'm . . . fine. How did you get this number?"

Josh laughs, one of those rich, rolling laughs I used to love. "It's on your website. I tried your old cell number, but I'm guessing you changed it?"

"Um, no. I didn't."

"Oh." His voice is tinged with surprise. Then, quieter: "You blocked me."

Well, Libby did. She deleted his number from my phone and blocked his ass (her words, not mine). And if he's just realizing this now, it means he's never tried to contact me.

My mind floats back to the last time his voice was in my ear, muffled from the long distance. *We need to go our separate ways.* I'd crumpled to the floor, sobbing, begging him not to do this, telling him that I loved him, that I would always love him.

To which he responded, *First love isn't meant to last forever.*

That was when I knew: he'd fallen for someone else. Exactly what I'd feared all those times he "forgot" our planned call or FaceTime. I'll never forget that sickening twist in my gut at the image of my Josh kissing someone else, undressing someone else, loving someone else.

GiGi always said to never ask a question when you already know the answer, but I'd needed to hear him say it out loud. So I asked.

Is there someone else?

Followed by the longest pause of my life.

Yes.

Shaking my head, I bring myself back to the present.

"Can I help you with something?" My voice sounds stiff and formal, and I clear my throat.

"I'm in Chicago," he says. "I was wondering if you wanted to meet for coffee."

"Coffee?" I repeat dumbly.

Across the office, Libby is mouthing *Hang up! Hang up!*

"Yeah, it'd be nice to catch up," Josh says in my ear.

His voice sounds exactly like I remember: dark chocolate with a hint of gravel. That voice used to *do* things to me. For years, just hearing it was enough to make me melt into a puddle of love and lust. Now, it makes me feel on edge, like my hackles are rising.

But for some reason I can't explain, I hear myself say, "Sure."

Libby mouths, *No! No! No!* and waves her hands like she's trying to stop me from jumping off a bridge.

"How's Sunday?" Josh asks.

"Sunday," I repeat, like a robot. "Let me check my schedule."

Libby lunges toward me, trying to grab the phone out of my hand. I swat her away. She grabs a piece of my hair and yanks, making me nearly shout.

"Can I put you on hold for one second?" I say, glaring at my sister.

Josh says sure. As soon I do, Libby is right in my face.

"You can't be serious! You're going out with the guy who threw you away like garbage?"

I take a deep breath. "I'm not going *out* with him. We're two old friends meeting for coffee."

She snorts. "Yeah, two old friends who used to bang."

I roll my eyes, but now I'm replaying memories of me and Josh in bed, in the shower, in the back seat of his dad's BMW. Mouth, hands, skin; my back arching and toes curling. Yes, he was an asshole. But he was also the first and only man to give me an orgasm.

Which ought to be reason enough to *never* see him again—he wrecked me so thoroughly that I haven't been in a real relationship since. But I have to admit, I'm curious about what he's been up to. I haven't seen or heard from him in five years; Libby blocked him on all my social media platforms after the breakup. I wouldn't mind hearing about his parents and older sister, either. They were like my extra family, and losing them was almost as hard as losing him.

As for Josh, I'm suddenly desperate to know what he's done with his life. *How long did he stay in Australia? Did he end up studying the Great Barrier Reef? Is he still with the girl he dumped me for?* Even though it won't change the past, I feel morbidly fascinated, like it's a cold case I'm dying to pick apart.

But I don't want to admit any of that to Libby.

"It'll be good practice for my challenge," I say to her. "Maybe I can use it as one of my twelve dates."

"Absolutely *not*," Libby says. "The dates have to be with someone you've never met. Plus, Josh is awful. He's the evil ex-boyfriend who shows up in romance novels just when the heroine is about to meet her true love! Literally!"

"We're not living in a romance novel," I remind her.

"You are—or you will be as soon as I get your profile set up! You just need to be patient."

"I appreciate the big-sister protective vibe. I do. But, Libs, you have to trust that I know what I'm doing."

Maybe part of the reason I've never been able to move on is because I never got any actual closure with Josh. Like a spreadsheet tab that's still open.

"And what *are* you doing?" she asks me, raising an eyebrow.

I don't answer. Instead, I take a deep breath and pick up the phone. "Josh? Sorry about that."

"No worries. Does Sunday work?"

He's always been persistent—when he wanted something, he would laser focus on it. For the longest time, that something was me and the goals we shared: marriage, kids, a house in the northern suburbs, balancing our two careers, and being together as long as we both shall live.

But he could also be easily distracted. I watched him try a dozen different hobbies during our years together: bagpipes, unicycling, watercolors, bird-watching. He'd lock onto them obsessively, then discard them and move on to something else. I should've been ready for that to happen to me, too.

"You still there?" Josh says, and I realize I haven't answered.

My hands are shaking. My chest is tight. It was much easier when I could pretend like Josh didn't exist.

But isn't that the whole point of Lou's challenge? To push myself? I don't want to spend my life avoiding uncomfortable situations.

So I clear my throat again and say, "Should we say ten o'clock at Stan's on Broadway and Aldine?"

"Sounds great," Josh says. "Can't wait to see you."

Nine

LIBBY

UGH. JUST UGH.

I cannot believe Josh Goddamn Jacobson had the nerve to call my sister after all these years. It took every fiber of my being not to rip the phone from her hands and hang up on him myself.

After the call, Hannah got all quiet and withdrawn, and I felt a familiar fire stirring in my belly. I had to get out of there before I said something I'd regret—so I'm taking myself out to lunch, spending calories and cash I can't afford.

My anger builds with every step as I weave between the summer tourists walking down Chicago Avenue. Where are all these people in the winter, when it takes guts and courage to be here, braving the elements? I wish they'd leave and take Josh with them.

Even if I had forgiven that asshole for breaking my sister's heart (which I haven't), I'd still hate him for cockblocking dozens of novels I could have loved. I seriously don't understand why so many contemporary romance authors name their love interests *Josh*. All guys with *J* names suck and Josh is the worst *J* name of all.

I've tried to purge my memory of the last time we talked, before he practically destroyed Hannah. If I hadn't flown down to Gainesville to help her pick up the pieces, she might still be curled in a ball on the floor, unable to speak, her eyes hollow and her face streaked with tears. Seeing her like that was the most terrifying experience of my life.

Hannah nearly failed out of college that semester; she hardly ate, she stopped running, she wouldn't even leave her apartment. She was a shell of herself for months—hell, she's still not fully back to normal. There used to be a light in her eyes. My sister fucking twinkled. But Josh stole that from her. And now he's back.

Ugh.

When I imagined helping Hannah write her love story this summer, it was *not* a second-chance romance. That's one trope we're not going anywhere near. Sexy cowboy? Sure. One bed? No problem. Secret millionaire—now, that would solve everything!

I'll never understand the fascination people have with second-chance love stories. If the relationship didn't work out the first time, why would the second time be any different? The problems aren't going to magically disappear. And people don't change.

Especially men. Especially Josh.

I'm about to step into the crosswalk when the light changes to red. I stop and scan the row of restaurants up ahead, looking for the Flaco's Tacos sign.

But it's something else that catches my eye—a tattered piece of paper taped to the pole. In big block letters it says COWORKING SPACE. RENT A DESK BY THE DAY.

A thought occurs to me: *We've got desks. We've got a lot of empty desks.*

And then my mind spins off in a totally new direction.

BY THE TIME I head back to work—my stomach full and happy from lunch, my mind buzzing with ideas about renting out our unused office space—I'm feeling better.

"What are you smiling about?" Hannah asks as I walk into our office.

"Just trying to think of ways to save our business and sabotage your coffee date," I tell her.

She frowns. "I told you, it's not a date—it's two old friends meeting for coffee."

"You don't even like coffee," I say.

If Josh knew her anymore, he would know that, too. He'd have suggested that they meet for that gross grass juice she likes.

"Libby," Hannah says, giving me one of her "don't be so dramatic" looks.

"Hannah," I say, sassing her back. "That boy *destroyed* you. Time may have dulled the memory, but—"

"I haven't forgotten," Hannah says.

"Then why?"

My sister looks up at me, and I can see her trying to put her thoughts into words. I know people can be sentimental about their first love—and that's what terrifies me.

If Hannah won't protect her heart, I'll have to do it for her. Starting with finding her a tall, handsome drink of water to make Josh look like the pathetic piece of shit he is.

"Meet me in the conference room in ten minutes," I say, and walk back out of the office.

HANNAH IS RIGHT on time, of course. Scott—nosy as ever—has joined us, too. I stand at the head of the table and clear my throat as the presentation I prepared comes to life on the flat-screen TV. My sister groans at the title of the cover slide: "Project Find Hannah a HEA."

"According to my research," I say, "there are seventeen different dating apps on the market—and three matchmaking services, which are irrelevant since we can't afford them."

I flip through several slides featuring apps I researched and rejected, pausing for a beat on the Jdate logo. While Hannah and I are both Jewish, she was never as into it as I was. Our one summer at Camp Sabra was life changing for me; I loved everything from singing the *hamotzi* before meals to making tie-dye challah covers at arts and crafts. But my sister was miserable and homesick from the start.

"I considered this one to help you find your *beshert*," I continue, "before deciding on the perfect app that really speaks your love language. And the winner is . . ."

Scott humors me and does a drumroll on the table as I click to the next slide for the big reveal.

"One+One," I say. The logo has two blue number ones on either side of a pink heart with a plus sign at the center. "This app collects a ton of data and makes the matches based on math and science, not just the luck of a swipe."

Hannah leans forward, and I can tell she's intrigued.

"They have an eighty-seven percent success rate," I tell her. "And when you go to people's profiles, you can see how their answers compare to yours and how compatible you are with each other based on the app's custom formula. Cool, right?"

My sister doesn't respond.

"Come on, Han. You've got to take this seriously."

"I am," she says. "I seriously trust you."

The smile she gives me softens the blow, and I suppose it's not all bad that she's leaving this in my hands. It would be decidedly less fun if she was micromanaging my every decision. And her reaction is more mature than mine was yesterday, when she showed me the training schedule she put together for us. (There may have been tears.)

"Okay," I say, clicking to the last slide. "Next steps."

I show her the to-do list for us to get her profile up and running before the check-in next week with Lou: a "fun and flirty" photo shoot, and answering the personality, lifestyle, and demographic questions the app uses for its data points.

Since I know organization relaxes my sister, I even mapped out the timeline with a different first date each week. For fun (and maybe a little bit of manifesting . . .), I added a final date—a wedding—next summer.

"There is no way in hell I'm getting married next summer," Hannah says.

"You could be engaged," I say, arching my eyebrows. My sister rolls her eyes, but I can see it now. Me, standing by Hannah's side as she marches down the aisle toward her leading man, whose name does not start with a *J*.

Ten

HANNAH

IT'S SUNDAY MORNING. *THE* SUNDAY MORNING. THE DAY I SEE Josh again.

To combat the jitters, I start the day with my run, focusing on speed work while listening to a particularly gruesome murder podcast. After showering, I do my Crush Your Comfort Zone journaling, spending way too much time ruminating over the question *If your comfort zone was a tree, what kind would it be?* because . . . weird.

After, I spend a good hour debating what to wear, until Libby, who somehow knows what I'm doing through her big-sister telepathy, calls out that I don't need to look cute if it isn't a date.

And it isn't. So I hang the pretty sundress back in the closet, put on shorts and a sleeveless shirt, and ignore the identical side-eyes from Libby and her devil cat as I head out the door.

Stan's donut and coffee shop is just a few blocks from where we live, so I'll be early, which is typical for me. Josh was always the opposite. The night of our senior prom, he was two hours late. He'd gotten distracted by an emergency with his hermit crab, and he apologized so profusely that I couldn't hold it against him. I thought it was sweet he cared so much about little Edward Scissorhands (who was fine, just molting).

That's the thing with Josh: he doesn't have a cruel bone in his body. As much as my sister likes to paint him as a villain, he'd never harm a living creature on purpose, including me. His last words to me the day he dumped me were *I'm so sorry, Hannah. I really am.* And I believe he was.

Didn't make it any easier for me, though.

My chest aches with the memory, and I swallow as I turn down Broadway, passing the elementary school and a cozy bookstore. Instead of focusing on the way we ended, I think back to our beginning.

We were in eighth grade and my appendix had ruptured, putting me in the hospital. Josh and I were in the same English class, and the teacher asked for someone to drop off my homework. We weren't really friends, but he volunteered. He showed up with said homework, plus a battered copy of *The Devil in the White City*, a book about serial killer H. H. Holmes, who lured women to their death during the 1893 world's fair in Chicago. Josh sat by my hospital bed and read to me for hours about the torture rooms, acid vats, and crematorium in Holmes's so-called Murder Castle. He stayed until the nurses kicked him out, then came back the next day.

And that was it. The beginning of the closest friendship of my life.

Come to think of it, that's what launched my fascination with true crime. A pitiful reminder that a huge portion of my personality traces back to Josh.

We were fifteen when I realized I loved him. I didn't just want to hang out with him as a friend and watch Tim Burton movies and talk about how Danny Elfman was the best film composer of our time. I wanted to hold his hand and kiss him and snuggle with him under a blanket. One day, while riding the Ferris wheel at Navy Pier, I worked up the courage to take his hand, thread my fingers through his. And to my utter relief, he smiled and said, *I've been wanting to do this for so long.*

Back in those days, Josh had braces and acne, and he was shorter than me; the popular girls teased me for dating him. That all changed by senior year. He ended up six feet tall with dark hair, blue eyes, and a dimple. Those other girls were suddenly interested in him, but he didn't seem to notice. Before and after his glow-up, I felt like the luckiest girl on the planet.

We applied to college together and decided on the University of Florida, where Josh became friends with everyone, invited to every party—and I was happy to ride his coattails. Most people just knew me as Josh's girlfriend, and on more than one occasion I overheard someone asking, "Why is he with *her?*"

Josh never made me feel that way, though. My parents' divorce should have made me suspicious of love, but I never doubted Josh. Which just goes to show that I can't trust my own instincts.

I've reached Stan's, five minutes early, and am considering a loop around the block, but the place is packed, so I get in line.

And then I hear something.

"Banana! Hey, over here." It's Josh. He's sitting at a table with two cups of coffee and two donuts. Waving.

I freeze, and time slows as I clock the ways he's changed. His hair is still dark and wavy, but longer than he used to wear it. His eyes are still as sparkling and blue as the lake on a summer day, but his face is tanned and a bit weathered, like he's spent time outside over the years. There's something else different about him, too, something intangible. He's comfortable in his own skin, I suppose. Self-assured in a way that he wasn't before.

Swallowing hard, I force myself to walk over to him. When I reach his table, he stands, and . . . was he always this tall? And broad? Or has he somehow grown since college?

"Hey," I say, waving awkwardly.

Josh opens his arms and pulls me into a hug. And *oh*, he smells good. Just a whiff and I'm tumbling backward in time, sixteen years old and wearing his hoodie to bed because I wanted to be surrounded by his smell all night long.

I pull away, my heart beating too quickly. Josh smiles down at me, his dimple creasing his cheek. He has faint laugh lines around his mouth and eyes that I've never seen before, and that shakes me: the passage of time, etched on his face. I used to know him better than anyone in the world, and now I don't know him at all.

"It's so good to see you," he says, and it sounds genuine.

"You, too," I say. "Although I didn't expect you to be here before me."

His grin widens. "I knew it would be busy, so I ordered. Iced dirty chai and a Nutella donut. I hope that's okay?"

I rarely drink anything caffeinated anymore (it makes me anxious), but I'm flustered that he remembers what I used to order.

"Thanks," I say, and we both sit. "How long are you in town?"

"I moved back. Started a job here."

"A job? So you didn't . . ." I stare at him, confused. "What happened to coral reef ecology?"

"That's what I study. Just finished my PhD at UCSD."

Damn. Have to admit, I'm impressed.

"And now you're . . . in Chicago? There's no coral reef here."

He laughs again. "The job's at Shedd Aquarium. They have research scientists on staff—I'm studying the effects of climate change on coral reef biological niches as water temperatures rise. I'll be helping to create a new exhibit, developing educational offerings, that sort of thing."

My head is spinning. "I can't believe you live here now. In Chicago."

"Yeah, I'm staying with my parents while I look for my own place."

I take a sip of my coffee. This is *so* weird.

"Congratulations," I say, forcing a smile to cover my bewilderment.

"Thanks. What about you—how's the Freedman Group? How are Libby and GiGi?"

My face falls. "My grandma passed away three years ago."

His smile disappears. "Oh, Hannah. I'm so sorry. That must have been awful for you and Libby."

The genuine concern in his voice makes my eyes prickle with tears. "Yeah. It was. It still is. We miss her every day."

"Of course you do," he says. "I'm so sorry. I loved GiGi."

"She loved you, too."

It's partially true; GiGi thought Josh had a good head on his shoulders. But I remember her warning me that I ought to figure myself out before committing to someone. I should have listened.

"Anyway," I say, clearing my throat. "Libby and I are running the company together, trying to keep it from falling into ruin."

I don't know why I'm telling him this. It's just spilling out of me. Probably because of the way he's listening, with complete focus, attentive and earnest. I've been picking at my Nutella-filled donut and sipping my coffee, but his are untouched.

"Things aren't going well?" he asks, his forehead wrinkling in concern.

I shake my head. "We recently lost a huge client. But," I say, not wanting to sound like a loser in front of my ex-boyfriend, who has a freaking doctorate and a supercool job, "we have the opportunity to work with a great new client. Have you heard of that 'Crushing Your Comfort Zone' TED talk?"

He lights up. "Yes! I watched that. Lou—short for Louise, not Loser. You're going to be her PR company? That's amazing."

"She's making us follow her program before she hires us," I say, taking another bite of my donut. A little Nutella oozes out of my mouth, and I wipe it with a napkin. It's strange, how comfortable I feel around him already. *Just like two old friends.*

Libby's voice floats through my mind: *Two old friends who used to bang.*

Refocusing, I tell him about the results of our questionnaires.

"My weakness is in my social skills, obviously," I say.

"Why obviously?" He's looking at me with a perplexed expression, one dark eyebrow raised, like he truly doesn't get it.

"Oh, because I'm . . . you know. Socially awkward."

"No, you're not. You're great with people."

No, I want to say. *You're great with people and I followed you around like a lost puppy.*

"Well, her analysis revealed that I avoid new people and situations, so my challenge is to go on twelve dates with twelve men this summer. It'll be horrendous."

Something happens to his face as I say those words. It's

subtle, a brief shift in his expression. Like when someone pretends to throw a punch, and you can't help but flinch.

Then he leans back and runs a hand through his hair, and the smile returns to his face.

"And Libby's challenge?" he asks.

When I describe the Down & Dirty, he says, "I've always wanted to do one of those," and it hits me: my love for running started when we both joined the track team in high school. Another core personality trait linked to Josh.

"Same. I'm excited to do it with Libby and Scott."

"Scott?"

"Our office manager. Remember that video that went viral on YouTube years ago? The kid helping his mom try on outfits at Neiman Marcus? 'Great!' 'Not great!'" I imitate little Scott's high-pitched voice. "Anyway, that's him. Great Scott."

Josh is eyeing me, and I can tell there's something going on in his mind. Back when we were together, I'd sometimes say, "What?" before he said anything. Like I knew what he wanted to say before he did.

"So . . . who's the fourth member of your team?" he asks casually.

"I still have to find someone."

He grins at me.

I stare at him. "What?"

"I'll do it." He picks up his donut for the first time and takes a giant bite. His voice is muffled when he speaks again. "The Down & Dirty. I'll be on your team."

I burst out laughing. This is *so* Josh. He's a golden retriever, eager to go along with anything that sounds fun at a moment's notice.

"Thanks," I say, "but I didn't ask you."

"Well, you kinda did." He gives me a cheeky grin.

I shake my head. "I need to think about how to balance the team. We can't let just anyone join—"

"Come on, I'm not just *anyone*—"

"—and I should discuss it with Libby and Scott before making a decision."

"I'll be useful," he says, leaning forward. "You know I will. How tall is this Great Scott guy?"

"Maybe five eight, five nine."

"There you go. You need someone who has reach."

He has a point; the best Down & Dirty teams are made up of people with different skill sets. The women from my running group will have strengths similar to mine: excellent endurance, not-so-excellent upper-body strength. Libby has never done anything like this before, so it's hard to guess what her strengths will be. Scott is also a wild card. He could either blow us all away or whine through the whole thing.

We need someone tall and strong, who can heft the rest of the team over a twelve-foot wall, then pull himself over. We also need someone who will be relentlessly happy, even when we're all exhausted and in pain. Josh would fill both those roles.

But: Libby would murder me.

But *but*: she isn't here. And even though the Down & Dirty is about finishing, not winning, I'm competitive by nature. I want my team to do well.

"Okay, fine," I say.

He raises both arms to the sky and gives a victorious whoop. "Yes! This is going to be awesome."

His excited shout makes multiple heads turn our way. I catch the woman next to us checking Josh out, then glancing at me with an appraising look.

I should've worn the sundress. And maybe spent more time on my makeup.

"Are you seeing anyone?" I ask him abruptly.

He startles. "Um. You mean, am I in a relationship? No. I'm not. Not anymore."

He shifts in his seat, clearly uncomfortable, and I decide that it's not polite to ask for more details. I wouldn't want him asking about my relationship history. Not that there's much to say. *I've had sex with three people since you, and it was all terrible. I think you broke me.*

Clearing my throat, I ask, "How's your family? Are your parents still in Evanston?"

He nods, taking a long swallow from his coffee.

"How's Suzanne?" I ask. That's his sister, five years older. "Drew must be, what, seven by now?"

His eyes light up at the mention of his nephew. "He turned eight last month. And Suz and Eric have a little girl now, too. Zella. She's four. Want to see a picture?"

"Of course," I say.

He pulls out his phone and swipes to a picture of himself between Drew and a little dark-haired girl.

"She's adorable. And he's so grown up," I say, struck by how much time has passed.

Eight years ago, I went with Josh to the hospital when Drew was born. We brought a blue teddy bear for him and tulips for Suzanne. At Drew's first birthday party, we gave him a set of wooden blocks, and Josh and I spent an hour building towers for him to knock down.

In the picture, Drew is holding a present. "Was this at his birthday party?" I ask Josh, desperate to shift my mind away from those memories.

He nods. "I made him an *amigurumi* monkey," he says, swiping to the next picture. Drew is holding a purple monkey that looks like it was made out of a chunky sweater.

"A *what*?"

"*Amigurumi*. A crocheted stuffed animal," he explains, like it's a perfectly normal thing for a twenty-seven-year-old man with an advanced degree to make. "When you're out on a research ship for weeks, there's a lot of downtime. Our cook taught me. Oh! That reminds me—I have something for you."

He reaches into a messenger bag draped over his chair, pulls something out, and sets it on the table between us.

My entire body stills.

"It's a meerkat," he says.

A crocheted meerkat, standing up on its hind legs in that peculiar stance they take when watching for predators.

But that's not all.

"He's wearing a suit," I say, my throat tightening. "And he has a briefcase."

Josh grins, his eyes sparking with delight. For a moment, he looks exactly like his teenage self. "Yeah, because of that time we went to the zoo and saw all the meerkats standing up together, facing the same direction. You said they looked like—"

"—a group of businessmen waiting for the train," I finish, my voice faint.

I pick up the meerkat, taking in the details. The little red tie. The briefcase with two gold knots for clasps.

"Josh, this is amazing. Thank you so much."

I mean it; it's a generous and thoughtful gift, and it must have taken hours to make. Hours in which he was thinking, specifically, about me. About a moment we shared a decade ago. *Why?*

When I look up, he's smiling fondly. "I'm glad you like it." He glances at his watch. "Crap, I need to get going. I promised Suzanne I'd watch the kids so she and Eric can go to the Cubs game."

This is also classic Josh, bouncing from one thing to the next like a pinball. We stand, and he pulls me into another hug. Again, that overwhelming, familiar smell. That sense of security and comfort and *home*. My eyes water, and I take a step back.

"It was good to see you," I say.

"You, too."

He hesitates, looking down at me. There's a question in his blue eyes. The air feels oddly intimate, the noise of the crowd fading away. All that exists is Josh, his dark hair falling across his forehead, his lips parting like he's about to speak—

Then he rocks back on his heels, and the moment is over.

"Let me know if you want to meet up to train for the Down & Dirty," he says.

I give myself a small shake. "Yes. I will."

Josh grabs a napkin and scribbles something on it, then hands it to me.

"In case you forgot," he says.

It's his phone number.

Which I still have memorized.

And then he's gone, leaving me alone in the crowd, feeling strangely rattled.

CRUSH YOUR COMFORT ZONE

THE ULTIMATE CHALLENGE COMPANION JOURNAL

WEEK 1

Before you can leave your comfort zone, you need to know it intimately. Why did your comfort zone develop? When? What purpose does it serve? Only after you understand this can we begin to explore our reasons for remaining stuck.

Today, write about the earliest time in your life that you remember finding comfort in this metaphorical zone.

Hannah, 6/5

It was the night of GiGi's annual holiday party for the Freedman Group—a big banquet at a hotel for all her employees and their families. Libby and I were around seven and five at the time, and Mom had dressed us in matching dresses with matching ribbons. All the adults thought we were so darling.

Libby was charming and delightful, as usual, but I was overwhelmed and tongue-tied. When an older man asked me what my name was, I froze up and couldn't respond. Libby answered for me: "Her name is Hannah, and she's shy."

I remember the warm rush of relief that followed, the comfort in knowing Libby would step in for me. But also the certainty that what she said was true, and always would be true: my name is Hannah and I am shy.

Eleven

LIBBY

AFTER A LONG AFTERNOON COLD-CALLING POTENTIAL clients (only two answered their phones, and they were both a decisive but polite *thanks, but no, thanks*), my day is about to get worse. Because today is the day we stop talking about working out and actually start doing it.

Hannah has put together a color-coded and organized torture—I mean, training—calendar, with exercises for endurance and strength and whatever other skills we'll need to complete all the obstacles on race day.

Which is not going to be easy, seeing how much I'm struggling with my first obstacle: Getting. These. Damn. Pants. Up. I'm in a stall in our office bathroom, using all my strength to work these suckers over my hips.

I let out a roaring grunt as I yank the spandex up the last few inches. The material snaps around my waist, squeezing my flesh like a vise. Next up: the sports bra Hannah insisted I buy during our "Sister Shopping Spree."

The whole experience was traumatic and took me back to the nightmare of my teenage years, when everyone who was anyone hung out at the mall. Since I couldn't fit into the sizes at the stores where my friends shopped, I'd pretend to be fascinated by the accessory section. I bought perfume from Victoria's Secret, a wallet from Abercrombie, and earrings from Hollister, just so I could walk out of the store carrying a bag.

I was not carrying a bag when we left Lululemon this past weekend. My lord. The wall of legging-clad mannequins was enough to give me a panic attack, and even if the tiny XXL pants fit, the prices were outrageous. Athleta was a little better. The store had mannequins of all shapes and sizes and I didn't feel like as much of an oddity. But still. I am not a fan. Of the pants, or the sports bra that is currently trying to hold me hostage.

The bra is stuck around my head, and *ugh*, why in the *ugh*. Were these things designed by misogynistic men trying to punish women? I can't—*ugh*.

One more twist, a tug, and my head is free. A little more shimmying and some strategic yanking and my poor girls are successfully smooshed. Mission accomplished?

I throw on an old BBYO T-shirt, pull my hair into a bun, and tie the laces of my brand-new On Cloud shoes. I'm as ready as I'll ever be—which is to say, not at all.

TWENTY MINUTES LATER, we're walking up the ramp that leads from Michigan Avenue to the lake path. I slow down under the guise of admiring the street art that marks the walls.

"You okay?" Hannah asks.

"I'm fine," I tell her, although my bright cheeks and erratic breathing might prove otherwise. If I'm struggling this much before we've even started on the path, there's no way I'll be ready to do that stupid race in twelve weeks.

We emerge at the top by Oak Street Beach, and I take a moment to soak in the view that makes our city so uniquely beautiful: the sun sparkling over the deep blue lake, so vast and huge Hannah used to think it was the ocean, nestled right up against the high-rise office and apartment buildings of downtown. The beach—with its golden sand, water gently lapping on the shore—is a slice of paradise amid the bustle of the big city.

I wish I could trade places with the beachgoers—the ones lying out on the sand, reading—not the ones playing volleyball.

Hannah grabs my hand and leads me away from the water, toward the two-lane path that runs parallel to the shore down the length of the entire city. My chest tightens as bikers and runners whoosh by. It feels like we're about to merge into speeding traffic.

An octogenarian who looks like Betty White (may she rest in peace) speed walks past us, looking as fresh as a daisy, which feels like a slap in the face when I'm struggling so much.

This is pointless—literally everyone is in better shape than I am. And it's not like three months is going to change anything. I am who I am, even if the world wants me to be someone else.

"It's not fair I have to do this," I say, dangerously close to whining.

"Hey, I'm doing a challenge, too," Hannah says, picking up the pace.

"Yeah, but yours was based on the answers of your quiz."

Hannah gives me a questioning look. "Yours was, too."

I scoff, then say, "Lou took one look at me and knew she was going to make me work out."

"On your left!" a biker calls out as he speeds by, barely

missing me. My heart literally seizes—watch me croak out here because an ambulance can't get to me on the path.

"Libs," Hannah says, steering me back into the walking lane. "That's not true."

"It is," I tell her. "You wouldn't understand—people don't judge you at first sight."

"People judge me all the time," Hannah says, pulling my elbow harder. "I'm awkward and weird and you know it. Plus, this isn't a weight thing."

"Everything's a weight thing," I tell her, even though it's wasting precious oxygen. My sister has been thin and pretty her whole life; she can walk into any clothing store and know they'll have her size. Her body is not the first thing people notice about her, and she's never had to worry about people judging her based on one quick look.

Me, on the other hand? I'm either invisible or gawked at.

"Libby," she says again. "Look at me."

I stop and look at my sister, even though we're standing smack in the middle of the running path. As people fly by us, I hear whispers in their quick, measured breaths and the rhythm of their sneakers hitting the pavement.

"This isn't about the way you look," Hannah says. "Which is beautiful, by the way. It's about stepping outside of your comfort zone, and you've got to admit, we're"—she glances down at her watch—"about three-quarters of a mile past your comfort zone."

"We haven't even gone a whole mile yet?" I ask, my breathing getting shallower.

"Come on," Hannah says, nudging my shoulder to get moving. "Let's talk about something fun to distract ourselves. The case I was listening to this morning on *Murder on the Mind* had a decapitated victim—"

"No murder," I say, interrupting her.

"Suit yourself. But it was really gory and good."

My sister gives me a sinister smile and I wonder—not for the first time—how in the world we came from the same gene pool.

"Want to tell me about the meet-cute in whatever you're reading?" Hannah asks, even though she wants to hear about fake love stories (her words, not mine) about as much as I want to hear about real murders.

While I appreciate the offer, I have a better idea.

"How about we get started on *your* meet-cute?" I ask.

Hannah groans but doesn't say no.

"I can ask you some of the questions for your profile," I suggest, taking my phone out of my newly purchased athleisure fanny pack.

"If you can hold your phone and talk, we aren't moving fast enough," Hannah says, a lecturing lilt to her voice.

"I thought this wasn't a race," I say, mimicking the words she used to try to make me feel better this morning. "It's just moving our bodies, right?"

Hannah gives me a side-eye but keeps walking.

"Okay," I say, glancing down at the list in my Notes app. I'll ease her in with something fun and silly. "If you were a fruit, what kind would you be?"

Hannah looks at me with an expression that's equal parts confusion and incredulity.

"How in the world will that help me find a soulmate?" she challenges.

"It's all about the data," I tell her. "Like, maybe apples are compatible with oranges, or cherries with bananas, or—never mind. I'll say you're a pineapple. Prickly on the outside, but sweet inside."

Hannah shakes her head and I look back to the list. "What are you passionate about?"

"Murder and running," Hannah says without giving it any thought.

"That makes you sound like a sadomasochist—and you don't want to attract a serial killer, do you?"

Hannah shrugs. "At least we'd have something to talk about."

I scan the list of questions—I can answer a few for her, like what she eats for breakfast (yogurt and a banana), if she's a morning person or a night owl (early bird), and the worst fad she ever participated in (a tie between French bangs and platform sneakers).

"Name a place you'd like to travel," I ask.

"Australia," she says without hesitation.

My stomach tightens; I imagine this has something to do with Josh. When Hannah got back from meeting him for coffee the other day, she gave me the CliffsNotes. It strikes me as odd that the guy who said "the ocean has given my life meaning" has moved back to Chicago.

Whatever he has up his sleeve, I'm not going to let him fuck with my sister. I protected her from him once, and I'm willing to do it again. The memory gives me a queasy feeling in the pit of my stomach, which I ignore, moving on to the next question.

"What's your ideal night out?" I ask.

"Is this you or the app asking?"

"The app," I tell her. "But it'll be good for me to know for planning your dates."

"If we're talking about my ideal night out with a *stranger*," she says, putting emphasis on the word, "then it would be doing an activity so we don't end up sitting around a table with nothing to do but stare and talk to each other." She shivers, as if just the thought is terrifying.

"What kind of activity?" I ask, recalling cute date scenes I've read. "Bowling? A wine and painting class? A museum?"

"Anything that isn't dinner or drinks," Hannah says.

I make a mental note to research romantic things to do in Chicago. Hannah may be approaching these dates as a means to accomplishing her goal, but I actually want her to fall in love.

The alert on her watch startles me out of our easy conversation.

"We've done two miles," Hannah says.

"Huh," I say. Maybe there is something to the idea of distraction.

"Want to hear about the obstacles we'll be doing on race day?" she asks.

I don't, but I can tell she wants a break from the dating questions.

"Go ahead."

She beams and starts sharing the details she's clearly been waiting to tell me about: how the Down & Dirty is a 5K race interspersed with ten different obstacles—things like crawling through mud under a barbed-wire cage, hauling sandbags up a hill, climbing a twelve-foot wall with the help of your teammates, and carrying your partner across one hundred yards.

I gulp, my panic growing with every new obstacle she describes. Unless there's a forklift involved, there's not enough training in the world that can help me heave myself over a twelve-foot wall.

"If you can't complete an obstacle," Hannah says, a warning in her tone, "you have to do thirty burpees."

"Thirty?" I gasp. I can't even do two.

"That's why we're taking this training seriously." Hannah glances over at me. "It'll be hard for me, too, Libs. My running experience won't help with these obstacles."

I look out toward the lake so she doesn't see me roll my eyes. I know she means well, but the last thing I need is another body positivity lecture.

We're both quiet, walking in comfortable silence until we're interrupted by an overly excited woman running in the opposite direction. It's Katy, a blond, bouncy cheerleader type who was in Hannah's running group. She stops right in front of us, jogging in place (God forbid her heart rate drops) and says a quick hello to Hannah before continuing her run.

"Is she the one you asked to join our team?" I ask once Katy is out of earshot—which only takes a few seconds.

"No," Hannah says, and I exhale in relief. I don't think I can handle that much pep when we're in the literal trenches.

Beside me, my sister brings her finger to her mouth and starts worrying her cuticle.

"Han?" I ask. "What's wrong?"

"Nothing," she says, her voice an octave higher.

"Hannah . . . what did you do?"

"Well," she says, stalling. "We needed a fourth. And I didn't exactly ask him—but I couldn't say no, and it really will be good for our team."

"Who will be good for the team?" I ask, dread welling in the pit of my stomach.

A puff of air leaves Hannah's lips, and the sound it carries sounds an awful lot like *Josh*.

"You didn't." I gasp, horrified.

"Let's keep moving," Hannah says, picking up the pace again.

I scurry after her. "What on earth were you thinking?"

"I wasn't thinking," Hannah admits. "But he offered . . . It'll be fine."

Fine, my ass.

"He's athletic and strong—which will help us, especially for the wall climb and the Ladder of Doom—and he's got that . . ."

A whisper of a smile crosses Hannah's face and I hope she's not thinking of that asshat's muscles. It was one thing to know he'd moved back to Chicago—it's a big city—but this stupid race is going to give him a built-in excuse to see my sister.

He'll probably talk her into going running with him—get her all hot and sweaty on the streets before he tries to get her all hot and sweaty between the sheets. *Ugh.* No. He can't do this. Especially not now, when Hannah is about to embark on a journey to find her one true love.

"You're not going to train with him, are you?" I ask.

"What? No. I mean, I don't know. We're on the same team."

Which is a nonanswer if I ever heard one. But following that logic, he's also on *my* team. Which means I could train with them, keep an eye on them, and make sure the one and only secret I've ever kept from my sister doesn't come out.

Hannah's smart watch beeps.

"Two and a half miles," she says, and I realize we've accidentally picked up our pace.

Apparently nothing makes time fly like pure rage.

Twelve

HANNAH

"I HATE YOU."

Those are Libby's first words to me as I peek in her bedroom. We've completed a full week of training for the Down & Dirty, a steadily increasing program I developed of high-intensity interval training, endurance, and strength. I'm also throwing in some unique exercises recommended in the Down & Dirty training forums; yesterday we went to a playground near our apartment to practice the monkey bars.

"It's time for our Saturday morning workout!" I say, trying to sound cheery.

I'm rewarded with a groan from the lump of blankets on her bed.

"My body is on fire," Libby says, her voice muffled. "I hurt in places that I didn't even know it was possible to hurt. My shins hurt. My scalp hurts. The little, tiny muscles around my vagina *hurt*."

Stifling a laugh, I walk into the gloom of her bedroom and push back her curtains. Morning sunshine bathes the room in glorious golden light, and I sigh happily. But when I turn back around, Libby is frowning at me from her nest of covers on the bed. Next to her, her cat glares like he would scratch my eyes out if he had the chance.

"It's normal to be sore after doing something new and different," I say.

"Normal?" she moans. "My palms are blistered and my armpits are killing me!"

Mine, too, but it's a good hurt, in my opinion. A sign that our bodies are changing in response to the challenge.

"Today's workout is just an interval walk-run. It'll help with your muscle soreness," I promise.

Libby groans again. "All I can do right now is walk-*hobble*. It hurt to sit on the toilet last night. *The toilet, Hannah.*"

To her credit, she climbs out of bed, wincing. Libby can be dramatic, but she's not faking this; she looks miserable, and I feel a twinge of guilt for pushing her too hard. My big sister has always been such a force of nature that sometimes I forget she's not invincible.

"Okay," I say, acquiescing. "But we still need to do some physical activity today. How about yoga?"

Her mouth twists in a horrified grimace. "The one time I did yoga, I spent the whole class trying desperately not to queef."

"Everyone queefs during yoga," I say, shrugging. "First, let me get you some Advil and coffee. In thirty minutes, we'll start."

AN HOUR LATER, we're at the end of our yoga workout, lying flat on our backs in Shavasana pose (now dubbed the thank-fuck-it's-over pose by Libby). On the TV, my favorite virtual yoga teacher, Lyn Liao, encourages us to imagine our bodies floating on the surface of a vast, empty ocean. Easy for her, given that she's doing yoga on a beach in Kauai while we're on our living room floor.

When I open my eyes and glance over at my sister, she looks exhausted but somehow radiant.

"How're you feeling?" I ask her.

She opens her eyes a slit. "Better, actually."

"I'm proud of you." I smile.

She rolls her eyes. "Blah blah blah. I still hate you."

"Don't hate *me*—this is Lou's fault!"

"Lou, short for Louise, not Loser," she says, mimicking Lou's voice. "Short for lunatic is more like it."

"Or ludicrous," I say, laughing.

"Lugubrious," she says.

"Lu . . ."—I search for a word—". . . brication."

"Gross," Libby says, weakly slapping at my hand.

I catch her pinky finger in mine and we stay there, our pinkies linked, floating together.

WHEN WE EVENTUALLY get up, I can tell Libby's not quite as stiff. While she showers, I head to the kitchen to wash dishes from the feast she cooked us last night. My sister is taking her commitment to fueling our workouts seriously. She's always fed us well, but this week she's added more protein, colorful vegetables, and complex carbs to the menu. I've had to remind her that our grocery budget has shrunk along with the pay cut we're taking.

Despite the yoga session, I'm restless and fidgety. I need to do something more intense or I'll feel this way all day.

An idea pops into my mind, and my heart thumps. Ever since I saw Josh, he's been on my mind—not in the background, where he's been for the past five years, but front and center. *Josh. Josh. Josh.* A drumbeat in my head. I keep thinking about him, then ordering myself *not* to think about him, which makes me think about him even more.

Maybe the only way to interrupt that cycle is to see him. I'm supposed to be stepping outside my comfort zone, and it would be *more* comfortable to pretend like Josh doesn't exist. So seeing him again would count as crushing that comfort zone.

That's logical, right?

No, I tell myself. *Don't.*

But when I hear my sister turn on the shower, I grab my phone and text him.

Hannah: Thinking of going for a run. Any interest in joining me?

He replies almost instantly. When and where?

I take a deep breath. At the zoo. In an hour.

Josh: I'll be there

I ARRIVE AT our designated meeting spot by the benches outside the Lincoln Park Zoo, and lo and behold, Josh is waiting in a T-shirt and running shorts, stretching his quads.

And damn, those are some nice quads. Tan and muscular and just the right amount of dark hair.

I mentally smack myself. *Stop it.*

At that moment, Josh sees me. I lift my hand in a dorky wave, and he smiles. The familiar dimple pops. The new laugh lines around his eyes crease, and in the space of a single heartbeat, I'm flooded with conflicting desires: run away or run toward him; smile or burst into tears; curl into a fetal position or jump in excitement.

A memory crystallizes: the day I returned from a two-week trip to Israel with GiGi and Libby. Josh met us at O'Hare with a poster that said WELCOME HOME BANANA. We all-out sprinted to each other, colliding in a heap of laughter and kisses.

Now it's an awkward wave and a smile from a distance.

"Hi!" he says as I get closer. He seems like he's about to pull me into a hug, so I stay a few feet away.

"Ready?" I say.

He blinks, clearly surprised by my abruptness. "Lead the way."

THE ZOO IS swamped with tourists, other runners, elderly ladies in walking groups, and moms pushing strollers. Josh is right at my side, and because of that I run faster than usual. He hardly seems winded, which I tell myself is because he's six inches taller than me.

I set off on my usual loop through the zoo, past a snow leopard sunning on a rock, past hulking camels and chattering monkeys. We circle through the boardwalk near the south end, where a series of ponds are flanked by reeds and grasses. Geese and ducks drift lazily across the water, birds chirp overhead, bees hover near wildflowers—and in the distance, the Chicago skyline, shimmering in the late morning sunshine.

The contrast of those jutting skyscrapers with the lush

natural garden is so beautiful, my breath catches. GiGi used to tell us about the Great Chicago Fire, in 1871, when—as legend says—Mrs. O'Leary was milking her cow and knocked over her lantern. Hot winds whipped the blaze into a frenzy that ended up destroying more than two thousand acres of the fledgling city.

But the people of Chicago didn't allow this to stop them; they rebuilt, bigger and better than before. If our city can make a comeback after such a devastating loss, so can the Freedman Group.

"Is everything okay?" Josh asks, interrupting my thoughts.

I look at him, realizing that we've been running in silence. "Oh. Sorry. Just thinking."

"No worries. I respect the QHT," he says. Quiet Hannah Time. He coined that term for my prolonged silences in high school; it became our shorthand when I needed to be with my own thoughts, because he tended to burst in with random conversational tidbits when I was silent for even a moment.

"Something's different about you," I say, apropos of nothing. "Both times we've met, at Stan's and now here, you arrived before me. What gives?"

He doesn't answer immediately, and I sneak a glance at him. He's got his thinking face on, those thick, dark eyebrows pulled tightly together, lips pressed into a line.

I feel like I overstepped, and I say, "You don't have to answer that—"

"I got diagnosed with ADHD."

I almost trip over my own feet. "You did? When?"

He nods, his eyebrows a tight knot. "When I went to Australia. I was really struggling in my studies. Forgetting to turn in assignments. Missing tests and meetings. It was . . . a rough time."

I hold back a bitter laugh. *He* had a rough time? He wasn't the one left behind with an apartment he couldn't afford and a life he didn't know how to live on his own.

"I hadn't realized how much I relied on you," he continues as we turn off the boardwalk and reenter the zoo proper. "I couldn't keep up. My adviser finally pulled me aside and said that she knew I was smart enough to do the work, so there must be something else going on. She suggested I get evaluated."

Josh was always smart and creative, but also scattered and distractible. And yes, I did help him stay organized, but it never bothered me, because he kept me grounded, stopped me from disappearing into my own anxious mind. I'd manage his schedule and remind him to turn in assignments; he'd order for me at restaurants or tell the waiter if something was wrong with my meal. Back then, it felt like a good partnership.

We pass the zebras and I slow down, wanting to be able to talk without losing my breath.

"So, are you on medication?" I ask.

"Would that make you think less of me?" he says in a wry tone.

"Of course not. No judgment whatsoever. Sorry if it felt that way."

He sighs. "No, I know. It's just, there's still a stigma about ADHD, especially in adults. Some people think it's an excuse to get drugs, or that I just need to 'work harder and stay focused,' like my dad always said."

I remember his dad saying that, and how much it hurt Josh.

"I'm sorry," I say again, meaning it. Then I share something with him that only Libby knows. "I take medication for anxiety and depression. I've been on it for four and a half years."

He goes quiet. I imagine him doing the math in his head. That was not long after he broke up with me.

"Does it help?" he asks, giving me a quick glance before looking away again.

"Overall, yes," I say. "I still have anxious thoughts running through my head, but the medication . . . it turns the volume down. And therapy helped me recognize that those thoughts aren't true."

"Example?"

He's listening with the full force of his attention, and because of that, my words keep spilling out. "Well. I sometimes think everyone hates me and they're just pretending to like me. Or—or that the people I love are going to leave when I need them most." My eyes are stinging, and I blink.

I can tell Josh is looking at me, but I can't meet his eyes. This already feels way too vulnerable. My dad left; Josh left. Obviously, it still hurts.

"Enough about me," I say, picking up my pace. "Is your medication helpful?"

He nods. "It flips a switch in my brain—instead of taking all my energy to do one simple task, avoiding it until the last minute, I can just . . . do it. At first, I couldn't believe this was how regular people got to feel *all* the time."

"I felt that way, too, when my meds started working. Like, is this what normal feels like?" I steer us past a couple pushing a stroller. "I mean, I'm not cured—"

"Me neither," he says, flashing me a smirk that makes me feel briefly off-balance. "But I've learned ways to compensate—

like crocheting in meetings. When my hands are busy, my brain can focus."

I stifle a laugh. "Grandma Josh, sitting in a serious academic meeting, crochet needle and yarn in hand."

"Next I want to learn to knit," he says, dead serious.

"Will you go by Nana? Grammy?"

"I prefer Meemaw, actually." Another smirky grin. "I also have a whole system of checklists and alarms in my phone. I set three reminders to meet you the other day for coffee. That's why I was there early. Plus, I mean, I *wanted* to see you."

His words make me glow inside. But I don't allow myself to examine that feeling too closely. We're rounding the corner back to where we started and slow to a walk, both of us breathing hard.

Josh's hair is curling around the edges, his skin glistening. The sight thrusts me back in time: freshman year in college, running together around campus, caught in a rainstorm. Splashing in puddles, my hair dripping wet, Josh pulling me in for a kiss, whispering in my ear that he wanted to take me back to his dorm and peel off my clothes and kiss me everywhere else, too.

My chest constricts; suddenly, I'm close to crying.

"Good run. We should do this again sometime," he says.

It was a good run, but I'm not sure I can handle being around him. I wish I could snap my fingers and be as nonchalant as he is. To him, our relationship is probably ancient history; to me, it's the wound that never closed over.

Why did you leave me?

The question is on the tip of my tongue, but I tamp it down and fold my arms, holding myself together against the onslaught of another memory.

"Why?" I demand, more harshly than intended. Why does he want to see me now, after all these years?

He stops walking and looks at me seriously, his dark eyebrows drawing together. Josh's thinking face. "We're on the same Down & Dirty team, so we should train together sometimes," he says. Then, quieter: "And I'd like to . . . spend time with you, I guess. You're the best friend I've ever had."

A lump forms in my throat. It's true for me, too. Josh is the only person who's ever made me feel so comfortable, so accepted, so free to be myself—except for my sister, which isn't quite the same.

I could use a friend like that again.

"Okay," I say, keeping my arms folded. If he tries to hug me like he did at the coffee shop, I might cry. "We can try to be friends."

His face breaks into a smile, his dimple winking. "I'll take that."

CRUSH YOUR COMFORT ZONE

THE ULTIMATE CHALLENGE COMPANION JOURNAL

WEEK 2

This week, we continue getting to know your comfort zone.

First, imagine your comfort zone as an actual, physical space. Is it indoors or outdoors? Is it light and airy, or dim and cozy? Are you alone, or is anyone else there with you?

Write about what you have imagined.

Hannah, 6/12

I'm running on a path in a forest at sunrise. It's so quiet that all I can hear is the sound of my own breath; my footfalls are dampened by the carpet of soft leaves under my feet. And there's a sense that I have all the time in the world, that I don't have anything else to do in this moment but run. No to-do list; no worries. I get to choose the path, too. Run whatever direction I want.

It's funny, because in real life I'd never go running alone in a forest. I wouldn't feel calm or safe; I'd feel nervous and vulnerable. And I'd never be able to wipe my brain free of all thoughts.

Which makes me wonder if maybe the comfort of this imaginary scenario is more about the fact that I'm free from all expectations. No one is around, dictating what I do. I don't have to answer to anyone but myself. I can go where I want to go.

Thirteen

LIBBY

LOU IS COMING TO THE OFFICE THIS MORNING FOR OUR FIRST official check-in—and I'm nauseous with nerves. It's like that dream where I'm not prepared for a huge math test, because instead of studying, I've been staring at Hot Math Teacher all semester, thinking of him plus me, minus all our clothing.

My palms are sweaty as I reach for the blue pen from the rainbow of colored pens I have splayed out on my desk—one for each page. Hopefully this will make it less obvious that I filled out most of the entries this morning. I don't want Lou to think I'm not taking this seriously, but honestly, I don't know how writing about my feelings is supposed to help me get in better shape.

Our assignments for the first week are all about getting to know our comfort zones—which at least is something I'm intimately familiar with.

When did your comfort zone develop?

In the womb, I write, then switch the blue pen for a purple one and turn the page.

Describe the sensory experience of your
comfort zone: sights, sounds, smells, and feelings.

I close my eyes and a feeling of calm washes over me. I'm curled up on our couch, a paperback romance novel in hand, Mr. Darcy wedged in the curve of my legs, purring softly. The love of my cat might be the closest I get to experiencing true love—the little man is not happy unless part of him is touching part of me.

As far as smells, there's something sweet in the oven; salted oatmeal raisin cookies at the magic point when the outer layer puffs up and turns a perfect shade of brown. The scene is so vivid that my mouth actually starts to water.

"Ready, sisters?" Great Scott pops his head into our office, interrupting.

I look at the time on my computer. *Shit.* Lou is going to be here any minute.

"Did you download the app?" I ask Hannah, who is sitting at her desk, her eyebrows furrowed in concentration. She's deep in one of her Excel spreadsheets.

"Hmm?" Hannah says, looking up.

"The app," I remind her. "You have to download it and log in."

"Oh yeah," Hannah says. "I did that this morning. We'll be fine; the meeting's going to be great."

I stand up and give my shirt a subtle stretch so it's not so clingy. "Easy for you to say. I don't have anything to show for my progress yet. *Ow.*" I wince at the pain in my side from turning too fast.

"Nothing to show, eh?" Hannah smiles like a proud trainer. "Those burning muscles beg to differ."

I sigh and try to do one of the stretches Hannah said was supposed to help, but it just makes the pain more pronounced.

My sister planned a different exercise for us every day—interval training with jogging and walking, planks and push-ups. Hannah keeps reminding me to be patient, that we're taking baby steps—and that's exactly how I feel. Like a baby.

Every single one of the activities has been a struggle. The other day I was mortified when a five-year-old boy watched us "deadhang" (seriously, could they find a better name for that?!) on the monkey bars at our neighborhood playground. We were supposed to go for thirty seconds; I barely made it ten. After I picked myself up off the woodchip-covered ground, the kid did his own deadhang, smirking at me until after we left to walk home.

Another day, Hannah made us dunk our hands in an ice bath for two minutes before squeezing a stress ball for thirty seconds. My finger bones are still cold just thinking about it. It was pure torture, but she says it's important to practice our grip strength this way, because we'll be wet and freezing through most of the Down & Dirty. *Yay?*

"The lady of the hour has arrived," Scott announces through the intercom system.

"Let's do this," Hannah says, and I follow her, one painful step at a time.

LOU LOOKS AS glamorous as always. Her blond hair is so shiny it's like it was literally spun from gold, and she's wearing pink everywhere, from her lipstick down to her peep-toe heels. She clearly has a signature style, and it makes me wonder what *her* comfort zone is—if it's an over-the-top walk-in closet or whatever chichi salon pampers and plucks her to perfection.

I wince as I take my seat next to Hannah, and Lou gives me a knowing smile. Normally, I'd be embarrassed—sitting shouldn't be that hard—but hopefully my proof of pain will make up for my barely filled-out journal.

Lou claps her hands like a teacher calling the room to attention. "All right, ladies," she says. "Let's see what y'all have done."

I show her the training schedule that "I" put together, and Lou seems impressed. We can't let her know that Hannah is the one who actually did it, but we do tell her Hannah has been joining me on my workouts, and that she's going to be on my Down & Dirty team, along with Great Scott and an old "friend" of Hannah's from college.

Part of me wants to let it slip that Josh is an old flame in hopes that Lou will forbid Hannah from seeing him in the spirit of the challenge, but Hannah would murder me (and she knows the most painful ways to do it), so I keep my mouth shut.

"This is music to my ears," Lou says. "And I love that you're doing it with your sister. Crushing your comfort zone works better when you have the support and encouragement of loved ones."

"I definitely have that," I tell her.

"It's too bad you can't help your sister with her dates!" Lou says, winking.

Beside me, Hannah gulps, and I kick her under the table.

"No way," I say. "The dates are all Hannah."

Lou's eyebrows arch, and I wonder how high they would go if she knew that we aren't exactly "walking her walk."

"Which dating app did you settle on?" she asks Hannah.

"One+One," Hannah says, pulling the app up on her phone. She slides it across the table to Lou, who flips through the screens, muttering the occasional "ooh" and "lovely" as she goes.

Hannah's cheeks are flushed; she's leaning so far back into the chair it's like she's trying to become one with the fabric. And me? I'm sitting on the edge of my seat, proud of the work of art that is my sister's dating profile.

I crafted the entire story: picking out which questions to answer, writing the responses, styling and shooting every one of the gorgeous pictures.

"This profile really captures you," Lou says to Hannah, and I bite my lip to stop myself from taking credit.

"Libby took the photos," Hannah tells her.

"You two," Lou says, her voice dripping with praise. "Just the kind of partnership I want working on my team. Your grandmother would be so proud."

I steal a glance at Hannah. Lou didn't know our grandmother, did she? Although I suppose we're doing a good enough job that any grandmother would be impressed, and if Lou did her research, which I assume she did, then she knows our grandmother started the Freedman Group.

When I look back at Lou, she has her nose buried in the app again.

"A pineapple," she says, laughing. "And this one. Wow." Lou looks up at Hannah and places a hand over her heart. "I love the vulnerability of admitting you want a stronger relationship than the one your parents had. It's clear you've really been doing the work of this challenge. Good job, you."

Lou slides Hannah's phone back across the table and stands, beaming down at us with undeserved pride. "Until next time, my chickadees—keep crushing y'all's comfort zones!"

And with that, she walks out of the conference room, leaving a scent of gardenias in her wake. I feel a twinge of guilt for deceiving Lou—but we *are* doing the things she asked. Just not exactly in the way she wanted.

Great Scott, who was clearly waiting in the wings, is quick to take Lou's spot across from Hannah and me.

"So . . ." he says, as if he hadn't been eavesdropping.

"One week down, eleven to go," Hannah says, deleting the app. Her profile is loaded on my phone, since I'll be doing the swiping and the influx of notifications would stress her out.

"Lou's a little scary, right?" Scott says. "I mean, don't get me wrong, she's fucking fabulous, but also a little . . ." He holds his hands up and waves his fingers, opening his mouth as if he's a meme of someone screaming.

"She's definitely intimidating," I agree.

Hannah stands and smooths her shirt. "I've got spreadsheets calling my name," she says. "Next time Lou comes in, we should have something to show her. Maybe the target market analysis?"

"Great idea," I tell my sister, even though my attention is already focused on the dating app. Now that Hannah's profile has Lou's stamp of approval, it's time to let the swiping begin!

The first guy looks like he's stoned; swipe left.

The second guy is covered in tattoos—hot, but not Hannah's type; swipe left.

A hat in every picture? Swipe left. Five foot three? Swipe left. A name that starts with a *J*? Can't swipe left fast enough! What is wrong with their algorithm? These matches are—*oh my*.

Now, this guy looks like a good candidate. His name is Tony, which starts with one of the twenty-five acceptable letters; he has a full head of dark, wavy hair, and he looks like he wears a suit to work every day. Swipe right!

There are a few more swipe lefts, and then a guy named Paul catches my eye. The first picture is of him on a sailboat and I immediately swipe right, imagining Hannah and me (and Paul) out on the lake.

My daydream is interrupted by a boinging sound as a heart pops onto the screen with the words: 1+1 = 2! Somebody likes you!

My heart races. I have my first match! A moment later, a message arrives.

PAULG: Hey, gorgeous

And just like that, my bubble bursts. I don't have my first match. Hannah does.

If I'm going to message these men as my sister, I have to think and act like her. And I can't act like Hannah if I feel like myself.

I close my eyes and take three purposeful, cleansing breaths. "I am beautiful," I tell myself-as-Hannah. "I love murder, but in a nonthreatening way. I am stupidly smart and crazy athletic. I am rational and logical and think carefully about everything I say before I say it. I am Hannah."

I repeat my sister's name until it feels like my own. And

then I open my eyes and flirt back with Paul as if I really am Hannah.

HANNAHF: Hey, handsome

Well, maybe not exactly like Hannah.

Fourteen

HANNAH

I HAVE MY FIRST DATE TODAY.

Until now, this challenge has felt somewhat abstract. Yes, I've watched Libby set up my profile on that stupid app, and yes, I pretended to be fully invested in the whole thing in front of Lou. But internally, I've been a card-carrying citizen of the land of denial.

No more.

"Okay, it's time," Libby says, facing me across our office. "You ready?"

My stomach flips over. "No."

"It's going to be *fine*. Rob is very nice." She picks up her phone, scrolls to the app, and rattles off information. "Thirty-two, six foot one, a Chicago native. Rescue dog named Bartholomew. Hobbies include playing board games and cooking recipes passed down by his Italian grandmother. He's cute, right?"

She turns the phone to show me his picture.

"He's a generic white guy," I say flatly. "Nothing about him stands out at all."

Libby huffs. "Not everyone needs to look like a Disney prince."

"That's not what I mean. It's better if there are identifying characteristics. Piercings, tattoos, facial hair, birthmarks. Just in case . . ."

"Stop," Libby says, knowing exactly where my mind is going. "Not every man is a murderer."

"Sure, but no one suspects the ordinary-looking white guys, so they're the ones who keep on killing, and killing, and killing . . ."

My sister sets the phone down and takes my hands in hers. "Han. It's going to be okay. You're meeting him in a public place, and it's just a drink."

I freeze. "What? I told you no drinks or dinners. You promised!"

She at least has the decency to look apologetic. "We couldn't make anything else work out. It's just a quick drink to see if you're compatible."

My breathing goes shallow. Those chattering monkeys who live in my brain double and triple and quadruple until my mind is nothing more than a string of panicked thoughts. *I hate walking into bars by myself. What if he doesn't show up? What will we talk about? What if I get sick or spill my drink or blurt out something ridiculous?*

I know it doesn't make sense. I know. I *know*. But anxiety isn't rational. And sure, Libby's been talking to this guy on the app, but it's easy to seem nice online. Aside from all my normal (ha!) anxieties about meeting a new person, there's a small but *not-zero* possibility that he's a predator.

"I hate you," I whisper to her.

"But I *loooooove* you!" she responds, giving me two thumbs-ups as she ushers me out the door.

As we pass the front desk, Great Scott looks up from his phone and puts his hand on his heart.

"Go with God," he says solemnly.

A FEW MINUTES later, I'm sitting at a table at Tavern on Rush, across from Rob. The bar is packed with older men and younger women, and the vibe is everything I hate: dark, loud, crowded. It's also fancier than I expected, and I feel underdressed in my vintage Nirvana T-shirt, denim skirt, and Converse. Within a few minutes, I have a headache from the competing noises of conversation and clinking glasses.

And Rob? Not a thing in his profile appears to be true. He's maybe an inch taller than me, not six foot one. And there's no way he's thirty-two—the pictures on his profile were probably from a decade and about four inches of hairline ago. Not that I'm judging his appearance, but I don't like that he misrepresented himself.

Oh, and the rescue dog? He gave it back to the shelter because it was too needy.

Asshole.

The one positive is that Rob is a talker, which at least keeps me from having to think of much to say.

Here's how our conversation is going:

Upon noticing my T-shirt: "Oh, you like Nirvana? Name ten songs." When I can't, he scoffs and says, "Figures," then launches into a diatribe about the ridiculousness of *bandwagon fans*.

On the subject of movies: "Who's your favorite *Star Wars*

character?" When I say I like Rose Tico, he mutters, "Typical," and lectures me about how Hollywood's obsession with political correctness has destroyed the *Star Wars* universe.

Regarding his work: "I'm an entrepreneur. You ever hear of the gig economy?" then he rambles until I tune him out (but I'm pretty sure he does DoorDash and Uber Eats).

When the server brings our drinks: "It's about time, Usain Bolt," with an exaggerated eye roll in my direction, which I do not reciprocate.

About his family: "My mom always said I look like a young Harrison Ford. Do you see it?" Obviously waiting for me to say I do, which I don't.

Finally, he excuses himself to go to the bathroom. I'd like to do the same, but I'm not stupid enough to leave my half-full glass of pinot grigio with a man who has no identifying features.

I pick up my phone. There's a text from Libby.

Libby: Is it going well??? Is Rob amazing??? 😄 🖤 🍹

Sighing, I respond.

Hannah: I've said maybe thirty words

Libby: So that's a yes??? 😗 😍

I'll fill her in when I get home—and talk to her about vetting future dates better. At least it's almost over. I put my phone down on the table and massage my neck. Rob has been boring and overbearing, but nothing horrific has happened. If anything good has come out of this date, it's that I think I can get through the next eleven, especially if I give Libby some feedback.

My phone buzzes again, and I pick it up, expecting another text from my sister.

But it's from Josh, and as I read the first message, several others appear.

> **Josh:** Remember in our junior year in high school when we snuck out and went to the graveyard one night

> **Josh:** To see that mausoleum that was supposedly haunted and when we got there a possum ran out from behind a gravestone and scared the living daylights out of me

> **Josh:** And you fell on the ground laughing until you peed your pants a little

> **Josh:** And then you changed in my car into a pair of old sweatpants I kept in the trunk and they were gigantic on you so you had to pull the drawstring so tight and tied a knot I could never get out

> **Josh:** Anyway, how are you?

A laugh bubbles out of me, despite the headache. This stream-of-consciousness texting is so very Josh. He used to send me things like this all the time, along with random GIFs or memes to make me laugh.

It's strange to remember I was once that kind of girl, spontaneous enough to sneak out at night with her boyfriend, to fall on the ground laughing.

My chest feels strangely warm. Which I do *not* want to happen with regard to Josh.

So I shut that feeling down.

Hannah: I'm on a date, actually

Josh: Ah

Josh: OK

Josh: Understood

Josh: Bye

The warmth in my chest curdles. Now I feel bad. I'm debating how to respond when another text arrives.

Josh: So yeah, my meds have worn off for the day. Obvi. Sorry for bugging you.

I can practically feel him cringing on the other end of that message. And suddenly I want him to know that I appreciated his texts. That they made me laugh for the first time all day.

Hannah: You're not bugging me. The date is terrible. He's in the bathroom and I'm trying to decide if I should make a run for it. But that's rude, right?

Josh: Depends. How terrible? Like, flossing his teeth at the table terrible? Or like, racist and sexist and homophobic terrible?

Hannah: More like, patronizing and won't stop talking about himself

Josh: ~~Hmmm~~

Josh: Well

Josh: I can give you a rescue call in a bit

Josh: If that would be helpful?

I can see Rob coming back from the bathroom, wiping his wet hands on his pants (ew), so I quickly respond to Josh before putting my phone down:

Hannah: Yes please!

"I have an idea," Rob says, picking up his drink and draining the rest of it. "We should go dancing."

I blink at him. This was not part of the plan. "I don't—"

"Have you been to the Hangge-Uppe? It's right across the street."

"No, I don't really—"

"If you get in early, there isn't a cover. One level is current music, the other level is all eighties, and it's great," he says. I wish I was quick-witted enough to make a snarky remark about him liking the eighties level because he was *born* during that decade, but I'm tongue-tied as usual, and he steamrolls right over me: "Come on, you owe me for buying drinks."

I'm racking my mind for some excuse when my phone rings.

"Hello?" I say, answering.

"Hannah! Darling! I'm so chuffed I caught you!" It's Josh, but he's affected a deep, plummy British accent, and he's speaking so loudly that I hold the phone away from my ear. "Your aunt Penelope has been in a terrible accident."

I sneak a glance at Rob, who has a concerned look on his face; he's heard everything.

"Oh dear," I say awkwardly. "Poor Aunt Penelope. Is she all right?"

"No! She's on her deathbed! In the ICU! Darling, the entire family is gathering. Please do come. She adored you so. She's always said that trip you two took to old Paris"—he says it "Paree," fake French accent and all—"was the highlight of her golden years."

I'm trying to figure out what fictional family member of mine Josh is pretending to be—my father? do I have a British father now?—when he gives an exaggerated sob over the phone.

"My sweet Penelope. Fifty years together, Hannah darling! I don't know what I'll do without her."

Rob is staring at me. I can't tell if he's buying this or not, but I figure I have to play along.

"I'm so sorry, Uncle . . . Ferdinand." *Ferdinand?* I mentally slap myself. "I'll get there as soon as I can. Please tell Aunt Pen to hang on for me."

Josh sniffs into the phone. "Of course, dear. Do hurry. Tallyho!"

I end the call and turn back to Rob, hoping I look like a shocked, grieving niece. "I—I'm so sorry. I need to get going."

I see the exact moment it dawns on him that the call was fake. His eyebrows drop and his lips twist in a sneer. "Bitch."

"Hey!" I say, shocked enough that the next words slip out: "What the hell is wrong with you?"

"What the hell is wrong with *you*?" He gets right in my face, his eyes glinting with something nasty, and I take a step back, terrified.

Our server walks by, and when Rob sees her, he steps away, smoothing his shirt. "You're not even that hot, anyway," he says to me.

And stalks away without paying.

I LEAVE THE bar—after settling our bill, Rob's three drinks to my one—and call Josh.

"Did it work?" he asks.

"Yes, but he figured out we were faking it!"

"How?" he says, sounding so surprised that I burst into a laugh.

"Aunt Penelope? Old *Paree*?" I say, stifling a giggle. "Josh, you could have pretended to be my brother or something."

"What would've been the fun in that?"

"Plus, that *accent*—I told you years ago to never, ever try any accents, remember?"

"Och, the wee lass has wounded me," he says in a terrible Scottish brogue, then switches to something I assume is trying to be Russian: "I am expert at accent. I learn from KGB—"

"Stop!" I'm laughing so hard I have to lean against a building to catch my breath.

Usually, I'd call an Uber, but that's not in the budget anymore. Luckily it's a warm June evening, the sun low enough that the streets are bathed in shadows, the breeze carrying the faintly crisp scent of the lake.

Once I start walking again, I ask him about his day, and he tells me about a project he's working on. Every summer, researchers from the Shedd take a group of high school students to study marine biology in the Bahamas. Josh is developing a new educational track focusing on coral reef conservation.

His enthusiasm for his work bursts out of him—he was never this passionate about anything we studied in college, or about his future as a financial planner.

And that's when it hits me.

Have I ever been this passionate about my work? I've been working for the Freedman Group for four years, and I'm not sure I've ever created anything I've been truly excited about. A strangely wistful feeling washes over me.

"Sorry, I'm talking your ear off," Josh says. "Tell me about your day. How's this summer challenge going?"

I describe the journaling and the training with Libby. An ambulance wails by, and I put my finger to my ear.

"I should warn you," I tell him as I pass Hotel Lincoln, dodging the throngs of people heading out for the night. "Libby's not thrilled about having you on our D&D team."

"Our *world-class* D&D team," he says.

"But since I'm in charge of the training program, she's going to have to deal with it. That's our trade: I do the training program; she coordinates the dates for me."

"Sounds fair."

"As long as she's more careful about who she sets me up with. Rob was sketchy. But it's over! One down, eleven to go."

There's a pause. Our easy back-and-forth has stalled out.

"Josh? You still there?"

He clears his throat. "Yeah, sorry. It's a little weird knowing that you're going out with twelve men this summer."

Anger flashes inside me, white-hot and surprising. He's the one who left *me*; he's the one who fell for somebody else.

"You don't get to say that to me," I say, then swallow down my anger, softening the edge in my words. "We're friends, Josh. Right?"

He's quiet for a moment, then says in a firm voice, "Right. Just want you to be safe." Another pause. "Anyway, we should go running again soon, friend. And I have an idea of where we should go."

My interest is piqued. "Where?"

"You'll see."

I hesitate, frowning; I hate not knowing what to expect.

"Come on," Josh urges. "It'll be fun. I promise."

So, I take a breath and remind myself to take a step away from comfort, toward growth. "Sure. Okay."

Fifteen

LIBBY

I'M SITTING ON THE COUCH, READING THE LATEST COHO book, when the front door opens and Hannah walks in. It's late, after ten, which I hope is a good sign.

"How was Hot First Date Guy?" I ask, not bothering to hide my excitement.

Hannah lets the front door slam shut. Mr. Darcy's back arches, his fur puffs up, and he darts down the hall, making a beeline for my room. The cat may not be able to read a novel, but he can sure as hell read a room.

"So . . ." I say. "Not a love connection?"

My sister turns slowly toward me, her eyes sparking with fury. If looks could kill, I'd be dead on the couch—which would be great fodder for one of her murder podcasts. *Sister killed over good intentions.*

"I . . . You . . . He . . ." Hannah can't get her words out.

"He . . . was super handsome and charming?" I say hopefully.

"Ugh." Hannah flops down at the opposite end of the couch. I stretch my legs to gently poke her and she recoils.

"Libby," she snaps, her voice as full of fury as her stare. "I am putting a lot of trust in you."

"I know," I tell her. She's trusting me with her time, her life, *and* her heart.

"Do you?" Hannah asks. "How much do you know about the guy you sent me out with? On a date which, by the way, was everything I told you I didn't want."

"I'm sorry," I tell her. "I did try, but he was insistent that I—that you—meet him at Tavern."

"And you didn't think that was a red flag?" she asks, her eyes growing wide. She's looking at me like I don't know what I'm doing—which, in my defense, I don't. Sure, I read more romance novels than the average person, but I haven't been on a proper date since Obama's second term.

"He seemed like a good guy," I say in my defense.

"What exactly did you know about him?" she asks.

"He's tall," I say, stalling. I've been messaging with a few different men, and it's hard to keep them all straight. "He's a runner. And he has a good job."

"Did you look him up on LinkedIn?" Hannah fires back, and I shake my head. "So, you just took his word for it?"

I shrug. "He looked nice."

"He was not nice—he started the date off rude and patronizing, and ended it being rude and threatening."

"Threatening?"

Hannah groans as if she can't bear to recount the date for me. "You have to be more careful," she says. "Cross-check everything on LinkedIn, Facebook, and Instagram. Google these guys and look for warning signs. Please. You don't want to find me dismembered in someone's crawl space, do you?"

"Of course not, I would die," I tell her. "At least you're home safe."

"No thanks to you," she says. "Josh saved me."

Fucking Josh. I'm glad he came to the rescue tonight, but I'll murder him if he screws this up for Hannah. She deserves to find someone who puts her first, who loves her more than any stupid dream job.

"I'm sorry," I say. "I promise I'll do better. It can only go up from here, right?"

My sister looks at me, and I can see her thoughts playing out over her face. She's not sure she can trust me, but she knows she has to complete this challenge if we're going to save the business. She also knows that if I don't find the guys and plan the dates, she'll have to.

Hannah sighs and stands. "Be ready for the trifecta to-morrow morning at seven a.m. Push-ups, squats, and jump rope. And maybe grip strength."

I nod, accepting my punishment—and the fact that I've got eleven more chances to find my sister her *beshert*.

I HAVE EVERY intention of going to sleep—but after I brush my teeth, wash my face, and climb into bed, I open the One+One app. Swiping left and right is more addicting than TikTok.

There are two new messages from guys I swiped right on earlier—one of them a six foot two lawyer. At least, he claims to be.

I study this guy, Brandon, and try to glean something from his picture. Is the sparkle in his eyes devious or enchant-ing? His smile sinister or sincere? It must be exhausting for

Hannah, being so suspicious of every person who crosses her path.

It should be easy enough to find out if this guy really is a lawyer, but I have no clue how my sister thinks I'm supposed to fact-check how tall a man is. Better to just assume they're fibbing a bit. No one tells the full truth—men add inches to their height (and their length); women subtract digits from the scale and their age. It's what people do. Just last month I rounded down a good twenty pounds when I went to renew my license.

I click on the possibly tall lawyer's message.

BRANDONB: Wassup?

Oy. *Do better, Brandon.*

I close the message without responding.

The second message is from a guy named Adam. Out of the hundreds of profiles I've skimmed over the last few days, his stood out. He's cute in that nerdy, Jewish-boy-next-door way, with curly brown hair, glasses, and a neatly trimmed beard. I swiped right even though he's only five nine, which is shorter than Hannah's requirements—especially if he rounded up—but his answers to the questions on his profile were so witty and charming I couldn't help but like him.

For the question about the last place he traveled, Adam said wherever the last book he read was set. Automatic bonus points that he reads, and also, I completely agree! A good book can absolutely transport you to another place.

As far as his favorite night out, Adam wrote that he prefers a quiet night in with a bottle of good red wine and a dinner that he and his date cook together (he'll do the dishes).

After that he wrote something about trading favorite songs on the stereo and dancing in the living room. Total swoon—the date sounds like something ripped from the pages of a romance novel.

It also sounds like Hannah's nightmare. At least for a first date.

I tap to read his message, hoping he has something more interesting than "hello." I swear, these men have no imagination.

ADAMR: Hello

I frown, disappointed—until I read his second message, sent two minutes after the first one.

ADAMR: Sorry. I'm awful at opening lines—but I have to tell you, I'm excellent at opening jars.

This makes me laugh, but I'm not quite sure how to respond. I fluff up my pillows and settle back, trying to think what Helen Hoang or Jasmine Guillory would write if they were drafting a meet-cute between Adam and me.

Between Adam and Hannah. *This is for Hannah*, I remind myself.

I consider saying something about women being strong enough to open their own jars, thank you very much . . . but I don't want to scare him away. I consider asking what kinds of jars he likes to open, but that's lame. Although maybe that will get him talking about what he likes to cook . . .

HANNAHF: What was the last jar you opened?

I hit send, and before I can close out of the message, three dots appear. He's online? At 11:11 on a Friday night? Forget that I am, too, but I wonder what that says about him.

ADAMR: Don't judge me . . . but it was a jar of marinara sauce

He's two for two with getting a laugh out of me. Which is good. Hannah likes funny guys; she was always laughing around Josh.

HANNAHF: Why would I judge you for that?

ADAMR: Because homemade sauce is so much better. But this was an emergency situation.

HANNAHF: Ahhh. A pasta emergency. Those can be very dangerous. I hope you're okay.

ADAMR: Everyone survived

I wonder if "everyone" was him and another woman, someone else he met on the app.

HANNAHF: Serious question

ADAMR: Shoot

HANNAHF: You mentioned you wash dishes

ADAMR: I do . . .

HANNAHF: Okay. So, when you're putting silverware in the dishwasher, do you put your utensils in face up or down? And why.

ADAMR: Going straight for the make or break questions, huh?

HANNAHF: Hey, I don't want to waste either of our time . . .

ADAMR: Well, I usually hand wash them. But if I'm going to use the dishwasher, sharp points down. Always.

HANNAHF: Always?

ADAMR: I could tell you the story, but I'd rather show you the scar sometime. Five stitches in my palm.

HANNAHF: Ouch

ADAMR: So, what do you think?

HANNAHF: About your scar?

ADAMR: About me showing you sometime. Maybe tomorrow night?

My heart flutters, and for a moment, it feels like he asked me out. Not Hannah. And while I wish I could say yes, I just promised I'd get to know more about these men before I send her out with them.

I crack my knuckles, excited to continue our conversation. Back when I dabbled in online dating, this was the part I loved. I'm a pro at the art of witty banter—especially when there's a screen between me and the man I'm talking to. It's the in-person stuff that brings my insecurities raging to the forefront.

I've always been aware of the way society sees women like me, but the rejection hurts when it comes from a person you thought you had a connection with—a person you thought was in the bathroom until the waitress tells you he paid for his half of the bill and got his order to go before leaving.

At least I don't have to worry that Adam will be disappointed with the woman he eventually gets to meet in person.

HANNAHF: LOL. Has that pickup line ever worked for you?

ADAMR: Hey, I told you I wasn't good at opening lines

HANNAHF: Or closing ones, apparently

I send a smiley face so he knows I'm trying to be flirty, not rude.

HANNAHF: As much as I'd love to see your scar in person, I can't tomorrow night

ADAMR: I understand

HANNAHF: Maybe next weekend?

That should be enough time to complete Hannah's stalking requirements.

ADAMR: I'm out of town the next two weekends

I frown, more disappointed than I have a right to be; I have a good feeling about this guy. Although, on the bright side . . . if his and Hannah's first date has to be delayed, that means more time for me to talk to him. To make sure he's a good match for my sister.

HANNAHF: I guess that means you'll have to make our first date worth the wait

ADAMR: Challenge accepted

ADAMR: Speaking of work, I have an early morning tomorrow. I'd better run.

The word "run" sends shivers down my arms. I glance at the clock and realize it's after midnight; tomorrow's workout with Hannah is going to be even harder if I don't get some sleep.

HANNAHF: Yeah, I'd better go, too

ADAMR: It's been fun chatting with you, Hannah

HANNAHF: You too. Good night.

ADAMR: Night

I plug my phone in and turn off my lamp. There's a giant smile on my face, and I feel the same way I do when I get caught up in the swoony part of a good romance novel.

Only this time, I'm helping to write the love story.

CRUSH YOUR COMFORT ZONE

THE ULTIMATE CHALLENGE COMPANION JOURNAL

WEEK 3

This week, we will explore how other people in our lives helped to create our comfort zones. Today, start by writing about a parent, or parental figure, who was a source of comfort to you in your early life.

Hannah, 6/19

It's funny, because my first thought wasn't my parents—I thought about Libby. Mom and Dad never seemed reliable enough for me to turn to for comfort, especially after the divorce.

Libby was, though. I remember so many nights when I couldn't sleep because my mind was racing, or I heard a spooky sound, or Mom and Dad had fought, and I crawled into bed with Libby. She'd grumble a little but she never said no. Sometimes she'd make me sleep top-to-tail which would put my face level with her feet. Is it weird that the memory of my sister's feet still makes me feel safe? Just the knowledge that she was there, I guess. That she would always be there.

Sixteen

HANNAH

"OOOH! I FOUND ANOTHER GOOD ONE!" LIBBY SAYS.

I glance up from my computer screen, where I'm running numbers on the media and spending habits of Lou's target market, and see Libby holding out her phone, a proud smile on her face.

This is the fifth time in the last hour that she's said this about a potential match. The fact that she's gotten so many "good ones" so quickly seems suspicious.

"What makes him so great?" I ask.

"He wrote that his mom is his best friend. Aw."

"Meaning he lives in her basement and she does his laundry," Great Scott chimes in. He's over in the corner, doing pull-ups on a bar we mounted so we can incorporate some Down & Dirty training at work, counting reps under his breath: "Nine, ten . . ."

I glance at Libby's screen and see a picture of the man holding up a fish he recently caught.

"Immediately no," I say.

She huffs. "Why?"

"Never date a man who proudly displays dead animals," Scott says between breaths. "Fifteen . . . sixteen."

He's only slightly winded and I'm mildly annoyed that he can do these so easily. The privilege of testosterone and upper-body muscle mass. I've never been able to do even one.

"Exactly," I say. "He's like, 'Look at this innocent fish I lured to its death. Maybe I should do the same with a woman.' Next thing you know, *you're* the one wrapped in foil in his freezer."

Libby makes a disgusted face and keeps swiping.

"You don't know how lucky you are," she says. "I never got this many matches when I was on the apps."

I catch a note of hurt in her voice. My sister is the loveliest, most generous, most creative human in the world. And she's objectively gorgeous—all luscious soft curves and creamy skin. She's been hurt by some truly awful guys, though.

"Any man who overlooks you is missing out," I tell her. "Remember: *If someone treats you badly, it's a reflection on them, not on you.*"

That's something GiGi used to say. Libby recognizes it, and her eyes fill with tears. "I'll keep looking."

I go back to my spreadsheet, and when I glance over again, I see Libby working on the pitch deck for one of the few prospective clients that agreed to a meeting with us. On impulse, I roll over to her desk and take a closer look at her computer screen. The press kit she's working on is good, but there's something missing.

"What if we mocked this up to show how the headline would appear in a newspaper, on Facebook, and on Instagram?" I suggest.

"No, that won't work," Libby says without looking at me.

I swallow and try not to feel like my idea is a pesky fly she's flicked away. "We could try and visualize how the campaign could expand their reach on social media."

"You work on your stuff and I'll work on mine, and tomorrow we'll share what we've got."

I swallow. She's right. This is what we do: divide and conquer according to our respective strengths. Even as a kid, Libby was praised for her artwork, her fashion sense, the little plays she'd write for us to perform for our parents and GiGi. I was praised for acing my math tests, for getting good grades, and for keeping my room organized.

It doesn't make sense for us to duplicate our efforts by working on the same tasks. The fact that I feel mildly stifled is irrelevant; everyone feels like this at work sometimes.

"Oh, and by the way," Libby says, turning around. "I'm working on a plan to bring in some extra cash."

"That's . . . good," I say; we definitely need the money—I'm nervous about the electric bill this summer since Libby likes the AC blasting.

"We have all this extra space in the office, so we're going to rent it out. You know, like a coworking space? Twelve people are already interested."

I blink. She's bringing strangers into our office? To work here? With us? Questions flood my mind: *How did she find these people? Will there be a vetting process? Background checks? Will they clean up after themselves?*

And most of all: Why didn't she talk to me about this before doing it?

"But—"

"It'll be fine, Han," she says, turning back to her work. "Trust me."

And what can I say to that? Nothing.

WHEN THE CLOCK turns to five, I discreetly slip out the door, telling Libby I'll meet her at home. It's time for me to meet Josh for this "special run" he's planned, and I don't need my sister telling me it's a terrible idea.

I already know that. But I can't keep myself from doing it anyway.

A FEW MINUTES later, I'm in Josh's car, heading south down Halsted.

"So . . . when are you going to tell me where we're going?" I ask. My knees are bouncing with nerves.

"Patience, grasshopper," he says, his dimple showing.

It's not just the surprise making me anxious; being in a car with Josh is unsettling. Not only does he own a car I've never seen before (a silver Accord he apparently bought in grad school), but it's strange being this close to him, in a confined space, with no one else around.

I can smell him.

I can hear that hint of gravel in his voice when he laughs.

I can see the individual flecks of stubble on his jaw. The finger-combed waves in his dark hair. The cracked skin on his knuckles as his fingers drum the steering wheel. He always had dry skin; I was always buying him hand cream, which he would promptly lose.

My chest aches. These little intimacies—details I know so well but am not entitled to anymore—bring a rush of emotion. Nostalgia? Sorrow? I don't know.

Ever since Josh reappeared in my life, I've been dancing around one question: *Why did you leave?*

Obviously our relationship didn't matter as much to him

as it did to me, but that begs another question: If I wasn't important enough to keep, why did he stay with me so long?

Maybe Josh dated me for all those years because it was easy. Because *I* made it easy. I never got upset when he was late for a date or got distracted in the middle of a conversation; I kept him on track with school. Then, as soon as we were separated by thousands of miles and he had to make an effort to connect with me, he moved on to someone else.

"Sorry to interrupt the QHT," he says, "but we're almost there. Close your eyes, please."

"Close my—"

"Trust the process, Banana," he says seriously. "It'll be worth it."

Josh is impossible to resist when he's like this. Obediently, I close my eyes.

"Give me a hint." I need to know *something* or my anxiety will keep climbing.

"I'm taking you to a place," he says in a dramatic voice, "where dozens of young women were tortured and killed, their bodies disposed of in quicklime or cremated—"

"The Murder Castle!" I say, delighted. "We're going to the site of H. H. Holmes's hotel? How'd you figure out where it was?"

"I have my methods." He pauses. "My methods being Google. I figure we can visit the site, then run through the area and talk about all the horrific things he did to his victims."

"Sounds great." And not just the activity—the fact that he remembers this part of our history together.

Friends, I remind myself. *He wants to be friends.*

He pulls the car to a stop, then parks. "Keep your eyes closed. I'll be right back."

I hear his door opening and closing; a few seconds later, my door opens. His hand touches mine, warm and rough, and my heart stutters. It's too familiar, this touch. Too painfully familiar.

I yank my hand away.

"Sorry," he says, sounding awkward. "I wanted to help you out of the car."

I give a shaky laugh. "Okay, lead the way."

With his hands lightly touching my shoulders, he walks me in some unknown direction. I feel cement under my feet, then grass.

"Okay," Josh says. "Here we are!"

I open my eyes and blink in the evening sun. I'm standing on a scraggly lawn littered with trash, next to a beige building with at least one broken window. Across the street is a discount grocery store. There's a graffiti-covered overpass in the other direction.

I hesitate. "You're sure we're in the right place?"

"This is the correct address. The hotel was right here," he says, indicating the run-down building. "It's a post office now, I guess. And . . ." He scratches his head. "Yeah."

"It's really interesting." I'm not sure what else to say.

We stand in awkward silence. An old fast-food bag rolls by like a tumbleweed in a Western movie. I'm not sure what I expected, but it wasn't this. The past century has swept away all evidence of Holmes and his many victims. There's not even a plaque commemorating the place where dozens of people lost their lives at the hands of a madman.

I wrap my arms around myself, feeling strangely wistful. Life passes so quickly. Once we're gone, the impact we had on the world fades, too.

Not that I'm living the kind of life that will leave a mark. But GiGi did. Which is why we need to keep the flame of the Freedman Group burning in her honor. My eyes fill with tears, and Josh must notice, because he steps closer. "Hey. You okay?"

I take a step away, forcing myself back to reality. "Just wondering if you still want to run around here?"

"Of course not," he says firmly. "Let's get back in the car."

We do, and he pulls away, staring straight ahead. A flush is creeping up the back of his neck. He's embarrassed, I realize. He was excited to share something with me—a joint memory, something unique to our friendship—and it didn't turn out like he hoped. While I was pondering the meaning of life, he was feeling stupid for taking me to stare at a run-down post office.

"It was cool to see the location," I say, tentative. "Crazy to think Chicago has changed so much."

But he's still twitchy, his knuckles white as he grips the steering wheel.

"Josh, it's okay—"

"I'm sorry," he says abruptly. "It was dumb of me to bring you here. But you know, typical Josh, not thinking things through. Getting all excited and not paying attention to the details."

The way he says those words—it almost sounds like he's reciting something he's been told.

"Do people say that about you?" I ask.

"Sometimes. I mean, yeah. And it's true. One of the many reasons I'm difficult to live with."

A flicker of indignation makes me sit up straight. "Wait. Who told you that?"

He exhales and shakes his head. "My ex-girlfriend," he says. It's strange to hear those words, to remember that Josh has had this entire life I know nothing about. "And I can't blame her. I'm not detail oriented. I'd forget to pick up what she needed at the grocery store—"

"Everyone does that sometimes—"

"Put expensive cheese in the cupboard instead of the fridge—"

"That's an honest mistake—"

"Get absorbed in something at work and lose track of time and not answer her texts and rush into the restaurant fifteen minutes late to her birthday party." He shrugs. "See? Difficult to live with."

"Josh, that's—" I sputter, feeling defensive of him. "That's complete bullshit."

He shakes his head, his jaw tight. "It's not, and you know it. Remember that business calculus class we took in college? I would've failed if not for you. And even now, with meds and lists and reminders, I'll always be scattered and disorganized."

"But that's not the whole truth about you," I say. "You're also creative, and funny and engaging, and incredibly thoughtful—"

"You don't have to—"

"Maybe you don't remember what to get at the grocery store, but you remember specific things about people, for years! Like that meerkat you made me. And when you planned this run—"

"That totally bombed."

"—it meant a lot to me." My voice echoes in the quiet car, earnest in a way that makes me feel exposed. This cuts too close to admitting how much I care about him, how much I missed him. "And about this ex-girlfriend. Everyone has imperfections. I'm sure she did, too. But if she couldn't handle your weaknesses or appreciate your strengths, that reflects on her. Not you."

It's similar to what I told Libby, and I'm grateful for my grandmother's wisdom, which has come in handy twice today. Not that any of it seems to have gotten through to Josh. He's staring straight ahead, his fingers tapping on the steering wheel while we wait for the light to turn green.

"To be fair," he says after a beat, "once I fell asleep in the middle of a conversation with her. She was telling me about an issue at work and I just . . ." He closes his eyes and pretends to fall asleep, letting out a snore.

I crack a smile. "Okay, yeah, that would be a little annoying."

He's broken the tension; Josh has always been good at that, but now I wonder if he thinks he needs to be funny and charming to compensate for what he sees as his flaws.

I lean my head against the back of the seat, hesitating before I ask the next question. "So. This ex-girlfriend . . ."

"Kayla. We broke up almost a year ago," he says, his voice even. "But we lived together for a year before that, and I was going to ask her to marry me. Bought a ring and everything."

My chest constricts. Josh saving up for a ring, planning a proposal. All the things I thought he would do for me.

But also, an unexpected swell of sympathy. Josh got his heart broken by the person he thought he was going to spend his life with. I know all too well how that feels. I could point that out, rub his face in it. *Doesn't feel great, does it?*

But it's obvious that he's still hurting. And it's clear that he doesn't want to talk about it anymore. Neither do I. Hearing about Josh's past relationship reminds me that we have successfully avoided talking about *our* relationship—particularly how it ended. If we're going to try being friends, we can't leave this hanging between us. I'm not sure I'm ready to face it yet, but I'm not ready to go home and call it a day, either.

He turns up Lakeshore Drive and I gaze out the window at Lake Michigan, dotted with white sailboats. The evening sun has turned the clouds cotton-candy pink, the blush reflected in the glistening water.

"How about we head to the lake path?" I ask after a pause. "I always run north of downtown, so it'd be fun to check out the south end."

He gives me a grateful smile. "I'd really like that."

And off we go.

Seventeen

LIBBY

THE NEXT WEEK, OUR OFFICE IS BUZZING WITH NEW ENERGY, thanks to the dozen people who are renting desk space. I knew coworking was popular, but I was surprised by all the interest. And it's a win-win: our renters are paying a nominal fee while making the office feel like a thriving business instead of a fledgling one.

Hannah and I are sitting in the conference room, halfway through a quarterly account review with the owners of Bagelville, one of our few remaining clients. For all the time we spend trying to make them happy—an impossible task—you'd think we'd have a high retainer. But no. GiGi signed them as a favor to a friend, and they balk every time we suggest upping their scope. At least they give us a discount on their bagels.

"What I don't understand," Mr. Schwartz is saying, "is why the *Reader* hasn't covered us once this month!"

"Not even once," his son, the junior Schwartz, echoes. He's fifty-something to his father's seventy-something, and the two men look like they could be caricatures of old Jewish men, one with gray hair and the other with none.

"I don't even know what we're paying you for," the elder Mr. Schwartz says.

I cross my legs and shift in my seat, trying to ignore the fact that my bladder is about to explode from all the water Hannah has me drinking. I don't understand the benefit of drinking a gallon a day when every ounce goes straight through me.

"Well?" the senior Mr. Schwartz says, getting more impatient by the second.

Hannah looks at me; usually I'm the one who talks clients down when they get irrational, but it's taking every ounce of concentration not to pee my pants. I'm still trying to think of what to say when Hannah jumps in.

"If you want to guarantee coverage in the *Reader*," she says in a calmer voice than I would have been able to muster, "then you'll have to pay for an ad."

"Yes," I pipe in. "You know what they say, advertising is what you pay for; publicity is what you pray for!"

The Mr. Schwartzes and Hannah look at me like I've lost my marbles. Oh, fuck it. I've got to go.

"Excuse me," I mutter, trying to get up from my seat without causing further distraction—or pain. Hannah says the muscle aches will ease as I get stronger, but so far, all this exercise has been a literal pain in my ass. And my side. And my quads.

"Gentlemen," Hannah says, calling their attention back to her. "While you weren't in the *Reader* this month, you did get coverage in other outlets. Let's look at your social media stats for the quarter."

As I waddle to the bathroom, I think about all the work we put into this client for barely any money—and zero appreciation. I don't know how GiGi did it for all those years. Probably because she loved public relations on a soul-deep level.

While there are parts of this job that I love—the creativity and interaction with people; the satisfaction of raising awareness for issues and products I care about; getting people to think about things in new and different ways—hawking bagels isn't one of them. And the business side of things is just so stressful. It's hard to find joy in the things you do love when you have to worry about keeping the lights on. Literally.

Hannah was up past midnight last night, trying to finagle the Bagelville analytics from this past quarter into something more impressive, but there are only so many ways to spin a story about Chicago bagels that rival their more famous New York cousins.

I felt guilty I couldn't be more help to my sister, but I stayed up with her in solidarity, using the time to work on a competitive deck, gathering information about services provided by other PR firms in Chicago. I was hoping to find something that we're missing, to give a practical—and fixable—reason that we can't seem to attract a single new client.

Of all the three dozen prospective clients we've reached out to over the past few weeks, only two agreed to meet with us, and both left our offices seemingly unimpressed. Which is why we can't afford to lose the bagel business. Even if they're only paying us pennies, they're pennies we need.

By the time I make my way back to the conference room, where the Mr. Schwartzes are still sitting with identical disgruntled expressions, Hannah is only on her second page of stats, sharing the reach of the few articles we managed to get placed in the last three months.

I'm nodding at something smart she said when my phone buzzes. I look down to see a message from Adam. Thank god; something to get me through the next ten slides.

ADAMR: Having a good day?

HANNAHF: I would give it a 5 out of 10

The rating scale is something new. I'm trying to infuse more Hannah into our conversations. This is as mathy as I get, and it's been fun rating things with Adam. So far, we've decided that Fox News gets a 3 out of 10, NPR gets an 8 out of 10, and vanilla lattes get a 9 out of 10.

Nothing has gotten a perfect 10 yet. After much discussion, we agreed that honor should be reserved for the most transcendent things. The kind of things that stop time because they are just that good or beautiful or delicious.

ADAMR: Ouch. At least there's room for improvement?

HANNAHF: I guess. How about you?

ADAMR: Well, it was a 6 out of 10 . . . but now that I'm talking to you, it's jumped to an 8

Swoon. Who knew numbers could be so damn sexy? As much as I want to type back something cute, like "What would it take to get it to a 10?" I don't. Because if I do, and Adam responds with something like "You coming over for dinner tonight," I won't be able to say yes. It wouldn't leave enough time for me to get Hannah up to speed on all the things Adam and I have talked about over the last week, like his first crush (the cantor at his temple), his favorite place to go as a kid (Camp Chickawah), and the best vacation he recently took (the beach in Destin, Florida).

Thanks to the stalking Hannah has me doing, I already knew about that trip—both the beautiful white sand beaches and the even more beautiful woman he went with. Adam's ex-girlfriend is stunning—just as slim as my sister, but with more curves and bigger boobs. And according to the photographic evidence, always dressed to the nines.

It was a good reality check: as much fun as I'm having talking with Adam, it's clear that he's the kind of man who dates leading ladies. Not sidekicks.

Which is irrelevant, anyway, since I'm setting him up with my sister.

"Isn't that right, Libby?" Hannah says, looking at me with desperation in her eyes.

I startle, remembering where I am. In our conference room. With our clients. Our *paying* clients.

"Absolutely," I say, even though I have no idea what she's talking about. I close out of the One+One app and turn my phone facedown so I can focus on the meeting and doing my part to help save our business.

Eighteen

HANNAH

ANOTHER DAY, ANOTHER DATE. THANKFULLY, LIBBY LISTENED to me and planned something active this time: pickleball. While I wouldn't say I'm looking forward to this date, I'm not outright dreading it. I might not have crushed my comfort zone—I might not have even stepped fully out of it—but I'm at least straddling the border.

Libby told me about the guy before I left, but I've already forgotten everything except that his name is Landon. Hopefully we won't have to talk except to razz each other about our serves.

I'm walking to the pickleball courts in a neighborhood park about a mile south of our apartment, listening to *Murder on the Mind* to calm my pre-date anxiety. This season, they're discussing the disappearance of a young woman from Tennessee whose remains were found scattered in various national parks. A family in Yosemite found her femur; a couple in Glacier found her jawbone. It's fascinating.

"Hey, all, we have some big, *big* news," Serena, one of the cohosts, says.

"That's right!" Preeti, the other cohost, chimes in. "We're publishing . . ."

Together, they shout: "A BOOK!"

I gasp out loud; a man passing me on the sidewalk startles.

"Sorry," I say to him, pointing to my bone-conduction headphones. Serena and Preeti are discussing the details, and I'm so excited I can hardly stand it. Impulsively, I pull out my phone. I mentioned the podcast to Josh on our last run, and he texted me the other day that he'd started listening.

Hannah: Guess what? Serena and Preeti are publishing their own book!!!

He doesn't respond right away, which is fine—he might still be at work. I pocket my phone and keep walking. A thought pops into my mind: I wish I was meeting Josh for pickleball, instead of some random guy.

Nope, I tell myself. *Not going to allow that kind of thinking.*

But then my phone buzzes in my pocket, and I pull it out, excited to hear what he thinks.

Josh: nice

That one-word response is like a pin stuck into a balloon. Instantly, I deflate.

Not a big deal, I tell myself. *He probably hasn't really been listening to the podcast, anyway.*

Shaking it off, I reach the park. My anxiety spikes, that familiar buzzing in my brain, but I force myself onward.

LANDON IS A tall guy with ginger hair and freckles, a nice smile, and an athletic build. He's easy enough to talk to, which is a welcome change from Rob, and after some introductions, we start playing.

As I send off my first serve, I realize I feel so much more relaxed here than sitting at a bar. Maybe I don't hate dating. With the right activity and person, it could be, dare I say, fun?

The first game I win by only two points. It's nice having a well-matched opponent, and we're both playing hard and enjoying it. After some good-natured trash talk, we launch into game two.

When I win the second game, Landon says the sun is in his eyes. We switch sides, and I win the third game, too—this time by six points.

Now the excuses really start coming in: he couldn't find his usual pickleball paddle, so he borrowed a friend's and "it's just off, I can't explain it"; it was leg day yesterday at the gym and he might have partially torn his hamstring; he wore the wrong shoes and they don't have enough tread on the court.

Still, he insists on playing one more game. I consider holding back and letting him win since he clearly thinks he has something to prove, but then I think about my last journal entry, how staying in my comfort zone is allowing me to remain afraid, to stay quiet, to play small. And something new pops into my head: *Why shrink myself down so he can feel big?*

During the fourth match, Landon brings his A game, but so do I. We're neck and neck, and we're having fun, laughing and shit-talking each other. But then I fire off a beautiful cross-court dink, which gives me the win.

And then I witness a grown man throwing a temper tantrum.

Landon chucks his paddle across the court, cursing as he

stomps away, ranting that pickleball isn't even a real sport anyway.

"Good game," I say as we both pack up.

Landon stuffs his paddle and balls in his duffel bag, shoots me a glare, and says, "You know, it's not attractive when a woman is so competitive."

My cheeks heat. My first instinct is to feel embarrassed for being so intense about a silly game. But I didn't cheat, and I wasn't a dick about winning. If the tables were turned and he'd beaten me four times, I might have been frustrated, but I would've been a good sport.

As he turns to go, I think about Generic Rob and how I wish I'd stood up to him more.

"You know," I say, trying to keep my voice from shaking, "it's not attractive when a man can't handle a competitive woman."

Landon flinches but doesn't turn around. I have no idea if my point landed.

I'm still glad I said it.

I'M WALKING HOME when I check my phone and see three new texts from Josh, right below his one-word nonanswer.

Josh: Banana! Sorry! I was wrapped up in a project for work. WOW! SUPER COOL ABOUT THAT BOOK! When's it coming out? I'm almost done with season one of the podcast and I'm obsessed.

Josh: Give me a call?

Josh: If you want

He answers on the first ring. "Hey! I was just thinking about you."

"Yeah?" My smile grows. "What are you doing?"

"Don't make fun of me."

"Never."

"Remember that swing on my parents' back porch?"

"Of course." We used to sit out there on warm summer evenings, drinking peach Fresca, which his mom bought in bulk because it was my favorite.

"I'm sitting on that porch swing, knitting my first hat. It's for my niece, Zella—"

"Aw, she's gonna love it, Meemaw!"

He chuckles. "And I just finished the last episode of season one of *Murder on the Mind*."

"Wasn't that ending phenomenal?" I say, excited. "Could you believe the part about the fingerprints—"

"On the windowpane? I know! How did the police miss that?"

"Well, the detective was—"

"In on the whole thing," he finishes. "Totally agree."

I slow my pace, not wanting to get home too soon. "So, how's the knitting going? That's a useful skill. Remind me to get on your team when the zombie apocalypse happens."

"Got to keep warm while being chased by the undead."

I laugh. "Are hats hard to make?"

"Not if I crochet one—that only takes a couple hours. This is harder, though. I keep dropping stitches. Plus, my mom's dog keeps trying to get me to play with him."

"Toby?" I ask, referring to the floppy-eared basset hound I remember from our teenage years.

"Nah, he crossed the rainbow bridge a few years ago. This

one's a spaniel mix. He's up on the swing with me, practically in my lap."

I can picture the scene so clearly, but in my imagination, it's me on the porch swing next to Josh, my feet on his lap. I can almost feel the breeze through the old red maple tree, almost hear the squirrels chattering in its branches.

"That sounds like a perfect evening," I say.

"It'd be better if you were here."

Emotion rolls over me, sweetly painful. It's like homesickness, and I guess that makes sense. I spent almost as much time at Josh's house as my own in junior high and high school—his mom and dad were the stable, responsible parents I never had. I ate countless dinners at his family's dining room table, watched hundreds of movies in their family room. We lost our virginity in Josh's childhood bedroom, and now *that* memory flashes through my mind with such intensity I can't breathe.

It was a summer afternoon after we'd graduated from high school, and his parents were at work. Our make-out session got so hot and heavy that I, who had been nervous to take this next step even though we'd done almost everything else, practically begged him to take my pants off. It was awkward and fumbling, yes, but also earnest and vulnerable and fun; Josh was so concerned about me and my enjoyment that he kept stopping, asking if I was okay, if everything felt good, if he needed to slow down or try something else—more respectful and conscientious as a teenager than most full-fledged adult men. Afterward, we lay in his bed, curled toward each other, foreheads touching, and I remember knowing—down to my bones—that I had found my forever person.

It always felt like that between us. Puzzle pieces snapping together, a key sliding into a lock. *Click.*

At least, that's how it felt to me.

If I was wrong about something that felt so right, how can I trust myself about anything ever again?

I should ask him why. Why he left, why he threw me away, why he never came back. But I can't talk about this with him. It's still too raw, even after all these years.

"Josh," I whisper, squeezing my eyes shut. "I have to go."

And then I end the call and start running.

WHEN I WALK into our apartment an hour later, I'm still so tangled up emotionally that I can't process it. Libby is on the couch watching *Notting Hill*. The apartment smells delicious, and I see a plate of freshly made cookies sitting on the coffee table.

"How was it?" Libby asks, smiling. But then her expression shifts to concern. "Han? What happened?"

I shake my head, the lump in my throat so huge I can't get words out.

"Hey, hey," Libby says, her voice soothing. "Come here."

She pauses the movie and shoos her demon cat off the couch so I can slump down next to her. Then she puts a throw pillow on her lap and I lay my head on it, feeling like I can't even support my own weight.

"Was it that bad?" Libby asks, stroking my hair.

I can't answer. My throat still feels swollen, my chest locked. But my sister's fingers in my hair are familiar and soothing— she's been doing this since we were tiny—and slowly the tightness begins to dissipate.

Once I can manage words, I say, "Can I have a cookie?"

She slides the plate close so I can grab one.

As I eat the cookie (salted chocolate chip pecan), my mind

drifts back to all the ways that Libby came through for me after the horrible breakup with Josh. She flew down to Florida and stayed for three weeks, cooking me meals, reminding me to shower and change my clothes and go outside at least once a day. She listened when I needed to talk and never once made me feel silly for crying. She's the one who made my appointment with student health; from there I got connected with the doctor and therapist who helped me stay on track after she returned to Chicago.

My eyes fill with tears, but this time, they're tears of gratitude. For my big sister and her beautiful heart. And all the countless ways she's shown up for me over the years.

"I need to tell you something," Libby says in a careful voice, her fingers stalling in my hair. "You're turning into Sir Flakes-a-Lot again."

"Rude!" I huff. That's what she called me in junior high when my dandruff acted up.

"You should start using your medicated shampoo."

"Okay, I will," I say, sighing in exasperation. If anything encapsulates the experience of being the little sister, it's this moment, swinging from gratitude to annoyance at being bossed around. "But don't stop playing with my hair."

She doesn't, and we stay like this for the next hour: Libby's fingers running through my hair, both of us eating cookies as we watch Julia Roberts tell Hugh Grant that she's just a girl, standing in front of a boy, asking him to love her.

I feel safe and peaceful, but there's a nagging voice in the back of my mind that sounds a lot like Lou, warning me that I've hopped right back into my comfort zone. Quiet, afraid, and small.

At this rate, I'll never get out of it.

Nineteen

LIBBY

THE NEXT SATURDAY MORNING, I'M SITTING AT THE KITCHEN table, attempting to write in my journal. At yesterday's virtual check-in, Lou reminded us that she'll be reviewing our daily entries when she comes in next. I'm trying to figure out how to answer a prompt from last week—*write about a romantic relationship in your early years and how it contributed to your comfort zone*—when Hannah comes out, looking sporty chic in her running shorts and tank top.

I'm grateful for the distraction, because every positive romantic experience I can think of isn't mine—it's from the life of a fictional character in a book I've read. If I were to write about my own life, it would be how my bad experiences convinced me that it's better, safer, to stay snug inside my comfort zone, vicariously living through moments in my favorite books.

"Where are you off to?" I ask Hannah.

"Just for a run."

It's supposed to be our rest day, but my sister doesn't be-

lieve in rest. I'm grateful for the day off—our training schedule keeps getting more and more intense, doing more reps and
going longer distances.

"Well, you look cute," I tell her.

"This?" Hannah says, looking down at her outfit. "Nothing special."

Hmm. I set down my sparkly blue gel pen and look back up
at my sister. She's right—there's nothing special about her outfit. But there's something different . . .

She turns to head toward the kitchen, her ponytail swish-
ing behind her, and it hits me: my sister *never* wears a ponytail
when she's running alone. Either she *wants* to get kidnapped
today, or more likely, she isn't running alone.

Josh.

I lean forward and shift my torso, just enough to make
sure the muscle burn is really gone.

Turns out Hannah was right. While the exercises are still
really freaking hard, I'm able to do a little more each time. Yesterday I made it fifteen seconds on the deadhang, and I survived eight reps of the push-ups, planks, and jump rope. I even
did two falling stars—which is kind of like a reverse pull-up.

And as much as I was looking forward to this well-earned
day off, I've read enough second-chance romance novels to
know that it just takes one romantic moment (ew) to fall back
in love (double ew).

"You know what?" I say, standing up. "I think I'll go
with you."

Mr. Darcy gives me a dirty look for disrupting his slumber
before curling up on the couch like a cinnamon roll.

"Wait, what?" Hannah says. Her eyes go wide, and I narrow

mine, trying to discern the true meaning of her surprise—if she's impressed that I want to join, or if she's annoyed that I'll be interrupting her Josh time.

"I'll be ready in three minutes," I call over my shoulder as I head to my room, leaving my sister stumped. And Josh cock-blocked.

Libby, 1. Josh, 0.

THIRTY MINUTES LATER, Hannah and I are walking across the bridge near Lincoln Park that arches over Lakeshore Drive. I've never gotten to the lake path this way, and it's exhilarating, having the traffic speed by beneath our feet.

Once we're safely on the other side, I spot none other than Josh Goddamn Jacobson, stretching like a tall Adonis.

As much as I hate to admit it, time has been good to Josh—he's got the dark-hair-and-blue-eyes combination that is always striking. Not to mention those damn dimples. If he was less good-looking, I bet Hannah wouldn't have let him back in her life so easily. But attractive men can get away with anything.

After an awkward hello—they hug, he and I nod—our little trio gets started on the path, heading north toward Evanston.

"Let's start with a warm-up," Hannah says, for my benefit, I'm sure.

It doesn't take long for the three of us to drop into a triangle formation, with Josh and Hannah speed walking neck and neck, and me trailing behind in more of a walk-run. My breaths are ragged, my feet moving so fast I'm worried I might trip. For the first time in weeks, my old fear about the ambulance not being able to reach me resurfaces.

Every once in a while, Hannah looks back to check on me,

and I give her what hopefully looks more like a smile than a grimace. I can't hear what they're talking about, but Hannah sure seems to be laughing a lot. I don't remember Josh being *that* funny.

He's nowhere near as funny as Adam, that's for sure. The other day Adam made me literally laugh out loud when he told me—*HannahF*—about one of his regular customers. Harvey, a widower in his eighties, recently scheduled three different dates at the diner—one for breakfast, another for lunch, and a third for dinner. When he realized the diner wasn't open for dinner, he got visibly upset—so Adam agreed to stay open late and cook them something special.

I cackled when Adam told me that after all that, the man only left him a two-dollar tip.

Hannah laughs again, and she and Josh pick up their pace. I try to do the same so I can eavesdrop, but it's futile. My legs feel like rubber and I'm terrified my heart is going to beat out of my chest.

The stretch of lake path between us gets wider and wider, until there's a gap the length of a city bus between us. They're still walking, but it's faster than the speed of my running, and Hannah's barely breaking a sweat.

In this moment, it's glaringly obvious just how much she's been slowing down for our walks. We aren't working out together like she said. It's more like she's babysitting her out-of-shape big sister.

The path starts to rise into a slight hill, and I'm doing my best to keep up, but my lungs are burning, the arches of my feet are throbbing, and—*ow!*—a cramp in my side finally stops me.

I bend over in pain, my breaths erratic. This is ridiculous.

I shouldn't be here. I am not an athlete. I was crazy for thinking I could handle this.

The drops of sweat sliding down my face are about to get joined by tears when I see a pair of men's orange-and-blue Brooks running shoes in my field of vision.

"You okay?" Josh asks.

"Just dandy," I reply between shallow breaths.

"Wait here," Josh says. As if I'm in any condition to move.

Moments later, he's back. "Here," he says, handing me an ice-cold water bottle.

I use the last ounce of energy I have to wave his hand away. I'm not desperate enough to accept help from him.

To prove that I'm okay, I stand back up. Too quickly, it seems, because the earth wobbles beneath my feet.

"Careful," Josh says, reaching out his stupid muscular arm to steady me.

It takes a beat for my equilibrium to return. As soon as it does, I shrug away from his touch, walking to the side of the path so we aren't in the way of other runners, athletes who don't practically faint twenty minutes into their workout. Luckily there's a bench, and I collapse onto it—right in the middle, so Josh doesn't think about sitting next to me.

"Where's my sister?" I ask, looking back up the hill at the path ahead of us.

"I told her we'd catch up," Josh says.

I narrow my eyes at him. Hannah wouldn't leave me. Plus, she'd never run off alone when she's wearing a ponytail. If she gets kidnapped, I'll . . .

"Here," Josh says, pushing the water bottle toward me again. "You'll feel better."

I shake my head, not sure what makes me angrier: that Josh is being nice or that I don't have the energy to tell him to fuck off.

Reluctantly, I take the bottle. The water feels like cool relief sliding down my throat, and I realize that, unfortunately, Josh was right. I do feel better. I take another greedy sip, then wipe the back of my hand over my lips before putting the lid back on the bottle.

"You're welcome," he says with a know-it-all smile on his stupid face.

I scowl. Normally, I'm a very polite person—but Josh Jacobson brings out the worst in me. Or the best, if you look at it in terms of the lengths I'm willing to go to protect my sister.

Speaking of . . .

"I don't like that you're back," I tell him. "In this town. Or in my sister's life."

"I figured as much," Josh says, his voice even.

"But you're still here, trying to weasel your way back into her life." I hate the way he's looking down at me, as if he's bored by this conversation, so I shift my gaze back toward the path, where bikers and runners and joggers are all speeding past us.

"Hannah's a grown woman," Josh says. "It's her choice—it should have always been her choice."

I bite my lip to hold back all the things I want to say to him. To remind him that he's the one who left her, the one who sent my sister into a tailspin of heartbreak and depression.

"Why can't you leave her alone? I'm sure there's no shortage of women who'd leap at a chance to be used and discarded by you. Just move on, Josh."

He opens his mouth like he's about to fire back at me. But then he stops, swallows, and takes a step back, kicking at a pebble in the path. "It's interesting . . ."

"What?" I snap.

"That Hannah is the person I hurt, but you're the one who's still angry."

"Damn right I'm still angry," I say, my voice sharp. "You were off living your best life in Australia while Hannah was falling apart. You treated her like she was disposable—"

"I know. Believe me, I know—I've had five years to reflect on how I treated Hannah, and I'm doing my best to make it right." He looks down at me, his eyes piercing. "Are you?"

I shake my head. This isn't about me. "Do you have any idea what you did to her?"

As I say the words, I'm transported back to those days, to that feeling of utter helplessness as I watched my baby sister fall apart. "I'll never forgive you for that. Never."

My voice cracks on the last word, and my eyes unexpectedly well with tears. I turn away so Josh doesn't see any sign of weakness.

"I don't blame you," he says quietly, and when I look up at him, I swear I see tears in his eyes, too. "I probably wouldn't forgive me, either."

For a split second, something inside me shifts—if this was a romance novel, I'd probably be rooting for him now; I've always been a sucker for a repentant hero. But this is real life, and no amount of repentance will erase what he did to Hannah.

"Do you care about her?" I ask, looking up at him from my bench. "Do you want her to be happy?"

"Of course. Believe it or not, that's something we have in common."

"Then promise me you'll leave her alone." My voice wavers again, and Josh's face softens. Damn him for being sympathetic.

"I can't promise you that," he says. "But I can promise you that I'll leave any decisions about me and Hannah completely in her hands. Okay?"

My body goes rigid; I don't like this. At all.

But what can I do? I can't physically prevent him from spending time with Hannah. At least if he leaves it up to her, I can help her see the situation more clearly. And I still have ten more chances to set her up with a guy who will make her forget all about Josh Jacobson.

"Fine," I say, folding my arms. "Leave it up to Hannah."

"Fine." He nods once, and we both go quiet. He puts his hands on his hips and turns away from me, staring out at the horizon. I wonder if he wishes he could be out on the water instead of here with me. I remember his family used to have a sailboat—one of his few redeeming qualities.

I close my eyes and focus on the warmth of the sun beating down on me, while the lake breeze brushes against my damp skin. A cacophony of sounds swell in harmony with the beating of my heart (which is slightly less erratic). The hum of traffic coming from Lakeshore Drive on one side, the distant crashing of waves on the other.

"Feeling better?" Josh asks, breaking the silence. "Ready to keep going?"

I look at him, then at the long path ahead. I think I've worked out more than enough for today.

"You go ahead," I tell him. "I'm going to catch a ride home."

"You sure?" Josh asks.

I nod. "Thanks for the water."

"Anytime," he says, flashing me that golden-boy smile that would probably let him get away with murder. Literally.

I watch as he runs off, his long legs taking him up the hill. He'll catch up with Hannah in no time. I don't know if I can trust him to keep his promise, but I also don't know what other choice I have.

My bladder constricts, reminding me I need to find both a bathroom and air-conditioning. *Stat.* I take out my phone and order an Uber.

While I'm waiting for Richard to pick me up in his blue Impala, my phone buzzes. I smile for the first time all afternoon when I see it's a message from Adam.

ADAMR: Serious question

My stomach drops. Has he realized the woman he's been talking with is not the woman in the picture?

HANNAHF: I can't promise a serious answer . . .

ADAMR: What's your opinion on gefilte fish?

HANNAHF: A solid 6 out of 10. Four points for flavor, and two for the tradition of it all.

ADAMR: Fair enough

HANNAHF: But if we're rating Jewish holiday food, matzo brie comes in at a 9/10.

ADAMR: Syrup or sour cream?

HANNAHF: Always syrup

ADAMR: I knew I liked you

I swoon a little—he likes me. And I like him, too. For Hannah. She'll love him.

ADAMR: I wanted to message you earlier, but the brunch crowd was rowdy today. The last group just cleared out.

HANNAHF: Brunching is serious business. And it's not really brunch if it doesn't cross over to lunchtime.

ADAMR: True! But if we're talking about combining meals, I have to say I prefer breakfast for dinner instead of combining it with lunch.

HANNAHF: Breakfast is good any time of the day

ADAMR: Now you're just trying to butter me up!

ADAMR: How has your day been?

HANNAHF: Not bad. Just heading home from a run on the lake.

I hit send, taking note of how nice it is that I am both telling the truth and acting like Hannah. But if he asks me to rate the run, I'm going to have to give him Hannah's answer (8 out of 10) and not mine (3 out of 10).

Oh well. I'd much rather be me right now, messaging Adam from the back seat of this Uber, than sweating out in the hot sun with Hannah and Josh.

That asshole better keep his promise.

CRUSH YOUR COMFORT ZONE

THE ULTIMATE CHALLENGE COMPANION JOURNAL

WEEK 4

While our comfort zones do keep us safe, they can also stifle us. Today, consider one way you stay in your comfort zone, and what positive emotions are associated with that. Then dig deeper, and explore if there are any negative emotions below the surface. Write about those.

Hannah, 6/26

A simple example of staying in my comfort zone: passing off a client call to Libby, something that happens nearly every day at work. My first impulse is to feel relieved and grateful, too.

But underneath that, I'm frustrated with myself. Embarrassed that I'm an adult woman who gets anxious doing something so ordinary.

And deeper still, I feel a little . . . claustrophobic. Like I'm in a small, windowless room with a ceiling so low I can't even stand up straight. I feel restless, like I want to stretch, to see how tall I could stand if I didn't put limits on myself.

Twenty

HANNAH

"READY TO GO?" I CALL TO LIBBY AS I LACE UP MY RUNNING shoes.

It's a Wednesday evening and we're meeting Josh and Scott for our first workout with the entire Down & Dirty team. We're going to North Avenue Beach, not far from downtown—a wide swath of sand popular with sunbathers and volleyball players—so we can practice running, squatting, and crawling in sand and water.

I'm excited for the workout. Less so about seeing Josh again. My emotions are still all over the place when it comes to him, and I appreciated having Libby as a buffer on our last run.

It was strange when he fell back to help her, though—not the helping part; that's a very Josh thing to do. But when he caught back up with me, he seemed on edge; we parted awkwardly and haven't spoken since.

Another reason it'll be nice to have Libby and Scott at the workout today.

Libby still hasn't come out of her room, so I head across the hall, calling, "Libs?"

She's facedown on the bed in her exercise clothes, fast asleep. My heart swells with affection and pride; she's been working so hard and making great progress, even if she can't see it.

Her evil cat is perched on the pillow beside her, his yellow eyes glinting with spite. I want to tell him to chill out; no way am I going to wake Libby up. Rest is important when you're training, and we already went on a walk today and did the stairs by the river at lunch.

I gently close her door behind me and head to the kitchen, then send a text to the group chat for our D&D team.

Hannah: Libby isn't going to make it for tonight's workout. Either of you still want to go?

Scott's reply comes back instantly: I'm out

I roll my eyes, unsurprised. Scott prefers the controlled environment of a gym, not outside "among the unwashed masses," as he told me.

Josh's response arrives next: I'm still game

A tremor of uncertainty runs through me. It's smarter to avoid being alone with him. But if I back out now, it will just make things more awkward.

Okay, I reply. See you soon.

AN HOUR LATER, Josh and I are sprinting down the lake path. I chickened out by suggesting we run instead of doing the planned workout, because it'd be easier to avoid talking. I've purposefully kept a pace so brisk that it's impossible to do anything but focus on the pounding of my feet on the pavement, the burning in my lungs and legs. If Josh realizes why I'm running this fast, he hasn't let on. He's stayed right next to me as we head down the path, dodging other runners and walkers.

We've covered five miles in less than forty minutes, and my body is screaming for me to stop. I refuse to listen. But then Josh slows abruptly.

"Can we walk"—he gasps—"for a minute?"

He winces in pain, and I put on the brakes. "Are you okay?"

"It's my"—he sucks in a breath—"hip flexor." Another breath. "Sorry."

"No, I'm sorry," I say between my own rapid breaths. Now that I've slowed down, my body is protesting the punishment I just gave it. I'll pay for this tomorrow. "Do you need to sit down?"

We're not far from Navy Pier, a strip of land the size of ten football fields jutting out into the lake, site of the Ferris wheel that's an iconic part of the Chicago lakefront. The place is a tourist trap—full of chain restaurants and gift shops—but there are benches, bathrooms, and water.

"That would be great," Josh says.

I snag a bench while Josh goes to buy water. And as I stare up at the giant wheel where Josh and I held hands for the first time, all the tender sweetness of that moment rushes back: the anticipation, the full-body tingles when his fingers interlaced with mine. My chest aches with that particular pain only memories of Josh can create.

The Centennial Wheel has been rebuilt since back then; it's bigger and nicer, with climate-controlled gondolas. Being here feels like a metaphor; our old relationship torn down and discarded, something different erected in its place. And I'm not sure how I feel about that.

I wonder if he remembers. Probably not. Holding hands is not a monumental event in most people's lives.

Josh returns and sits heavily next to me on the bench, his face tightening with pain.

"You sure you're okay?" I ask.

"Yeah, it's a lingering injury. Flares up when I run too fast."

I'm about to apologize again when he lifts the bottom edge of his shirt to wipe the sweat on his face, revealing nearly all his torso. Tan skin and a broad chest; a sprinkling of dark hair that funnels into a line down his flat stomach and disappears into his running shorts . . .

My mouth goes dry. The last time I saw this much of Josh, his metabolism was so fast he couldn't gain weight or put on much muscle. I loved his body, of course I did, but it was . . . not like this. We had an inside joke that he hadn't fully completed puberty yet.

He has now.

I avert my eyes, but it's too late. Now I'm thinking about what's in those shorts. And wondering if anything is different down there, too.

Damn it.

My cheeks are burning hot; it's been so, so long since I've had thoughts like this, about anyone. Attraction. Lust. I put my water bottle to my lips and take a long swig, trying to cool myself off.

"Thirsty?" Josh asks, a teasing lilt to his voice.

"Uh . . ." Flustered, I search for something else to talk about. "How's work?"

"Good," he says, lighting up. "Remember that project I told you about, the summer program for the high school kids?

Looks like I'll be joining the trip to the Bahamas on our research vessel later this summer, so I can get a feel for how it works."

He continues, telling me all the details, but my mind is stuck on the image of Josh on a boat wearing swim trunks and no shirt, his glorious torso exposed for all and sundry to enjoy. Then he starts talking about how he got scuba certified, and I'm imagining him in a wet suit, peeling down the top, his golden skin dappled with water droplets.

He takes a drink, and I can't help staring at his throat, the way it bobs as he swallows. My eyes drift down to the dark V of sweat that makes his shirt cling to his chest.

I glance away as he lowers his water bottle.

"How's work for you?" he asks.

"Good. Fine."

"But . . ." he prods, like he knows I have something else to say. He probably does; I wouldn't be surprised if he can still read me.

I shrug, thinking back to the conversation Libby and I had about the presentation, when I suggested we mock up a social post. I was trying to stick a toe out of my occupation-related comfort zone, but it was clear that didn't work for her. And I can't afford to upset the balance of our partnership—not now, with things as precarious as they are.

Josh nudges me. "Hey. Want to ride the Ferris wheel?"

No. No, I do not. The last thing I want is to be in an enclosed space that reminds me of the first time I touched this man—or any human being—in a romantic way.

"It's getting late. I should probably head home," I say.

Josh pulls something out of his pocket. Tickets. He's grinning, his dimple winking. "Oops. Already bought them."

This is classic Josh, fun and spontaneous, assuming I'll go along with him.

Before I can answer, my phone buzzes, and I pull it out of my pocket.

Libby: You went to work out with Josh? You should've woken me up. CALL ME!!!!

My spine straightens in indignation. I feel like my five-year-old self, stamping my foot when my big sister would try to tell me what to do. *You're not the boss of me!* I may not be willing to confront Libby about switching up our roles at work, but I'm going to exert my independence in this.

I stuff my phone back in my pocket and look up at Josh. "Let's do it."

JOSH BOUGHT TICKETS for two cycles, which means we'll have more than thirty minutes alone together. As our gondola lifts, the sounds of city traffic fade away, until all I hear is the squawk of seagulls and distant music from the pier below. It's magical. This giant wheel, gently tilting us toward the clouds.

My breath catches as I take in the view: the skyline to the west, all sharp spires and square edges, the setting sun casting streaks of gold between the buildings. And to the east, Lake Michigan, painted with orange and pink, stretching to the horizon. Below us, the marina is full of boats bobbing gently. Love for my beautiful city fills me to the brim; I never want to live anywhere else.

"I wanted to talk to you about something," Josh says.

He's unusually serious, and my muscles tighten.

"That's ominous," I say with an awkward laugh.

He doesn't laugh, just exhales and runs a hand through his thick, dark hair. It looks like he's wrestling with something, and I wait, holding my breath.

"I want to apologize for the way I left you, back in college," he says.

It takes me a moment to process what he's said. He's not sorry that he left. He's sorry for the *way* he left. And of course, he brings this up now, when I can't leave.

Before I can respond, he continues, "I don't expect you to forgive me, and I won't make excuses for my behavior. But I want to explain a few things. If that's okay with you."

"Go ahead," I say, my voice tight. The air in the gondola feels stuffy, and I focus my eyes on the lake, shining in the evening sun.

"I don't know if you knew this," Josh says, "but I was deeply unhappy during our junior year."

I blink, stunned. We must have gone to a hundred parties that year, and Josh was the life of each and every one, always smiling and joking around.

"You were?" I ask. "Why?"

He sighs and leans back against his seat. "I felt . . . trapped, I guess. Like the world was pressing in on me and I couldn't take a breath. My whole life was planned out for me, and I'd never had the opportunity to think about how I actually wanted to live. The closer we got to graduation, the more stuck I felt."

I feel sick—and not just because of the implication that he must have felt stuck with *me*, too. How did I miss this? That the person I loved better than anyone in the world felt this way?

"I had no idea," I whisper.

He shakes his head. "There was no way you could know. I pretended everything was fine, I kept going out and making people laugh and saying all the right things, but I was kind of dying inside. The study-abroad program seemed like a long shot, but when that acceptance letter came, it was like an escape hatch opened. I could breathe again."

Despite how upset I am, my heart aches at the thought of young, college-age Josh, overwhelmed and alone.

But he wasn't alone; he could have talked to me. He *should* have talked to me. Anger sparks in my chest, and I turn to him.

"Why didn't you say anything? We were more than just girlfriend and boyfriend. We were *best friends*. You didn't even give me a chance to try to understand."

"That's my biggest regret, not communicating with you," he says, looking at the floor. "But at the time, I mean, I hardly understood what I was feeling. I didn't know how to separate our relationship from the plan we'd mapped out for our lives, so instead of talking to you, I just . . . ran away. It was immature and selfish—"

"Damn right it was," I say, my anger building. "You had a thousand opportunities to tell me. You—you basically lied to me for months. It was a shitty thing to do, Josh. Dishonest and cowardly and so fucking cruel."

He nods, taking the hit like he knows he deserves it. "There's no excuse—"

"You rented an apartment with me," I continue, years of hurt bubbling over. "I thought we had our whole life planned out, and you were trying to figure out how to escape. It wasn't fair to me. It wasn't fair to *us*—to the history we shared."

"I know," he says quietly.

"And even worse—you kept stringing me along! You should've

broken up with me when you left. I spent that entire semester missing you, trying to survive with this massive hole in the fabric of my life, and meanwhile, you were moving on to another girl."

He looks up sharply. "What are you talking about? I wouldn't do that, Hannah."

I scoff. "Yes, you did. You told me over the phone when you dumped me."

He blinks. Stares at me for a few seconds. Then drops his eyes to the floor. "I . . . that wasn't true."

I suck in a breath. "What?"

"There wasn't anyone else."

"Why did you say it, then? Why would you—"

The realization washes over me, and I slump against the seat, my mind reeling. He wanted to stay in Australia, to continue his studies, and he didn't know how else to make me understand that we were really, truly over.

He opens his mouth like he's about to speak, then closes it again.

"What?" I prod.

But he just shakes his head. To his credit, he looks deeply ashamed.

I don't know how to process this revelation, on top of everything else. The wounds are so deep they're practically etched on my bones. Should I be glad that he didn't leave me for another girl, just for another life?

My eyes fill with tears, and I angrily wipe them away.

"When your ex broke up with you," I say, facing him, "did you have any warning?"

His jaw muscle flexes. "Hannah, I—"

"You bought a ring, so you were hoping to marry her. *Plan-*

ning on it. Right?" He nods, and I press on, unable to stop. "How did that feel, to have your world turned upside down? Did you feel stupid? Worthless? Discarded?"

He closes his eyes, his forehead knitting in pain. Even though it hurts to realize that he's thinking about another woman, at least he'll understand what it was like for me.

"It hurt when Kayla left, of course it did," he says, opening his eyes, "but looking back, it's clear that we weren't right for each other. I'm sure you feel the same way about us, and I don't blame you."

Several emotions hit me at once: relief that Josh isn't still in love with Kayla; a twinge of hurt that he thinks *we* weren't meant for each other, either. And on top of that, frustration. Because he still doesn't *get it*. He thinks that when he left me, my broken heart healed, that I realized we were better off apart.

"Josh," I say, "I've never been glad that you left. I've never, not for one moment, been glad that we didn't end up together."

"That's not—"

"I mean, intellectually I know it's a good thing, because you didn't want to be with me, but I have never had that thought in my brain: it's a good thing Josh left. Never, ever, ever."

"Hannah—"

"Do you honestly not understand what you did to me? It didn't just *hurt* when you left. It fucking destroyed me. It was like—like getting my legs cut off and everyone around me is telling me to get up and walk and I'm looking down at my missing legs thinking, how? How am I ever going to walk again?"

"Hannah, please let me—"

"No, I need to say this. I understand that it was a tough time for you, and I'm sorry for that. I really am. But, Josh, you broke me. I've never been the same. And I know it was the right thing for *you* because you found your dream career. You moved on. Fine, you and Kayla didn't work out, but at least you've been able to *have* healthy relationships. I'm completely stunted—"

"No, you're not—"

"You wouldn't know! You haven't been here!" I'm freely crying now, unable to stop the tears rolling down my cheeks. "You haven't seen me try to date other people and realize it's not going to work, it's never going to work, because I'm still stuck on my high school sweetheart. Do you have any idea how embarrassing that is—"

"It's not—"

"—and how pathetic I feel? I've never even had an orgasm with anyone but you!"

Josh stares at me, wide-eyed with shock. I break off, breathing hard, and slump against the seat, wishing I could dissolve into it. I have never felt so stupid and small in my entire life. *I'm still stuck on my high school sweetheart.* I didn't want him to know that. Ever.

"I'm sorry," I say after a beat. "That was inappropriate of me. I'm—"

"Hannah." Josh moves to the opposite bench in the gondola and faces me, his knees outside mine, almost touching. "Hannah," he says again, so softly it brings fresh tears to my eyes. "I'm sorry. I am *so* sorry. You didn't deserve any of this. You're the most—" He breaks off, running his hands over his face like he's disgusted with himself. "I hate that I did this to you. I told myself you were better off without me. That I fucked up so thoroughly there was no chance of ever setting things right again."

I don't like the way he's condemning himself for a mistake he made as a twenty-one-year-old. I'm not blameless, either. What kind of girlfriend—what kind of *best* friend—doesn't notice that her favorite person is miserable?

"Josh, we both—"

"If I could somehow rewind my life and do things differently, I would in a nanosecond," he says, locking eyes with mine. His dark hair falls across his forehead, making him seem boyish, earnest. It's impossible to look away. "If I could do it all over again, do you want to know what I would've done?"

I nod, wordless.

He takes my hands, cupping both of mine inside both of his, and the sweet familiarity of that touch makes me ache with longing. He's gazing at me with those eyes I know so well: lake blue, ringed with dark lashes, eyes that used to love me. My heart lodges in my throat, waiting for him to say the words I've wanted to hear for the past five years: *I would have stayed. Leaving you was the worst decision I've ever made.*

Then he speaks, his voice steady, his words measured. "I would've come to you and said, 'Hannah. I have this crazy, impossible dream, and I want to pursue it. I know this might hurt you, and I know it'll ruin all our plans. But I need to take this opportunity so I don't wake up one day, twenty years down the road, and realize that life has passed me by. That I never made a deliberate, independent decision of my own.'"

My stomach twists. I think back to that moment when he walked into our new apartment and announced he was going to Australia, how blindsided I felt. If he'd said it this way, if he'd laid it all out there, it still would've hurt like a motherfucker. But at least it would've been honest.

Josh is watching me, gauging my reaction. And I realize

what he's offering: not an apology, exactly, because he doesn't regret his decisions. No, this is a chance for each of us to say what we should have said then, to communicate with the maturity we didn't have at the time.

I swallow hard.

"If I could go back in time," I say carefully, "and respond to you with what I know now, I would have said: 'Josh. You're the most important person to me in the entire world. And I want you to be happy. Even if that means you need to leave.'" I take a shaky breath, ordering myself not to cry again. "'Even if that means we aren't together.'"

As I say the words, I realize they're true. More than anything, I would have wanted Josh to follow his heart. Those words wouldn't have saved me from pain. But they would've saved me from years of confusion, years of wondering what I did wrong. Maybe I would have been able to move on and love someone else.

Josh shifts over to my side of the gondola and puts his arm around me. It's not a romantic gesture, it's a comforting one—for me, but maybe for him, too. I lean against his shoulder, breathing in his familiar scent, appreciating the solid warmth of his body against me.

After a moment, he speaks, his voice vibrating from his chest into mine. "We held hands here for the first time. On the old Ferris wheel. Do you remember?"

"I remember everything."

My voice sounds tired, and I am. Tired of the way my first relationship has continued to hang over my life, coloring everything I believe about myself and the world, all these years later. My sister is right; I need to move past Josh and on to my next chapter.

Maybe now I can finally, finally let go.

"I really am sorry," he says quietly.

I nod. "Me, too."

We sit like that, staring at the night sky and the lake and the city lights, until our ride comes to an end.

Twenty-One

LIBBY

A FEW DAYS LATER, HANNAH, MR. DARCY, AND I ARE SITTING on the couch watching *My Big Fat Greek Wedding*—one of my favorite movies because I can relate to Toula Portokalos more than to the typical rom-com heroine. I went with the obvious, yet delicious, Greek pairing for our dinner with a trio of dips (hummus, tzatziki, and feta), Greek salad with grilled chicken, and spanakopita from Trader Joe's.

We're almost to the point where Aunt Voula tells the story about the lump on her neck when my phone buzzes. I peel my eyes away from the TV and see the One+One alert; a new message from Adam. My stomach flutters. I hadn't expected to hear from him much—he's been dealing with some family stuff—but we've still been chatting a lot. A lot as in multiple times a day.

Every morning, he sends me Hannah's daily horoscope. I accidentally told him I believe in that stuff, even though Hannah does not—but at least I remembered to give him her birthday instead of mine. We chat on and off throughout the day, and then before I go to bed, he asks how my day went (even though he already knows most of it) and wishes me sweet dreams.

I imagine this is what it feels like to have a real boyfriend.

I look back at Hannah, whose eyes are focused in the direction of the TV, but it doesn't seem like she's actually watching. She's been distracted lately, and I hope it's not because of Josh. She told me about their ride on the Ferris wheel, when he apologized for breaking her heart. I told her it's about damn time, but also that I hoped she wasn't planning on forgiving him.

She mumbled something about how he was young and didn't mean to hurt her. Which is total bullshit. And the fact that he's got her thinking that makes me realize Josh knew what he was doing when he promised he'd let Hannah make all the decisions when it came to their relationship. The man knows how to manipulate my sister.

Of course, I can't tell her that, because Hannah immediately gets defensive every time I bring up Josh. All I can do is double down on finding her a new match. One who is smart and kind and thoughtful, who will put her first.

My phone buzzes again with another message from Adam. As much as I don't want to give up talking to him, I know the time is coming to pass him on to Hannah.

But it doesn't have to be tonight.

I let out a giant yawn that hopefully isn't so big she doubts its sincerity. "I'm beat," I say.

Hannah looks at me like I just told her I was going to go jump off the roof naked. "But this is the funniest scene," she says, flabbergasted.

"It's okay," I say, yawning again. "I've seen it before."

My sister narrows her eyes; clearly, she doesn't buy this pathetic act of mine. But it's too risky to message Adam out here.

The other night, Hannah caught me smiling down at my phone and I panicked and told her I was texting Suji, a woman who's been renting a desk from us. It wasn't a total lie; Suji did message me last week to see if I wanted to go out to lunch, but I'm trying to be good about saving money. We grabbed coffee instead, and we've been doing it almost every day since.

I didn't realize how much I'd started to dread going into the office until I started looking forward to it—thanks, in part, to Suji. And the constant chatting with Adam.

It's strange being so happy.

One more yawn, and I stand up. Mr. Darcy looks at me like I've lost my marbles, too.

"Good night," I tell them both and head back to my room, opening the One+One app as I go.

ADAMR: For the record, aging parents are 6/10

ADAMR: I mean, the fact that they're still here and kicking is like 9/10. But it can be a lot.

ADAMR: Anyway, how have you been?

I climb on my bed and lean against the wall of pillows, feeling like a teenage girl with a crush. And it hits me: I have a crush on Adam.

Well, shit.

This is not good. It's really, really not good. Especially since he doesn't even know I exist. He knows Hannah, or the Hannah I've been pretending to be.

So, for the life of me, I don't know why I'm still smiling. And why I'm tapping out a new message to him. But if I stop now, it would be like stopping a book with only a few pages left. And I have to know how this story ends, even if it ends with me standing alone in a puddle of tears.

HANNAHF: Hi! Are your parents doing okay?

ADAMR: They'll be fine. Just having a hard time realizing there are things they can't do anymore.

HANNAHF: Like what?

ADAMR: Driving. Running the restaurant. Changing lightbulbs in the ceiling. Juggling with knives.

HANNAHF: With knives?!?

ADAMR: Just seeing if you were paying attention. ;)

HANNAHF: To every word

Cringe. That was too much. Hannah is not the type of girl who openly swoons—and this whole thing will fall apart if Adam meets the real Hannah and realizes she's nothing like the girl he's been talking to. I need to start acting more like my sister. *Stat.*

I close my eyes and take a focused breath. *Hannah.* My beautiful, smart, athletic, logical, slightly murdery sister. Once

I feel a little more Hannah-y, I open my eyes and try to get our conversation back on a safe track.

HANNAHF: Are your parents still married?

ADAMR: Forty years

ADAMR: They were older parents when they had me

ADAMR: How about you? Your parents.

HANNAHF: They're married . . .

HANNAHF: . . . to other people

ADAMR: Ahh

HANNAHF: It's okay. They're happy, I guess. We aren't close. But my sister is all the family I need.

My eyes unexpectedly well with tears. Hannah and I have been through a lot together, especially the last few years. And now I feel all this pressure to make everything okay for her, even though I have a sinking feeling we're in over our heads with these challenges, with Josh being back in the picture, and the business slipping away from us.

ADAMR: Is your sister older or younger?

I type "younger" out of habit, then catch myself and go back to type "older."

ADAMR: And you two are close?

HANNAHF: She's my best friend

It's weird putting words about me in my sister's mouth, but I'm pretty sure she would say something similar. I still have the "best friends forever" bracelet she gave me when she was twelve and I was fourteen. Our last summer at Camp Sabra.

ADAMR: Nice. I always wanted a sibling. It would definitely make all this parent stuff easier.

HANNAHF: Maybe it's not too late . . .

HANNAHF: Women are having children older all the time. I think a woman in the UK had a kid at eighty!

ADAMR: Oh god, that's terrifying. I can just picture my mom breaking the news to me and saying—well, you wouldn't give me a grandchild . . .

HANNAHF: Ha! Isn't it crazy how society can be evolved in so many ways, yet parents are still pressuring their kids to procreate?

ADAMR: Seriously. I think my parents were more disappointed than I was when my wedding didn't happen.

His wedding?
There were a lot of pictures with that pretty fashionista on his Instagram, but I'm pretty sure I would remember if he'd brought up a wedding or an almost-wife.

The revelation is enough to make me question everything he's told me, everything I thought I was starting to feel. It's a good reminder of how easy it is to hide things about yourself when you're chatting with someone online.

And yes, I'm aware that I'm hiding something even bigger from him.

For a brief moment, I imagine a world where Adam isn't really Adam—that he has a Hot First Cousin or Hot Best Friend who is chatting for him, just like I'm messaging him on behalf of Hannah. I can picture it, me standing in the wings, watching as the real Adam and the real Hannah sit together at a romantic, candlelit table. I'll feel that weird combination of happy and sad—until I spot someone standing off to the other side, almost hidden in the dark shadows.

We'll lock eyes, and something in me will recognize something in him. We'll walk toward each other, unable to ignore the pull between us. And now that our work is done, now that the real Adam and the real Hannah are together, the two of us imposters can live out our own love story. A double Cyrano.

I sigh, reminding myself that my life is not, and will never be, a romance novel.

Looking back at Adam's last message, I'm not sure how to respond to this casual truth bomb.

Two minutes pass.

I'm still trying to find the right words when Adam breaks the digital silence.

ADAMR: Btw—calling off a wedding is 2/10.

ADAMR: Although I suppose it's better than marrying the wrong person

I readjust the pillows behind me, feeling more at ease with the conversation since it seems he's comfortable talking about it.

HANNAHF: How long ago did that happen?

ADAMR: It'll be two years in August

Long enough that Adam likely isn't looking for a rebound fling. I couldn't put Hannah through something like that. I relax even more.

HANNAHF: And you called it off?

ADAMR: Not exactly . . .

Over the next thirty minutes, I'm captivated by the story Adam tells me about his ex, Sarah. They'd been together for three years before he proposed. Of course, I asked how he popped the question, and it sounded super romantic—he re-created their first date, right down to being seated at the same exact table. When the waiter brought their dessert, the words "Will you marry me?" were written in chocolate along the plate. Adam got down on one knee right there, in front of everyone.

It's the kind of grand gesture I would love but that would make Hannah want to shrivel up and disappear. If their relationship ever gets to the proposal stage, I'll make sure to tell Adam that less is more when it comes to my sister.

Adam tells me that he and Sarah started planning the wedding right away—they picked the date and the venue, tasted all the hors d'oeuvres and the cake. But instead of it bringing them closer together, Adam felt a distance growing between them. He assumed it was the stress and pressure of the wedding; her parents were pretty controlling about the whole thing. But since they were paying for most of it, he let it go.

The night of the rehearsal dinner, though, something happened. His parents hosted the dinner at his family's diner. It wasn't fancy—the restaurant had seen better days—but everything was made with love, and his parents spent hours preparing the place.

It meant a lot to Adam to start the wedding weekend off there, but his future in-laws were less than impressed. They practically said as much, and his future wife didn't say anything to defend him or his family. After the guests left, Adam and Sarah fought; she implied that she hoped he'd stop working for the family restaurant and get a job that was more suited to the life they wanted to live together.

The life *she* wanted them to live together.

Before they could talk things through, her bridesmaids swept her away to the hotel where she was sleeping for the night. Adam was shaken, but he told himself they'd work through it together. After all, they were about to commit to each other for better or worse.

The next morning, Adam stood in front of two hundred guests, anxiously awaiting his bride. Fifteen minutes after she was supposed to walk down the aisle, the doors opened. The wedding planner walked in and gave him a note from Sarah that simply said, *I'm sorry.*

The next week, when he was supposed to be on his honeymoon, Adam moved out of the fancy condo he and Sarah had bought downtown, and into the apartment above the restaurant, where his parents had lived when they were first married.

AS HE FINISHES typing out the story, my heart hurts for him. I don't want him to misinterpret my silence, so I type back a quick response.

> HANNAHF: I'm sorry you went through all that

> ADAMR: You know what they say, that which doesn't kill you makes you stronger

> HANNAHF: Do you really believe that?

I've been thinking lately about the lasting impact of painful moments. It didn't kill me all the times my mom told me I had "such a pretty face." And it didn't kill me when J. J. Lyons was willing to make out with me sophomore year so he could cop a feel but didn't want to be seen in public together. I survived all those moments, but they left scars.

> ADAMR: Well, I'm still here, aren't I?

> ADAMR: And besides, if I was married, I wouldn't have been on this app to meet you

I send back a smiley face, because sometimes, the right words just don't exist.

> ADAMR: Speaking of meeting you, I would love to. In person.

My heart swells—until I remember that he doesn't want to meet *me*. He wants to meet the woman in the pictures on the profile. I exhale, then give Adam an answer in my sister's language.

HANNAHF: That would be 10/10

It's getting late and we both have to work in the morning, but we settle on plans to meet next Friday. That gives me enough time to prepare Hannah. And to prepare myself for letting him go.

For the first time since this whole challenge began, I consider writing in the journal. But my life feels so . . . I don't know. Unimportant. It's not like I have a story worth documenting. Now, Anne Frank? She had a reason to write in her diary. But Libby Anne Freedman? Not so much.

This whole journal thing just feels so forced and inauthentic. If Lou wanted to know how I was feeling about things in my life, I would tell her. But talking to a person is different than writing to myself. It would feel less weird if I wrote the entries like a letter to her.

Which isn't a bad idea. I mean, she's going to read them anyway.

I grab my favorite sparkly gel pen and open to the blank page for tomorrow's entry.

CRUSH YOUR COMFORT ZONE

WEEK 5

Comfort is not inherently bad. In fact, comfort zones serve a vital purpose in our early years by protecting us. But they become a problem when our desire to remain comfortable prevents us from growing, from achieving our potential.

Today, write about a time in your early life when you did step out of your comfort zone and something scary happened. What did that teach you?

Libby, July 3

Dear Lou,

When I was in second or third grade, my Girl Scout troop went on a camping trip, which was definitely outside my comfort zone. And the hike we went on was REALLY outside it.

The path through the trees was narrow, and I quickly fell to the back of the line. Even though I tried my hardest, I couldn't keep up. I lost sight of the group and made a wrong turn. (Insert a joke about taking the path less traveled.)

It took two hours before they found me; the sun set and I was terrified in the dark, thinking a bear was going to eat me. Meanwhile, I really had to pee and ended up relieving myself in a patch of poison ivy.

So that whole experience confirmed my belief that it's better to stick to things I'm good at and enjoy. Also, to stay on the freaking path. It's there to be followed!

Twenty-Two

HANNAH

IT'S THE NIGHT BEFORE THE FOURTH OF JULY AND I HAVE AN-other date—one I'm actually looking forward to. I've gone out with two other men in the past couple of weeks, and it's getting easier. One was axe throwing with a big, burly guy named Gunnar; the other was a tandem bike ride with a guy named Mateo. They were both fine; no sparks, but nothing terrible, either. It's like exposure therapy, I guess, when people with arachnophobia let spiders walk all over them, or people with a fear of heights stand near the edge of a tall building.

For tonight's date, I'm meeting Danny at Grant Park down-town for swing dancing under the stars, with a live band and everything. There's a lesson at eight, then the dancing starts at nine o'clock.

But first, I'm meeting Josh for a drink at the Congress Plaza Hotel. He sent me a text about it the other day, told me that H. H. Holmes used to hang out in that very lobby to scout for his victims—wide-eyed, small-town women who had moved to Chicago looking for work. I suggested we grab a drink to-night before my date.

He has a date tonight, too. A fundraising banquet for the aquarium. And yes, I'll admit to feeling a twinge of *something* when he mentioned that. Not exactly jealousy. It was more the realization that this is what we are: friends, moving on in life, pursuing other people. It's weird. But in a good way, I think. After our Ferris wheel conversation, I finally feel able to move on.

"I'm heading out," I call to Libby.

She pokes her head out of her bedroom. "Oh, you look so pretty!"

I'm wearing a summer dress, flowery and fluttery; perfect for dancing. It's a bit outside my usual fashion-related comfort zone, which is the point.

"Thanks!" I say. "Hopefully the weather holds so the dance doesn't get canceled."

We've had on-and-off-again rain showers all day, but last I checked, it's supposed to be clear tonight.

"Have fun! I have a good feeling about Danny." She pauses, then continues in a flat voice: "Say hi to Josh for me."

I'M A BLOCK away from the hotel when the heavens unleash a sudden burst of rain. I gasp and start running. I didn't bring an umbrella, and soon my hair and shoulders are dappled with water.

"Banana!" I look up and see Josh coming around the corner; he has an umbrella, bless him. He's wearing a dark suit and tie, looking so handsome my chest aches. His date will be impressed.

When he reaches me, he puts the umbrella over my head.

"Thanks for rescuing me," I say.

"My pleasure."

Under the umbrella, we're close enough that I can smell him, and it's not his usual scent. He's wearing cologne, something piney and warm that his date will no doubt appreciate.

Again, that twinge of something that is not jealousy.

"You look nice," I say, smiling up at him. Friends can compliment each other, right?

"You, too," he says, grinning down at me. He hasn't shaved in a few days, and the scruff looks unfairly good on him, all masculine and rough. "You wore a dress like that to our spring fling junior year, right?"

I blink, surprised he remembers. But before I can answer, a truck whooshes by on the road, sending a puddle splashing all over us.

The cold water hits me like a sheet of ice, and I shriek. I was wet before, but now I'm *soaked*; when I look down, my bra is visible through my dress. Even worse, my dress is splotched with mud.

"Jerk," Josh mutters, his eyes following the truck. His beautiful suit and white shirt are sopping wet and dirty; he even has flecks of mud on his cheek.

Panicky thoughts fill my mind; I can't show up to my date looking like this, but there's not enough time to go home, shower, and change. "Shit, shit, *shit*. I don't know what to do."

Josh's eyes light up.

"What?" I say.

"Come on." He grabs my hand and tugs me toward the lobby doors of the hotel.

"What are you doing?" I ask, confused.

"I have an idea, just trust me," he says, not looking back.

Usually I would, because this is Josh, and this is what Josh does, what he's always done, pulling me along in his wake. But something rears up inside me and I stop, yanking my hand out of his.

He looks back at me, confused. "What's wrong?"

"Tell me your idea," I say. "You always do this—expect me to go along with you. Like when you planned that run, or when you bought those Ferris wheel tickets. But I don't like surprises, Josh. Communicate with me. Explain what you're thinking."

I never would've said anything like this back when we were dating. Maybe not even a few weeks ago. But all this comfort-zone journaling has made me realize how often I stay quiet in order to keep the peace.

Josh's dark eyebrows pull together in a frown. He's silent for so long that I begin to get nervous; did I upset him?

"You're right," he says finally, surprising me. "That's a bad habit of mine and I'm sorry."

"It-it's okay," I stammer.

"I'm not trying to steamroll you—it's more that my brain is racing ahead, and I have trouble slowing down to explain myself. But that's not fair to you." He pauses, thinking. "Here's my idea: if the hotel has laundry services and an open room, maybe we can clean up here. Let's see if they can launder our clothes, and we'll each take a shower. We might be a little late for our dates, but it'll be faster than us going home and changing."

"There's no way they'll be able to launder our clothes that quickly," I say.

"Just . . . will you let me ask?"

I sigh. "Okay."

JOSH IS ABLE to sweet-talk the concierge into giving him everything he wants. Why yes, they do have a room we can use to clean up in. Yes, they do have laundry services on-site, and yes, of course they'll rush it for Josh with his dimple and sparkling blue eyes.

I wonder if this is what life is like for Josh, easy-breezy, getting whatever he asks for with a wink and a smile. I have to admit, it's convenient.

Josh's date starts before mine, so he gets cleaned up first. I'm sitting on the bed in a hotel robe, trying not to think about him showering just a few feet away. To distract myself, I text Libby to see if she can message Danny on the app to let him know I might be late.

"Banana?" Josh's voice echoes from the bathroom.

"Yeah?" I ask, looking up from the phone.

"Can you bring me that shampoo?"

The room was made up so hastily for us that the housekeeper hadn't fully stocked it yet; she handed us a couple of tiny bottles of shampoo and conditioner, which are now sitting on the dresser next to the bed.

"One second," I say, grabbing them and heading into the bathroom.

As soon as I open the door, it hits me like the steam billowing out: Josh is behind that white shower curtain. Naked. An image flashes through my mind of us in the shower of his freshman dorm, giggling and kissing as we soaped each other up, Josh's hands on my body, sliding down between my—

Stop it. Friends don't picture friends naked.

"Can you give them to me?" Josh sticks his arm out of the curtain, his hand outstretched.

Swallowing, I step toward him and place the small bottles in his hand. I intend to step away quickly, but . . . I don't. Something unexpected shivers down my legs. Pure, old-fashioned lust.

"You know," Josh says, "we could save water if you joined me."

My breath catches. "I don't—"

"I'm kidding."

But is he? He's still reaching his hand out, like an invitation.

My impulse is to laugh and step away, go back out to the room and wait until it's my turn to shower. Say goodbye and meet my date. Spend the rest of the night imagining Josh with a beautiful woman in an evening gown. Maybe kissing her good night. Maybe more than that.

That's the easy choice, the *comfortable* choice. But am I not supposed to be pushing the boundaries of my comfort zone?

Never mind that I am absolutely burning with desire to see Josh naked.

Taking a deep breath, I drop my robe and step into the shower.

The first thing I see, coming into view in the steamy air between us, is Josh's face. Dark, wet hair falling across his forehead, a shocked expression in his eyes. He does not let his gaze drift downward on my body, not even an inch.

"Hannah . . ."

"Just conserving water," I say.

"Of course," he says, his voice faint.

I'm painfully aware of him. He's doing a valiant job of maintaining eye contact, but I don't have that kind of self-control. My eyes drip down the length of his body, and the sight unleashes a whirlwind of memories. I know the exact place on his chest where my head will fit, the ticklish areas on his rib cage, the angle of his jaw where he loves to be kissed. But there's a scar on his collarbone that I've never seen before, and he's muscular and tan and so damn masculine it makes me ache between my legs. Familiar and new, all at the same time.

And also. He's getting hard.

Quickly, I lift my eyes back up to his face. His cheeks are flushed.

"Don't mind that," he says, giving an awkward laugh. "It's an involuntary response."

I nod. "Of course."

I'm sure I'm blushing all over. Showering with my ex-boyfriend, who took it upon himself to learn my body, to discover what made me feel good and memorize my responses. What was I thinking? What the actual hell is wrong with me?

I need to distract myself, so I turn to face the water spray, grab the washcloth, and rub the small bar of soap against it, making a lather. Robotically, I wash my arms, trying to forget that Josh is inches behind me and maybe still has an erection and probably is staring at my backside. Maybe he's thinking that I'm not as youthful as I once was, or noticing the weird pimples I sometimes get on my shoulders or that strange mole on my lower back. My only thought now is to get this over with as soon as possible.

When I try to reach my back, Josh says, "Can I help?"

I stiffen. "Sure."

He takes the washcloth and rubs it across my shoulder blades, down my spine. All I feel is the gentle scrub of cloth against me, not his hand, and in this position—still facing the spray, with Josh behind me—I can almost pretend like he's not there. I take the shampoo, lather it into my hair, then close my eyes and rinse under the water.

As I step back from the spray, squeezing the excess water from my hair, Josh breaks his silence.

"You're beautiful," he says, so quietly that it's almost like he's talking to himself. He's behind me, just over my left shoulder.

I go still.

"I knew you were beautiful," he goes on. "I remember it well. But my memories didn't do you justice. Not even close."

His hands rest on my shoulders, his fingers slippery and wet, sending shivers down my arms.

"I need to confess something," he says.

My heart pounds, and I want to turn around, but I'm frozen, the shower hitting the front of me, Josh behind me.

"You said in the lobby," he goes on, "that I always come up with plans and expect you to go along with me. You're right—and I'm working on communicating better."

He runs his hands across the tops of my shoulders to my neck. I bite my lip to keep from sighing.

"So I need to tell you, Hannah. About what I've been doing this summer."

"Okay?" I'm not sure where he's going with this.

"I'm trying to win you back," he whispers, and presses his lips to the curve of my neck. Warmth spreads down my body, lighting me up like a candle.

"Oh," I say faintly. "Why?"

He slides his hands down my arms until they reach my hands, and he threads our fingers together. He doesn't bring his body against mine—there are still several inches between us—and judging by his shallow breathing, there's a reason for that. A big, thick, hard reason.

"Why?" he repeats, sighing. "Because you're the standard."

"What does that mean?"

"You are the standard by which I measure every other woman I've ever met. Not just women—everyone, period. Does this person make me happy like Hannah Freedman? Is this person as interesting as Hannah Freedman? Can I be myself around this person, like I could with Hannah Freedman? Everyone gets measured against you."

"And how do they measure?"

"They come up short. Every time." He kisses my neck again, making me shiver. "So, I realized: if I'm comparing everyone to Hannah Freedman, maybe I should go back and get the real thing."

I tilt my head, inviting him to kiss more, which he does. A soft cry escapes my lips at the feeling of his warm mouth, his rough stubble against my skin.

"Don't make that sound," he says, his voice strained. "I'm barely holding myself together as it is."

"Maybe I want you to fall apart."

He sighs but doesn't make a move, so I suppose that's a no.

After a beat, he speaks. "I've been thinking about something you said the other day. That you haven't had an . . . orgasm since me."

I give an embarrassed laugh, my cheeks warming. "Oh god. Josh. That's—ugh. I *have* had an orgasm since you. Just not with anyone I've dated. I've had plenty on my own."

He groans, and I feel him rest his head against the back of mine, holding it there, his fingers tight on my shoulders. "That's . . . fuck. Don't put that image in my mind."

"You're the one who brought it up." I grab the bottle of conditioner and squeeze some in my hand, then in my hair.

I feel Josh's hands joining mine, helping me work the conditioner through the tangled strands. The rasp of his fingers against my scalp nearly makes my knees buckle.

"Why haven't you been able to . . . come," he says softly, "with anyone else?"

I take a steadying breath as he continues to massage my scalp. "I'm not sure. I have a hard time relaxing, I guess. And then I get self-conscious that I'm taking too long, and then I feel anxious and it becomes this vicious cycle. Like there's something wrong inside me, like my body doesn't work like it's supposed to."

His hands stiffen in my hair. "Did someone say that to you?"

"Not in so many words, but—"

"Who?" He sounds pissed.

"Just a guy. No one important."

His name was Mitch and he was a fellow runner. We went out for two months before we had sex, and he did his best to make it good for me—really gave it the old college try—but everything felt so awkward, so foreign. I kept thinking about how I didn't really know him, and wondering if he was bored or annoyed, and eventually I told him I was fine, he could just finish up. The relationship fizzled soon after that.

"Asshole," Josh mutters.

"He wasn't, though. He was actually pretty nice."

I step into the spray again, rinsing the conditioner out of my hair, and Josh's hands fall away. I'm embarrassed talking about this, about my failure to have any other romantic relationship after him.

But then Josh wraps his hand around my arm and spins

me. Now we're facing off in the shower, inches apart, steam billowing around us. He's looking down at me, water droplets caught on his dark lashes, a fierce urgency in his eyes.

"You deserve better than that," he says. "Better than some 'pretty nice' guy who doesn't spend the time to make you fall apart and beg for more."

Warmth pools between my thighs; Josh was always so patient, so focused on my experience, and I didn't realize, back then, how rare that was. If I tensed up or got frustrated with myself, he would say things like, *We're not in a hurry. There's nothing I'd rather be doing. I love making you feel good.* And then I could relax and let myself fall, knowing that Josh would catch me.

I want that, I do. But the thought of trusting him again? Terrifying.

His eyes—so dark, almost navy blue in the dim light—flick between my mouth and my eyes, like he can't decide what to focus on. "I know I don't deserve another chance. But I'm asking for one anyway. Hannah, please. Let me prove I can be what you deserve."

I'm alight with different feelings—my heart is aching, wanting him to pull me into a hug and hold me. But my body is on fire with lust, wanting him to push me against the wall and spread my legs and take me.

"Don't decide right now," he continues. "Take some time to think about it. I care too much about you to have a quickie and then go our separate ways tonight."

I blink up at him, startled. "Wait. We're naked in the shower together and you're telling me that you *don't* want to have sex with me?"

He gives a pained laugh and glances down at himself. "I

want to. Obviously. But I don't want to steamroll you; you should decide what *you* want. If we're going to do this, I want us both to be all in. Understand?"

"Yes. But—" I take a shaky breath. "But don't make me walk out of here with nothing but words, Josh. Give me something to think about."

His eyes spark with desire. "That," he says, "I can do."

He captures my mouth like he's been craving this, like I'm the sweetest thing he's ever tasted. A groan rumbles between us—from me or him or both of us, I have no idea—and memories crash over me in waves. The thousands of kisses we've shared, the familiar rhythm and slide of lips and tongues and mingled breaths. It's a miracle. A blessed relief. Like climbing into your own bed after a journey away from home; like that first day of spring after a cold, dark winter. Josh's soft, warm kisses alternate with deep, desperate strokes, and then he's teasing me, his teeth nipping against my bottom lip.

I'm so lost in this kiss that I hardly notice his hands moving, running down my back. I wait for them to slide lower, but he stops at my waist. His thumb traces the old scar from my appendix, like he's remembering how it brought us together. Then he runs his hands to my shoulders, down the sides of my ribs, skirting the edges of my breasts but not wrapping around to cup them. We make a perfect A shape here in this shower—mouths touching, hands reaching, but the rest of our bodies separated, like we know if we get any closer, we won't be able to stop.

It's agonizing, being touched like this, his hands all over me but not going where I want them. I know why he's holding back. *If we're going to do this, I want us both to be all in.* And that's smart, that's the right thing to do, but my decision-making skills are fuzzy right now. Especially as I kiss his lush, warm mouth and run my hands across his shoulders, appreciating the bulk of his deltoids and biceps, trailing my hands down his back, dipping my fingers into the gulley of his spine, then lower, lower—

There's a knock and we jump apart.

"Laundry service!" a muffled voice calls.

Josh pulls away, his chest rising and falling rapidly. "Just a moment," he shouts.

He gives me one last kiss, then steps past me, wrapping a towel around himself as he heads out to get our clothes.

JOSH DRESSES IN the bedroom, and I get ready in the bathroom. My mind is buzzing, frenetic. I can't believe how close I came to begging him. Now that my adrenaline-fueled lust has faded, I'm glad I didn't. He's right; I need to think about this. Just because I want his body doesn't mean I should jump into a relationship with him. He said he wants us to be "all in," which is all very well and good for him—but he's not the one who was dumped and left behind. Can I trust that he won't do that again someday? I want to, but I'm not sure I can.

When I come out of the bathroom, Josh is sitting on the bed, fully dressed, his hands on his knees. When he sees me, his eyes drift down my body and the dress I can now admit I put on because I thought he might like it.

"I'm going to lose my mind tonight, knowing you're out with someone else," he says.

"Me? You're doing the same thing."

He shakes his head. "Want to see my date?" He pulls up something on his phone—the Shedd Aquarium's board of directors—and points to a picture of an older woman with silver hair and a bright smile. "This is Elaine. Her husband passed away a few months ago. I asked her to come with me so neither of us had to show up alone. If I'd thought you would've come with me, I would've asked you in a heartbeat."

Before I can respond, he leans in and kisses my forehead. His lips are warm against my skin, and it takes all my strength not to take his face in my hands and guide his mouth to mine.

"Think about what I said, okay?" he tells me as he straightens up. "No pressure. No rush. I'll wait."

And then he's gone, leaving me breathless, late for a date, with a decision to make.

Twenty-Three

LIBBY

HANNAH'S DATE WITH ADAM IS TOMORROW, AND MY STOM-
ach has been in knots all day. The whole evening is going to be
filled with so many potential land mines—if she says or does
anything that contradicts our conversations, he'll know she's
not me. That I'm not her.

For all the other dates, I've emailed Hannah a list of bullet
points about each guy. But since there are three weeks of chat
to cover, I decided we should do this one over dinner.

"Something smells good," Hannah says, coming out of the
bathroom after her post-run shower. Her hair is wrapped in
a towel and she smells like the mango bodywash she's used
since high school.

"I hope it tastes good," I tell her as I give the zoodles a
quick stir.

"What are we going to watch while we eat?" Hannah asks,
opening the drawer to get out the silverware.

"I was actually thinking we could talk," I tell her.

A fork falls out of her hand, landing with a clang in the

drawer. I feel her eyes on me, so I turn and offer what I hope is a reassuring smile.

"It's nothing bad. I just want to tell you about the guy you're meeting tomorrow."

Hannah looks relieved. "Is this the guy who's had you smiling the last few days?"

The last few weeks. Not that she needs to know that.

"He's funny," I say, hoping she doesn't notice I'm not exactly answering her question. "I think you're going to like him."

"If you say so," Hannah says. So far, none of her first dates have led to a second date. But at least she hasn't come home as distraught as she did after that first one.

The air fryer beeps and I transfer the shrimp to the serving bowl before bringing the spicy peanut zoodles to the table, where the cucumber salad is already plated in individual blue-and-white bowls. I have fortune cookies for dessert, since I decided to go all in on a Chinese theme. Even though it's just a Thursday night dinner for two, it's still fun to make an occasion out of it.

"So, tell me about this guy," Hannah says as she takes a seat.

I smile. There are so many adjectives I could use to describe Adam: cute, charming, funny, caring, humble, sensitive, and a word that's something kind of like loyalty, but more than that. A quality in a person who puts his family's needs before his own. Altruistic, maybe?

"He's a chef," I tell Hannah, figuring it's safe to start with the basics. "He runs a diner in Wicker Park that's been in his family for generations."

"Hmm," Hannah says, looking up. "Zoodles are good, by the way."

"Thanks," I say. "Luck of the draw—I picked a random recipe on Pinterest. Didn't even check the reviews first."

"Your bravery knows no bounds," she teases.

"Maybe I'll write about it in my journal tonight."

Hannah rolls her eyes. "Libs, the journal is for your feelings, not your recipes."

I don't feel like trying to explain how it all seems tied together in my head, so I shrug it off and get back to the subject at hand.

"Anyway," I say. "Your date tomorrow night. With Adam."

"Yes, tell me more about this NJB," she says, using the acronym for a nice Jewish boy.

"I sent you an email with some of the things we've talked about," I tell her. "He's chatty, so we've covered a lot of ground . . ."

Hannah's eyebrows arch as she reaches for her phone. I brace myself for her reaction when she sees the length of the email.

"Elizabeth Anne!" Hannah says, her eyes growing wide. "This isn't an email—it's a novel!"

"It's not that long," I say, focusing my concentration on my zoodles.

Hannah shakes her head as she scrolls. And scrolls. And scrolls. Maybe I did write a lot, but it's the details that can make or break a deception like this. I watch my sister's face as she reads, her lips curving in the hint of a smile. She laughs, and I'm filled with relief—and something else, sharp and stinging. I knew she'd like Adam, and I know he'll like her, too.

"Serious question," Hannah says, setting the phone down. "Do you want to go out on this date?"

I bark out a laugh. "Don't be crazy."

"Libby, you clearly like this guy."

"I do," I tell her. "I like him for you. And he likes you back."

"You're the one he's been talking to," Hannah says. She's trying to logic me into a confession that I'm not going to make.

"He's been talking to me pretending to be you," I tell her. "The whole thing is very meta. By the way, he's into numbers, too—we do this little game where we rate things out of ten."

Hannah lets out a dramatic, all-knowing sigh. "You should go on this date."

"Don't be ridiculous," I say, slipping into my big-sister lecture voice. "If I showed up, it would be like catfishing him. And I can't—*you* can't—do that to him. Plus, I really think you're going to like him."

"I don't know . . ."

"If you don't like him, you won't have to see him again. But you have to go on this date."

Hannah sighs again, this time in defeat. I know she wouldn't do something to purposefully hurt someone's feelings. Adam's or mine.

"What are we doing on this date?" she asks, and I relax a little, knowing I won.

I tell her that Adam and I planned the evening together—they're going to meet after work at my favorite coffee shop, and then walk to the Southport Art Festival. It's got all the ingredients for romance: a moonlit stroll, admiring local art—maybe trying on some jewelry as cover bands serenade them with love songs from the eighties and nineties. And then, when they get married, the same band can play the reception. Their love story is practically writing itself. As long as Hannah doesn't screw this up.

"Promise me you'll read the email," I say, finishing. "You don't have to memorize it all, just the sections I bolded."

My phone buzzes, and I look down, surprised to see Adam's name on the screen.

"It's him, isn't it?" Hannah says.

I look up, trying to wipe the smile off my face. "No," I lie.

"Your cheeks are getting all splotchy and your ears are red," my sister says.

"The zoodles are spicy," I tell her. "I used sriracha."

"Just admit you like the guy."

"Thanks for doing the dishes," I say, ignoring both her accusation and the truth behind it.

"Libby," she says, a playful warning tone to her voice. But I can't tell her that yes, of course, I would love to go on this date with Adam. But Hannah's pictures are what he swiped right on—and while he clearly likes my personality, physical compatibility matters.

"We're not done talking about this," Hannah says.

"Good night, seester," I say, heading back to my room.

"It's not even nine o'clock!" she calls after me.

I close the door and try not to think about the metaphorical one that's about to shut forever. This is the last night I'll be able to talk to Adam. I already miss him—which I know is ridiculous.

But it'll all be worth it when Hannah realizes how good a relationship with a good man can be, and leaves Josh in the rearview mirror. Kind of like Adam is about to be in mine.

Twenty-Four

HANNAH

IT'S FRIDAY AFTERNOON AND THE OFFICE IS SO NOISY I FEEL like my head is going to explode. All the extra people Libby brought in have altered the entire atmosphere. It wouldn't be so bad if they kept to themselves, but they're so damn *friendly*. Whenever I go to the bathroom or fill my water bottle, there's someone around. Smiling. Trying to converse with me. It's like living in the uncanny valley. It must take a certain kind of extroverted weirdo to voluntarily pay for the privilege of working around strangers.

Libby loves it; she's in her element, making friends and getting to know everyone. Great Scott calls them "squatters" and gives them the side-eye whenever they try to talk with him, but he also loves gossip and spends all day blatantly eavesdropping on their conversations.

We need the money; I did the budget yesterday, and these desk fillers are keeping our lights on. Not that it's enough—I had a mild panic attack yesterday when the woman who runs GiGi's scholarship emailed to remind me to deposit the funds for the next six months. I had to drain our emergency account to cover it. Which means I'll need to cut back even further on Libby's and my salaries.

So, I'm doing what I usually do when my brain is on overload: staring at spreadsheets and listening to true crime.

Serena and Preeti are wrapping up the case of the missing Tennessee girl (it was her boyfriend, but his parents covered it up by dispersing the remains across several national parks). Then they switch gears.

"We've had a lot of interest about our book," Serena says, "and we want to thank you all for your support. It's coming out next summer and we're so excited to tell you more about it."

Preeti chimes in. "It'll be a fun challenge—juggling this podcast, plus promoting the book."

They go on, but my mind stays on Preeti's words. On a whim, I pick up my phone and text Josh.

Hannah: Wouldn't it be cool to do the PR for the Murder on the Mind book?

I haven't seen Josh since our (*ahem*) meeting at the Congress Plaza Hotel last week, but we've been texting several times a day. And while I'm trying to not think about the physical experience of being in that shower with him (though it may have led to a few naughty dreams), I *am* thinking about what he said to me.

I'm trying to win you back.

He hasn't brought it up again, but I can tell he's waiting for my answer.

I'm at a crossroads, and I don't know which path to take. It's not just the free-falling terror of placing my heart in Josh's hands and trusting him not to break it again. This affects my sister, too. And our business. If I'm dating Josh, I don't think I can keep going on dates with other people. I wouldn't be okay with that if our situations were reversed.

But Libby has put in so much effort on our challenges, not only training for the Down & Dirty, but scheduling my dates. She's on the app constantly, messaging at all hours of the day. Probably because she has a teensy crush on this Adam guy I'm going out with tonight. But still. I can't back out on her.

My phone buzzes—a text from Josh—followed by several others in his usual texting style.

Josh: YES! You should pitch them.

Josh: Is that what it's called?

Josh: Pitching? Like a sales pitch. Not a baseball pitch.

Josh: obvi

Josh: Idk but you should do it

I have to laugh, even though it'll never happen. Libby and I have never done PR for a book, which, now that I think about it, is strange, given how much Libby loves to read. But book releases are usually smaller projects, and GiGi never did them, so they haven't been on our radar.

Hannah: That was more of a rhetorical question. We're focusing on trying to win bigger budget clients, like Lou. But it's cool to think about.

Josh: I didn't mean you, plural, should pitch them

Josh: I meant you, singular

Josh: You, Hannah Jane Freedman, would be an amazing publicist for Serena and Preeti

I set the phone down, shaking my head. No way I can do it on my own. I'm about to explain that to Josh when Great Scott sends a phone call through to my line, and the rest of my day goes up in flames.

EVERY ONCE IN a while, we have an emergency at the Freedman Group. I'm aware these aren't actual emergencies—no one is going to bleed out or suffocate if we don't manage this PR crisis—but if it matters to our clients, it matters to us.

And in this case, it matters to our *client's* clients, since it's their data that has been leaked.

MySole is a tech start-up that makes an instrumented insole for runners so they can optimize their gait. We connected with them because their new CEO is the son of the infamous Mr. Rooney of UnderRooneys, the company that dumped us and forced us to grovel for Lou's business. In contrast to my feelings for the older Mr. Rooney, I genuinely respect the younger Rooney as a person. Plus, I think the technology is awesome.

Today, though, the company that secures MySole's cloud was hacked, spilling their clients' names, ages, heights, weights, and other health information. We need to do damage control, ASAP.

Libby's already gone home; she said she wasn't feeling well.

My first thought is to call her and beg her to come back. Anxiety is chattering away in my mind, reminding me that I can't do this on my own, detailing all the things that could go wrong. But I take a deep breath, call Libby, and tell her I've got it under control.

To my surprise, she agrees, on the condition that I send her the copy to look over before we send it to the client.

Next thing I know, I'm on the phone with MySole's CEO, Noah Rooney. He's understandably frantic about the data leak, plus he's on his way to O'Hare to catch a flight to Minneapolis.

"I don't know what to do," he's saying into the phone, panicky. "Our clients are never going to trust us again."

"They *will* trust you," I tell him in my most confident voice. "It's not the mistake that damns you, but your response to it."

That's a GiGi-ism, and it feels good rolling off my lips.

"Tell me honestly: Do I need to stay in Chicago to deal with this?" Noah asks. "Because this weekend I'm planning to ask a very important woman a very important question."

I straighten up; even more reason for me to take this off his plate. "Absolutely not. I'll draft an official statement while you're on the plane. With your approval, we can have it sent to all your customers tonight."

"You're sure?"

"This is what you pay us for, remember? We've got this."

He thanks me, we both hang up, and I get to work.

I'M WAITING FOR some information from a software engineer at MySole when my calendar pings with a reminder.

MEET ADAM, 7:00PM

Ugh. It's currently 6:35 p.m. There's no possible way I can leave right now.

I text my sister: I'm still working. Can you reschedule tonight's date?

My phone immediately rings.

"Hannah!" Libby wails. "You can't cancel at the last minute!"

"I'm not finished cleaning up this mess," I say, rubbing my temples. It's bizarre that I even have to explain; she should understand. "We can't risk losing another paying client and we *especially* can't risk being known as the kind of company that doesn't show up when the stakes are high."

My voice is snippier than I intended—headache plus stress plus the inevitable feeling of guilt for letting my sister down. But staying here and finishing my work is the right thing to do.

"Adam's a great guy," Libby says, her voice tinged with disapproval. "He doesn't deserve to be stood up."

"I'm not standing him up! Message him and let him know I have a work emergency and ask if we can reschedule—"

"Han, that's not—"

"Tell him I'm sorry," I say. "But I need to go. I have work to do."

I end the call, proud of myself for standing my ground. Proud of myself for handling this crisis, too. I give myself a figurative pat on the back, plus a hat tip to Lou. My dating challenge might be silly, but the journaling is making a difference.

Beneath those thoughts there's a deeper current, something not so easy to explain. I'm relieved to have an excuse to skip the date tonight. It feels disingenuous to go out with someone when I have feelings for someone else.

I lean back in my chair and take a deep breath. Yes, I have feelings for Josh.

What's more, I'm going to have to face them. To make a decision.

Just not tonight.

Twenty-Five

LIBBY

IT TURNS OUT THE ONLY THING MORE STRESSFUL THAN HANnah going out with Adam is Hannah *not* going out with Adam.

All day, I've been a nervous wreck. I played every possible scenario through my head: that they don't hit it off and the date ends in disaster; that it's love at first sight and they run away to get married and I lose both of them; that Adam somehow realizes it wasn't Hannah he's been talking to.

The one scenario I didn't consider was that my sister would back out of the date. And now poor, sweet Adam is going to get stood up. I know it's for a good reason—the whole point of this challenge is to save our family business. But Adam . . .

I check the time on my phone. He and Hannah are supposed to be meeting in fifteen minutes, so Adam is on his way, if he's not there already.

When we were messaging a few weeks ago, he told me he's always early to everything. It stems from an experience one morning in seventh grade when he had an upset stomach and was late walking into a school assembly. They had a guest speaker, some ex-military guy turned self-help/motivational speaker. The jerk made an example out of teenage Adam, calling him onto the stage to apologize, then ranting that tardiness was a sign you didn't respect or value anyone else's time.

Adam hasn't been late to a single thing since.

Which means I better do something fast.

My heart constricts at the thought of Adam sitting alone at a table, waiting for a date that isn't going to show. Just like his wedding day. *Ugh.* I can't believe Hannah is doing this to him.

For a reason I can't explain, I'm compelled to go myself, to make sure he's okay. Or to see if he's not. The coffee shop is just a few blocks away, so I grab my purse and head out the door.

I walk there in half the time it usually takes and stop outside to catch my breath. Once my heart has settled to a normal rate, I force myself to look inside the window. It's just like I imagined it, Adam sitting alone at a table. Only he's cuter in real life than in his photos. A lot cuter.

He's wearing a light blue button-up shirt, the collar loose and the sleeves rolled up to show his tan forearms. His brown hair is short on the sides and curly on top, his beard neat and trimmed, his lips full and soft. There's a warmth to him that none of his pictures captured. He just looks so . . . so kind. Like you want to sit down and tell him everything about yourself.

I smile in spite of myself, then remember why I'm there. I check the time again—two minutes until Hannah was supposed to meet him. I open the One+One app, my finger poised over the message icon, but I can't do it. Not yet.

Before I can talk myself out of it, I walk inside. The bell above the door is tiny, but the noise it emits is so loud it might as well be a cymbal in a marching band, cutting through the din of people talking and the whir of the espresso machine.

My cheeks flush as every person in the place turns toward

me—including Adam, sitting alone at the table in the back. His face lights up in a smile, but it fades when he sees I'm not the woman he's been waiting for.

It takes everything in me to keep my own smile in place, to pretend his disappointment doesn't sting. I make my way to the counter—since I'm here, I might as well get something to drink.

My phone feels heavy in my hands; I need to message Adam and let him know that Hannah won't be coming after all, but I don't want him to get up and leave quite yet.

"Can I help you?" the barista asks.

As I place my order for a medium sugar-free vanilla latte and white chocolate macadamia nut cookie, I notice the woman at the table next to Adam's is gathering her belongings to leave.

"On second thought, make that two cookies," I say, on impulse.

Taking a deep breath, I settle at the now empty table beside Adam. He looks up and gives me a polite smile before furrowing his brow and looking down at his phone. Hannah is officially late.

I pick up my own phone and open the One+One app.

HANNAHF: Hey...

Out of the corner of my eye, I watch as Adam's face lights up at the sight of Hannah's name.

ADAMR: Hi! This place is really cute, I've got a table for us in the back.

HANNAHF: Shoot, I was hoping to catch you before you got there

212

Adam's face falls.

"Order for Libby!" the barista calls.

I stand, grateful for the perfect timing. Before I head back to the table, I type out the next message.

> HANNAHF: I'm so sorry, an emergency at work came up. A client had a data leak and it's a mess. I was hoping to have everything wrapped up so I could leave, but it looks like I'm going to be here a few more hours. Any chance we can reschedule?

I hit send on the message, then walk back to the table with my latte and cookies. Adam's eyebrows are pulled together; he looks disappointed, but not devastated or mad, which is good. I watch as he types a response, making sure to tilt my phone up so he doesn't see his own message appear on my screen.

> ADAMR: Data leaks are 1/10

> ADAMR: And no problem, we can reschedule

> HANNAHF: Thank you so much, and again, I am SO sorry

> ADAMR: Good luck

I watch as he sets his phone down, his mouth dipping into a slight frown. He has such nice lips. The man even looks adorable when he's sad. He taps his fingers against the table, and I can tell he's debating what to do next. I don't want him to leave.

"Excuse me," I say, my voice coming out a little froggy.

Adam looks up. He meets my eyes and smiles, and warmth spreads through my body. For one brief, beautiful moment, I imagine another world where this could be a serendipitous meeting, where Adam could get to know me for me. And maybe even like me.

"Yes?" he says, and I blush, realizing I've forgotten to speak.

"They accidentally gave me two cookies," I tell him, pushing the plate toward the middle of my table. "Would you like one?"

"What a lucky mistake," Adam says.

"Very lucky," I tell him, even though luck had nothing to do with it. "They're white chocolate with macadamia nuts."

Adam's eyes go wide as he leans closer. My breath hitches and I wait for him to say the words I know he's going to say, the same thing he told Hannah the first time I brought up my—her—favorite cookie.

"You know, white chocolate isn't really chocolate," he says, his voice low. The words seem to hum against my skin. "There's no cocoa in it, just sugar and butter. And sometimes a little vanilla."

I shrug and pinch a piece off one of the cookies. "Those are some of my favorite ingredients."

"Do you cook?" he asks.

"I dabble. How about you?"

"A little more than dabble," Adam says. He dips his head and looks back up at me in a gesture that feels shockingly familiar, even though I'm seeing it for the first time. Like he's uncomfortable talking about himself. "It's what I do professionally."

"A chef," I say, although I know he doesn't like to claim that professional title.

"More like a cook," he says, one corner of his mouth rising in a self-deprecating smile. "I didn't go to culinary school, I just learned the ropes growing up in the kitchen at my parents' restaurant. I run the place now."

"What kind of restaurant?" I ask.

It feels a little like cheating because I already know so much about him, but since society puts people who look like me at a disadvantage, I figure it's okay to use what I know to steer the conversation.

"A diner in Wicker Park. Nothing fancy, but we make a mean breakfast."

"Hey, don't knock the most important meal of the day," I tell him. "Other than dessert."

I nudge the plate toward him and he takes the second cookie.

"Thank you," he says. "I'm Adam, by the way."

"Libby."

He settles back in his chair and takes a bite of his cookie. "Nice to meet you, Libby. What do you do, other than dabbling in cooking and cheering up random strangers in coffee shops?"

My heart literally flutters. I'm cheering him up!

"I work in PR," I tell him, grateful that he and Hannah haven't gotten that deep about work-related things. When we messaged about Hannah's job in the early days, I just said that she runs finance and analytics for her family business. *Boring stuff that isn't fun to talk about.*

"Public relations?" Adam asks. "That's something I know nothing about."

I laugh. "Most people don't. But that's probably for the best. It would be a lot harder to manipulate public opinion if the public was aware they were being manipulated."

"So how do I know that you aren't manipulating me right now?" Adam says, his eyes twinkling as he grins.

I choke on my iced latte. It takes me a second to recover,

and Adam looks like he's ready to leap up and deliver the Heimlich if it's needed.

"Went down the wrong way," I tell him once I catch my breath.

"My bad joke didn't help," Adam says, handing me a napkin. I take it and attempt to elegantly dab the corners of my mouth. "So how do you do what you do? Or are you like a magician and you can't reveal your secrets?"

"No magic," I tell him. At least none that we have. "And as far as what I do, it's different every day."

"That must be nice." There's a wistful tone to his voice, and I wonder if he's happy with the restaurant. I know it's a lot of work, but he hasn't said much about whether he likes it or not. "Maybe I should hire you for the diner—our reputation could use a refresh."

"Are you telling me you have a bad reputation?" I ask, dropping my voice in a way that I hope comes across as flirty.

"Oh no," Adam says, chuckling. "Nothing like that. It's a great place, a lot of history. It's just a little . . . I don't know, stodgy? Now that I'm in charge, I just feel like shaking things up."

"That makes sense," I tell him. This is something new that he hasn't told Hannah yet, and I'm honored he's telling me. Libby.

"If you do want to talk PR options for your diner," I say, "give me a call."

I reach into my purse and pull out one of my business cards.

He takes the card and studies it for a moment, then looks back up at me.

"So, Libby in PR," Adam says. "How do you feel about art?"

AN HOUR LATER, we're on a moonlit stroll down Southport Avenue. The road is closed to traffic, with booths running down the middle of the street, featuring everything from fine art to funnel cakes. It's exactly the way I imagined it—only it's me walking with Adam, not Hannah.

It takes everything I have not to give the art ratings; a 4/10 for the scenic vista (pretty, but boring), 6/10 for the impressionist paintings, and an 8/10 for the mixed-media portraits. But it's a painting of old Chicago on fire that leaves me breathless. It seems like something GiGi would like, for its beauty and the reminder of our beloved city that came back from the ashes. It would be the perfect centerpiece for the wall in our lobby if only I (a) had that kind of money to spend and (b) was confident enough that the walls would still be ours after Labor Day.

I push all that from my mind and join Adam as he continues the cookie theme of our night, buying us each a biscotto from a vendor.

He hands me one, and I take a bite. It's crunchy and cinnamony and tastes an awful lot like GiGi's famous mandel bread. "What's the difference between biscotti and mandel bread?" I ask.

Adam's eyebrows do a little dance, and the expression seems familiar. He fits the picture I had of him so perfectly. "They're almost the same," he says. "Except in my opinion, mandel bread is better. It's got a higher fat content, so it's richer, not so dry. But for some reason, biscotti gets all the attention."

"That's actually a perfect example of what PR can do," I tell Adam as we dodge a man walking a massive Great Dane. Adam's shoulder bumps against mine, and that brief contact sends another golden burst of warmth through me. I catch a whiff of his scent, clean and woodsy, and my skin tingles.

Stay focused, I remind myself.

"For being so similar, the two have very different public images, right?" I continue, and he nods. "The fancier name could have something to do with it, but more likely, someone had an idea to position biscotti as the perfect companion to coffee—and voilà! One small change can completely alter the way people perceive something."

Adam pauses, gazing at my face for a moment, like he's studying me.

My cheeks heat up under his focused attention. "What?"

He grins and looks away, ducking his head. "Nothing. But if that's what PR can do, then I'll definitely be calling you."

HOURS LATER, WHEN I'm finally climbing into bed, I can't stop smiling. We stayed at the fest until almost ten o'clock—I didn't buy anything (Hannah put the fear of God into me with the bleak state of our budget), but Adam bought a bowl that was made out of an old vinyl record. When we parted ways, Adam said he'd give me a call next week to talk about my PR ideas for his diner.

It was the best first non-date I've ever been on. As much as I thought I already knew Adam, I didn't know how good he would smell, or the way his laugh rumbles in his throat before coming out in rolling waves, or the way he taps his fingers like there's music playing inside his head.

I flop against the pillows and Mr. Darcy curls against me. I'm going to stop messaging Adam as Hannah, I decide as I give my cat a good scratch around the ears. Of course, they'll still talk a bit to try to reschedule their date, but *spoiler alert*: Hannah's going to be really busy the next several weeks and I'm afraid they might not be able to find time to meet.

In the meantime, I'll keep talking to him. As myself. As long as he reaches out like he said he would.

It was refreshing tonight, talking to him without pretending to be someone else. I didn't have to talk about murder or math or exercise. And judging by the number of laughs and smiles there were, and the fact that he invited me to go to the fest with him, I think he liked talking to me, too.

My phone buzzes and I grab it—imagining a text from Adam, asking when we can meet again.

My heart leaps at the sight of his name on the screen, but then crashes, landing with a thud in the pit of my stomach.

He messaged Hannah through the app. Not me.

ADAMR: Just checking in. Hope you aren't still at work.

I swallow down my disappointment. Of course, he's checking on Hannah.

She came home around ten thirty, but I stayed in my room. I haven't decided how much I'm actually going to tell her about what happened. She already accused me of having feelings for Adam, but after tonight, that flicker of a crush feels more real. And even more complicated.

Tapping my phone, I answer.

HANNAHF: Hey. I got home a little bit ago. Crisis hopefully averted.

ADAMR: That's good to hear!

HANNAHF: I'm sorry again about canceling so late. What did you end up doing?

I hit send and bite my lip, waiting for his response, wondering if he'll tell Hannah about our evening.

ADAMR: Not much

Those two words pull the plug on my night and send all my glowy, happy feelings circling down the drain.

Not much.

I shouldn't be surprised. Even if Adam had fun with me tonight, it doesn't mean anything. Adam's just another in my long list of unrequited crushes who put me smack in the middle of the friend zone—when we said good night, he said he'd call me about my PR ideas. Nothing else.

Life would be so much easier if attraction was mental instead of physical. If men were turned on by a great personality instead of a great body. I close out the app and turn off my lamp, no longer looking forward to whatever dreams I'll be dreaming tonight.

CRUSH YOUR COMFORT ZONE

WEEK 6

We've reached the midpoint of the challenge, which can sometimes feel like a very dark place. You've come so far, but you still have so far to go.

Remember: the middle of the journey is where the growth begins. You're just not seeing it yet.

Today, take a moment to write about the deepest fear in your mind right now.

Hannah, 7/10

My deepest fear? Josh. I'm terrified to move forward with him, but I'm terrified to NOT move forward with him. Being with him feels like I've found a long-lost piece of myself, like I'm finally whole. But I've also gotten used to living without that piece; I've adapted. If I let him in, what happens if it doesn't work out between us? I don't know if I can survive having that piece ripped away again.

The thought of trusting him is scary, and the point of this whole challenge is to do things that scare me. But when it comes to Josh, what exactly is my comfort zone? It used to be him, when we were together, so maybe I shouldn't return there. But being alone is far more comfortable now, so getting back together with Josh will be stepping away from that.

I don't know what the right decision is, but I do know that I want to be braver. Maybe that's my answer.

Twenty-Six

HANNAH

LOU BREEZES INTO OUR CONFERENCE ROOM AT ELEVEN ON the dot for our scheduled check-in. She's a sparkling cotton-candy vision in her pink pencil skirt, pink blouse, and rose-gold jewelry.

"My girls!" she says, spreading her arms beatifically. "How are y'all doing?"

Under the table, Libby links my pinky finger with hers, a silent reminder that we're in this together.

"Great, thanks," Libby says. "How are you?"

"Just peachy, sweetheart," Lou says, smiling. "Your office sure is bustling with activity. How lovely. Anyway! I can't wait to hear about the progress y'all have made. Hannah, shall we start with you?"

I hesitate briefly; while I've been doing the required components of the challenge—the dates, reading Lou's book, journaling—I'm also wrestling with a decision that could mean dropping out: getting back together with Josh.

I've written down all the potential pitfalls in my journal: the risk of being hurt again, fracturing my relationship with my sister, harming our business. It's my attempt to sort my tangled-up emotions into neat sentences, lists, bullet points. The irony is not lost on me that I'm using Lou's program to decide if I'm going to keep going with her program.

"I've gone on five dates so far," I tell her. Rob the Generic White Guy, Landon the Sore Loser, Gunnar the Axe Thrower, Mateo the Tandem Cyclist, and Danny the Dancer. It would have been six if I hadn't canceled on Adam last week. I'm not sure Libby has fully forgiven me for that one; she's been guarded ever since.

Lou raises one perfectly arched eyebrow. "Only five? We're on week six."

"She has another date tomorrow," Libby chimes in.

I didn't know about this, but I nod and mumble, "Yes, tomorrow."

"All right," Lou says, tossing her blond bob. "Keep an eye on your pace, darlin'. There's a reason we do these challenges in twelve weeks, not twelve days or twelve months—it's the sweet spot for making a lasting difference in your life. Change needs time, yes, but it also needs a time*line*. Oh, I like that! I should use that on the podcast." She grins, holding her hands out to me. "Let's see your journal."

I reluctantly slide it across the table, hoping she doesn't see everything I've written about Josh. Lou flips through the journal quickly, and I'm relieved to see that she's just checking that I've filled the pages.

"Well, well, well," she says, nodding. "Someone is taking this seriously. I'm impressed, Hannah. How are you feeling? Has it made a difference?"

This is a question I can answer honestly. "Yes, it has," I say. "I'm more aware of why I'm staying in my comfort zone. And I wouldn't say I've crushed it, but I've realized that I'm suffocating myself by staying safe."

Lou's eyes widen, like I've said something profound. "You're right—safety can be suffocating. Proud of you, girl."

"Can I ask a question?" I say. Lou nods, and I go on. "What if . . . I end up liking one of the guys I meet and want to stop dating anyone else? How would that affect the challenge?"

Next to me, I can feel Libby's suspicious gaze on the side of my face.

"Hypothetically," I add quickly.

"There are no hypotheticals in life," Lou says, shaking her head. "Just facts. But then we attach emotions to those facts. That's what complicates things. Understand?"

I do not. But before I can ask for clarification, Lou turns to my sister. "Now, Libby! How's it going with those workouts, getting ready for your big race?"

Libby describes the training program, and Lou smiles. "Marvelous. Now let's see that journal."

As Lou flips through Libby's journal, her smile dims. I only get a few glimpses of the pages, but I can tell that they're mostly blank.

Lou slides it back to Libby, sighing. "This can only change your life if you allow it, dear. You must be a full participant."

Libby nods, looking chastened. "I understand."

Lou's pink lips press together, and my pulse quickens. What if she decides to drop us, right here, right now?

"Girls, what I'm seeing here isn't unusual. You're in the murky middle—far enough in that you feel like you've been doing it forever, but you still can't see the finish line. The true challenge is maintaining your commitment even when it's not exciting and new anymore. I promise if you do, you'll be rewarded. And that"—she glances at Libby—"includes taking the journaling seriously."

I nod—the middle of the race is always where your mettle is tested, where you see if your weeks of training will pay off.

"We understand," Libby tells Lou, then motions to the screen on the wall where her keynote presentation is queued up. "If you have time, we'd love to show you our preliminary thoughts for your PR plan."

"Go ahead," Lou says, nodding.

Libby runs through the slides, and Lou fires off questions and comments while I do my best to jot them down on my notepad. Within fifteen minutes, she's poked holes in our carefully constructed strategy, which is going to mean hours of additional work. Better to know now than miss the mark on the final presentation.

When Libby finishes, she looks as dazed as I feel. "Thank you for the feedback. We'll make those adjustments."

"Keep up the good work, dolls," Lou says, standing. "Now, remember what I said about taking my program seriously. *All* of it—not just the easy parts."

And with that, she flutters out of the room.

"Whew, that was intense," Libby says, laughing awkwardly. "But, bright side, we only have to convince her we're doing those damn challenges for another six weeks!"

She stands, but I put my hand on her arm and stop her. "Libs, she's right. You're only doing the easy part of your challenge."

"Easy part?" Libby scoffs. "I'm busting my ass six days a week—literally! Meanwhile, you're putting in the bare minimum effort on your dates, just checking them off your list."

"Hey! I'm—"

"And what was that question about falling for one of the guys? You better tell me if *that* happens."

I swallow. I was hoping Lou could give me some guidance on what to do about Josh, but I can't tell Libby that.

She turns to go, but I don't release her arm. "You've been doing the physical work," I say, "but that's only part of the program. The journaling has made an actual, measurable difference for me."

"How?" Libby's eyes spark with challenge.

I open my mouth, then realize that there isn't much I can tell her. I'm not ready to talk about Josh yet. And the other changes I've seen in myself? All the tiny decisions to speak up instead of staying quiet, the infinitesimal shifts toward bravery? None of those are that impressive.

"You know that crisis with MySole?" I ask, grasping for something she'll understand. "I know you were upset about my canceling the date, but you have to admit—I handled that crisis like a boss. There's no way I could've done that a few weeks ago."

"Okay, yes, that was great," she says. "I'm happy that it's working for you. But I've tried, and journaling just isn't my thing."

I study Libby, the stubborn set of her jaw, the tension in her shoulders. I have the distinct sense that beneath this resistance, my confident, badass sister is scared. Scared to face her comfort zone, to consider why it developed in the first place. Scared to take a cold, hard look at the wounds she's trying to protect.

"Libs?" I say, tentative. "I know it's—"

"Stop looking at me like that." She huffs and rolls her eyes. "It's just that I've been doing this stupid training for six weeks, and I haven't made any progress—"

"What? You've made *tons* of progress! You're way better at those monkey bars—"

"I'm not even close to being prepared for the Down & Dirty! And *now* Lou's saying that all that work isn't good enough? On top of everything else, I have to write in some stupid journal about my stupid feelings?"

"Yes, to understand what's causing them—"

"What's the point? Even if we complete the challenges, she's not going to give us her business if she doesn't like our ideas—and she just blew our entire PR plan to bits. What if we give this everything we've got and still lose everything?"

She breaks off, her eyes filling with tears. It's a rare glimpse of vulnerability, and it makes me feel off-balance; this isn't my role as the little sister.

"What would GiGi tell us, if she were here?" I ask.

Libby shakes her head. "She never would've let things get this bad."

I lean back in my chair, thinking. "Remember the big financial crisis in 2008? GiGi told us she came close to folding. But she said that if you want to be in business for a long time, you've got to learn to ride the waves. That ups and downs are a part of life—"

"So, keep your eyes on the horizon and keep moving forward," Libby finishes, nodding.

"That's what we'll do, right?" I say, needing my big sister's reassurance.

Libby exhales, and her expression shifts from doubt to determination. I can't deny that it makes me feel better.

"We're Ruth Freedman's granddaughters," she says. "We finish what we start."

Twenty-Seven

LIBBY

TRUE TO HIS WORD, ADAM EMAILED ME MONDAY MORNING
and said he'd love to talk about hiring us to do PR for his restaurant. I waited a few hours to write back, not wanting to
seem too eager. But in the days since then, it's been a flurry of
emails with questions and details about the history of the restaurant and his goals for the future.

The conversation switched to text messaging yesterday
when he sent me photos from inside the restaurant. The
place really has seen better days—it's shabby, and not in the
chic way.

Most of our texts have been work related, but the more
friendly we get and the more we message, the more worried I
am about accidentally mixing up the chat threads and reply-
ing to a HannahF thread as Libby, or vice versa.

My plan on quitting One+One cold turkey didn't work;
Adam is still messaging HannahF on the app, although not as
frequently.

This afternoon, we've been talking about how to breathe new life into some of his menu items. I make sure I'm on our text thread before I type a new message.

Libby: Remind me again what your most popular dish is?

Adam: Probably a tie between the latkes and the smoked salmon Benny

Libby: Have you ever thought about combining the two? Using a latke as the base for the Benedict instead of an English muffin?

Adam: 🤯

Adam: I know what I'll be serving for brunch this weekend! I'll call it the Libby Special.

Swoon.

Libby: Don't laugh, but I've always wanted to have something named after me. And I can't think of anything better than fried potatoes and smoked fish!

He sends a winky face, which sends me into a spiral. Is the emoji flirty or friendly? I'm stumped into silence and the seconds keep piling on top of one another.

I picture Adam leaning against the counter at the restaurant, running a hand through his curly hair, waiting for my response.

ADAMR: Hey, what are you doing this weekend?

My heart leaps at the prospect of Adam inviting me over for brunch to sample my namesake dish—until I realize the message isn't on our text thread. It's on the One+One app.

I switch back to our text thread. Hannah doesn't have to reply to him right away. Besides, she's busy. All weekend.

Libby: You'll have to let me know if people like it . . .

I'm about to suggest he have Harvey try the new Benedict out on his next date when I remember that HannahF knows about the octogenarian Romeo, not me.

Adam: What do you think about featuring a different Benny each week?

Libby: I think that's a great idea—give people a reason to keep coming back.

Adam: You're so smart

I smile at the compliment, even though a part of me yearns for a more superficial compliment—that I'm beautiful, that I have pretty eyes or great boobs—which, let's face it, I do.

Flipping back over to the One+One app, I figure I've made Adam wait long enough for Hannah.

HANNAHF: Hey! I'm going out of town this weekend.
To Milwaukee for Summerfest.

That's not true, of course. Hannah will be in town, going on a rock-climbing date with SethM, an accountant who is tall and athletic and has great reviews on LinkedIn and Yelp.

ADAMR: Sweet! Music festivals are 9/10.

HANNAHF: True. But porta potties are 2/10.

ADAMR: LOL

Adam: What's your favorite thing to cook?

Adam: Doesn't have to be for breakfast

It takes me a minute to realize that Adam is talking to me, Libby, not Hannah. This is exhausting—being two different people is hard enough without trying to be them at the same exact time.

Also, did he just casually take our conversation from professional to personal? I mean, it's work adjacent, since it's still about food. He could be mining for ideas, not trying to get to know me better . . .

God, my brain is exhausting sometimes. I look back down at the empty message field, taunting me to come up with a clever reply.

Libby: I'm an equal opportunity cook . . . I don't like to play favorites.

Adam: Fair enough

Adam: Then what's the last thing you cooked?

Libby: I tried a new pasta recipe last night with zucchini and feta—I'm taking the carbing up part of training very seriously

Adam: What are you training for?

Shit. Apparently if I don't overthink something, I under-think it. I could have told Adam about the pasta without admitting that I'm training for an event I have no business participating in. The last thing I want is for him to picture me in workout gear, huffing and puffing my way through the ob-stacle course. Maybe I can make it sound like it's not a big deal. He doesn't have to know details.

Libby: Just a race. I'm doing it with my sister.

Adam: Like a 5k?

Libby: I wish. That would be easier.

I switch over to One+One, hoping that a message from Hannah will distract him into forgetting about me and my stupid race.

HANNAHF: What's the last concert you went to?

Adam: A 10k?

Crap. I hate admitting the truth so much that I can't even be excited that he wrote me back instead of answering Hannah first.

I crack my knuckles and take a deep breath.

Libby: Don't laugh. But it's the Down and Dirty.

Adam: The obstacle course race?

Adam: Why would I laugh? That's awesome!

Libby: Maybe. But training is less than awesome.

Adam: Or maybe you're just doing it wrong . . .

Libby: Please tell me you aren't about to mansplain my own training to me

Adam: Oh, god no!

The three dots appear again, and I wait, hoping he has a good explanation. This is exactly why I don't like talking about this—people take one look at me and assume that I couldn't possibly do something athletic. But they don't know all the work I've done. All the work Hannah has done to help me. I haven't lost much weight, but my clothes are a little looser, and I've been able to push myself further the last few weeks.

Plus, I'm not as nervous to try new things. We tried yoga again, and I didn't hate it. And I would have enjoyed the Pilates class if I hadn't been terrified I'd get stuck in that contraption with my legs up in the air.

Adam: What I meant to say was that training can be fun

Adam: Have you heard of the Chi-Town Ninja Gym?

I haven't, but my good friend Google can surely help me out. I do a quick search and see that it's a place where kids have birthday parties.

Libby: The kids' place?

Adam: It's not just for kids. Wed nights they have adult open gym.

Libby: Cool

My stomach flips as the word hangs there, so very un-cool.

Adam: I've actually been wanting to check it out

Adam: We could go together next week if you want?

Is he asking me out?! Or is this just a friends thing? It's definitely not a professional thing. So it must be a friends thing.

Adam: What do you think?

I'm thinking so many things that I can't keep them straight. But it would be really fun to hang out with Adam. Even as friends.

So I stop thinking, and reply before I change my mind.

Libby: Why not! Let's do it.

"What are you smiling at?" Hannah asks as she walks back into our shared office.

Busted.

"Oh, just an inside joke," I tell her, knowing it's a cop-out. Plus, inside jokes are things you have with friends—and I don't have many of those anymore. Other than my sister.

"With who?"

I panic and say, "Suji." We haven't hung out other than grabbing coffee at the office, but she's funny and easy to talk to.

"Oh?" Hannah clearly doesn't believe me.

"Yeah," I tell her. "We're going to grab a drink on Wednesday night to talk about an idea she had about us hosting a networking event here. We can sell tickets and hopefully bring in more renters."

The lie comes out so easily, I wonder if I should be worried. This life of duplicity is rubbing off on me, and not in a good way.

Before Hannah can ask any more questions, she gets distracted by her own phone. I look back down at mine, where there's one last message from Adam. A message that sends me tumbling from my perch on top of cloud nine.

Adam: Perfect! You'll see how much fun training can be.

His words make me realize that I won't just be hanging out with Adam. I'll be hanging from ropes with him. More accurately—struggling to get up ropes with him.

Maybe I can write back and say I got the date wrong, and I have a prior commitment this Wednesday. And the next Wednesday, and every Wednesday until the end of time.

I pick up my phone, poised to text him an excuse, but something stops me. The journal prompt from this morning asked about the last thing I did that pushed me outside my comfort zone. I haven't been able to answer it yet, since I don't think trying a new pasta recipe counts.

This non-date outing would definitely do the trick. It doesn't get much farther out of my comfort zone than (a) doing something athletic that's (b) in front of people and (c) with one of those people being a cute guy I have a not-so-tiny crush on.

Maybe I am starting to grow. Just a little bit.

CRUSH YOUR COMFORT ZONE

THE ULTIMATE CHALLENGE COMPANION JOURNAL

WEEK 7

I want you to imagine a wounded animal, out in the wild; where would it retreat? To a safe space, a cave, where it can lick its wounds, rest, and recuperate before heading back out again. That's the important part: the heading back out. Unfortunately, many of us have become stuck.

Today, write about a wound in your past that caused you to retreat into the safety of your present-day comfort zone.

Libby, July 17

Hi, Lou.

Maybe the reason I've been avoiding this journal is because I've been pretending my wounds don't exist. I'm the queen of covering up pain with a smile or joke—but I know that if I want to grow, I have to face the things that have hurt me.

Like when I was seven and my mom wouldn't even let me try on a two-piece swimsuit. When I was thirteen and couldn't find a single romance novel with a character who wasn't skinny. Every day on the bus when strangers avoid eye contact when I'm walking down the aisle, looking for a seat.

On their own, none of these "wounds" are that big or tragic— but after living in this body for twenty-nine years, the comments and actions have added up, like a million paper cuts. I'm tired of letting them hurt me.

Twenty-Eight

HANNAH

I'M STANDING ON MICHIGAN AVE. IN THE OPPRESSIVE JULY heat, eating a quick and cheap lunch (a hot dog—the peppers, tomato, and pickle spear tumbling from my poppyseed bun as I scarf it down) when a text arrives from Josh.

Josh: Come sailing with me today

Longing corkscrews through my chest, sharp and searing. I've spent the past couple of weeks thinking about him, deliberating, but it comes down to this: I miss him. I want to see him, to hear his voice. To breathe the same air.

Maybe there's a way to take baby steps toward being together. I want to give him a chance, but I also don't want to rush things.

Hannah: I've been thinking about what you said at the hotel. About us. And

I bite my lip, hesitating. Part of me wishes I could throw

caution to the wind and go for it with Josh now. Do what *I* want, instead of worrying about what my sister will think, or what's best for our business.

But I can't; responsibility is one of the most important values I learned from GiGi. I continue typing.

Hannah: And I want to try again. With you. But I need to finish my dating challenge this summer before I feel comfortable moving forward. Is it okay if we take things slow until then?

I take a deep breath and press send.

Josh: Of course

Josh: I just want to spend time with you

Josh: speaking of which

Josh: Sailing?

I exhale, relieved at his easy response. He knows where I stand, so nothing will happen. Plus, sailing sounds amazing— the city feels swampy with humidity today, and I have such fond memories of being out on Josh's family sailboat. His mom would pack a picnic lunch and his dad would enlist us as his crew, teaching us about all the different knots, how to trim the sails and tell what direction the wind is blowing.

Libby is heading out tonight with Suji to plan their big networking event, and it sounds like she'll be gone for hours.

Hannah: Sounds fun. When?

Josh: Let's say 5pm

Josh: At the Montrose marina

Josh: You remember where that is?

Josh: I'll bring dinner

My smile grows as I type.

Hannah: Can't wait!

A FEW HOURS later, Josh and I are miles away from land, cutting across the water, white sails unfurled. The lake is like crushed diamonds sparkling on a clear blue canvas, the muggy city long forgotten as wind whips my hair and cool spray hits my face.

Josh had to remind me of all the sailing basics as he navigated us out of the marina. I feel like an awkward landlubber, losing my balance, stumbling over ropes. Josh, on the other hand, has come alive. He apparently spent lots of time sailing near Brisbane during his year abroad, then around San Diego during grad school. And it shows: he's confident, steady as he adjusts the tension, tightening his grip on the rope so the sail captures the wind and we pick up speed.

I can't keep my eyes off him. His dark hair tousled by the wind, his eyes sparkling, and his dimple winking. The wind pulls the fabric of his T-shirt against his broad shoulders and chest, his shorts against his thighs. I flash back to the shower, that big, golden body right there in front of me, and warmth spreads down my legs.

Josh doesn't seem similarly affected by me. He's grinning and chatting, his usual pleasant self, definitely not drowning in lust like I am. So I try very hard to stop thinking about the rasp of his stubble against my neck, his warm mouth on mine.

It's smarter to take things slow.

When we reach a spot with no one else around, Josh hands me one of the ropes and tells me to hold it loosely, easing the tension until we're bobbing on gentle waves. From here, the skyline looks like a jumble of children's blocks, hazy and indistinct.

My stomach growls, and Josh looks up from where he's dropping the anchor.

"Hungry?" he says, grinning.

"Starving."

Josh heads down to the cabin, where he's piled towels and our backpacks. Then he freezes. "Shit."

"What's wrong?"

He turns around, a horrified look on his face. "I forgot the food. I packed this whole picnic basket with sandwiches and fruit and drinks . . . God, I'm an idiot. I am *such* an idiot."

"It's not that big of a deal—"

"It *is* a big deal. I was trying to impress you."

"I am impressed!"

"My stupid brain," he mutters.

"Hey! I like your brain. We can grab something to eat later."

He runs his hand over his face, looking so frustrated that it makes my heart twist. He planned this for me; he put in effort to do something special.

I think for a minute. "I might have some food in my bag. And your mom always kept stuff in the cabin, right? Let's see what we can figure out."

Eventually, we're able to put together a smorgasbord of sorts: two protein bars from my bag (only slightly smashed), a package of beef jerky, a can of trail mix from the cabin, and some Jolly Ranchers. I brought my emotional support water bottle, of course, so we share that.

We eat sitting on the edge of the bow, our legs dangling over the side. It's a casual position, like two old friends hanging out, but this close to him, I have to concentrate on my breathing so I don't betray the fact that my body is lighting up, my fingers aching to reach out and touch him.

Josh tells me about his research on a type of coral in the Bahamas that withstands rising water temperature better than other species.

"Half of the world's coral reefs are already dead," he's saying, "and if we don't do something to change things, ninety percent will be gone by . . ."

His words fade away and I follow his gaze to my lap, where the wind has lifted my cover-up to expose my thighs and the edge of my bikini bottom.

"By?" I prompt.

He drags his gaze away like it's physically painful. "By 2050," he finishes, then swallows.

Maybe he's not as unaffected as I thought. Memories from our shower together flash through my mind: Josh's fingers in my hair, his soapy hands on my body, the ache between my legs.

"Do you remember our first kiss?" I ask.

His eyes flick up to meet mine. "Of course. At the play-ground near my parents' house."

We were each on a swing, twisting ourselves around until the chains were in knots, then letting our feet go so we could spin until we were dizzy. After we'd slowed down, he reached out, grabbed the chains of my swing, and pulled me close.

"I was so nervous," I say.

"Me, too."

"Is that why you waited so long to kiss me?" From the day we first held hands on the Ferris wheel to that first kiss was almost two months. "I remember thinking maybe you didn't want to."

The corner of his lip curls up, bringing out a whisper of his dimple. I want to lick it.

"Oh, I wanted to," he says. "But I was doing research in preparation."

"Research!" I burst out laughing. "Like what?"

"I googled 'how to kiss a girl' and took notes. The ideal lip-to-tongue ratio. How to breathe while kissing. What to do with your noses so they don't mash together."

I double over laughing, holding on to the metal railing so I don't tip over.

"I didn't know what I was doing!" Josh protests.

"Lip-to-tongue ratio," I wheeze.

He shakes his head, grinning. "Don't make fun of me."

"I'm not! I think it's cute."

"Yay. Cute." He rolls his eyes. "Exactly what every teenage boy wants the girl of his dreams to say about him. I just . . . wanted our first kiss to be perfect."

"It was," I say, smiling. The world around us faded away, like we were encased in a golden, shimmery bubble. "So, when we got to second base, did you research that, too? Did you google 'how to touch a girl's boobs'?"

He chuckles. "No. I figured that out all on my own."

"Well done."

"But I did google 'how to finger my girlfriend.'"

The laughter dies abruptly in my throat. His eyes seem darker now, and a pulse of heat shoots through me.

"You did?"

He gives a slow nod.

I'm flashing back to that moment—his hands fumbling to unbutton my jeans, sliding into my underwear. That first touch of his hand, *right there*; how it seemed to electrify me. The first time I came—it felt like some kind of miracle. I hadn't known my body could do that.

His eyes are intense as he watches me, cataloguing my expression as he slowly says, "I also googled 'how to go down on my girlfriend.'"

Another sharp burst of heat, low in my belly. I remember my surprise when he first headed downward on my body, how I told him I wasn't sure I was going to like it. He said he would stop at any time, but he wanted to try. I was nervous and it seemed to take a while, but when I came, it was *amazing*. I was speechless for fifteen minutes.

"I'm embarrassed to say I never googled any moves to try on you," I tell him, trying to keep my voice light. "Was I a disappointment?"

"Never."

He takes my hand, lacing his fingers with mine. My heart stutters to a stop. It feels so right, like our hands were designed to fit together.

"We were good together," I say softly, "weren't we? Sometimes, I wonder if I'm seeing the memories through rose-colored glasses. But it was really good, wasn't it?"

"You're the best I've ever had," he says. "And I don't just mean . . . physically. I mean you're the best conversation, the best companionship, the best friend and lover. It's why I never got over you. I've never loved anyone the way I love you."

I blink. *Love.* I'm not sure what to do with that. The present tense. But I feel it, too; like the love wasn't lost, just put in storage for a while. Now we've unboxed it, dusted it off, and it's as bright and beautiful as ever.

Lou's words at our last check-in float through my mind: *There are no hypotheticals in life. Just facts. But then we attach emotions to those facts. That's what complicates things.*

I think I understand now. The fact is, I love Josh. I always have. So, why am I letting my emotions—my fears—complicate things? Trusting him again, even though there are no guarantees that we'll work out, feels like the bravest thing I could ever do.

There's no way I can put all that into words. So instead, I lean in and kiss him.

Our kiss in the shower was desperate, heated, like we were afraid it could end at any moment. This kiss is slow and languid, like we have all the time in the world, and I suppose we do, bobbing in the middle of the lake with no one else around. His lips are warm and welcoming, and I close my eyes and follow his lead.

He may have googled how to do this years ago, but his movements now are born of experience, because Josh still knows exactly how to kiss me. Light presses of his lips against mine, just a hint of tongue. Heat crawls up my spine and curls into the center of me.

"I missed your hair," I murmur, running my hands through the soft waves. "You have such nice hair."

He hums. "I missed your hands in my hair."

Our kiss takes on a heavier rhythm, and his teeth scrape against my bottom lip. Shivers run down my body, and I let out a quiet groan.

"I missed *that*," he says. "That sound you make when you like something."

"You're the only person who's ever heard it."

He grins against my lips. "Does it make me a jealous bastard that I'm fucking thrilled to hear that?"

He pulls me into his lap sideways, my feet dangling off one side, my chest against his, my back pressed against the railing. He kisses me deeper, his hand cupping my jaw, which is something I always loved.

"I missed your mouth," I whisper. "So much, Josh. You have no idea."

"I do have some idea." His hand slides down until it's wrapped around my throat, a possessive gesture that makes my body pulse with need. This is a new side of Josh, blatantly masculine, taking what he wants, and I love it. My eyes roll back in my head as he tilts my chin up so he can kiss the other side of my neck, moving upward toward my ear, sucking on my earlobe and making me gasp.

His other hand drifts inside my cover-up to the bare skin at my waist, and he feels so rough and warm that I might spontaneously combust.

"I love the way every part of you fits perfectly in my hand," he murmurs.

And he shows me, palming my ass, my waist, up to my breast. I arch against him, wanting more. Wanting to be closer. Impulsively, I shift my weight and swing one leg over his lap so I'm straddling him. He's hard beneath me, and his breath hitches as I settle against him. The railing presses painfully against my back but I don't care; nothing could drag me from this moment. Still kissing him, I slide my hands under his shirt and run them up the long, taut lines of his torso. He takes a shuddering breath.

"I love the way you breathe when you're getting turned on," I say.

He gives a pained laugh. "*Getting* turned on? I'm trying to hold myself back."

"Don't."

"Don't . . . what?"

"Don't hold back."

He pulls away, just enough so he can catch my eye. "You know I'll wait as long as you need, right? I'll go slow. I'll be careful. I'll—"

"I don't want to go slow anymore."

His pupils dilate as his eyes search mine.

I smile. "And I don't want you to be careful."

It takes a second or two for that to hit him, but when it does, the world seems to tilt beneath us, and everything shifts. He crushes me with his hands, pure need radiating from his skin into mine. He fists my cover-up and yanks it over my head. My bikini top comes off next, peeled away and tossed somewhere behind him.

He takes a nipple in his mouth and I arch my back and groan.

"Is this really happening?" he murmurs, kissing my body with open-mouthed wonder.

I feel the same way, like this can't be real, like it's one of those dreams I have periodically about him, before I wake up hot and bothered and deeply frustrated.

"It's happening," I say, as much to myself as to him.

We're both desperate and frantic now, but still moving so in sync it's like we share one mind. Together, we bundle his shirt up and off his body, and then his chest is against mine, the heat of his skin in contrast to the cool breeze. He claims my mouth with deep strokes of his tongue, punctuated by sharp nips with his teeth.

Then my back presses into the railing and I squeak in pain. He pulls away, his eyebrows knit together in concern. "Are you okay?"

I gesture behind me, unable to speak. But he understands and spins us around, his back against the railing, my legs wrapped around his waist. This positions him perfectly against me, and I shift my weight to angle the pressure where I like it.

Groaning, he bites my shoulder gently. "I missed this. The way we move together."

He grinds against me, his hands gripping my hips so tight I might have bruises later, but I don't care. I haven't felt this way for so, so long, and I'm shocked to realize that I'm already close to climaxing. The pressure builds and Josh seems to understand just what I need, keeping up the same pace, his breaths quickening in time with mine. My eyes fall shut as a tingling warmth spreads over me.

I'm so close. My legs are trembling but I'm hovering on the edge, teetering like a tightrope walker, and I can feel myself getting frustrated, starting to worry, thinking, *Maybe I can't do this with him, either. Maybe there really is something wrong with me.* I push those thoughts away, but my arousal dims a fraction.

His hand drifts inside my bikini bottoms, and I shift my hips to guide him to the perfect spot. My breathing quickens as the entire world narrows to those few inches of my body.

Yes. This. But still I can't quite get there. I want to—it's just out of reach, deceptively close but slipping away, like I'm trying to catch a wisp of cloud.

It doesn't matter, I tell myself. This is still the best thing I've felt in years. I guide his hand back up to my breast, and he lets out a helpless sound. He's losing himself, his eyes lifted heavenward, hazy and unfocused.

"Josh," I say, trying to rouse him. "Josh. Do you have any condoms?"

He shakes his head like he's trying to make sense of what I'm saying. "Do I . . . Hannah. You said you didn't want anything to happen between us until the summer was over. I wasn't even expecting to kiss you."

I groan. "I want you."

He presses his forehead against mine. "I want you, too." Then he straightens up. "I might have one in my wallet. Say a prayer that it's not expired or ruined."

"I'll pray to any god that'll deliver a condom in my hour of need."

He chuckles, a little painfully. "Wait here. My wallet's down in the cabin." Then he pauses, his gaze hot as it sweeps over me. "No—come with me. I'm not fucking you against a fiberglass hull, no matter how badly I want to."

He eases me off him so we can both stand, then takes me by the hand and tugs me belowdecks. It's small but neat, with a kitchenette, a table, and a cushioned seating area. Josh finds his wallet, and I hold my breath.

"Hallelujah," he says, lifting a condom out.

I launch myself at him, greedy and desperate. He wraps one arm around me, and with the other, spreads a towel on the cushion before lowering me flat on my back, coming over me. The heat of him, the weight of him on top of me, is enough to make me nearly weep with gratitude.

"You, looking up at me," he whispers. "Your hair spread around you . . . you're the most beautiful . . . you're everything. You're perfect."

My heart swells and lifts. But the urgency building inside me doesn't want him to gaze too long. So, I nudge him, grinning, and say, "You're still wearing your shorts . . ."

He laughs, easing up slightly as I help him tug his shorts down. Then my bikini bottoms come off. He rolls the condom on as I watch, drinking in the sight of him, the hard planes of his body. His shoulders and his abs and his quads . . .

"What did you do to look like *this*?" I say, the words leaping out of my mouth. "You've always been gorgeous, but damn."

He quirks up one eyebrow, clearly pleased. "You want to hear about my training program? Chest and back on Mondays, arms and shoulders on Wednesdays—"

"No! Never mind! I'm desperate here."

And at that, he slides into me and we both let out identical sighs of relief. This, *this* . . . it's everything, fullness and stretching and glorious closeness. He laces my fingers with his, pulling my arms overhead, pinning me in place as he begins to move. The rest of the world ceases to exist except for this space, the gentle rolling of the boat, the muffled sounds of water lapping against it.

"I missed this," I say.

"Me, too." He's panting already. "But god, Hannah, I'm not

going to last. You're so . . . fuck. No. You're coming first. I didn't do all that research as a horny teenager for nothing."

He pulls out and crawls down my body until he's between my legs, and then he's tasting me, winding me tighter and tighter until I'm up on that tightrope again, my legs trembling with need.

"I'm so close," I whisper. "So, so close."

"I'm not in a hurry. Take your time." His hands reach up to my hips, and the feeling of them—big and rough—grounds me. I close my eyes as the familiar tingles work their way up my legs. *Yes.* But then a flash of panic rips through me; these feelings are too big, too scary. I'm going to split right down the middle. I want to bolt but I want to stay and I'm so damn terrified and so turned on I can't breathe.

I'm writhing, my feet scrabbling helplessly on the towel. His grip on my hips tightens, holding me in place, like he knows just what I need.

"Josh, I can't . . ." I babble. "I don't . . . Josh . . . no, no, nononono—"

My legs spasm and my back arches and I'm not even in my body; I'm an explosion of light somewhere overhead, and then I descend back into myself, crying out and rocking back and forth.

Before I've even come all the way down, he's building me up again, but this time it doesn't take as long. Soon I'm crying out, reaching down to run my hands through his hair as I shake. This climax is sweeter, like I'm bathed in golden honey, and I sigh in pleasure, letting my body relax into the soft surface beneath me.

"Thank you," I whisper, closing my eyes.

"Glad to be of service," he says. Then he nudges my legs apart with his knee, roughly. "But I'm not done with you."

My eyes fly open at the heat in his voice. Before I can respond he's inside me again, and this time he's not holding back. He's all long, deep, rolling thrusts, each one a relentless tug and pull deep in my core.

"I missed this—no, *you*," he says. "I missed *us*."

And I know what he means: these kisses, these touches, reminding ourselves of what we love about each other's bodies— those are wonderful. But what I missed most was bigger than all those individual parts; it's the entirety of him, of us together, all the years of our history, the friendship and passion and trust.

He lifts one of my legs to rest my ankle on his shoulder. With this new angle, he hits something different inside me, and I gasp.

"Hannah, Hannah," he chants, pressing his cheek against my calf. Then he lifts my other leg to his shoulder and the next thrust is so deep I whimper. He makes eye contact, checking in, and I nod. *Yes. More.* And he obliges, closing his eyes, his face tilted upward like he's praying, like he's trying to hold on as long as possible until—

Another climax hits me out of nowhere, and I cry out. Finally, Josh lets himself go, pulling me down until we're both drowning, then resurfacing, gasping for air in a world that finally makes sense again.

AFTER, HE PULLS me against him, my head resting on his chest in the spot that has always felt made for me.

"I'm still sorry I forgot dinner," he says, pressing a kiss to my forehead.

"Josh, it's really okay—"

"I know, but things have been stressful at work for you, and I wanted you to relax. To feel taken care of. For an evening, at least."

My heart warms like glowing coals. "I do feel relaxed. And you took care of me quite well. Triple well, one might say."

His chuckle vibrates between us. "I have a lot of time to make up for." He goes quiet. "Not to push this, but . . . where does this leave us?"

"Leave us?"

He runs his hand across my stomach, drawing lazy circles around my appendectomy scar. "You said before that you wanted to finish your challenge. And that's fine, I just—"

"I'm going to stop the dates," I say, and he exhales in relief.

But there's tension in his voice when he asks, "How will you explain that to Libby?"

I turn my body, propping myself up so I can see his face. He looks somehow boyish and utterly manly at the same time, that sharp jaw, that dimple, that gorgeous hair that is now a rumpled, tousled mess.

"I'm going to tell her the truth," I say.

"Which is . . ."

"That I just had mind-blowing sex with Joshua Andrew Jacobson," I say, laughing.

He smirks, all smug satisfaction for a moment, before his expression melts into something more vulnerable. "Which means what, exactly, for us?"

A thrum of anxiety runs through me. "I guess that depends on what you want."

"That's not obvious?" he says, motioning to our bodies, our legs tangled together, our skin glowing with a slight sheen of sweat.

"Spell it out for me." I need him to be clear; he's the one who left, and he's the one who came back.

He holds my gaze, tender and fierce. "I want you, Hannah. I want to take you to dinner and hold your hand and kiss you. I want to put a picture of you on my desk at work. I want to take you to bed, and I want to wake up with you in the morning and feed you breakfast and go running together. But if you're not ready for that—"

"I am."

Even as I say the words, though, a tiny voice whispers that I'm being stupid—that if things don't work out between us, it'll hurt like hell. That I'm being selfish, that I can't just do what *I* want, because this affects my sister and our future.

But there's another voice, too, reminding me to be brave, to take a risk, to follow my heart. I don't think it's Lou's voice. I think it's mine, steady and clear. And I'm going to listen.

"I want all those things," I tell him. "I want them with you."

"Now, *that* is the best thing I've heard in five years." He wraps his arms around me, all solid muscles and warm skin, and exhales a long, long breath, relaxing completely.

I wish I could relax, too. But I know what's coming next.

I have to tell Libby.

Twenty-Nine

LIBBY

IF HANNAH'S NOTICED THAT I STEPPED UP MY EFFORT TRAIN-
ing the last few days, she hasn't said anything. Not even when
I suggested stopping by the playground to do some extra
deadhangs and pull-ups after we did our scheduled interval
walk-run.

I expected her to question me, since I usually complain
about any activity that uses my body weight against me, but I
was willing to try anything to help prepare for this friend-date
or work-date or whatever this is with Adam.

Just my luck, the extra work backfired.

My armpits are achy as hell, and my palms are sore from
all the friction, which does not bode well for my surviving the
Ninja Gym.

"Hey!" Adam says as I walk in. The room smells like rubber and sweat, and I'm instantly transported back to my high
school gym, which is not a place or time that I'd particularly
like to revisit.

If it weren't for Adam, standing there with a bright smile
on his face, looking both athletic and adorably dorky in gym

shorts and a rec league T-shirt, I might have walked out before we made it past the reception desk. But alas, he's here early and I can't back out now.

"Hey," I say, not sure if I should go for a handshake or a hug. It's only awkward for a moment, because he leans in and gives me a nice, albeit platonic, hug.

He smells even better up close, that musky, manly scent I haven't stopped thinking about since the street fest last weekend. He feels strong and solid beneath my arms, and I can't help but notice his height; while too short for Hannah's standards, he's perfect for me. My head comes up to his shoulder, and I resist the urge to lay it there and close my eyes.

But we've got a terrifying obstacle course to get to.

After we check in and sign a very long, detailed waiver that I only skim for fear of spotting some kind of warning that I won't be able to unsee, a pumped-up guy named Billy gives us a quick tour and tells us the rules.

"Where should we start?" Adam asks, his eyes shining with excitement.

I scan the room from corner to corner, searching for anything that might be easy. My eyes land on a group of brightly colored shapes—circles and squares that look like they're meant to be jumped on, from one to the other. They're not as high as the steps by the river that Hannah and I practice going up and down for our training, and the foamish material looks a lot more forgiving than the concrete.

"How about those?" I suggest, pointing.

Adam turns to look in the direction I'm indicating, and his smile fades. "I . . . uh . . . I think that's the kids' section."

"Oh," I say, hoping my face doesn't look as red as it feels. "Suppose there's an age and weight limit on those."

I cringe, annoyed at myself for calling attention to my Achilles' heel. Luckily, Adam doesn't seem to notice.

"How about the balance beam?" he suggests. "Ease our way into the hard stuff."

"That sounds like a good plan," I agree, even though my throat constricts at the thought of "hard stuff."

The balance beam, it turns out, is not one of the solid, immovable kinds that I remember from the gymnastics birthday parties of my childhood. This one has a fulcrum in the middle so the beam rises and falls as you walk across it.

"Want to go first?" Adam asks.

"Sure," I say, hoping my voice doesn't reveal my nerves.

I take my time, squaring myself up in front of the beam, hoping the yoga Hannah and I have been doing has been helping my core and balance.

Kids do this all the time, I remind myself. It can't be that hard. Then again, it's easy to be fearless when you're young and have no idea how much there is to be afraid of.

Stop it, Libby.

I take a deep breath and think back to the quote on this morning's page in the journal. *Outer strength comes from inner strength.* It's almost like Lou knew where I would be at this moment in my journey.

I glance back at Adam, who gives me a reassuring smile. Then, with the wisdom of Lou in my mind, I take the first step out of my comfort zone and onto the balance beam. My legs wobble, and I instinctively bring my hands up to steady myself.

Once my feet feel stable, I move one foot in front of the other, walking up along with the slope of the beam. Before I know it, I'm halfway across, ready for the descent.

"You've got this," I hear Adam say from behind me, where he's watching at the end of the balance beam. I'm suddenly aware he's behind me. As in, staring at my behind. I reflexively squeeze my butt cheeks, wishing these leggings weren't so formfitting.

The thought derails me, and I sway before steadying myself. I'm hyperaware of my body as I put one foot in front of the other, leaping off the end of the beam.

"Nice!" Adam says, his voice full of what feels like undeserved pride.

We do the balance beam a few more times walking straight, then sideways. The last time, it's actually fun, and I find myself speed walking along the beam, jumping off at the end with a silly flourish.

As we head to the next activity, I realize that new things might just be scary simply because they're new. My training this summer has included so many things I thought I couldn't do—when in reality, I was just afraid to try. But once you've done it—and know you *can* do it—the fear no longer has power over you.

I want to take that power back.

Over the next thirty minutes, I make a conscious effort to focus on my inner strength and not my inner scaredy-cat. Adam and I take turns leaping down a row of slanted boards facing each other; it's almost like jumping from boulder to boulder. By the last time we sprint across, my feet are barely grazing the boards, hopping from one to the next.

We then decide to conquer a crazy wall-scaling challenge that looks like it could be one of the obstacles at the Down & Dirty. The two blue walls face each other, just a few feet between them. I insist that Adam go first so I can watch how he does it.

I'm almost giddy with excitement as Adam makes a running start, jumps on the trampoline, and lands midway up the wall, with one foot propping him up on either side of the narrow way. He makes it look easy as he uses his hands for support, moving his feet as he straddles the space between the two walls until he jumps down on the other side.

"That was insane," he says, running back around to the side where I'm trying to pump myself up. The space between the walls is so narrow, I hope it's wide enough for me to make it through. I will literally die of embarrassment if I get stuck. I have a sudden flash of paramedics sawing the wall in half to break me free. Or lathering me with butter so they can slide me out.

"Once you're up there, it's second nature," Adam says, clearly sensing my nerves. "Your body will know what to do."

"But getting up there . . ."

"Want to watch me do it one more time?"

I exhale in relief. "Yes, please."

He flashes a grin, then he's off, leaping up and landing on the wall. When he's halfway across, I walk up to the edge, subtly measuring myself against the width. I'm relieved to see it's not quite as narrow as it looks from a distance.

When Adam comes back, a little out of breath, with sweat glistening on his brow, I position myself at the starting point, then take off in a sprint toward the trampoline.

But I accidentally slow to a stop before I get there. My heart is pounding with fear and I freeze.

"Just try again," Adam says behind me, as if it's that easy.

As I retrace my steps, I imagine a world where it is that easy. Where I don't let hard things get the best of me. I can do this.

And I do. I run, getting faster as I approach the trampoline, but the second before I should be jumping—I stop.

I expect Adam to look disappointed when I turn around, but there's no judgment in his eyes.

"I don't know what's wrong with me," I tell him.

"I do," he says.

My heart sinks and I avert my eyes. I've gotten a lot stronger in the last six weeks, but I don't have enough strength to look Adam in the eye when he tells me all the things he thinks are wrong with me.

"You've got to shake the lead out," he says, and I look up, confused. His expression is so kind, I unexpectedly feel tears prick my eyes.

"It's something an old coach of mine said when he knew I could go faster," he continues. "The 'lead' is all the things you're carrying—you've got to shake them off, let go of anything holding you back. Just run and jump and fly."

"Run and jump and fly," I say, echoing him.

"But first you've got to shake the lead out," he says, and he demonstrates—shaking his hands and legs like an Olympic swimmer getting ready for a race. He manages to look cute even when he's acting ridiculous. "Come on," he says, his voice gently teasing. "Don't let me look stupid all by myself."

He ducks his head to meet my eyes and gives me the warmest, most encouraging smile, lighting me up from the inside.

I join him, shaking my arms and my legs like a lunatic. I imagine all the things I'm shaking off. The insecurity, the doubt, the fear—all tossed to the side, leaving me lighter and ready to fly.

"Ready to give it another go?" Adam asks.

"Ready," I say as I move into position, feeling determined.

This time, I start running and I don't stop. My feet hit the trampoline and I'm up in the air, propelling myself into the crevice of the wall. I catch myself, not quite as high as Adam got, but a good foot off the ground.

Just like he said, it's instinctual; my body seems to know where to put my hands and how to move my feet, one foot forward at a time as I make my way through the obstacle.

"You did it!" Adam says, as I come out the other side. He's there waiting for me and wraps me in a big hug. I resist for half a second, but when I realize he's just as sweaty as I am, I relax and allow myself to be held.

I close my eyes and savor the sensation of his arms around me, warm and solid and comforting. The feeling is both foreign and familiar, and my eyes well with tears as I realize it's been years since someone who wasn't Hannah hugged me.

"Want to do it again?" Adam asks as he pulls back from our sweaty embrace.

"Hell no," I say, wiping what could either be sweat or tears from the corner of my eye. "But thanks for helping me get up there."

"Anytime," he says, bumping his shoulder against mine. He keeps it there for a second, and I can't tell if the gesture is flirty, or bro-y.

"I think we've done everything except . . ." His voice trails off as he looks toward the mother of all Ninja challenges. A man with huge muscles is currently on the contraption, grunting as he moves himself up a ladderlike object five feet off the ground. It's like he's building the monkey bars as he's climbing across them.

My eyes go wide.

"Or . . ." he says, drawing out the word, "we could go get a drink?"

"Now you're talking."

ALL NIGHT, I'VE been reminding myself that this is not a date. When Adam grabbed my hand to help me balance, it was not a date. When he put his hand on my back as we walked toward the climbing ropes, it was not a date. And when he gave me a hug, it was not a date.

At best, we're two new friends hanging out; at worst, we're two business associates with a semi-shared interest that one of us happens to be faking. But as we walk down the steps to the river near State Street, I start to imagine a world where this could be a date.

For the first time since I started planning my sister's dates, I understand why she prefers to have an activity. There's automatically something to talk about, although Adam and I have never had a problem finding things to say to each other. Whether I'm talking to him as myself or as Hannah.

"This okay?" Adam asks, motioning toward City Winery, which has a patio that overlooks the Chicago River.

"Perfect."

I follow his lead, pausing to admire the view of the city lights reflecting on the water, the moon overhead peeking out between the clouds. A few boats float down the river, and couples stroll down the Riverwalk, hand in hand.

At the table, Adam takes a seat and I panic, not sure if I should sit in the chair next to his or across from him. I wish I'd sat first, so he could have decided where to sit.

"I'm just going to run to the ladies' room," I say, hurrying inside the main building.

Behind the safety of the locked door, I stare at my reflection in the mirror, face still flushed from the exertion of the gym, frizzy hair coming out of my ponytail. All the times I imagined myself on a date with Adam, I was wearing a dress and lipstick and high heels—even though I don't own a pair.

In some of those imagined dates, I'm confident and athletic and smart and beautiful like my sister—but inside, I'm still me. The thought of Hannah makes me uneasy. Even though she never seemed to have much interest in meeting Adam, I feel like I'm betraying her.

On impulse, and maybe because I'm a little crazy, I open the One+One app. It's been a few days since HannahF messaged AdamR with more excuses about how busy work was. Tonight's as good a night as any.

HANNAHF: Just saying hi! Hope your day has at least been an 8/10!

I hit send and instantly curse myself for being so self-destructive. No good can come from this. I stare at the screen, waiting for the dots that will let me know he's typing a reply, but they don't come. I put my phone back in my purse, then go to the bathroom and wash my hands.

Still no message from Adam.

Huh. Maybe this really is a date. I can't think of any other reason he wouldn't message Hannah back. He's sitting alone, with nothing else to do but admire the romantic moonlit view, because I left him. Like an idiot.

I head back outside and pause for a moment to watch Adam. He's perusing the menu, absently stroking his beard. Even in his sweaty T-shirt and shorts, his curls disheveled, he looks damn good. And so self-assured, like he knows exactly who he is and is content being himself.

My heart swells with hope; I want this to be a date. I really hope it is, but as I walk over to him, I decide not to press my luck, and take the seat across from his. Plus, it has the added bonus of being able to unabashedly look straight at him instead of awkward side glances.

"So," I say, suddenly shy. What do two people on a date even talk about?

"So," Adam says. "I've started a list of ideas."

"For what?" I ask, smiling.

"Fusion dishes for the restaurant," he says. My heart drops; okay, so we're back to professional mode. Then this isn't a date?

He hands me the menu, and I force a smile back on my face. "Seeing the wasabi tuna tacos here made me think about your latke Benedict idea. Which was brilliant."

"What do you have so far?" I ask.

Adam's eyebrows do their little dance, then he looks down and reads from the napkin where he scribbled out his ideas. "Well, for Asian fusion I was thinking about fried rice kishka or a crab rangoon with lox instead of crab." He looks up to see my reaction, and I give him what I hope is an encouraging smile. "Then I started thinking Italian . . . maybe a brisket lasagna."

"Hmm," I say, trying to wrap my mind around the flavor profiles. Barbecue and marinara sauce might go well together, but the cheese throws me off a bit.

"Scratch that one," Adam says, looking back down at his list. "And this one . . ." He scrunches up his face and twists the napkin, looking at it from another angle. "I can't read my writing."

"You may have missed your calling as a doctor," I say, grinning.

"Tell me about it," he says, the light momentarily leaving his eyes. "I thought about it once."

"Being a doctor?"

"Yeah. Every Jewish mother's dream except mine. My parents expected me to join the family business, and it didn't really matter that I wanted something different. Did you always want to go into PR?"

"Yes and no," I say honestly. "I wanted to be just like my grandmother. It was always such a huge deal when I'd visit her office when I was a little girl, seeing her name—our name—in big letters on the wall. She told me it would all be mine one day if I wanted it. Mine and my sister's."

"It's a blessing and a burden, isn't it?" Adam says. "Being born into a career."

"It is," I say, and the moment feels oddly somber. Having GiGi's business to run has been a blessing—I didn't have to stress about choosing a major or finding a job after college, and I get to work with my sister every day. But I suppose it's been a burden, too. The pressure to keep it going. To not lose everything she worked so hard to create.

"How about brisket tacos?" I suggest, trying to lighten the mood.

"Or brisket quesadillas," he says, his face lighting up again. "Brisket nachos?"

"Better than lox nachos," I say, laughing.

Our eyes meet across the table. His are warm brown, like maple syrup, with flecks of green around the pupil. They stay locked on mine for a moment, then drift downward, toward my mouth.

Startled, I look away.

Adam clears his throat and leans back in his chair. "Thanks

for the ideas," he says. "I feel inspired again, for the first time since . . . maybe ever."

"Happy to help—but don't feel like you have to totally reinvent yourself. From the preliminary research I've done, there's a lot to love about your diner. Sometimes people just want the mandel bread they know and love. You know?"

He nods. "So, you think I should hold back on the kishka fried rice?"

"Maybe start small. You could try to expand your clientele, get new people interested in what you provide—or better yet, give your current customers a new reason to come in. Like for dinner instead of brunch."

"Oh god, there's this one customer who would love if we opened for dinner," he says, then tells me the story I already know about Harvey, the ornery old guy who asked three women out on the same day, one for each meal.

As he talks, it dawns on me how royally I have screwed this up.

Even if Adam were interested in a relationship with me, it could never happen—I spent way too much time talking to him as Hannah. And if he became part of my life in any meaningful way, he'd have to meet my sister. And then he'd find out that our meeting wasn't the chance encounter he thought it was. That I orchestrated the whole thing.

The thought puts a damper on my mood, but if this is going to be my first and last kind-of-sort-of date with Adam, I should just enjoy the night for what it is. A fun side plot in Adam's story, before he eventually finds his leading lady.

Thirty

HANNAH

I'M STANDING IN OUR DARKENED KITCHEN, EATING RASPBER-ries out of the carton—so anxious about talking to my sister that I haven't washed the berries or turned on the light—when I hear her key in the lock.

Libby walks in. Her eyes are lit up and sparkling, her cheeks flushed. Then she sees me and winces, almost like she's embarrassed to have been caught.

"Oh, hey," she says, flicking on the light. "Didn't know you were home. What're you doing in the dark?"

I hold up the carton like an offering, like maybe this will keep my sister from reacting badly to the bomb I'm about to drop. "Eating raspberries."

She narrows her eyes; her big-sister spidey sense knows something's up. "What's going on?"

"Nothing, nothing." I put the raspberries back in the fridge, which allows me to break eye contact. My hands shake as I shut the door. "How were drinks with Suji?"

"It was—" She pauses. "It was good. We came up with some good ideas for the networking event."

Libby puts her purse down and toes off her shoes. Then she walks into the kitchen, pours herself a glass of water.

My stomach is in knots. I need to talk to her about Josh. But why is it so hard?

"What did you end up doing tonight?" Libby asks.

I swallow. "I . . . went sailing."

My sister's eyebrows shoot up, but before she can say anything, I start talking:

"I know you're not going to like this, but I'm a grown woman, okay?" I say. "I get to make my own decisions. That's not to say that I don't appreciate everything you did to help me, because I do, but here's the thing: I have a lot of skills now. My prefrontal cortex has fully developed. I've done *therapy.* So, I guess what I'm asking is for you to support me. No matter what happens."

I force myself to stop; my breathing is erratic.

"I"—Libby stares at me, her eyebrows still raised—"have no idea what you're talking about. Can you back up?"

I blink. And realize that I skipped over some key information.

"I went sailing with Josh tonight." Deep breath. In and out.

Her eyes widen. "Okay. Okay. That's fine. As long as you didn't—"

"We had sex," I blurt.

Her glass slips out of her hand, hitting the tile floor with a spectacular crash, sending shards flying across the room.

"How could you do that?" she shrieks.

I gasp. She doesn't have any shoes on, just ankle socks. "Don't move! I'll grab the broom."

"It was just a onetime thing, right?" She's wailing, oblivious to the broken glass. "One time to get it out of your system so you can move on?"

I bite my lip and look away, and she knows what that means.

"Hannah! You can't get back together with him. Are you out of your mind—"

"Stay still! You're going to get cut." I get the broom and carefully step across the floor, glass crunching under my shoes. I'm grateful for something to focus on so I don't have to see the disappointment on my sister's face.

"I can't believe this!" She's practically hyperventilating. "You know you can't trust him, right? You—"

"It's not your job to protect me," I cut in. Now that the proverbial bomb has dropped, I feel calmer. Like I can let the fear go and sink back into the logical side of my brain.

"But it *will* be my job to fix everything when it falls apart again," she says, "so I think I should have some say in the matter."

I shake my head, frustrated. Does she hear the words coming out of her mouth? Does she honestly think she has a say in who I choose to love?

She keeps ranting: "I just don't understand how, after everything he did to you, you can forgive him!"

"Well, I have," I say, keeping my voice calm. "And—"

"Forgiveness doesn't mean forgetting what he did. GiGi always said to forgive your enemies but remember their names—"

"Pretty sure it was JFK who said that—"

"Not the point!" she says, and I roll my eyes. "Someone has to hold Josh accountable for what he did, and if you won't, I will."

"You're not holding anyone accountable; you're just holding a grudge," I say. "Oh, and you're bleeding."

I point at her ankle, where there's a two-inch slice of red from a flying piece of glass.

"What?" she gasps.

I bend down to inspect the cut; it doesn't look deep. "I'll get a Band-Aid," I say, and reach around to the drawer where we keep the first aid supplies. Crouching again, I apply it to my sister's ankle as she hisses in pain. Then I sweep up the rest of the glass, grateful for a moment of silence.

"It's not so fun, is it?" Libby says quietly. "Picking up the pieces."

"I don't mind."

She huffs, shaking her head. "It's a metaphor, Han. God, your brain is so literal! I'm saying that *I* had to pick up the pieces of your life when Josh left you. *I* had to put on the Band-Aids. And it was awful. *Awful.* I never want to see you hurt like that again."

Her voice trembles, and my heart softens. Libby's always seemed so competent, so in control. So bossy, too, but I suppose that's the role of a big sister.

"I appreciate what you did," I say, "but this is my life, Libs."

Her eyes flash. "Yes, but it affects me, too. If you back out of the challenge—"

"You're the one who pushed for us to do it in the first place. I didn't even want to!" My temper is flaring, and I try to tamp it down.

She throws up her hands. "Don't you dare put this on me. We agreed to do this. Together."

"Right, *together*," I say, unable to keep the snark out of my voice. "Meaning you pushed and pushed until I finally caved."

Hurt flashes across Libby's face, and I instantly regret my words.

"Well," she says, before I can apologize, "it's too late to change our minds. So, what now? Are you going to tell Lou you dropped out so you can bump uglies with some dickhead who's obsessed with underwater plants?"

"Coral aren't plants! They're animals," I say, jabbing a finger in her direction. "And that's not the point! I'm going to explain to Lou that even though I haven't *technically* completed the challenge, I have accomplished the *intent* of it. Getting back together with Josh requires more bravery than going on a thousand dates. I've stepped out of my comfort zone—"

"Bullshit," Libby says, folding her arms. "You've stepped back *into* your comfort zone. You've regressed to being a teenager!"

"Not true." I march over to the table where my journal is sitting, then pick it up and wave it at her. "I've been journaling about this—"

"You were journaling about it but not talking to your *sister*, who also happens to be your roommate and business partner? How long has this been going on?"

"It's been building over the past few weeks," I tell her, and continue before she can interrupt me again. "So much of Lou's program is listening to our own voice, not someone else's. I feel good about getting back together with Josh, but even if I didn't, it still wouldn't be your decision." I don't tell her that my original plan was to wait until the end of the summer. "But you wouldn't understand, because you're not even doing the journaling!"

"I *started* to, but you wouldn't know that because you haven't even *asked* me about it. You've been too busy falling back in love with a literal *rectum* of a man!"

We face off, breathing heavily, and I notice what she's wearing. Leggings and a T-shirt. I glance over near the door where she left her shoes.

Her *running* shoes.

"Wait. Where did you say you went tonight?"

She blinks. "I went . . . out for drinks with Suji. Don't change the subject."

"Which bar?"

"Um. Dublin's."

She is so lying. "What did you have to drink?"

"A . . . vodka soda. And she had an old-fashioned."

"Fantastic. Show me the pictures," I say.

"What? I didn't—we didn't take any pictures."

"At no time in your life have you ever had a drink with anyone and not taken pictures. Pictures of the drinks, pictures of your friend taking a sip, pictures of you and your friend holding your drinks. That's, like, ninety percent of your Instagram."

Not that she does this often, anymore.

She shrugs. "I forgot."

"Liar, liar, pants on fire," I say, fully reverting back to the child she's accusing me of being.

"I don't care, I don't care, I can buy another pair."

"Elizabeth Anne Freedman. Where. Were. You?"

I stare my sister down, taking advantage of the inch of height I have on her. To my utter surprise, she crumbles.

"Okay! Fine!" She throws up her hands. "I went to a Ninja Gym with Adam."

"You . . . huh?" Nothing could have prepared me for this answer. "Adam? The guy I was supposed to go out with?"

She gives a guilty shrug. "When you stood him up, I went and talked to him because I felt so bad about it, and we hit it off."

"I *knew* it!" I say, fist pumping the air. "I knew you were into him! You went on a date with him? Libby! Oh my god, that's amazing. Why didn't you tell me?" I point at her. "Wait— why *didn't* you tell me? You're such a hypocrite, getting mad at me for not telling you about Josh while you're out dating my matches!"

Despite my words, I'm smiling. I couldn't be more excited for her.

Libby, however, doesn't share my excitement. Sighing, she goes into the living room and flops on the couch. Her cat appears, as if summoned via a portal from the underworld, and curls up on her stomach. Libby throws an arm across her face, like she's trying to hide.

"It wasn't a date. He's a prospective client, and we've been talking about some PR ideas for his diner."

"But you met at a Ninja Gym? I'm confused."

"We were talking about PR stuff the other day, and I mentioned the Down & Dirty. Adam said the Ninja Gym would be a good place to practice for some of the obstacles."

She says this like it's a normal thing for her to do, which it is not. My mind has officially been blown.

"Move," I say, shoving her legs off the couch so I can sit. "I want details. Was it fun? Do you like him? Did he kiss you? Are you going out again?"

She groans and rolls away. "There's nothing to say. We met. We had a drink. I came home."

"You had a drink? That's a date."

"No, it—"

"Text him and say you had a good time!" I tell her. "Where's your phone?"

I lunge for her phone, which is sitting on the coffee table, but she grabs it at the same time.

"Let go!" she says, trying to wrestle it out of my hands. We're in a tug-of-war with an eight-hundred-dollar iPhone. "I'm not texting him! I don't want to look desperate."

"It's not desperate to say you had a good time after a date."

"It wasn't a date!" she shouts, her voice cracking on the last word.

I let go of her phone. Libby slumps back. Her cat scampers to the top of the couch and hisses at me.

"It wasn't a date," she whispers. Her eyes are red, like she's on the verge of tears.

"Okay, sorry." I swallow. "I'm just excited for you. Kind of like how I wish you'd be excited for me about Josh. You're the one who loves romance. You should be all over this!"

She sits up, eyes blazing. "And you're the one who's always telling me that romance novels aren't real. Josh left you once, and he'll do it again. Like GiGi always said, when people show you who they are, believe them—"

"Maya Angelou," I mumble.

"What?"

"Maya Angelou said that."

"Well, GiGi wrote it in her notebook." Libby shakes her head, exasperated. "And no, I'm not excited about Adam because nothing's going to happen between us. Nothing ever happens, and it's never going to, because those kinds of things don't happen to people like me!"

She slumps back on the couch, covering her face with a throw pillow.

I'm speechless again, but this time because it's clear my sister is hurting. She has deep wounds related to men and love and trust that go back to some jerks in high school, and maybe even further, to our parents' divorce. Which makes me consider that her feelings about Josh aren't really about Josh at all, but about what he represents.

I gently set the throw pillow aside so I can see her face. "Libs. I appreciate everything you did for me when Josh and I broke up. I needed you then. But what I need now is for you to trust me. I hope it works out for Josh and me this time; I believe that it will. But if it doesn't, I'd like to know that I can come to you for support, and you won't say 'I told you so.'"

She sighs. "I promise I won't say 'I told you so.'"

Right. Meaning that she assumes things won't work out. But this is as close to supportive as I'm going to get—at least for now. I'll have to prove to her that Josh and I are in it for the long haul.

"Fair enough," I say, then smile widely. "And I'll be here, cheering as you and Adam fall in love."

In response, she smacks me in the head with the throw pillow.

CRUSH YOUR COMFORT ZONE

WEEK 8

When we get hurt, we're desperate to figure out why, so we can prevent it from happening again. But unfortunately, this desire to protect ourselves sometimes becomes another excuse to remain in the safety of our comfort zones.

Think about a wound in your past, and how you responded. What comfort zone have you remained in since then?

Hannah, 7/24

Well, the obvious wound is when Josh left me, back in college. Once I graduated and started working for GiGi, I really thought I had healed. Moved on. I had a job, an apartment, a built-in support system with my sister. I felt like my life was on track.

But looking back, I'm realizing that I never had to make any difficult decisions about my future—it was all decided for me. Working for GiGi allowed me to stay in a safe little bubble, which was probably what I needed at the time. Now that I'm back with Josh, though, I'm itching to spread my wings. To see what I'm capable of.

I'm just not sure how to do that without impacting my relationship with my sister. That's something I never, ever want to lose.

Thirty-One

LIBBY

THE NEXT MORNING, I WAKE WITH AN EMOTIONAL HANG-over. The talk with Hannah last night brought up so many stupid feelings. And it didn't help that I was already in such a weird place after the amazing not-a-date with Adam.

The logical side of me understands what Hannah was trying to say—it's her life, and she has the right to make her own decisions. But I'm literally sick over it. It's not just that I *think* she's making a mistake; I *know* it. Deep in my soul. And it's my job as a big sister to protect her.

And to protect myself—the walls in this apartment are so thin, I'm going to have to get noise-canceling headphones to block out all their sex noises. Hannah better hope that a fire doesn't break out while they're doing the nasty, because I could die alone in my bed if I don't hear the alarm.

The sound of Hannah's door opening and closing shakes that awful vision from my mind.

"See you at the office," she calls out, as if it's just another day.

But it's not as easy for me to pretend everything is okay.

My little sister is speeding toward the edge of a cliff, and her brakes are broken.

God, I hope they used a condom during their boat sex. The last thing she needs is to get knocked up by stupid Josh Jacobson.

My phone chimes with my last "you better get your ass out of bed" alarm, and I sit up, reaching for my phone. There are notifications from Instagram, and an alert for a new match on the One+One app, but no text from Adam. I know I have no right to be disappointed, especially since I didn't send him one last night, either. But if feelings were logical, they wouldn't be so hard to make sense of.

I open One+One and check out the new match, even though Hannah's stopping the challenge—and probably ruining our chances of saving the company. Watch this guy be the one who could make her forget all about Josh. One date too late.

Fortunately or unfortunately, the guy is average at best. He checks the tall box and having a professional job box, but he has a cat, and Hannah is not a cat person. I glance down at Mr. Darcy, curled up on the pillow beside me in a perfect loaf, his legs and tail tucked into his body. How is it possible there are people who don't love cats?

"Who's a good boy," I say, rubbing the soft fur between his ears. "You're a perfect ten, aren't you?"

The rating makes me think of Adam, and how I need to officially end things with him and Hannah. I open up the messages on the app, then crack my knuckles and start to type.

HANNAHF: Sorry I've been flaky lately. I know I said work has been busy—and it has. But I've also met someone and want to give it a chance to see where things go. I'm really sorry we never got to meet up in person, but I hope you find your 10/10.

As I hit send, relief washes over me. But there's sadness, too. Which, again, leaves me frustrated at my illogical feelings. There's no reason to be sad—it's not like I'll never see the guy again. At the end of last night, after an awkward yet wonderful hug, we agreed that Adam would come to the office next week to hear any ideas for the restaurant.

Now I just need to think of said ideas, and find a way to get Hannah out of the office for an hour.

FOUR DAYS LATER, I'm putting finishing touches on the deck for my meeting with Adam. Between working on the presentation, my training schedule, putting out an "emergency" press release about a new flavor of cream cheese at Bagelville in honor of Lollapalooza this weekend, and organizing the ticketed networking event with Suji, it's been a busy week. And somehow, I still found time to write in my journal every single day.

I'm surprised by how much I actually enjoy it—another thing I used to say I hated even though I'd never really tried it. I have half a dozen empty diaries people have given me over the years, but having a permanent record of my life has never been appealing. Part of the reason I read so much is to *escape* it.

But it turns out, writing to Lou has helped me process my feelings, to understand what she calls "the why behind the what."

It's a small change, and nowhere near where I'm supposed to be by this point. According to last night's prompt, I should be getting ready to transition from the comfort zone to the growth zone. But I still feel like the same old me.

"Your two o'clock is here," Great Scott says through the interoffice intercom.

I glance at the time on my computer—Adam is fifteen minutes early. Luckily Hannah also left early for her "lunch meeting," which I suspect is with stupid Josh.

I take a deep breath and grab my laptop before heading toward the lobby.

It's been a week since our night at the Ninja Gym, and I'm giddy at the thought of seeing Adam. He's been texting me every day, but he didn't respond to the message HannahF sent for a few days. When he did, he apologized for the delay, saying he hasn't been on the app much lately, and that he wished her all the best. That made me feel sad, and then inexplicably good.

Great Scott's eyebrows shoot up his forehead when he sees me coming around the corner. I can see his mind making the connection between the new dress that hugs my curves instead of trying to hide them, and my meeting with Adam—who looks damn good in dark jeans and a blue button-down shirt with a worn leather messenger bag slung over his shoulder.

"Hi," I say, giving him a quick hug. "Follow me."

Suji gives me a wave when we walk past—she knows a little about Adam. Not the part about me fake chatting with him on behalf of my sister, but about my crush on him and how he's hiring us to do the PR for his restaurant.

"This place is impressive," he says as he takes it all in.

"Thanks," I say, grateful for the people coworking here today. "It was my grandmother's pride and joy. And this is the best spot in the office."

I hold out my arm for him to enter the conference room, which looks over Michigan Avenue. He walks around the large table and looks out the picture window.

"Wow," he says. "You might be a little out of my league here."

I inhale a quick breath, taken aback—until I realize he's talking about the caliber of our office, not me, personally. But he is impressed with me professionally, and I have a feeling he would be even if there was no one else in the office.

"Can I tell you a secret?" I ask, lowering my voice.

Adam leans closer, and I catch a whiff of his cologne that makes my knees wobble.

"Those people out there?" I whisper, gathering myself. "They don't work here."

Adam looks confused.

"Well, they do work here, as in they work here, in this space, but they don't work for me. For us. They rent their desks—like a coworking office."

"Nice," Adam says. "And are these one of the perks of working here?"

He nods down to the silver tray on the credenza, where I filled our crystal decanter with ice water and put out the chocolate caramel pretzel bars one of our desk renters gave me as a thank-you gift. They paid extra to use the conference room last week and ended up securing funding for their future bakery/bookstore. Based on the bars, the bakery is going to be a smash hit—and we'll hopefully be able to manage their PR.

"Help yourself," I tell him. "They're from a bakery that'll be opening in a few months."

"Is this bakery going to sell mandel bread?" he says, his mouth quirking up in a crooked grin.

I laugh and try to suppress the little thrill that Adam and I have an inside joke.

"Should we get started?" I ask, pulling out a chair and motioning for him to take the one beside me. It's a big room for a meeting with just the two of us, so I decided it would be better just to share my computer screen than project up on the TV. I clear my throat, trying not to think about Adam's smile when I made it through the climbing wall, or how good his arms felt when he hugged me.

"As I mentioned the other night," I say, shaking myself, "you can take one of two strategies—focus on getting new people in the door, or getting current customers to come more often."

Adam's phone buzzes on the table, but he ignores it, his warm brown eyes staying focused on me and the presentation—which starts with the current state of the diner. I'm hoping he won't be offended by my assessment.

"Now, based on the photos you sent me," I say, treading carefully, "it wouldn't be bad to freshen the space up a bit. There's definitely a vintage feel to the place."

"Should we go more modern?" Adam asks.

"Not necessarily," I tell him. "But you could be more vintage-chic than vintage-old."

"Got it," Adam says, jotting the word "chic" down in his Moleskine notebook like a dutiful student.

"You don't want to change too much too fast, but a lot can be said for a fresh coat of paint and maybe having the booths re-covered."

Over the next twenty minutes, I take Adam through the ideas in my proposal. According to the financials he shared, the diner does the most business on Saturday and Sunday brunch.

While they're open for breakfast and lunch the rest of the week, business isn't great.

I suggest opening for dinner one or two nights a week and making each one a unique experience, possibly trying out theme nights.

"Theme nights like people dressing up?" Adam asks, his eyebrows rising.

"No," I say, laughing at the image of people eating bagels and lox while wearing period costumes. "I'm thinking events—like you can host a puzzle night, where there's a different jigsaw puzzle at every table. And maybe if people complete the puzzle before they leave, they get a free dessert."

"Like one of these magic bars," Adam says, taking the last bite of his.

"You could have monthly events—like speed dating, where people switch tables after each course. Or a book club with custom cocktails to go along with the book."

"Ooh." Adam's eyes shine as he scribbles something in his notebook. "I love that."

His excitement is contagious, and I continue to spitball. "For your older clientele, people who are retired, you could have game days—like a mahjong brunch or a gin rummy game once a week where you have gin cocktails on special."

Adam is nodding, writing furiously in his notebook, his curls falling across his forehead. I busy my hands with my pen so I don't accidentally reach over to see if his hair is as soft as it looks.

"Another idea that really embraces the old-fashioned vibe is starting a supper club—like a Sunday night family dinner for people who don't have family around."

"I like it," Adam says, tapping his index finger against his chin. My eyes narrow in on his face, my heart beating in time with his finger as I study his lips, his light brown beard surrounding them. Hannah was right; I have it bad. And she doesn't even know the half of it. "Maybe we start with the gin rummy night. Easy to do and I know some of my regular customers—like Harold—would be up for it."

"I can't wait to meet the famous Harold," I tell him. "I wonder who he'll choose to be his date."

"Do you think we could do one this weekend?" Adam asks, his excitement palpable.

I pause, considering how much work goes into planning an event. "If we keep it simple, we could make it something of a soft launch. We could put out a press release, maybe invite some influencers to attend and post about it. And if you have a budget, you could run an ad—but it's not necessary."

Adam shakes his head, and it takes me a moment to realize he's impressed, not disappointed. "You're really good at this," he says, and my stomach flutters with the compliment.

"I hope so," I say. "Otherwise I might be in need of a new job."

He chuckles, but I gulp with the realization that even if I am good at this, my sister and I still might be in search of new jobs soon. And I'm not quite sure how I feel about that. Devastated about losing GiGi's business, yes, but also maybe a little . . . excited? What could I do if I didn't have the Freedman Group?

Stop, I tell myself, instantly shutting the thought down. This isn't just my career and livelihood—it's Hannah's, too. She's counting on me.

Refocusing, I smile at Adam. "How about an event on Friday night?"

"Let's do it," Adam says, and we jump into planning mode.

Thirty-Two

HANNAH

JOSH HAS PLANNED AN EPIC DATE FOR US THIS EVENING: kayaking the Chicago River, then dinner, then a hotel reservation tonight, since he's still staying with his parents and I'm not ready to have sex at my apartment with my sister in the next room.

We're in a rented double kayak, skimming across the surface of the river, slicing through the heart of downtown. Buildings rise sharply on either side of us like steep canyon walls, their windows gleaming in the evening sun. Down here, the air is cooler, the traffic muffled by the sounds of water and birds calling as they swoop above us. The sky overhead is so blue my chest aches.

Josh is in back, providing power, while I steer up front. As we make a turn past a riverboat full of tourists, he asks, "So . . . did you email them?"

He means Serena and Preeti. Instantly, the butterflies in my stomach take flight. "Yes. Right after lunch."

It took me six drafts to get the email right, and a few hours to work up the guts to send it. I introduced myself and said that if they need a publicist, I'd love to be considered. I explained that I have plenty of experience in PR, but none as a book publicist, so I would do it pro bono in exchange for an endorsement if they're happy with my services.

I don't think I would've done it without Josh's encouragement.

"Well done," he says. "I know that wasn't easy."

"I've been stress-checking my inbox every ten minutes. I keep reminding myself that they'll need a day or two to decide, but I'm still so nervous! I know, it's silly—"

"It's not silly," he says, knocking his paddle gently against mine. "It's brave."

I smile and dig my paddle into the water, propelling us past a riverfront restaurant, where couples sip their drinks and eat dinner, their conversation floating on the breeze. Behind me, Josh hums something off-key. My heart soars with contentment; I get to be with this man. I get to share a kayak with him. And later, a bed.

"What?" he says.

Confused, I twist around to look at him. "I didn't say anything."

His eyes crinkle with laughter. "I could hear you thinking."

I smile and continue paddling, trying to put what I'm feeling into words. "I was thinking about how we're . . . here. Just kayaking on the river."

And to anyone else, that probably wouldn't make sense, but Josh says, "Like all those years we weren't together didn't exist."

"Exactly. Like they were outside the space-time continuum and we've finally returned to our real lives."

We pass under a bridge, and a shadow falls across us for a

moment before we burst into the sunlight again, dazzling me. I stare up at a massive redbrick building topped by a clock tower.

"Have you heard the theory that every decision we make splits the timeline into different versions?" I ask.

"Yeah. Like, today I drove in from Evanston but in a different reality, maybe I took the train. It makes you wonder—"

"If there would've been a terrible train accident? Someone on the tracks?"

He snorts a laugh and uses his paddle to lightly splash me with water. "No, Miss Intrusive Thoughts, but thanks for that mental image. You know the movie *Sliding Doors*, with Gwyneth Paltrow?"

"Young Gwyneth, pre-Goop," I say, nodding. "We watched it with your mom—remember?"

Josh laughs. "Oh yeah. She kept an eagle eye on us so we didn't get up to any hanky-panky under the blanket."

"How is Jeannie, anyway?" I ask. "What does she think about us being back together?"

When he doesn't answer, I glance back at him. His face has a pinched look, his eyebrows pulled together.

"What?" I ask, my stomach knotting. "You haven't told your parents?"

"No, I have."

"And?"

His forehead furrows, and my heart sinks.

"They're not happy about us being together?" I say, almost whispering. It feels like a knife in the back. I loved Jeannie and Karl.

He hesitates, then shrugs. "It's more that—well. I'm staying with them right now, so . . ."

He's avoiding my question, but I'm not sure I want to know

the answer, so I continue paddling, searching for something to lighten the mood. "Remember Gwyneth in *Emma*? I loved movie days in AP English."

"Agree, although that age gap between Emma and Knightley always creeped me out—"

"Maybe not as weird as Alicia Silverstone kissing her stepbrother," I say.

Now we're on to *Clueless*, which is based on *Emma*, and Josh says, "I mean, it was young Paul Rudd. I probably would've kissed him, too."

I twist around, laughing. "His character had the same name as you—"

"Ew, *Josh*?" He mimes gagging. "Guys named Josh are the worst."

I tilt my head, surprised. "Did you hear Libby say that?"

"No—but it seems to be universally acknowledged among women. Anyone named Josh is a walking red flag." He doesn't seem bothered, just mildly amused.

"Well, that's unfair," I say, offended on his behalf.

He gives a noble sigh and makes a long stroke with his paddle. "I didn't ask to be a Josh—I was born one. All I can do now is try and break the stigma."

I turn my face up to the sun as I paddle, enjoying the sensation of gliding through the water. We're almost to the pull-out point, and I'm sad we can't stay out here all night.

"So, Gwyneth ends up being hit by a van just as she declares her love for her perfect match, right?" I ask, bringing us back to *Sliding Doors*. I've always loved this about our conversations, the way we flit from one topic to the next, connected by inside jokes and shared history.

"Well, yes," Josh says, "but in the other timeline, she meets her perfect match anyway, like they were destined for each other. Which made me wonder about us. If we would've ended up together, no matter what decisions we made along the way."

"I like that."

Maybe we both needed to learn some lessons before we were ready to be together again. And no matter what happens in the future, we'll find our way back to each other.

We reach the pullout spot and Josh hops out of the kayak, splashing in the shallow water as he pulls the kayak ashore, then takes my hand and helps me out. As I step up to dry ground, my phone chimes in my backpack: a new email.

"Oh my god," I gasp, yanking my phone out. "It's from Serena and Preeti."

"Open it!"

"I—I can't! You do it," I say, shoving the phone toward him.

He catches it, fumbling. "Your passcode still the same?"

I nod, too stressed to speak. My body is vibrating with anxiety.

"*Hi, Hannah!*" Josh reads. "There's an exclamation point after your name. *Hi, Hannah*, exclamation point. *We're thrilled you reached out to us.* No exclamation point there—"

"Just read it!"

"I am—sheesh." He clears his throat. "*We've been considering hiring an outside publicist and we've met with several—*"

"Of course they have," I say, my heart sinking. "That makes sense—"

"Hold up, Banana. There's more. *We've met with several PR agencies, but there's something intriguing about working with a loyal fan like yourself. Can we set up a time to chat? We're free tomorrow any time before noon, eastern. Xoxo, Serena & Preeti.* They used an ampersand, not the spelled-out word."

He looks over at me, but I can't respond. I've frozen into an ice sculpture of myself.

"Did you hear that?" he asks gently.

"I . . . yes. Yes." I look up at him, bewildered. "They want to chat? With me?"

"Affirmative."

"I need to reply," I say, frantic. "If we're going to talk tomorrow, I need to reply now. Can I—just one second. Sorry, I'll be quick."

"No worries, I'll take the kayak back."

Josh heads off, dragging our kayak behind him to the rental place. I find a bench and sit, typing my response with shaking hands.

Serena and Preeti,
I'm so thrilled that you're interested in chatting. Tomorrow works great. Shall we say 10am?
All my best,
Hannah

As soon as I press send, panic hits me like a fist to the chest. I have hours of work before I'll be ready for this. I pull up my Notes app and start a to-do list. I'm thoroughly absorbed when Josh sits next to me, and I look up with a start.

"Oh shit. What time is our dinner reservation?"

He shakes his head. "Just canceled it."

"What? No—we should still go. You've been so excited about this place. I'll work after."

Even as I say the words, my panic grows. Not only do I not have time, I'm not sure I have the *ability*. I've never done anything like this on my own, but the thought of getting Libby involved makes me feel all prickly inside: she might try to take over the project, or she won't understand why it means so much to me and why I agreed to do it pro bono when we're desperate for money.

But without her, I might completely humiliate myself. I probably will.

Josh crouches in front of me, and I meet his eyes. They're bottomless blue and full of an emotion I haven't seen in so long: confidence. In me. I'd forgotten that this is how he used to look at me, all the time. Like I could do anything. And I always knew that he would be right by my side, cheering me on, as I did it.

"What do you think," he says slowly, "about going back to your place? I'll help you prepare for tomorrow. I can get us takeout while you work."

My shoulders drop with relief. "You don't mind?"

"There's nothing I'd rather do."

"Thank you!" I throw my arms around him. Then something occurs to me, and I pull back. "Can we go somewhere else? I'm not sure when Libby will be home, but I . . . I don't want her to know about the Serena and Preeti thing yet."

It's not that I plan on keeping it from her forever. I'll explain everything if Serena and Preeti decide to hire me. I mean, us.

Josh nods. "Let's swing by your place and get your laptop, then we can go to the hotel and work."

"But if we're alone in a hotel room, I'll want to tear off your clothes and do dirty things to you for *hours*!" I wail. "I won't get any work done and neither of us will get any sleep."

He bursts out laughing, then stifles it as he sees the panic on my face. "Then we'll go to a coffee shop or something."

"What about the hotel reservation?"

"I'll change it."

"It's too late to get a refund!"

He presses his forehead against mine. "Hannah. Let me take care of it. And then let me take care of you. Okay?"

"Okay." I kiss him, hard on the mouth, but force myself to stop before I get too swept away. "I would really like to kiss you more, but—"

"You have work to do," he says, taking my hand. "Let's go."

Thirty-Three

LIBBY

IT'S FRIDAY. THE BIG NIGHT. MY FIRST EVENT AT ADAM'S diner.

Everything for the gin and rummy evening came together so quickly—several local papers were happy to break up the Lollapalooza buzz, and we managed to get coverage in the *Reader*, *Block Club Chicago*, and a few online outlets.

I left the office around three so I could help Adam set up. He's as nervous as I am excited, which I understand given the pressure to do right by a family business that's been entrusted to you.

What I don't get is the pressure I'm putting on myself and my outfit. I keep reminding myself that this is professional, not personal. But I want to look good, especially if any press comes to the event.

After changing outfits four times, I settle on a pair of dark blue jeans that make my butt look amazing even though they're a little tight in the waist, and a floral blouse that's long enough to cover my belly but also shows a little cleavage. Heels would be over-the-top—and I'm not coordinated enough to walk in them—so I settle on some strappy black sandals, grateful I gave myself a pedicure last weekend.

I get off the bus half a block from the diner and give the butterflies in my stomach a moment to settle before walking inside. I see Adam through the window, moving around the empty restaurant, comfortable and confident.

A car honks as it passes by, startling me and capturing Adam's attention. He turns and looks outside, his face lighting up when he sees me.

My heart lifts. He's been texting all day with an hourly countdown to the kickoff . . . or whatever it's called when the first hand is dealt in gin. He's got high hopes for this event, and I hope it exceeds—or at least meets—his expectations.

"Hey!" Adam says, opening the door. The bell chimes a friendly tone as I walk inside. "Welcome!"

"This place is great," I tell him, meaning it. The diner feels less stodgy than the photos made it look. There's a well-loved warmth to the space, the air saturated with decades of baked goods and greasy comfort food. My stomach growls, and I realize I forgot to grab lunch.

Red booths line the walls, with two- and four-top tables filling the rest of the space. There's a full bar in the back and a semi-open kitchen behind it. I walk over to the front counter, where old family photos line the wall.

"Is this your dad?" I ask, pointing to a black-and-white photo of a man who looks an awful lot like Adam, standing in front of the diner with his arm around a woman.

"That's actually my grandfather," Adam says. "This one's my dad." He points to a color photo: a man who looks like a carbon copy of the first one, with a slightly rounder face and a little less hair, carrying what can only be a tiny Adam on his shoulders.

"Strong family genes," I say.

"We look more alike than we are," Adam says. "My grandfather was a master in the kitchen—it seems the cooking genes get watered down generation by generation."

"We're always our own harshest critics," I say, repeating the words GiGi said to me so many times. It didn't always resonate in the moment, but I hope Adam takes it to heart.

"Should we get started?" he asks, rubbing his hands together.

"Let's do it!"

With two of us working, the room is turned into a quasi casino in no time. We place a fresh deck of cards on every table, and string red and black streamers featuring hearts, diamonds, clubs, and spades along the walls. It's cheesy, but that's kind of the point.

When our work is done, Adam looks around the room, proud of the minor transformation. Then he looks at his watch. "That didn't take as long as I thought it would."

He's right. We have almost an hour before the event starts.

"Should we have a drink?" he suggests, making his way behind the bar. "You can test out one of the specials—how do you feel about gin?"

"It makes me feel ginvincible," I say, then inwardly cringe, hoping he isn't one of those people who hates puns.

But Adam grins, his eyebrows doing their trademark dance. "Then let the fun be-gin! What can I make you?"

He hands me a copy of the special menu we came up with, featuring a gin and tonic, a gin fizz, and a French 75 on the gin side; and a dark and stormy, a rum runner, and a mai tai on the rummy side.

"Let's go with a French 75," I say.

"Good choice," Adam says, grabbing the shaker from a shelf. "Delicious, but simple—there are only four ingredients."

"That's about seventy-one less than I would have guessed."

Another smile, and I swear my insides turn to liquid. I can't help but imagine an alternate reality where we could be an us. A couple like Hannah and (gag!) Josh.

Adam measures out gin, lemon juice, and simple syrup before pouring them into the shaker.

"See? Easy-peasy," he says, placing the lid on the shaker. "Now you shake."

And shake he does—not just the shaker. He gets his entire body into it, doing a crazy dance to whatever music is in his head.

I snort a laugh and cover my mouth, but it's too late—he heard it.

"Is there something funny about the way I shake a drink?" he asks, mouth falling open in mock surprise. "Show me how it's done, then."

He holds the shaker out to me, his eyes twinkling, but I shake my head. I have already embarrassed myself enough in front of this man—but the little Lou in my mind is telling me I need to get my butt off the sidelines and into the game of life.

"Oh, fine," I say, taking the shaker from Adam. I raise my arm, ready to shake, but something stops me. "I need music."

"Good idea," Adam says, grabbing his phone. A few taps, and "Shake It Off" starts playing from the speakers. I sway to the beat and twist my wrist, shaking the shaker as Taylor

Swift sings, and he joins in, until we're both dancing like two dorky teenagers at a high school dance.

By the end of the song, we're both breathless and smiling, and I hand the shaker back to him. "Think we're good?"

"I think you're great," he says. Our fingers brush as he grips the shaker, and our eyes lock.

My heart stops. I'm frozen in place, unable to look away from the heat in his eyes, slowly melting me from the inside out.

Quickly, I pull my hand away from the shaker, bringing my icy fingers to my face in an attempt to bring myself back down to room temperature. I need to get a hold of myself.

Adam grabs two champagne glasses and pours equal amounts from the shaker into both flutes before topping them with champagne. "Last step is the garnish," he says.

"I don't need anything fancy," I tell him.

"Nonsense," Adam says, grabbing a lemon from a bowl of fruit on the bar. "If I'm going to impress you, I've got to pull out all the stops."

My cheeks flush, but Adam doesn't seem to notice as he dips a sharp knife into the skin of the lemon, spinning the fruit around in his hand.

"Careful," I say. "You don't want another scar."

He stops and looks up at me, tilting his head. "Did I tell you about my scar?" he asks, twisting his right palm toward me.

My stomach drops. Dishwashers haven't come up in our conversations—he told HannahF about his accident and the reason he always loads silverware facing down.

"You didn't," I say, quickly landing on some version of the truth. "But I noticed it the other day—and that knife looks pretty sharp."

"I'll be careful," he says, his eyes on mine as he swivels the knife back and forth. He completes the last cut and holds up two perfectly twisted slices of lemon rind. He places one on each of the glasses before handing me one.

"Cheers to a great event," I say.

"And to Harvey getting lucky," Adam says, a glint of mischief in his eyes.

Harvey's not the only one who would like to get lucky, I think, and before I can scold myself for having inappropriate thoughts about a client, the bell on the front door chimes— the first rummy player has arrived. Thirty minutes early.

THE REST OF the night flies by. Adam is constantly in motion— helping out behind the bar and in the kitchen, even settling a hearty debate over whether the dealer should deal seven or ten cards.

I helped where I could at the beginning, but when one player didn't show, I got roped into taking their spot in the game. It was fun—and I accidentally won three out of four hands.

A highlight of the evening was meeting Harvey, who was as extra as I imagined. The man had the balls to bring three different dates to complete his foursome. His table was behind mine, and I heard him tell the ladies that he would go home with whoever won the most hands. For their sake, I hope he was the big winner and got to take himself home.

Once the last player clears out and Adam sends his staff home, it's just the two of us.

"Wow," he says, locking the door. "That was . . ."

I barely stop myself from saying "ten out of ten." Instead, I say, "Incredible."

"I feel like celebrating," he says. "Have another drink with me?"

"Sure," I say, trying not to get my hopes too high. He just wants to celebrate, and I'm here. "Another French 75?"

"I've got a better idea. Come with me."

He grabs my hand, and my entire body sparks with electricity. But there's no time for me to be flustered—he's pulling me through the kitchen, out a back door, and up a flight of stairs. I don't realize he's taking me to the apartment above the restaurant until he opens the door, leading me into his living room.

"Oh," I say.

Adam drops my hand and heads down a hallway. As soon as he disappears from sight, I stare at my palm, wondering what kind of receptors under my skin could make holding hands with a cute guy make my insides go haywire. At least the feeling distracts me from wondering what's going on, and why he brought me up here.

He returns a moment later, carrying a bottle of wine.

"Do you like red?" he asks.

"I do," I tell him.

He nods, as if this is important information he's filing away. "Great," he says. "A customer brought me this bottle— it's French. Maybe we can do a theme with French everything. French wine. French fries. French bread."

French kissing, I think.

He's close enough now that I can smell him—woodsy and warm. His curls fall across his forehead, and I put my hands behind my back to remind myself not to reach out and brush them away.

"So, what do you think?" Adam asks.

I blink, realizing I missed something he said. He's now only inches away, and I'm captivated by the sight of him: the flecks of green in his brown eyes, the lock of hair that's fallen across his forehead, the way his lips part.

"I think . . ."

I don't know what I'm thinking. There are no words in this moment. Just him and me and the space between us, which is getting smaller and smaller until we're a breath apart. And then his lips are on mine, soft and tentative.

I freeze, afraid that one wrong move will break the spell.

Adam hesitates, too, and I don't want him to think that I don't want this, that I don't want him. So, I stop thinking and do what I've been dreaming about since my first conversation with Adam two months ago. I press my lips back against his, opening my mouth in an invitation.

Adam deepens the kiss, cupping my face with one hand, pulling me closer until our tongues meet, sending a shiver down my thighs. The rough scratch of his beard tickles, and my lips curve into a smile. He tastes sweet, like champagne and possibility, and I can't believe this is happening.

I close my eyes, afraid that if I open them, I'll wake up and be anywhere but here: standing in Adam's apartment, his arms around me as the summer sky moves from dusk to night, the sound of traffic on the street outside. Kissing. A lot.

Just in case this turns out to be my active imagination again, I let my hands drift up and down his back, feeling the muscles I knew were hiding beneath his shirt. He flexes under my touch and gives my bottom lip a playful bite before moving down to the curve of my neck, sending desire racing along my skin like flames. He traces kisses along my collarbone and up to my jaw before finding my mouth again, lips open and wanting.

His hands drop down to my waist and keep going until he's cupping my butt, pulling me against him. He wedges his leg between mine and I can feel his arousal. The physical reaction he's getting from kissing me. *Libby.*

I wish I could swallow this man whole.

Of all the times I imagined doing this with Adam, I wasn't really me. I was Hannah. But she's not here. I am. I'm dying to touch his skin, so I slip my hands under his shirt and he lets out a hum of pleasure. Our kisses become more urgent, a little desperate, and heat licks up and down my spine. One of his hands is buried in my hair, and the other is exploring my curves, sliding from my waist up my rib cage to my breast, and I mentally curse the fabric of my shirt and bra that separates his hand from my skin.

Adam's hands drift back down to my waist and slip beneath my shirt, and I sigh with gratitude. Every nerve ending in my body is alive, awake for the first time in years, and they are all saying, *Take me, I'm yours.*

His fingers dance along the hem of my shirt. I'm lost in this moment, drowning in pleasure—until I feel the sensation of air against my bare back.

And it hits me like a lightning bolt to my brain. He's taking my shirt off. My shirt. The shirt that's covering my too-tight jeans.

Panic slices through the haze of desire. *No.* He can't. I can't. We can't.

I step back, pulling my shirt down, wishing it was an invisibility cloak. I shouldn't have let myself get carried away by the booze and the magic of the night. I know how this story ends. The way it always ends. With a guy getting his kicks in private, but not wanting to be seen with me in public.

"Libby?" Adam asks, reaching for me.

I take another step back, shaking my head. "I should get going."

Adam's forehead wrinkles. He looks hurt and confused. "Did I misread this? I'm so sorry. I thought . . ."

"You didn't do anything wrong," I say, interrupting him. "I just . . . it's late. And I'm pretty tired."

He exhales a deep breath and runs his fingers through his hair. His curls look so soft, and I curse myself for missing the chance to run my fingers through them. But the moment and the opportunity are gone.

I wish there was a way to explain that it's not him, it's me, without sounding like a generic line. We still have to work together.

"Thanks for a great night," I tell him. "I'll reach out with next steps."

Adam flinches, and I realize how corporate and unfeeling I sound.

"For the public relations," I add. "Not . . . our relations." God, I need to stop talking. "Thank you again, really."

And before I can say anything to make this goodbye more awkward than it already is, I slip out the door and down the stairs into the dark, lonely night.

CRUSH YOUR COMFORT ZONE

THE ULTIMATE CHALLENGE COMPANION JOURNAL

WEEK 9

When we get hurt, we're desperate to figure out why, so we can prevent it from happening again. If there isn't a clear cause, we often turn inward and (falsely) assume it was our fault.

But just because we believe something doesn't mean it's true. This lie we tell ourselves becomes another excuse to remain in the safety of our comfort zones.

Today, I want you to dig deep. What lie do you believe about yourself because of your wound?

Libby, July 31

Hi, Lou.

If you ask my sister, she'd say the lie I believe is that I don't deserve love. Specifically, the romantic, soul-blending love that people write books about.

When you've never seen someone who looks like you play the leading lady in a romantic movie, it's difficult to imagine yourself in that role. People my size play the quirky best friend, the comic relief, the wise sister.

Maybe that's why I panicked last night with Adam. I've been thinking about it nonstop and feeling so stupid about it, so embarrassed, but also wondering if it was for the best. No reason to go down a road that I know won't have a happy ending.

Thirty-Four

HANNAH

JOSH AND I ARE SITTING ON A BLANKET UNDER A TREE IN Grant Park, each of us focused on our own tasks. I'm on my laptop, and he's crocheting a rainbow-colored blanket while listening to an online lecture. We've been meeting a couple of afternoons per week to work together outside, listening to music and stopping occasionally to chat (or sneak a kiss).

Usually, it's relaxing, but today, I'm sweating. And not just because August has arrived in Chicago, bringing with it the oppressive heat and humidity that almost make me miss the freezing wind and snow of winter.

I'm stressing about the financial situation of the Freed-man Group.

My email inbox has been nothing but bad news: the rent for our office space is increasing next month; a client is going bankrupt, so they won't be sending our final payment; the quote to fix the broken refrigerator in our break room is double what I budgeted for. As it was, we barely had enough money to keep the lights on through Labor Day, but even that might be a stretch now.

Josh reaches over and pulls my hand away from my mouth. "Careful," he says gently, and I notice for the first time that I've chewed on my cuticle until it's bleeding. "You okay?"

Sighing, I set my laptop aside and stretch out on the blanket, staring up at the green canopy of trees above us. "I hate money."

Josh chuckles, not unkindly, and says, "Yeah. Money sucks."

"I hate not having enough of it," I say. "I hate having so many expenses, and so many complicated sources of revenue. It's a full-time job to keep track of it all, and it's sucking my life away."

"Like the machine in *The Princess Bride*?"

"Exactly."

Josh sets aside his crocheting, turns off the lecture, and lies next to me. "You know you don't have to be responsible for all of it. For managing all the finances by yourself."

I huff. "Right, like Libby could handle it. She can barely remember to pay her own credit card bill."

In fact, I set a reminder in my calendar to double-check for her, ever since she forgot one month and had to pay an enormous fee.

"Still, you could talk to her about it," Josh says.

"Talking won't help. I'm the only one who knows the ins and outs of our budget, and that's fine—"

"Doesn't sound fine—"

"—but someone has to do it and that someone might as well be me." I roll onto my side, facing him. It's past five o'clock now, the time we usually say goodbye and each head to our respective homes. But as I let my eyes drift down his lean, strong body, I'm desperate to spend more time with him. Naked.

Those shoulders. Those thighs. I want to bite them.

"Horny eyes," Josh says, grinning at me. "I mean, I get it. It's been difficult to get alone time."

Guilt shimmers through me; it was my fault we didn't use the hotel reservation Josh made. Though the call with Serena and Preeti went well. They seemed to like my ideas about a mailing featuring clues about the book, as if it was a cold case, and they were impressed with the list of influencers Josh helped me gather. But the more days that pass without hearing from them, the more sure I am that they're going with someone with more experience. Probably a good thing I didn't tell Libby about it.

"You should come to my place," I blurt out. "And you should stay over."

His dark eyebrows lift. "Won't Libby be there?"

"Yes, but . . ." I shrug. "She needs to get over it. You're my boyfriend."

His eyes light up. I haven't used that word in front of him yet, though he's called me his girlfriend a few times.

He grabs my hips and pulls me against him, making my skin flush with heat. "I'd love to."

"And guess what? I have a box of your clothes from college that you can change into."

He bursts out laughing. "How serial killer of you. What's in it?"

"I don't remember," I say, but he makes a face that says, *Sure ya don't,* and I sigh. "Your old Cubs hoodie, a pair of basketball shorts, and some T-shirts."

After he went to Australia, I wore that hoodie almost every day and slept in the T-shirts until Libby threatened to burn them in a giant Josh-related funeral pyre. So I hid them.

Libby probably has no idea they're still buried in the back of my closet.

"I wondered where those went," he muses. "What've you been doing with my clothes all these years? Freaky things, hopefully."

My cheeks heat up, and he grins, delighted.

"Anyway," I say, shaking my head. "Come over. I've been hoping for a redo on that shower. And this time, I want you to push me against the wall and have your way with me."

A HALF AN hour later, we burst through the door of my apartment, laughing. When I spot my sister in the kitchen, the laughter dies in my throat.

"Hi," I say, trying to act casual. "What's for dinner?"

Libby narrows her eyes. "I didn't make enough for three."

A blatant lie. Something's bubbling in a saucepan; the air fryer is going, and there's a huge salad on the counter. As is her custom, my sister has cooked enough to feed a dozen starving rugby players.

I fold my arms. "Oh, come on. You've made plenty—"

"It's okay, I'm not hungry," Josh cuts in.

"Wonderful," Libby says.

I glare at her. She's being flat-out rude, and I can tell she's making Josh uncomfortable. "Libby, you—"

"You have a cat?" Josh interrupts, brightening. "You didn't tell me!"

"Watch out, that cat hates everyone but Libby," I say.

And indeed, the cat is stalking toward Josh, sizing him up like prey.

"He's an excellent judge of character," Libby says. There's a devious gleam in her eyes, like she's waiting for her Patronus to deliver the scratch she wishes she could.

But to my utter shock, when Josh stoops down to pick up the cat, the little devil allows it. Not only that, he lets Josh flip him on his back and hold him like a baby, curled against Josh's chest.

"What's your name, handsome?" Josh says to the cat.

My sister appears to be frozen halfway between shock and rage; I can practically see white-hot flames of anger radiating from her body.

"Mr. Darcy," I answer, when Libby doesn't.

"Great name," Josh says, smiling at the cat. "'You have bewitched me, body and soul, and I love, I love, I love you,'" he quotes, then scratches the cat's ears. "You're a sweetheart. I bet you're so misunderstood, aren't you?"

And the damn thing starts purring.

Libby is still staring, but she's melting a little. She's like a proud mama with that cat.

"Come on, little man," Josh says to the cat. "We'll hang out while the girls eat."

He's turning to go when Libby exhales and says, "Come and have some dinner, Josh."

Josh catches my eye, silently asking if this is a test. I nod, feeling cautiously optimistic. And when my sister pulls an extra plate out of the cupboard, I hold myself back from cheering.

"All right," Libby says in a resigned voice. "Let's eat."

Thirty-Five

LIBBY

OUR CHECK-IN WITH LOU EARLIER THIS WEEK WENT REALLY well. It's strange how connected I feel to her even though I know next to nothing about her. I suppose ours is like most of my relationships—unrequited and mostly in my head.

Lou seems impressed with our progress—both in our challenges and in our refined strategic approach for her PR plan. It felt good to have our efforts acknowledged, and her confidence gives me hope about our chances of winning her business—which is good, since Hannah seems even more stressed than usual about our finances. But the biggest impact of her visit was on Great Scott.

When Lou questioned him about his training, he admitted he hasn't been doing much of anything. With Lou as his witness, he agreed to one training session with us a week. Lou reminded him that, as a member of our four-person Down & Dirty team, he should carry his weight.

Which brings us to the beach today. It was supposed to be all four of us, but Josh had plans with his mom. As much as I'm trying to be supportive of Hannah, I wasn't sad about it.

Hannah and I are meeting Scott at the beach near North Avenue—and of course, Hannah decided we should turn our walk there into more interval training.

"Run for ninety seconds?" she asks as we veer onto the lake path near Diversey. It's crowded, even for a Saturday, and the path is filled with people running, biking, or rollerblading.

Without complaining, I pick up the pace, moving from a speed walk to a jog and finally a run. We pass a young woman who seems to be on a leisurely stroll, which gives me a little thrill. Passing people is a new experience for me.

I keep my breathing slow and steady, exhaling with every stride and swinging my arms close to my core the way Hannah taught me. We pass another speed walker, and I accidentally pick up the pace even more as we take the corner of the path and the city comes into view. The iconic skyline is made of so many different buildings: some short and wide, others tall and narrow. Some vintage and shabby, others vintage and intricate or modern and sleek. The variety makes me think of all the different kinds of people out on the lake path, including me. I suppose I belong here, just like everyone else.

The muscles in my legs are burning, but it hurts in the good way I used to think Hannah was lying about. I didn't believe pain could feel good until I experienced that satisfying ache, the proof of all the work I've been doing.

Hannah shows no sign of slowing down. This feels like a long freaking ninety seconds, so I start counting in my head. *One Mississippi, two Mississippi, three Mississippi.* When I get to thirty, I know she's messing with me.

"Is your watch broken?" I ask, slowing to a jog.

"Nope," Hannah says smugly, "but you just ran for two and a half minutes."

She lifts her hand and I reluctantly give her a high five. It's hard to be miffed at her when I'm so proud of myself. Nine weeks ago, I could barely walk one leg of the lake path. I've come a long way, getting stronger even if I'm not getting any skinnier.

"Want to go another ninety?" she asks.

"Don't press your luck," I tell her.

We walk in companionable silence, enjoying the beautiful morning. The breeze coming off the lake makes up for the heat of the August sun shining down on us.

I've missed this. My sister is one of the few people in the world I can just be with, and the last few weeks have been tense with the weight of secrets between us. Who knows how long she avoided telling me about Josh. And I was hiding the truth about my feelings for Adam.

Although I was hiding that from myself, too.

Adam sent me two texts the night I ran away like a crazy person after kissing him. One to make sure I got home safely, another a few minutes later, apologizing if he did anything wrong.

I sent back a short reply to the first, letting him know I made it home. But I didn't acknowledge the second. I couldn't. Everything I tried to say felt wrong. Plus, I can't explain what happened when I don't understand it myself.

One moment I was in my body, my skin thrumming with every word, every touch, every look, and every kiss. The next, I was in my head, catapulted back in time. I was six years old, listening as my mom told me that "curvy girls like us" don't get Prince Charming. I was twelve, hearing my dad complaining about how the local news anchor had put on weight, saying she should be taken off the air. I was fifteen, standing alone in the gym because every boy I'd asked to the Sadie Hawkins dance had turned me down. I was seventeen, trying not to cry when Alex Taylor told me that he liked my personality but he wasn't attracted to me.

It doesn't take a rocket scientist or a therapist to realize that when I pulled away from Adam, I was protecting myself. I've been doing that my whole life. Just like porcupines have their needles and skunks have their smell, I've got my sharp wit and sense of humor. But in that moment with Adam, I didn't even have those. I felt so naked and exposed I had to run away. I was too close to confronting that so-called lie of mine.

"What do you think?" Hannah says, breaking my silent reverie.

I look at my sister, hoping for context. What did I miss?

"You weren't listening, were you?"

I shrug an apology and my sister rolls her eyes and says, "We're here."

I can hear the music thumping from Castaways, the giant ship-shaped bar at North Avenue Beach. It's got the vibe of a club after midnight, even though it's just barely eleven a.m.

"You're sure you don't want to just, I don't know, lay out like a normal beach person?" I ask, hopefully.

"Come on," Hannah says. "This'll be fun." And it sounds like she really believes it.

I follow her, trudging through the sand, away from the rental beach chairs and umbrellas, toward Scott, who is lounging on an old FREE BRITNEY beach towel.

For the next thirty minutes, Hannah leads us, her two reluctant followers, through a series of drills performed in the lake at various water depths, so we can "take advantage of the natural resistance of the sand and water." Which is nothing compared to the resistance that's going on in my head.

I can't stop thinking about Adam and the mess I made of things.

We finish up by lying on our backs in the water—which is deceptively relaxing for how terrifying the obstacle is going to be. "Water crossing" sounded benign until Hannah explained that we'd be floating one hundred yards on our backs under a chain-link fence that's like six inches above the water.

Today, I'm grateful there's nothing between me and the clouds. I close my eyes and try to imagine the crosshatch of the fence above me, and just the thought feels suffocating. I wonder if there are built-in safety escapes along the way if someone (aka me) has a panic attack.

Maybe that's what happened the other night. Although I'm not sure that would be more or less embarrassing than the other excuses I've invented for myself.

"Hey," Scott whispers, floating into me.

"What?" I hiss. He's been complaining every step of every exercise, and I wonder if I was this annoying to Hannah in the beginning. I have a feeling I owe her a big apology.

"Spill the tea already," he says.

"What tea?" I ask, playing dumb.

"Don't be coy with me," Scott says. "I'm out here, getting my hair wet with lake water, to support you two."

"You're out here because Lou scared you into it."

Scott shivers beside me. "I'll do anything that woman tells me to do."

"Same," I agree.

Hannah's still floating peacefully with her eyes closed, almost like she's asleep.

"So, what happened with your boy toy?" Scott asks.

The question catches me so off guard I sit up, forgetting I'm in the middle of Lake Michigan, in water that's at least four feet deep. It takes a second to get my feet underneath me, and when I do, I give Scott a death glare.

"I don't have a boy toy," I insist.

"That cute, nerdy guy who came to the office," Scott says. "He was definitely into you—and don't tell me the feeling isn't mutual."

"Adam?" I ask, as if there could be anyone else. "He's a client. A *paying* client, not even a pro bono one."

"Pro-boner, maybe . . ." Scott mutters. It's loud enough to catch Hannah's attention.

She props herself up, looking at me with surprise. I haven't told her anything about the event a few nights ago, other than it went well.

"I—you don't know what you're talking about," I say, making my way back to the beach. The resistance of the water is no joke, and I'm tired of everything being such a struggle.

"Libby," Hannah says, coming after me.

"I want to go home," I tell her.

"Wait," she says, catching up to me. "Sit and dry off."

I don't have the energy to argue, so I let her lead me back toward our towels to sit.

"Talk to me," Hannah says as she laces her fingers between mine, giving my hand a squeeze—the sign I usually give her to let her know she's not alone. My heart constricts and I look up at the clear blue sky, hoping gravity will suck my tears back into their ducts. No such luck.

Salty tears slide down my cheeks, and I hope Hannah

thinks they're sweat or remnants of lake water. I'm the older sister; I'm supposed to be the strong one.

She leans her head on my shoulder, and we both stare out at the sun glistening on the water. The lapping waves of Lake Michigan might as well be the ocean. I wonder if another set of sisters is sitting on a similar shoreline on the other side, staring out at the opposite view.

It's quiet in that city sort of way, where the wind is loud, carrying with it sounds of people laughing, music playing, traffic humming. A kind of white noise that lets you know you're not alone.

Scott sits on my other side—on my towel, even though his is just inches away—and the moment shifts.

"How are things going with Adam?" Hannah asks, her voice cautious.

"They're not," I tell her.

"I'm sorry," she says. "It's his loss."

An image of Adam flashes through my mind, his smile fading, his eyes growing wide and confused. His arms reaching for me as I turned away.

"So . . . if we were to rank this guy as Great or Not Great, where would he fall?" Scott asks. I swear, he never misses an opportunity to remind us of his quasi fame.

"He's great," Hannah says, answering for me.

"He really is," I tell them. "But I wasn't. I was Not Great."

I feel Hannah's eyes on me, but I keep mine focused on the whitecaps of the waves. For some reason, it seems important for her to know Adam wasn't like the others. All the guys I've crushed on who turned down my awkward advances.

"Did something happen?" she asks.

"Something almost happened," I admit. "But I stopped it."

"Why?" Hannah asks.

I shrug, not wanting to voice the possibilities that have been running laps around my mind: wondering if he was actually attracted to me; if he wanted to pursue a relationship or if he was just caught up in the moment. Maybe he'd had too much to drink and I was conveniently there.

Scott breaks the silence. "A few years ago, I hooked up with a guy who was *not hot*."

I choke out a laugh. "Am I supposed to be the not-hot guy in this story?"

"Irrelevant," he says. "As I was saying, he was short, had more hair on his chest than his head. He had a gap in his teeth and this weird laugh, like 'he-he-he.' But I couldn't take my eyes off him."

"Like a freak show?" I ask.

Hannah tweaks my side, so I stop talking and let Scott finish his story.

"Listen, what the guy lacked in looks, he made up for in confidence. He believed he was all that, and every single person in the room believed he was, too. When you're confident—"

"I'm not confident," I say, stating the obvious.

"Gurrrl," Scott says. "You should see yourself when you're in the zone. When you're working an event or a conference room, you're on fire and you know it. You're magnetic. If I swung your way, I'd totally do you."

"Uh, thanks?"

"You're totally welcome," Scott says. "But my point is that physical attraction can grow out of emotional attraction. You just have to own it."

Before I can respond, Great Scott leans over and gives me

a kiss on the cheek, then pops up and grabs his towel (which he's kept perfectly dry by sitting on mine).

"I'm off, chickadees," he says, imitating Lou's voice. "I've got a pro-boner client of my own to attend to. Toodles!"

And with that, he's gone. Leaving my sister and me in the wake of his unsuspecting wisdom.

"I was totally the ugly guy in that story," I say once he's out of earshot.

Hannah sighs. "I wish you could see yourself the way I do."

"With scraped palms and knees," I say, showing her my battle scars from the last few weeks of training.

"Those are signs you tried something new," she says. "It shows you've got grit, and that you're brave. It's all part of what makes you beautiful."

"You just think that because you love me," I tell her.

"You're easy to love," Hannah says. "And if Adam is as great as you've said he is, he'll see that, too."

"He's that great," I agree. "But I *really* screwed up."

"You know, there's this thing called second chances . . ."

I glance over at my sister, who has a dreamy smile on her face. "I'm sorry I haven't asked how things are going with Josh. But it's kind of obvious—you're glowing."

"That's just sweat," she says, playfully wiping her brow.

"No, it's happiness," I say. "And I'm happy for you."

"Wait—are you actually being supportive of my relationship with Josh?" Hannah asks, not bothering to hide her shock.

I press my lips together. "I wouldn't go that far. But if he keeps making you happy, maybe I'll consider forgiving him. In a few decades."

Hannah laughs, playfully knocking her shoulder against mine.

We're both quiet, and my mind drifts to our grandmother, the way it often does.

"I wonder what GiGi would think of this mess we've made," I say.

Hannah stiffens beside me. "Actually . . . I've been meaning to talk to you about that."

"Is everything okay?" I ask, concerned.

She bites her lip, hesitating. "Well, I—"

A volleyball sails toward me, and I shriek, throwing my hands up to block myself from being hit in the face.

"Sorry about that!" a teenage boy calls, running up to us.

I toss him the ball. "No worries," I say, then turn to my sister. "What were you saying?"

Hannah blinks. "Oh. We just need to be careful about the budget, okay? If the squatters are using our printers, they should pitch in for ink and paper." She stands, wrapping her towel around her. "What do you say we catch an Uber home?"

"Nah," I say. "Let's walk."

Thirty-Six

HANNAH

I'M HIDING IN ONE OF THE BATHROOM STALLS AT WORK WITH my phone, calling Josh's number and silently praying that he picks up.

Then he does: "Banana! I was just thinking about you. How—"

"Serena and Preeti said yes," I blurt. "They sent me an email saying they'd love to work with me."

A pause. "They did?"

"They did."

I hear a full-throated whoop so loud I cover the phone with my hand, just in case my sister, Great Scott, and the NPCs hear it echoing throughout the office.

"I'm so proud of you!" Josh shouts. Then in a muffled voice, like he's speaking to someone else: "Sorry, sorry—I'll leave." To me, with an embarrassed chuckle, "I just startled every person and animal in the area. But god*damn*, Hannah, that's incredible! How are you feeling?"

"Shocked," I say.

"I'm not. Not at all." He's a bit out of breath, like he's walking up a flight of stairs. "I want to hear all about it, but I don't want to be distracted and there's a lot going on here."

"I totally understand."

"Save tonight for me, will you? We should celebrate; go to dinner, drink some champagne," he says. "How about I get a hotel reservation? I want to get you naked and not have to worry about your sister in the next room."

A pulse of heat shoots through me. "I love this idea."

"Great. I'll see you tonight. Oh, and Hannah?"

"Yeah?"

"I am seriously so proud of you."

JOSH MANAGED TO get us a reservation at Nobu, a fancy sushi restaurant in the West Loop. Dinner is perfect—the food is delicious, the champagne is bubbly, and Josh is enthusiastic and attentive as I tell him all about my plans for Serena and Preeti's book. It's the perfect distraction from the overwhelming sense of impending doom I have regarding the financial state of the Freedman Group. And the fact that I'm too chicken to talk to my sister about any of it.

As the evening passes, I realize that this is the first real, grown-up dinner date we've ever been on. High school dances, college parties, pizza dinners, and movies at the discount theater were fun, but this is a whole new world. We're adults now, with real jobs and real responsibilities, and I keep smiling when I remember that he has chosen *me*.

Once we're both stuffed and a little tipsy, we walk to our hotel. Our room is beautiful, but as soon as the door locks behind us, we can only focus on each other—undressing, touching, tasting. It's all heat and desire and sweet, aching tenderness, and when it's over, we end up talking for hours because we don't want the night to end.

We're lying like we used to when we were teenagers, on our sides with our foreheads touching, whispering to each other in the dark as we fight off sleep. He's telling me about the apartment he's going to check out next week. It's in Old Town, halfway between my place and the aquarium, and close enough to the lake that he can easily go for a run.

"Do you want to see it?" he asks, finishing.

He says this so casually that it takes me a moment to realize what he's asking.

"You want me to come with you?"

Moonlight from the window glints off his eyes as he nods. "I want to make sure you'd feel comfortable spending the night. Spending *several* nights. And maybe, down the road . . ."

He trails off, breaking eye contact with me, a sure sign that he's struggling with what he wants to say next.

"Down the road?" I nudge his foot.

"Spending *all* the nights," he finishes, lifting his eyes to meet mine.

"Wait—are you asking me to move in with you?"

He shrugs, a flash of vulnerability in his expression. "Not yet. I know it's fast, but time is confusing, isn't it? We've only been back together for a few weeks . . . but we've been together since we were fifteen. I don't want to rush things—"

"But we don't want to waste any more time," I finish, and he nods. "I'd love to look at the apartment with you."

He exhales, relieved, and pulls me closer, until we're flush against each other, my head tucked under his chin. "Good, because I need to get out of my parents' house."

There's an unexpected edge in his voice; anger, maybe? Sadness?

"What's going on with them?" I ask, tentative. It hurts to think that they're unhappy that Josh and I are back together.

"It's . . . just been hard," he says stiffly, and then shifts the subject. "Have you talked to Libby? About Serena and Preeti, I mean."

"Not yet." I don't know how to explain it to her: my deep yearning to take the project and run with it, all by myself, to see what I can do on my own. But there's more at stake than my personal desires—and not just our business, either.

Now that Josh is back, I've been drifting away from my sister. I'm glad she opened up to me about Adam, but the very fact that I didn't already know shows that we're not as close as we should be. This project for Serena and Preeti will only widen that distance, and it'll be my fault.

Josh taps on my temple lightly. "Let me in," he says. "Please?"

I smile, realizing the QHT has gone on for a while. I'm not sure how to explain, so I shift my weight until I'm flat on my back. He does the same, and we lie side by side in bed, staring up at the dark ceiling above us.

"Have I told you much about when my dad left?" I ask.

"Just the basics."

"I was only seven, so I don't remember a lot." I pause, searching for the words. "But I do have one crystal clear memory. Libby and I were watching a movie and I went to ask my mom to make us some more popcorn. She was on the phone with a friend, talking about the divorce. She was crying."

I remember how disorienting that was, to see my mother in such a vulnerable state. I'd been sheltered from most of the tumult of the divorce by Libby.

"My mom didn't see me," I continue, "but I heard her say, 'Apparently he needs to follow his passion, whatever the fuck that means.' It was the first time I'd heard my mom swear, so that was shocking, but what stuck in my mind was the despair in her voice, the way she spat out those words. 'He needs to follow his *passion*.'"

My throat closes in and I can't speak anymore; I've journaled about my parents' divorce, but I haven't let myself feel many of those buried emotions. I know that the collapse of my parents' marriage is more complicated than this; they married too young and never worked well together. But I hope Josh understands what I'm trying to say, because I'm not sure I can put it into words.

I glance over at him. He's staring at the ceiling, his expression thoughtful. "You internalized your mom's words," he says. "That following your passion hurts the people you love."

I nod, grateful; he articulated it better than I ever could. "I want to work on Serena and Preeti's book and make it *my* project—but I can't shake this feeling of guilt, like I'm abandoning Libby." I swallow. My throat feels thick. "I know what it's like to be abandoned by someone chasing their dreams. And I—I can't do that to my sister."

Tears run down my cheeks, and Josh wraps his arms around me. I bury my face in his chest and breathe in his familiar scent.

"You're not abandoning her," he says. "You deserve a chance to do something *you* are passionate about. Libby would want you to be happy."

He's right, of course; I know that intellectually. But it's so difficult to break out of an established role—not just as business partners, but as sisters. Libby's always been the trailblazer, the leader. Since the day I was born, I've watched her, how she interacts with the world, molding myself around her.

"Talk to her," Josh urges. "Tell her how you feel—"

"She'll be upset—"

"Maybe."

"Definitely."

My stomach cramps at the thought of her reaction. Standing my ground with Libby about Josh was difficult enough. I don't know if I'm strong enough to bring up anything else.

He kisses my head. "All I'm saying is that you should give her the chance to support you."

I run my hands through his hair, gently scratching his scalp, and he closes his eyes and gives a contented sigh. My mind drifts back to our conversation on the Ferris wheel. I wish Josh had given *me* the chance to support him back in college. That feeling of being blindsided, of realizing that he'd planned a huge change without telling me, was the worst part.

My sister deserves better.

"I'll talk to her," I say eventually. Then, in a teasing voice: "How much do I owe you for this therapy session?"

He chuckles. "How much will you give me?"

"Anything," I say. "Everything."

He rolls me onto my back, pinning me down with the delicious heaviness of his body.

"You know I'm in love with you, right?" he says. There's a dark heat in his eyes that makes it difficult for me to breathe. "I never stopped loving you, but now I'm back *in* love with you."

"That's good," I say, "because I'm in love with you, too."

He kisses me, a deep, melting kiss that leaves me breathless. But when he pulls away, I swear I see tears in his eyes.

I touch his cheek, concerned. "You okay?"

His eyes fill with a raw pain that strikes my heart like a knife. What is he not telling me?

But then he blinks and it's gone.

"Being with you," he says, "is the only time I feel like I'm home."

I understand what he means—being in the right place with the right person at the right time. A sense of wholeness, like everything broken has been restored.

"Thank you for coming back to me," I tell him.

And then I do the only thing I can do in that moment: I bring his mouth to mine, and I close my eyes and let myself free-fall.

CRUSH YOUR COMFORT ZONE
THE ULTIMATE CHALLENGE COMPANION JOURNAL

WEEK 10

Thousands of years ago, fear was essential. Fear told us to run away from predators or stay away from a cliff. It kept us safe and alive. But in our modern world, we are rarely in actual, physical danger, so fear isn't keeping us safe anymore. It's holding us back.

Today, think about something you want to do, but haven't. If you had no fear, would you do it? What if you decided to do it anyway . . . even though you're scared?

Hannah, 8/7

The first thing that comes to mind is working on my own projects, without Libby. More than just the work for Serena and Preeti; building a whole career of my own. But whenever I think about that, a whole bunch of fears rush through my mind. I'm afraid of hurting Libby, first of all. Afraid of ruining our relationship.

But more than that, I'm afraid that if I try to do something on my own, I'll fail. I'll learn that I don't have the ability to do this and it was stupid for me to even try.

But if I didn't have any of those fears? Well, that's easy. I'd just do it.

So I guess the real question is: Can I do it anyway? Can I do it, even though I'm scared?

Thirty-Seven

LIBBY

IT'S TUESDAY NIGHT, AND I'M ALONE AT THE OFFICE. GREAT Scott left at five on the dot, and Hannah left soon after to meet up with Josh. I don't have anywhere to be—and besides, I'm on a roll, preparing for the next event with Adam.

We've been talking a bit—over email, not text—about the speed-dating event at the diner next weekend, where singles switch tables after each course. We're doing two seatings: an early-bird one for singles in their sixties and seventies, and a late one for the twenties-and-thirties crowd.

Our communication has been strictly professional—which could mean he's being respectful and following my lead, *or* he has just as much regret over what almost happened the other night as I do. As I did.

I'm still embarrassed, but I'm trying to forgive myself now that I understand what triggered my reaction. There's no going back and changing what happened, but I'm grateful I didn't bungle things so badly that we couldn't keep working together. And someday in the future, when I meet another guy I'm interested in, hopefully I'll be able to stay in the moment and out of my head.

But right now, my focus has to be on work and training. The race is in two weeks, and I am not ready. Mentally or physically.

The only thing I am ready for is my couch and my latest Book of the Month pick. My gaze drifts to the stack of papers at the corner of my desk, a contract for the working relationship, and an invoice for the first payment.

I'd been stalling on having Hannah draw up the paperwork, but once she knew about Adam and the events, I figured it would be good to go ahead and get paid for the work I'm doing. I was planning to send a courier over to the restaurant with it tomorrow. A decision that I now realize was driven by the fear of seeing him again.

It would be brave of me, not to mention more fiscally responsible, to take the bus and drop it off myself instead of paying someone else to deliver it. And it's not like Adam will be at the restaurant this late, anyway. I can just slide it under the door and leave without having to see him.

With that decided, I put the papers in a manila folder and grab a Post-it note from the dispenser on Hannah's desk. I scrawl *Sorry I missed you*, so Adam knows I'm not actively avoiding him—even though that's pretty much exactly what I'm doing.

TWENTY MINUTES LATER, I'm stepping off the bus near the diner, the envelope tucked under my arm. The temperature has dropped drastically, and I hope the dark clouds rolling in aren't a sign that I'm making a ginormous mistake.

My heart is beating so fast as I approach the door, you'd think I was trying to steal something instead of leaving it behind. I move quickly, racing against both the rain and the bus schedule so I can drop the papers off and get across the street before the next bus arrives.

The breeze rustles my skirt, lifting it slightly in the air. I yank it down, turning to make sure I didn't accidentally give anyone a free show. When I turn back, Adam is standing on the other side of the door, looking at me with those warm brown eyes that make me want to tell him all my secrets.

He opens the door, and this time, the bell feels more ominous than welcoming.

"Hi," he says, a question in his voice.

"I didn't think you'd be here," I say. Adam's lips—the ones I can still imagine pressed against mine—turn down. "I mean, the papers. I'm glad you are. For you to sign."

My words come spilling out in the wrong order, and Adam's forehead wrinkles, like he's not sure if he should laugh or give me a hug. God, what I would give for a hug from him right now.

"Want to come in for a drink?" Adam asks. His tone is casual; I still can't tell if he's happy to see me, or annoyed, or even just bored. "I've been perfecting my French 75."

Thunder rolls in the distance, and since the only thing worse than facing my fears with Adam is riding the CTA in soaking-wet clothes, I step inside.

Adam walks behind the bar and I take a seat at a stool on the other side, the knot in my stomach loosening ever so slightly as I watch him take out the ingredients. Time stretches as I wait for him to ask about the other night. I'm not brave enough to tell him the truth, but I also can't bring myself to tell him another lie.

"How've you been?" I ask, when the silence gets to be too much.

Adam looks up from the shaker and gives me a sad smile that both settles my stomach and gets my heart racing. This would be a lot easier if he wasn't so damn attractive.

"I've been okay," Adam says.

I stop myself from asking if he's talking about a 4 out of 10 okay, or a 6 out of 10 okay. Maybe it's for the best that things stopped before they had the chance to get started. It's hard to be authentic and in the moment around him when half of what I know is supposed to be someone else's memories.

Silence falls between us again. I watch as Adam picks up a lemon and twirls it around his fingers. The fingers on the hands that traveled up and down my back before landing on my butt, pulling me so close I could feel that he was just as worked up as I was.

"I'm sorry about the last time I was here," I say. "Letting things go too far."

"I respect if that's how you feel," he says. "But I wouldn't have minded it going a little further."

Adam's eyes flicker with a spark of something that looks like desire. Not just physical lust, but something deeper. More emotional.

I shiver under his stare, feeling seen. Not for what I look like, but for who I am. Heat rushes to my core, and for a moment, I'm in my head again. Only this time, the words playing on repeat are from Hannah, saying that I'm beautiful, and from Lou, encouraging me to crush my comfort zone.

Adam's eyes drift down, and I swear they linger on my lips. I know that look. I've never experienced it myself, but I have through plenty of characters. And in every book I've read, what happens next is inevitable.

Except in the book, the main character didn't already screw things up by giving the guy every reason to think she wasn't interested. Even though she is. I am. Very, very, very interested.

I accidentally lick my lips, calling even more attention to my mouth. Adam's gaze returns to mine, and I can see the question in his eyes.

The answer is a thousand times yes, but I can't find the words to explain my change of heart. So I go for it. Forcing myself out of my head and into my body, propelling myself off the barstool, leaning over toward Adam.

His head turns in surprise, and our noses collide instead of our lips. Embarrassed, I start to pull back, but he stops me. His hands are on both sides of my face, holding me steady as his lips find mine.

The kiss is gentle at first, like he's asking permission. Permission I eagerly grant, opening my mouth for him. We stay like that for a beautiful moment, lips and tongues intertwined, until he breaks the kiss, just long enough to hop over the bar so he's on my side.

I lean back into the stool, bringing him and his beautiful mouth with me. My legs part, making room for him to step closer.

Adam's hands are on my hips, his fingers inching closer to the waistline of my skirt. Before I can stop myself, I reach out and pinch his arm.

He flinches and steps back, looking as confused as I feel.

"Sorry," I say, leaning in for another kiss. "I had to make sure you were real."

"I'm definitely real," Adam says, pulling me close so I can feel how real he is. Soft in all the right places, and hard in all the right ones, too. "And I'm glad you are, too."

Thunder claps, shaking the building. We both jump—and I realize how dark it's gotten. With the lights on, we're on full display for anyone passing by.

"Upstairs?" Adam's voice rumbles through me, sending shivers down my spine.

"Good idea," I agree. "If someone sees us, you might knock Harvey off his pedestal as the ladies' man of this place."

Adam laughs. "He can keep the title—I've got the prize."

I lean in for another kiss, and Adam's hand drifts down my leg, slipping beneath the hem of my skirt.

Another clap of thunder startles us, and we break apart. Adam doesn't hesitate—he grabs my hand and leads me up the back stairs to his apartment. He hesitates at the first landing and looks back, but I give his hand a squeeze, letting him know I'm still with him.

His face breaks into a smile as bright as pure sunshine, and he flings the door open, pulling me through. Before the door even closes, he presses me against the wall, his body against mine.

"Is this okay?" Adam asks as his lips trace down my neck.

"Mm-hmm," I murmur. I don't think I could form words if I tried.

"And this?" he asks, sliding his hand under my skirt, cupping my ass.

I moan in response and arch my body toward him. His erection strains against his jeans, kicking my lust into overdrive.

"Bedroom," I manage to say, in case my intentions are anything less than crystal clear.

He smiles against my mouth, not breaking our kiss as he walks backward, leading us down a hall to his bedroom. Inside, he reaches for the light switch and turns it on, but I turn it off. I'm not ready to be that seen.

"Take these off?" I say, motioning to his pants.

"Happy to." Adam smiles down at me as my fingers fumble with the button on his jeans. He helps me, taking them off in one fell swoop.

When he slips off his shirt, I step back, taking him in, standing before me, wearing nothing but his boxer briefs. Lightning strikes outside, illuminating the room and giving me a glimpse of his body. The man is a sight to behold. His legs are skinny, but his chest is broad and covered with a smattering of hair. He's got a hint of a belly, and it's that little imperfection that gives me the confidence to step closer and let him see me.

When his hand reaches for the hem of my shirt, I flinch and suck in my stomach. Adam stops, sensing my hesitation, his eyes searching my face. I take a deep breath and remind myself that this is okay, that I'm okay and this is exactly where I want to be. That there's nothing to be afraid of.

The room illuminates again with another strike of lightning, and the skies seem to open, rain pouring down. The rhythmic pounding against the window helps me relax as Adam slips my shirt over my head. His eyes grow wide in appreciation as he takes in my body, my breasts, my nipples straining against the lacy fabric of the new bra I went and got fitted for last week. As if I knew—or hoped—I would end up right here.

"God, you're beautiful," Adam murmurs. His hands reach toward me, and the way he's looking at me like I'm a hard-earned prize, I almost believe him.

Feeling brazen, I reach behind me and unclasp my bra to help him along. His eyes darken with intensity as he sinks down, teasing my left breast with his hand, slipping the right one into his mouth. He switches sides, and I stumble toward the bed as my legs turn to jelly.

Leaning back on the bed, I pull him down with me so we're lying on our sides. His skin is soft and warm against mine; his hands feel rough as they travel down my body. I kiss him, thanking him for the way he makes me feel, like I'm worthy of his adoration.

We stay there for what feels like an eternity, exploring and tasting each other, until I'm light-headed and shaky, desperate to feel him inside me. I have a feeling this will be different from all the other times I've done this. Not that there've been that many.

"Do you have a condom?" I ask.

He nods and exhales a slow breath, as if he, too, can't believe we're here, about to do this. It only takes a moment for him to get a condom out of his nightstand drawer, but that's all it takes for my mind to go somewhere else.

Back to college, before my first time. I knew he was the wrong guy, but I wasn't patient enough to wait for the right one. I was anxious to get it over with, to lose the burden of the "virgin" label. I thought it would make me feel more like a woman, but it only left me feeling empty and used. Unloved and unlovable.

"Hey," Adam says, brushing his lips against mine as his hand slides down my hip, lowering my skirt. "Where'd you go?"

"I'm here," I say, but in my mind, I slip into my imagination, into the skin of someone else, an amalgamation of all my favorite romance heroines, full of confidence, eyes on the future and the pages ahead.

"Stay with me," Adam says. His kiss relaxes me, and when I feel him start to pull down my underwear, I don't tense up, and when he looks up at me, I smile and nod, urging him on.

I've never felt more naked, not just physically, but emotionally. The guys I've slept with in the past made me feel like I was the means to an end. They wanted to have sex, and I was there and willing.

But here with Adam, the way he keeps checking in on me . . . it feels like he wants to get closer to me. To connect with me. And I want that, too.

He presses me down against the bed, coming over me until we're chest to chest, limbs intertwined, his hardness pressing against my stomach.

"Hi," he says, gazing down at me with lusty eyes.

"Hi," I say, breaking into a goofy grin, ruining whatever seductive vibe this moment would hold if it were in a romance novel. But it's better than that, because it's real life.

Another flash of lightning, reflecting in Adam's eyes, crackling with desire.

"I'm glad you came back," he says, dipping his head to give me a kiss. He gently pushes my legs open, taking his length and running it up and down, teasing me, warming me up. When I can't take it anymore and he's slick with my desire, I reach down and guide him where I want him to be.

Adam keeps his eyes locked on mine as he pushes inside me, and I gasp at the fullness of him, stretching me, filling me. His face contorts in pleasure and he moans my name, and I melt. My name has never sounded so beautiful; I've never felt so beautiful. I imagine myself the way he sees me, and it's like I'm that heroine again. Not myself, but not not-myself, either.

I wrap my legs around him, arching up as he pulls back, matching him stroke for stroke. My eyes drift closed, and somehow I'm both inside and outside my body. Time slows and bends and stretches, and I have no sense of anything other this his body and mine.

"Libby," Adam says.

I open my eyes. His face is inches above mine, his eyes looking not just at me, but through me. Through all the layers I put on for the outside world, shattering my protective shield. He sees me, and he still wants me.

I tilt my head up, my mouth hungry for his. He changes his angle, then reaches down where our bodies meet, and uses his fingers to apply pressure in just the right spot. He's watching me closely, paying attention to every gasp and movement I make, studying me like I'm the only thing that matters. Like we're the only two people on the earth and nothing exists but us and this moment with the summer storm raging outside.

Lightning shatters the sky, followed by a roll of thunder, so close it makes the walls shudder, and I come undone. Warmth floods my body, lifting me up and away, soaring and tumbling through space.

He's right there with me, tensing before he shudders and collapses onto me. He kisses my neck as I relax, safe and warm in his arms.

He sighs, a satisfied sound. "You . . . are incredible," he says.

"You're not so bad yourself," I say, brushing his curls away from his forehead.

When he slides out, I feel empty again. He turns away to

take off the condom, and those few moments are enough for me to get in my head again: *What happens next? Does he want me to stay? Now that it's over, am I supposed to leave?*

I'm sitting up in bed, reaching for my discarded clothes, when Adam returns.

"Oh no you don't," he says, practically tackling me back into the bed, making me laugh. "I'm not letting you run away this time."

My heart expands as he pulls me against him, spooning me like I'm precious to him. We lie together, listening to the rain outside, the gentle rumbles of thunder as the storm moves away.

If this was one of my romance novels, this moment of bliss would be followed by a crisis that plunges the lovers into a dark night of the soul. But luckily, it's not a novel. It's life. My life.

After a minute, something else rumbles. My stomach.

"Hungry?" Adam asks.

I nod. "Lunch was a very long time ago."

"Well, lucky for you, you're with someone who knows how to cook. Wait here."

He pulls on his boxers and disappears. A few minutes later, he's back with two plates of the most perfectly scrambled eggs and toast. We sit in bed together, eating and laughing. As the night goes on, he disappears into the kitchen several times, bringing back string cheese, gelato, and finally, pizza rolls—which I tease him relentlessly about.

Long past midnight, when the storm has stopped and our cheeks are sore from laughing, Adam takes my plate away and kisses me, long and slow. Soon that turns into more, and we don't stop until once again we're both satiated. I have a brief thought that I should probably get home, but Adam wraps his arms around me and makes it clear that he wants me to stay right there, tucked against his chest.

And I have no problem with that. For the first time in my life, it doesn't feel like I'm imagining someone else's story. I'm living my own.

Thirty-Eight

HANNAH

I CAN'T MAKE OUR BUDGET WORK.

I've been staring at my spreadsheet so long that I'm certain there's a permanent black-and-white grid imprinted on my retinas, but no matter how hard I stare, these numbers aren't going to work for next month. It's mathematically impossible. Worry vibrates across my skin like static electricity. September's lease payment is due in three weeks and we don't have the funds to cover it.

Outside, I can hear the buzz of activity from the desk fillers, my sister's laugh floating above it all. Lately it seems that Libby is always out there with them, socializing, brainstorming ideas for more collaboration opportunities. I know she's trying to drum up income, but she doesn't seem to understand that a few hundred dollars here and there aren't going to solve a problem of this magnitude. We need actual clients with reliable payment schedules.

She breezes into our office, her earbuds in, talking on the phone. It sounds like she's wrapping up a call with a prospective client, and I watch her, trying to read her body language and expression to determine if it's going well.

"Thank you so much," Libby says. "We can't wait to hear your thoughts on the pitch." She sits at her desk, back to me. "Well, I don't see why not! Everyone *loves* unicorns."

Another prickle of irritation runs through me. What the hell is she talking about? Whatever it is, she didn't run it by me, didn't give me a chance to weigh in or contribute.

Great Scott's voice comes through the intercom system: "Visitor for Libby."

I push the button to respond. "She's almost done with a call. Who is it?"

"Someone she'll want to see." Scott sounds impatient, like this is a huge hassle rather than his actual job—for which we have docked our own salaries to pay him, I might add.

"Let him know that Libby will be out soon."

"What do you think I am, your secretary?" Scott huffs.

"Well, yeah—"

"You can go on back," Scott says to the visitor. "Down the hall, second door on the right."

Before I can remind him not to let random people into our office unannounced—he did that with Lou, and look where it's gotten us—someone knocks on our office door. Sighing, I push back from my desk and go to open it.

"Hello," I say, summoning up a smile. "How can I help you?"

"Hi, I'm looking for . . ." The man stops. He's staring at me with a strange expression, like I'm a puzzle he's trying to work out.

Is he a client Libby found without telling me? He's handsome, a few years older than me and a few inches taller, with brown curly hair and friendly eyes. In one hand, he's carrying a manila envelope, and in the other, a bouquet of flowers.

"Libby?" I turn toward my sister, using my eyes to transmit my questions: *Who is this man and how do we know him and why didn't you tell me he was coming by?*

Libby spins in her chair, taking her earbuds out. Her mouth falls open. "Adam?"

"Adam?" I repeat, confused.

"Libby?" he says.

I spin back around to face him. "Oh, *Adam*."

"Hannah?" he says. The bewilderment on his face has melted into pure shock.

He must recognize me from the dating app—I almost forgot Libby used my picture when she was talking to him. As me.

I glance at the flowers he's holding; Libby wasn't home when I went to bed last night, though she was there when I woke up.

Interesting.

"We're sisters and we work together," I say, pointing between Libby and me. I'm thrilled that Libby has been brave enough to move forward with him.

Adam gives an awkward laugh. "I'm sorry, but this is *such* a weird coincidence. Libby, I matched with Hannah on a dating app earlier this summer." He's looking at Libby now, an earnest expression in his eyes, like he doesn't want to upset her. "We never went out or anything. I had no idea she was your sister."

"Wait—you didn't tell him?" I say, spinning back to face my sister.

Libby's gone white as a ghost.

"Tell me what?" Adam says behind me.

Libby stands, taking a few slow steps forward like she's walking toward her executioner. "Adam, I . . . I can explain."

My stomach drops: he didn't know Libby was messaging him from my profile. That he was talking to her all along, never me. She never told him.

"Explain . . . what, exactly?" he says.

Libby takes a shaky breath. "I'm Hannah on the app."

"You're—huh?"

"I messaged you on the app as Hannah—"

"Why?" he asks, blinking.

"It's part of the challenge we're doing," I cut in, wanting to help. "I had to go out with twelve men in twelve weeks, but I hate meeting new people, so Libby volunteered to message the men and set up the dates. I had a work emergency the night we were supposed to go out, and then I got back together with my ex-boyfriend, so it ended up being a moot point. Anyway, Libby went and introduced herself to you."

Adam's still staring at Libby, like he's trying to make sense of all of this.

"But they gave you an extra cookie," he says to her. "And then you gave one to me."

I don't know what this means, but Libby must, because she bites her lip and winces.

"I thought that was just a coincidence—" Adam shakes his head, then says in a lower voice, "I thought you actually wanted to talk with me that night."

"I did!" Libby protests, her eyes widening. "I do."

"*You* were the one messaging me on the app?" Adam's forehead wrinkles in confusion.

Libby's big, brown eyes are full of apology. "That's how I knew you'd be at the café. But then I met you and . . ."

She trails off, shrugging helplessly.

"You kept messaging me as Hannah, though," Adam says, fidgeting with the bouquet. "Even after we met. Why?"

"I wanted to talk to you."

"You *were* talking to me. In real life." He sounds upset, and I don't blame him. Libby should have explained all of this weeks ago. I had no idea she'd continued to message with him from my profile on the app.

"I didn't know what was going on between us," Libby says, her voice wavering. "If it was professional or . . ."

Adam lifts the flowers; he looks flabbergasted. "You thought last night was *professional*?"

Libby blanches. "I'm really sorry, this is—"

"I don't know *what* this is," he cuts in, "but maybe you could figure it out and let me know? Because I thought . . . never mind. I should go."

"Wait," Libby says, "please don't—"

"I need time to think, to clear my head." He turns and walks away, taking the folder and flowers with him.

I expect Libby to follow, but she crumples into her chair, her head in her hands.

"Oh shit, oh shit, oh shit," she's whispering, over and over.

I kneel next to her, worried. "Libs?"

She looks up at me; her face is tear streaked. "I really screwed up."

Well, yes, but I'm not going to tell her that.

"It's going to be okay." I have no idea if that's true—if Adam is the kind of person who will be able to get over something like this—but I figure she needs encouragement now, not honesty.

"No, it won't," she says, shaking her head.

"It seems like he really likes you, Libs. He brought flowers! I'm sure once he gets a chance to digest this, he'll—"

"I slept with him last night," she blurts.

I blink. "You . . . as in, you had sex?"

She nods, miserably.

"Wow." I'm impressed; I know Libby has some hang-ups about getting naked. "How was it?"

She smacks me in the boob.

"Ow!" I yelp, twisting away. "So was it bad?"

"No! It was the opposite of bad. He's sexy and charming and a great kisser and last night was so, so nice." She buries her face in her hands again.

"Call him and explain what happened. If you're honest, he'll understand."

She shakes her head, still not looking up. "That's the thing, I haven't been honest. And integrity is really important to him—but it probably wouldn't have worked out anyway, so . . ."

And then she's crying, and I put my arms around her, my heart aching. I want to say something to make it all better, but I remember how Libby helped me back in college, when Josh left. She didn't make me talk; she didn't force-feed advice. She just took care of me, allowed me to process my emotions at my own pace.

"Let's head home, okay?" I say gently. "We can get takeout from Joy's and watch *Pride and Prejudice* and drink rosé all night. Then in the morning, we'll figure out what to do next."

She glances up, her eyes red. "Which *Pride and Prejudice*?"

I hesitate. One option is the six-episode BBC miniseries

with grumpy Colin Firth falling in a lake; the other is the two-hour movie with grumpy Matthew MacFadyen caught in the rain. I've sat through each dozens of times, and I'd prefer the *shorter* one, obviously. But tonight isn't about me.

"You choose," I say.

"Let's do the 2005 movie. But only if—"

"We can watch the hand-flex scene as many times as you want," I say, smiling.

"And the first proposal in the rain?"

I nod. "Sure."

"Thanks." Libby takes a shaky breath. "But don't you have plans with Josh?"

"He'll understand."

She makes a sour face. "Please don't tell him what happened."

"I won't. I'll just tell him I need some sister time."

And I do—the fact that things got this serious between Libby and Adam and I had no clue makes it clear that we've drifted further apart than I realized.

"Joy's and *P&P* and wine sounds good," she says, wiping her eyes. "Although that seems an awful lot like the comfort zone I'm supposed to be crushing."

I grab Libby's hand and pull her upright. "Sometimes your comfort zone is exactly what you need."

Thirty-Nine

LIBBY

I'VE HAD A LOT OF BAD DAYS IN MY LIFE. BUT TODAY—WHEN Adam walked into the office and saw Hannah, then me—was the worst by far.

I should have known this wouldn't end well. I was literally living out the miscommunication trope I despise in so many romance novels: when the couple has a problem that could be solved with one honest conversation, but instead, they ignore it, letting it simmer until it all boils over. I've literally thrown books across the room, shouting, "Just talk to each other, dammit!"

But now I understand why so many authors write this: because it's realistic. Opening up to someone you care about, having hard conversations that require vulnerability, can be terrifying. Which is exactly why I, a grown-ass woman, kept information from Adam that I knew would come out at some point.

It's nearly midnight, and I'm snuggled up in bed with Mr. Darcy purring on the pillow beside me, but I can't sleep. Hannah's suggestion to comfort myself with a favorite movie and meal was a nice distraction, but now, with nothing else to occupy my mind, I can't stop ruminating about everything that went wrong.

I wish I could go back in time and do it over, being braver from the start. Then maybe we could've lasted more than twenty-four hours. Our relationship was like a comet or a shooting star—whichever one it is that burns fast, then disappears.

This is what I get for trying to pretend I have main-character energy. Not everyone can be the steak. Someone has to be the mashed potatoes.

Mmm. Mashed potatoes. Is it too late for mashed potatoes? *Tonight, it's not.* I reach for my laptop and get as far as opening the food delivery website when I remember a journaling exercise I did the other day.

The question was about what we turned to for comfort when we were younger. At the time, I couldn't remember anything specific, so I wrote that Hannah and I always comforted each other. I realize now that isn't true. As the big sister, I felt like it was my responsibility to be there for her, to comfort her. Which left me to my own devices, finding a way to take care of myself.

A distant memory comes into focus. I'm eight years old, and Hannah and I are hiding in the pantry, finishing off a sleeve of Oreos. She was there for the game of it—the secretive nature of our NTNT moments, while I was laser focused on the cookies.

That day, I was mad at my dad because he'd made a comment about my shirt being too tight. My mom said it must have shrunk in the wash, but it hadn't shrunk. I'd gotten bigger.

I remember standing in there, a glimmer of light shining through the pantry door as I bit into the cookie. It tasted like comfort, but also revenge. I knew my turning to food would hurt my dad, but I didn't realize it was hurting me, too.

I'm tired of hiding away and avoiding my feelings by indulging myself with comfort food—cookies or mashed potatoes. Not that there's anything wrong with finding comfort in favorite foods; it's the habit of turning to those instead of confronting what's really going on that can be problematic.

I know what I need to do. Before I lose my nerve, I close the delivery website and open my email browser.

Adam,

I'm sorry. Those two little words are nowhere near enough, but they're all I've got. You trusted me, and I wasn't honest with you.

I don't know if it matters, but I wasn't trying to mislead you. I was protecting myself because I care about you, and that scared me. The last thing I ever wanted was to hurt you.

I'd be happy to introduce you to another publicist or an event planner who can step in and see the next three events through to completion.

Again, I'm sorry, and I'm grateful that I got to know you, even if it wasn't for very long.

Libby

Before I can overthink it, I hit send. I imagine the words turning into particles, speeding through the air, putting themselves back together in Adam's inbox.

He probably won't see it until the morning—and even then, I might not hear back from him for a while. Or ever.

My phone buzzes.

Adam: Hi

Before I can wonder if we're so cosmically connected that he was thinking about me at the exact moment I was thinking of him, my phone buzzes again.

Adam: Saw your email

I open the text thread and feel the familiar panic of trying to remember who I'm supposed to be while messaging Adam. But there's only one me now. The one who lied and manipulated him into thinking I was someone—someones, really— that I'm not.

Libby: Sorry, I know you wanted time. I just had to say how sorry I was. How sorry I am.

Adam: It's okay

My stomach flips. What exactly is okay?

Adam: Can I call you?

I exhale a slow breath. I don't think I can handle hearing his voice. Texting is better. Safer.

Libby: It's late. I don't want to wake Hannah up.

It feels weird typing her name out to him, but there's nothing to hide anymore.

Adam: That's right, you share an apartment, too?

Libby: Yup. She's my best friend. And my roommate. And my business partner.

Adam: There's so much I don't know about you

I can't tell if his words are an accusation, or just the sad truth.

Libby: I really am sorry

Adam: I'm not angry. I was upset at first, but now, I'm just hurt.

Libby: I'm even sorrier about that

My eyes well with tears, and I try to blink them away. I know how it feels to be hurt by someone you care about, and I never wanted to make Adam feel that way.

Adam: What hurts the most is that you didn't trust me enough to be honest, to show me who you really are

His words hit straight to my heart. He's right. It's not his fault that men in the past have let me down, starting with my father. The ironic part is that Adam's the first man who really saw me. Even though I was holding so many things back.

I stare at my phone—both grateful for the screen separating us and wishing it could transport me to his apartment in

Wicker Park. I think of him, lying in his soft bed. The pillow-top mattress made it feel like I was lying on a cloud. Or maybe that was because I was next to Adam.

Libby: I know it sounds like a line, but it really wasn't you. It was me.

They aren't the right words, but they're the only ones I have right now. Adam said he needed time; maybe I do, too. To work on myself, and get to a place where I'm not so afraid to let someone see me. All of me.

As much as I opened up to him last night, a part of me was holding back. Pretending to be someone I'm not. But there was a moment when I got a glimpse of how it could be. What the world feels and looks like outside my comfort zone. And it was both terrifying and freeing.

Adam: Well, when you're ready to trust me, I'd like to get to know the real you

I blink in surprise.

Libby: I thought you'd never want to see me again

Adam: Of course I do. I really like the part of you that I got to see. But I can't be with someone who won't share their whole self.

Libby: I think you saw my whole self last night. Twice, actually.

Adam: This isn't something you can joke away

Busted. But he's right. I journaled about this just last week—
my humor has always been my shield. I know that's what
Adam (and Lou) are asking me to put down, but I don't know
if I can. It's a part of me, as much as my brown hair and brown
eyes.

Libby: You're right. I'm sorry.

I imagine him running his hands through his hair, frustrated. Looking over at the right side of his bed, picturing me
there. Wanting me back? Thinking I'm not worth the effort?

Three dots appear on the screen and I hold my breath,
waiting for his response, hoping that he'll say again that it's
okay. That I'm forgiven, that we can move past this.

Adam: Listen, it's getting late and I think we both need
some time. But I would like to get to know the real Libby.
Maybe you can let me know when she's ready to show up.

I want to tell him he already knows the real me. That I was
more myself than I've ever been when I was talking to him on
the app as Hannah. Because I didn't have to worry about what
he thought of me, how he would judge me.

It's too much for me to explain in a text. And I'm not sure
it even makes sense. So, I just type back a simple message.

Libby: I understand. I'll let you know.

Adam: Goodnight

At least it's not goodbye.

Forty

HANNAH

IT'S A HOT AND HUMID FRIDAY MORNING, AND I'M HEADING to a doctor's appointment. I'm getting back on birth control, which seems like an important step, an acknowledgment that my relationship with Josh is serious.

I took the purple line up to the Evanston Medical Clinic, the same clinic I came to for my very first gynecologist appointment at age seventeen—when Libby told me I'd better get on birth control because she sure as hell wasn't going to help raise a little Josh Jr.

Dr. Segura is happy to see me, and surprised but pleased to hear that Josh and I are back together. She does my Pap smear, then answers my questions about contraceptive options including what to do when—in a few years down the road—we're ready to try for a baby. As I leave, she gives me a hug and tells me she'll be thrilled to see me someday for my first OB appointment.

Outside in the summer sunshine, I cross the parking lot, feeling buoyant and excited about the future. Josh is leaving tomorrow for the Bahamas on the aquarium-sponsored research trip, and we're going to spend the entire evening together, after Libby and I do our workout this afternoon.

"Hannah?"

It's a man, pushing a wheelchair toward the clinic. It takes me a moment to realize that it's Josh's dad, Karl.

I tense up; I've been nervous to see them again since Josh implied they aren't thrilled about us being together.

"Hi, Mr. Jacobson," I say, smiling tentatively. He looks so much like Josh, tall and broad shouldered, but with more gray in his hair.

Then I realize the woman in the wheelchair is Josh's mother. Startled, I take a quick step back.

"It's so nice to see you," Jeannie says, smiling up at me, her dimple like Josh's. There's a blanket on her lap, the rainbow blanket Josh was working on the other day. "I keep asking Joshua to bring you over—we're thrilled you two are back together, aren't we, Karl?"

Karl nods. "We certainly are."

"Thank you," I say, trying to cover my confusion. Josh hasn't mentioned anything about his mother having health problems. "How are you?"

"Well, it's been a rough road." She motions to herself like I know what's going on. "But it's made a world of difference to have Joshua back. I was so grateful when he said he'd move home during this whole ordeal."

My confusion blooms into full-blown worry. Does she have cancer? Was she in an accident? I look at Karl, hoping for a clue.

Realization dawns on his face. "Joshua didn't tell you?"

I shake my head.

"Jeannie has ALS," Karl says, his voice grave. "Lou Gehrig's disease? Diagnosed about six months ago."

"ALS . . ." I trail off, racking my brain.

"It's a progressive neurological disease," Jeannie says apologetically, like she's sorry to give me the news. "Remember the ice bucket challenge a few years ago?"

My heart drops; I remember enough to know this is bad. Weakness, paralysis, eventually death. No cure.

I can't speak. Jeannie has the kindest, most generous heart; she was like an extra mom during my teenage years. My eyes flood with tears, and I order myself not to cry. They shouldn't have to spend an ounce of energy comforting me.

"I'm so—I'm so sorry," I stammer. "I had no idea."

Jeannie and Karl glance at each other, and something wordless passes between them.

Then Karl says, "Joshua is . . . having a hard time with this."

"But he's seemed much better since you've been back in his life," Jeannie rushes to add.

"We thought he'd told you," Karl says.

They're gazing at me with such concern, and I can't let them worry about my feelings when they're the ones facing this devastating diagnosis.

"I'm sure he's been waiting for the right time," I say, going down on a knee so I'm at eye level with Jeannie.

It seems like they've been wanting to talk, because it all spills out as we stand there on the sidewalk. They tell me that Jeannie's symptoms aren't too advanced yet—she can still walk, she says proudly—but she tires easily, hence the wheelchair. She isn't having any difficulty breathing or swallowing, Karl says with a smile.

They just got back from a trip to Disney with their grandchildren, Zella and Drew, and they're going to New Zealand next month with their best friends—trying to get in all the bucket-list vacations before Jeannie can't travel.

As they talk, my mind keeps wandering back to Josh. This is what he's been dodging, every time his parents came up in conversation. Did he think I wouldn't be able to handle it? Did he think I wouldn't support him? Or maybe—and this makes my stomach churn—he didn't think I'd be around long enough for it to matter.

No, I tell myself. There has to be an explanation.

Eventually Karl glances at his watch—they need to get going. I give Jeannie a gentle hug, then straighten up for a bear hug from Karl.

As we go our separate ways, I have only one thought in my mind: I need to talk with Josh.

NOT LONG AFTER, I'm being led by a kind security guard through the administrative areas of the aquarium to Josh's office. After I left the clinic, I sent Josh a text asking if I could stop by; he responded OF COURSE, followed by a GIF of an excited golden retriever hopping up and down. My mind has been spiraling through possible reasons Josh would have kept this from me, but I'm trying to give him the benefit of the doubt and wait until he can explain.

When I reach his office, my hands are shaking with worry. Josh opens his door, a huge smile on his face.

"What's wrong?" he says, his smile fading into concern.

My eyes well up with tears. "I—I ran into your parents at the doctor's office."

Josh's face goes blank, and then he just . . . crumples. In a heartbeat, I know why he didn't tell me—it's not that he didn't want to; it's not that he was trying to keep things from me. He simply could not say the words.

I hold my arms out and he collapses into me, burying his face in my neck. With one foot, I nudge the door closed behind me for privacy.

"I'm so sorry," I whisper. "I'm so, so sorry about your mom."

His shoulders start to shake with silent tears. My heart is aching—for him and his entire family. Josh and his mother have a special bond, one I've always envied. Memories of them together fill my mind: making chocolate chip pancakes on Sunday mornings; Jeannie taking dozens of pictures at every school event; Jeannie clipping Josh's hair in the kitchen, asking me for my opinion on the length.

My chest constricts, and I squeeze Josh tighter. Nothing I say or do will make this better, but I can hold him while he cries. I can run my hands through his hair, and whisper in his ear that I'm here, that he isn't alone, that this is awful and so unfair.

Eventually, he pulls away, wiping his eyes with one hand. "I kept wanting to tell you," he says. "I'm sorry I didn't."

I hold his face in my hands, wishing I could transfer love right through my skin to his. "Do you want to talk about it now?"

"Yes. I do." He hesitates, motioning behind him. "But maybe not here . . ."

For the first time, I notice his office and suck in a shocked breath. It's a hovel of chaos: the floor covered with stacks of paper and folders, his desk piled with Coke Zero cans and take-out boxes, and under his desk, a basket full of tangled yarn and partially completed projects.

"I know it's bad," he says, visibly wilting. "But I can't deal with it. My brain is such a mess lately."

"I'm sure it's been overwhelming, helping your parents, trying to focus at work," I say, then hesitate, hoping this doesn't offend him. "Would it be helpful if I organized it a little for you? If that's inappropriate or rude, please let me know, but—"

"I would be so grateful," he cuts in. "Are you sure?"

I nod. "Absolutely."

His shoulders drop in relief. "Thank you."

Josh takes his afternoon medication, and for the next hour, we work together—returning file folders to his filing cabinet, sorting papers into piles to keep and recycle, filling the garbage can with trash. Josh is right by my side, and as we work, he tells me more about his mom.

His parents were downplaying how challenging it's been. Jeannie can only walk a few steps, Josh explains, and will be getting a power wheelchair soon. She can't do her own hair or makeup, so his dad has had to learn, and it's sweet but sad to watch them struggling together. Sometimes she needs help cutting her food or even bringing her fork to her mouth. She uses a machine at night to keep her lungs clear; eventually, she won't be able to breathe on her own. She keeps talking about a vacation to Italy next spring, but Josh doesn't think there's any way she'll be able to manage that. The doctor estimates she has two to three years, at the most.

"Your mom seemed happy you moved back home," I say, winding up a ball of yarn. We're sitting on the floor with our backs against his desk, our legs stretched out in front of us.

He nods, setting aside a half-finished scarf. "Yeah. I was supposed to do a postdoc fellowship at UCSD, but I wanted to be closer to home."

His words make me pause. I set the yarn in the basket as worry settles in my chest. Up until my conversation with his parents, I had this idea that he'd moved back to Chicago for me, because he wanted another chance. But of course he didn't take a job in a landlocked state to rekindle things with his old girlfriend. Did he reach out to me simply because I happened to be here?

I don't like where my mind is going, so I force myself to redirect. "So, working here at Shedd isn't ideal?"

He shakes his head. "No. I mean, I'm happy to be here now. I'd rather regret losing time building my academic career than regret not spending my mom's last years with her."

His words knock the wind out of me. It sounds like he has no intention of staying here permanently.

"After your mom . . ." I hesitate, stumbling over my words. "A few years down the road, do you think you'll end up back at UCSD?"

I know the answer before he speaks; I can see it on his face. It's the way he looked when he told me he was going to Australia. Determined; focused. I respect that, I do. But a sharp pain pricks my heart, nonetheless.

He tilts his head as he studies my face, his eyes all gentle concern. "Han—"

"I get it. I understand." But my eyes fill with tears, and I look away.

He shouldn't have to console *me*. He's losing his mother. He's changed his career plans to be near her. I'm not surprised; this is the kind of person he is, and I'm so damn proud of him for doing it.

But at the same time, I feel so . . . silly.

I've been planning a future for us, but this was all temporary for him. Although—didn't he imply that he wanted me to move in with him?

He tucks a strand of hair behind my ear. "Hey, talk to me. What's going on?"

I shake my head, fighting the emotions tightening my throat. "Nothing. It's just . . . I think I got the wrong impression about what's happening with us."

"Wait—you don't think—" He shifts his weight and faces me. "Let me be clear: I would want you to come with me."

I look up at him. "You would?"

"Of course! I want you to come wherever I go."

His words are reassuring and warm, and it feels so good to hear them. Except for one thing.

"But my work is here," I say.

"Sure, but you could get another job."

I give a short laugh of disbelief. "It's not just a job—it's my career. My family business. I can't just pack up and leave."

He studies me like he truly doesn't understand, a wrinkle forming between his dark eyebrows. "You've been telling me for weeks that you're unhappy working with your sister—"

"I wouldn't say unhappy—"

"Okay, but you've been wanting to make a change. That's why I've encouraged you to go for it with Serena and Preeti."

I blink. "You were doing all that to make it easier for me to leave my sister?"

"No! I mean, maybe." He runs a hand through his hair, flustered. "I want you to have a career you enjoy, and it wouldn't hurt if you had some flexibility. I want to build a life together—"

"But only if I change my life to accommodate yours," I say. "Only if I follow you."

It's not that I would never consider moving—it's more that he *assumed* I would follow him, without even a discussion. If we stay together, is this how it'll be—his career coming first?

His plans always taking precedence over mine? That's not the kind of partnership I want.

He hasn't answered, but I can see by way his jaw is set that he isn't budging on this.

"It's not fair to expect me to be the one who does all the bending," I say, hurt tinging my voice. "This is where I want to be—here, in Chicago, working with Libby, running GiGi's company together."

"And I need to be at a university that can support my research," he says. "This is my life's work—I thought you understood that. I thought you wanted to be with me."

"I do! But you're expecting me to choose between you and my sister."

His eyes flash with frustration. "And you're expecting me to give up my dreams so you can stay here and not chase yours."

His words punch me in the stomach. "But—my dreams are here," I stammer. "I'm doing exactly what I want to do."

"Are you serious?" He shakes his head, incredulous. "After everything you've told me about how stifled you feel at work?"

"I'm not stifled! I want to adjust our roles and responsibilities, but I have no intention of leaving. I'm not going to abandon my sister."

"And I'd never ask you to—but I don't want to lose you, Hannah. You've been the one bright spot in the middle of all this darkness. When we're together, it's the only time I can forget about everything that's happening with my mom."

I flinch; this isn't the compliment he means it to be. I don't want to be all sunshine and fun—a real relationship means sharing the dark times, too.

"But that's the issue," I say gently. This is difficult to tell him, but I think it's necessary. "The past few weeks have been fun, but they haven't been real—you haven't been real. You haven't let me in. You haven't allowed me to see what's going on inside you."

And it's all too similar to what happened in college—he was so unhappy, but he didn't tell me. The old feeling of abandonment wells up inside me, filling my lungs with panic. I can't go through that again. I can't spend the next few years falling deeper in love with him, only for him to disappear and leave me broken.

Josh slumps back against the desk. He looks so hopeless that my heart fractures right in two, because I feel the same way.

"I didn't mean to shut you out," he says, his voice bleak. "It was just nice to have something good. With you. Something easy."

Again, not a compliment. My old fears rush back—that Josh stayed with me all those years in high school and college because I made it easy for him. As soon as it became difficult— as soon as he had to work to keep connected with me—he let our relationship fall by the wayside.

My lungs ache, and I struggle to take a breath. "So, you got back together with me because it was . . . convenient?"

He frowns, but he doesn't deny it. "That's not—"

"I don't blame you," I say, holding up a hand. "You're going through a rough time; you wanted someone by your side. And you knew I would take you back."

"Hannah—"

"And I did, didn't I? You didn't even have to try very hard to convince me. It took—what, a month? A few runs, a shower together? I didn't make it much of a challenge."

I'm spiraling, and I force myself to take a breath. This isn't about me—none of it is. He's been grieving all summer and will continue to grieve as he loses his mother, little by little. Of course he would seek out comfort and familiarity.

I'm not angry with him. I'm just sad. So incredibly sad.

Josh reaches for my hand, but I move it away. I'm already splintering around the edges. If he touches me, I'll fracture.

"Maybe I haven't been real with you about what's going on with my mom," he says quietly. "But the way I feel about you is real. What we have together is real."

I shrug helplessly. "That's never been the problem—of course we care about each other. The problem is that we want different things out of life."

"I know what I want. I want to be with you."

"No, you want me to follow you. There's a difference. You don't want to change your plans for me."

"You don't want to change your plans for me, either," he says.

"I'm not the one who went to Australia!"

"Han. Come on. That was five years ago—"

"Exactly," I say. "And five years later, we're repeating the same pattern."

Josh opens his mouth, then shuts it again, because he knows it's true. Exhaling, I lean back against the desk, while he slumps forward, his head in his hands.

We both go quiet, and my eyes drift to the framed pictures on Josh's newly clean desk: a selfie of us together on the sailboat just a few weeks ago; a picture of us at a Halloween party in college, dressed up as Jack and Sally from *The Nightmare Before Christmas*; another of us at high school graduation in our caps and gowns. The sight calms me: all this history between us, it means something. Right?

But then Josh breaks the silence.

"Maybe we should take a step back," he says.

I look up, alarmed. "What does that mean?"

His face is usually so expressive, but not now. It's like he's pulled down the shades to block me from seeing inside. "Maybe we should reevaluate where our relationship is going."

I stare at him, unable to process this. "Where our . . . ? Hold on. Are you breaking up with me?"

"That's not—" He swallows. "I don't want that to happen. But . . ."

"But what?"

"If our lives are headed in opposite directions," he says, "then it would be better to figure that out now, before we get in too deep."

But I'm already in so deep I can't see the surface. My panic rises until it's nearly choking me. He's going to leave me. Again.

All I want is for him to wrap his arms around me and promise that he'll never leave me. That he'll do anything to stay with me. That he'll choose me.

But maybe that isn't the right thing to do, for either of us. If we keep acting like everything is fine, pretending like we don't have real issues to face, we'll just be kicking this down the road. At some point, Josh will want to move away. And I will want to stay.

I take a deep breath, ordering my heart to be strong.

"You're leaving for the Bahamas tomorrow," I say. "The Down & Dirty is the week after you get back. That gives us three weeks to think about what we want. After the race, we can talk again."

Setting aside everything to do with our jobs and locations, this might not be the best time for Josh to start a new relationship. I want to support him through the loss of his mom, but I'm not sure he wants that from me. Maybe he just wants easy and light.

"I think that's a good idea," he says.

Josh stands, dusting off his pants, then grabs my hand to tug me upright. He immediately pulls me into a hug, the perfect Josh hug, the kind I dreamt about during our years apart. I close my eyes and memorize the feeling of his arms around me, his cheek pressed into the top of my head, his familiar smell. Just in case this is the last time.

"I am so sorry about your mom," I whisper.

His arms tighten around me and the balance shifts between us, so he's leaning into me, and I'm holding him.

Eventually, he releases me and takes a step back, wiping his eyes. "I haven't really processed what's going on with my mom yet. I've hardly let myself think about it. So thanks for being here. Thanks for helping me tackle my office, too."

"I'm happy to help in any way I can," I say, meaning it.

He presses his lips together, rocking back on his heels, like he's struggling with something.

"What?" I say.

"I didn't say anything."

"I know, but I can hear you thinking."

His lips curve in a sad smile. "I just"—he shrugs—"love you."

My chest constricts. Somehow, I manage to say: "Be safe on your trip."

Then I give him one last smile, and head out.

Forty-One

LIBBY

SUJI AND I ARE TAKING WHAT'S BECOME OUR DAILY ICED coffee break. A little splurge I justify since it's better than going out to lunch every day like I used to. And it's been nice having a friend I'm not related to, whose happiness I don't feel responsible for.

"Doing anything fun this weekend?" she asks.

"Not sure I'd call it fun . . . but I'm supposed to climb the rock wall at Maggie Daley Park after work today with Hannah."

As soon as I say my sister's name, I realize I haven't seen or heard from her all day. She had a doctor's appointment this morning, but it's almost three o'clock.

"Sorry, just want to check in on my sister," I say, grabbing my phone.

My stomach clenches with worry as I imagine the worst-case scenarios: kidnapping, murder, hit-and-run. Hannah's true crime obsession is rubbing off on me.

Libby: Haven't seen you all day!

Moments later, my phone buzzes, and my whole body relaxes.

Hannah: I'll meet you by the park entrance at 5:30

"Everything okay?" Suji asks.

"Oh yeah," I say, slipping my phone back in my pocket. "Curse of being the big sister, you never stop worrying."

"I think that's supposed to be the curse of parents," Suji says. "At least with Korean parents—I'm thirty-two and my mom panics if she doesn't get a proof-of-life message every day."

I smile but can't really relate. Hannah and I talk to our parents every few weeks, mostly out of obligation. Come to think of it, I don't even think they know what's going on with the business.

"So, the rock-climbing wall is still on?"

"Possibly . . ."

Suji clearly reads the thinly veiled panic in my voice. "Afraid of heights?" she asks.

"More like scared about not getting off the ground."

I tell her that I agreed to meet Hannah there without checking the website—which I did this morning to see if there was a weight limit. It said that anyone could climb as long as they could fit in the harness and have a belayer of "equal or greater weight."

"I don't want to show up and find out that all the belayers working are lightweights," I say, my stomach twisting at the thought.

I can't handle a repeat of the Evanston Carnival for Meg McKeen's birthday party in fifth grade, when the safety bar wouldn't latch around me and I had to get off the ride in front of everyone.

"Hmm," Suji says, thinking. "You could always call ahead and ask? I assume they'll know the weights of the belayers working today."

It's such an obvious idea, but it calms me. "I could kiss you," I tell Suji, digging out my phone again.

TWENTY MINUTES LATER, I'm walking up to the park entrance, where I spot Hannah pacing in front of the sign. I swear, my sister has so much energy that it's physically impossible for her to sit still.

"There you are!" I call out, waving.

Thanks to Suji's brilliant idea, I found out there are not just one, but two belayers working today who have a good twenty pounds on me. Now I'm excited to see the view of the lake from the top of the wall. Or almost the top. I bet the view's even nice from halfway up.

At the sound of my voice, Hannah turns to face me. It looks like she's been crying—her eyes are red, her face pale. My eyes instantly well with tears, too. I can practically feel her emotions—an ache in my throat and tightness in my chest.

I fold her into my arms as she starts to cry.

"You're okay," I tell her, hoping that's true. "What's wrong?"

Hannah mumbles something, including one word that starts with a *J* and ends with an *osh*.

Rage instantly ignites inside me.

"What did that asshole do?" I ask, trying to keep the fury out of my voice. That piece of shit better not have hurt my sister.

"His mom," Hannah says through hiccups.

"Mrs. Jacobson?" I ask. From everything Hannah has told me in the past, the woman is lovely. "What did she do?"

"She's dying," Hannah says before dissolving into more tears.

"Oh no," I say, leading Hannah toward a bench. We sit down and Hannah rests her head on my shoulder. I rub her back as she cries, and as much as it hurts to see my sister upset, a tiny part of me feels good to be needed again.

Lately, Hannah hasn't had much use for me. She's been happy, which makes me happy, but I've been feeling a little lost without having to take care of her.

"I'm so sorry," I tell Hannah. "I know how much Mrs. Jacobson means to you."

But even as I say the words, something doesn't sit right. Yes, Hannah and Josh's mom were close back when Hannah was in high school, but as far as I know, she hasn't talked to the woman in years.

Sure enough, Hannah pulls back from my embrace, her eyes red and puffy. "That's not it," she says.

My stomach sinks. Hannah had a doctor's appointment this morning—maybe something is wrong with her?

"Han, what's going on?" I ask, my voice wobbling. My sister is the only person I have in this entire world—if I lose her . . . just the thought of living without her knocks the wind out of me.

"I can't sit anymore," Hannah says, leaping up from the bench as if it's on fire. She starts walking through the park toward the lake, and I rush to catch up.

"Hannah, stop," I plead. "You're scaring me."

My sister slows down, and with her eyes glistening with tears, she tells me everything: Josh didn't tell her about his mom's diagnosis (typical); he moved back to Chicago to be with her (which is the decent thing to do); he isn't going to stay in Chicago for good (not a surprise); he's eventually going to leave and pursue his dream career across the country (because he's an asshole and that's what assholes do).

"That asshole," I say, not bothering to temper my rage. My hands are balled into fists. I want to punch that piece of shit in his stupid perfect face.

"He's not being an asshole," Hannah says, shaking her head. "That's why it hurts so much—I can't blame him for any of it."

"Of course you can blame him! He's doing what *he* wants to do, which is what he's always done, treating you like an afterthought."

She flinches, and I know my words have hit home.

"His mom is dying," she says quietly. "He's shocked and grieving."

I shake my head, frustrated. "His personal tragedy isn't an excuse. You're not a secondary character in his life, existing to support his journey."

"That's not what's hap—"

"That's *exactly* what's happening," I say, my pace picking up along with my anger. "He makes you believe he's going to ride off into the sunset with you when he's just planning to ride off on his own again, leaving you behind. This is why I told you not to get involved with him! It's why I told him to break up with you the first time."

"You what?"

Hannah stops in the middle of the path, and it's only when I notice her expression—eyes wide, jaw dropped—that I realize what I accidentally admitted.

Fuck.

Forty-Two

HANNAH

THE GROUND BENEATH ME SEEMS TO TILT, THROWING ME off-balance.

"What did you say?" I whisper.

Libby folds her arms. "Josh was stringing you along after he left—you were miserable! And I knew *you* would never end things."

I'm struggling to process her words. *It's why I told him to break up with you the first time.* Maybe I should have guessed—Libby has never hidden her dislike for Josh—but she was the one person I thought was on my side back then.

"You *told* him to break up with me?" I ask.

"No—I mean, not at first," Libby says, a defensive set to her chin. "I was worried about you. And pissed at him for being such a shitty boyfriend. I called to talk some sense into him, get him to start calling you regularly, text you, send emails—anything! But then he said that he was going to extend his study abroad for another semester. And at that point, I—well. I told him he needed to end it with you."

"And he just . . . agreed?" I say, disbelief lacing my voice. I can't imagine Josh going along with it that easily. He may have been a little self-absorbed back then, but he's never been cruel.

Libby shifts her weight in her sneakers, clearly uncomfortable. "Well, no. He didn't want to. But god, Hannah, he was treating you so badly. I told him how miserable you were, and that the kindest thing would be to let you move on. I told him to"—she hesitates briefly—"make sure you understood it was over."

Another wave of disbelief rolls through me. Of course. All those years I spent believing that Josh had fallen for another girl—he denied it on the Ferris wheel but never explained why he'd said it.

"*You* told him to say that he'd met someone else," I whisper.

Libby looks at me, and for the first time since we started this conversation, I see an apology in her eyes. "I thought that would make it easier for you."

She reaches for my arm, like she wants to soften the blow, but I yank it away.

"Easier?" I spit out. "Do you have any idea how that felt? It wrecked me. I can't believe . . ."

My knees wobble; I stumble to a nearby bench and collapse, my head in my hands. A high-pitched ringing fills my ears. I'm vaguely aware that my sister is nearby, that she's saying something, but I can't grasp it.

My mind slowly focuses on her voice, and her words sharpen like glass.

". . . if things with Josh were going to end anyway, it's better to know now, isn't it? And on the bright side, we should be able to get the rest of your dates taken care of before the end of the challenge."

I lift my head and lock eyes with her. My shock morphs into something else, something hot and red and angry.

"Were you not listening to me at all?" I say, clenching my fists. "I get it: you hate Josh. But *I* love him, and I came to you because I'm terrified I'm going to lose him again. And losing *him* feels like losing *myself*. But you're happy about this?"

Libby takes a step back, her eyes wide. "Hannah, no. I care about you—"

"Do you?" I say. "Or do you just want to make sure I need you? Some kind of twisted emotional Munchausen by proxy?"

Not long ago, I looked Josh in the eye and told him that I'd never leave my sister. Right now, I want to move to the opposite side of the earth from her.

"I don't want to work with you anymore," I tell her, the words spilling out of me. Words that have been building up all summer. Maybe for years. "I'm sick of running *everything* the way you want to."

Libby's eyebrows shoot up. "What? We're a partnership—"

"A partnership with roles *you* decided. I'm so sick of dealing with all the financial stuff—"

"But you're good at—"

"Did you ever think that maybe I wanted a chance to come up with the ideas for our campaigns? To be creative? To talk with our clients—"

"You *never* want to talk with our clients," Libby cuts in. "You always expect me to take the lead—"

"You *like* taking the lead. You *like* being in charge. You don't want me to be my own person—"

"Oh, you want to talk about being your own person?" Libby's eyes are blazing. "Do you remember how you latched on to me after Mom and Dad divorced? My little shadow, following me everywhere, even when I was with my friends—"

"I was seven years old!" In an instant, I've ricocheted back to that childhood version of myself. I thought Libby liked having me around. I thought I was lucky to have a sister who not only tolerated but welcomed me.

Libby tosses her hair, her frustration growing. "It lasted until you were thirteen—until you met Josh and latched on to *him*. And then it was like I didn't even exist anymore! It was all Josh, all the time—"

My jaw drops. "You were jealous?"

"I was *worried*," Libby says. "You hardly had any other friends! Then he left, and you latched back on to me, and once again I had to let go of all *my* friends to take care of you—"

"I didn't ask you to do that," I say, defensiveness rising in my chest. "I never asked you to sacrifice your social life for me."

"Right. Like I was going to leave you alone every night—"

"Maybe you should have, if I was such a burden," I mutter.

"So you could watch creepy crime documentaries and hide from the world?" Libby throws her hands in the air. "Then Josh comes back and you latch on to him again. And now—surprise, surprise—it isn't working out. So you need me to swoop in and take care of you—"

"I don't want you to take care of me," I say, my voice sharp.

Libby scoffs. "What do you want me to do? Walk away like our parents did? Like Josh did? Maybe you should be grateful for the *one person* who has always stayed."

Her words feel like a slap. This conversation is spiraling out of control, and part of me wants to stop, to apologize, but another part is glad it's all coming out, all these words we've kept inside for years, flying through the air like arrows.

When I speak again, my voice is rough. "Well. I don't need you anymore."

Even as the words leave my mouth, I want to reach out and snatch them back. Because I do need her, of course I do, though part of me wishes I didn't. I'm twenty-seven years old. Shouldn't I be able to stand on my own two feet?

Libby presses her lips together, her eyes shining with tears. "You came running to *me* today."

"Because I wanted you to *listen*," I say, my voice cracking. "I'm breaking inside, and I thought my big sister would care."

"I do—"

"Whenever you do something bossy or overbearing," I say, needing to get these words out, "I always tell myself that you want the best for me. That you're trying to protect me. But maybe that's not true. Maybe it's never been true."

My sister's eyes widen; her cheeks flush, freckles standing out in angry splotches. A tiny voice whispers that I'm going too far, that I should stop before I say something I'll regret, but then I remember all the times I bit my tongue and let Libby take charge.

I square my shoulders and the words come roaring out: "You've kept me dependent on you because it makes *you* feel better about yourself. You *need* me to need you. Well, guess what? I'm done with that. I'm done with everything."

And I turn and run, knowing my sister can't catch me.

Forty-Three

LIBBY

I COULDN'T CATCH HANNAH IF I TRIED. AND IT'S CLEAR SHE doesn't want me to. That's what hurts the most.

My vision blurs with tears and I slump onto the bench, trying to make sense of all the words my sister just threw in my face.

How can she think I want anything but the best for her? I've been the opposite of selfish—literally everything I've done in the last five years has been for her. I used to have friends, I used to have a social life—I used to be in three book clubs! I had a standing brunch every Sunday with a group of girl-friends! I went to happy hours at least three days a week! I used to have a life.

And I'm not sorry for how I handled things with Josh. It was one of the hardest things I've ever done, but it was the right thing to do. If I hadn't, Hannah would have continued to let life pass her by, waiting for Josh to come back.

Now, five years later, history is repeating itself. But this time, I'm not going to be there to pick up the pieces of her broken heart. Not that she wants me to.

Two women walk by, laughing and talking as if their world is just full of sunshine and roses. They look alike, and I wonder if they're sisters; if they're both as happy as they seem, or if one of them is harboring hidden secrets and hurt.

My stomach twists at the fresh memory of Hannah's face, the devastation in her eyes, the pain and shock followed by pure rage.

Hannah has always been the one easy relationship in my life, the one person I didn't have to try with. But who knows how long she's been keeping her real feelings about our roles from me. Resenting me for being myself, for fulfilling my side of our partnership, when I had no idea she wanted anything to be different.

She doesn't want to work with me anymore.

The thought makes my head spin—she can't really mean that. She can't walk away from our business, from the plan we've had since we were little girls, imagining the day that we would take over GiGi's empire. It was our dream.

At least, it was my dream.

I realize now, too little, too late, that I never asked Hannah if it was *her* dream.

Frustrated, I stand up and start walking, directionless, kind of like my life.

AN HOUR LATER, I'm still wandering in circles around the park. I'm tired of being alone in my head; I wish there was someone, anyone, to talk to.

When I reach for my phone, it sinks in, just how small my life has become. This isn't something I feel comfortable talking to Suji about, and I haven't kept up with any other friends.

I have my sister and I have the Freedman Group. There's no one and nothing else.

Out of habit or desperation, I swipe over to the One+One app, but I can't talk to Adam anymore, either. Not as myself or as HannahF.

I flip back to the last text he sent, when he said he'd like to get to know the real me. But if he saw the real me, the way I acted today, he'd want nothing to do with me. And I wouldn't blame him.

My chest aches. There's no reason to keep this stupid app if I'm not helping my sister anymore. If I'm not using it to talk to Adam.

Before I can change my mind, I delete One+One from my phone, taking hours and hours of conversations with Adam about everything and nothing with it. Gone. Over.

I swipe over to the Uber app to call a ride home, but when I see Maggie Daley Park on the map, I stop.

Just because Hannah's giving up doesn't mean I should. I have the training schedule; I know what I need to do to stay on track. She probably expects me to quit without her nudging me.

There's a fire in my belly, and I get the tingling sensation that comes before a good idea. I'm going to dominate the Down & Dirty. I'm not doing it for Hannah. I'm not doing it for our business. I'm doing it for me.

Before I lose my nerve, I stand up, brush the dirt off my leggings, and walk back to Maggie Daley Park. I'm going to get my fat ass in a harness and climb that damn wall.

CRUSH YOUR COMFORT ZONE

WEEK 11

As you look back over the past eleven weeks, you should be realizing that you can't remain in your comfort zone and grow.

So what are you going to choose: comfort or growth?

Hannah, 8/14

I don't know, I don't know. Everything hurts right now and all I want is to feel better. Josh is gone and Libby isn't talking to me and I think it's my fault. I'm the one who brought up the issues that led to all of this.

I forced the discussion with Josh about our future; I could have stayed quiet and trusted that things would work out. Maybe I should have, because I don't know if he'll ever come back to me and it feels like a part of me has been ripped away and it all hurts so much I can't breathe.

And with Libby? Maybe I should have stayed quiet with her, too. Yes, I'm so angry at what she did and at the time it sure seemed like a good idea to tell her that. But I accidentally let WAY too much boil over. Now I don't have anyone and as much as I try to pretend that I don't like people, that's a big fat lie because I love two specific people with all my heart.

CRUSH YOUR COMFORT ZONE

THE ULTIMATE CHALLENGE COMPANION JOURNAL

Libby, August 14

Hi, Lou,

Honestly, I don't think I have much of a choice. My comfort zone has been crushed. Shattered is more like it.

I never realized how much my life revolves around being Hannah's big sister. Without that, I don't know who I am. Even the things that used to bring me comfort don't.

There is no comfort anymore. Is this what growth is supposed to feel like? Is that why they call it growing pains?

Whatever it is, I don't like it.

Forty-Four

HANNAH

I'M IN LIMBO—AND NOT THE PARTY GAME WHERE YOU BEND backward under a stick, though I do feel like I'm being forced closer and closer to the ground. I mean the space between two worlds, not fully part of one or the other. Or maybe that's purgatory; I'm hazy on Catholic theology, for obvious reasons.

Either way, this is the first time in my life that I've felt so untethered and alone.

Josh left for his research excursion; he sent a text letting me know he won't have consistent cell service, so I doubt I'll hear from him. It's all too similar to when he left for Australia; his absence is like a black hole, sucking me down. But I'm fighting it. I'm taking my medication and doing my journaling, trying to treat this like a relapse of any chronic disease, one I know how to manage.

But that doesn't change the fact that I'm so, so lonely.

I miss my sister at a cellular level. Like my physiology isn't working properly without her. We've fought before, of course—we're sisters; squabbling and bickering is our native tongue—but this is different. We're drifting past each other in our apartment like ghosts. This fight has weight, and it's smothering me.

I keep ruminating on everything she said—wondering how much of it was anger and how much she truly meant.

Yes, she saved me after Josh left in college, but I would've done the same for her in a heartbeat—she's just never given me the opportunity. She's always been so strong, almost annoyingly so, but maybe she felt like she had no other option. No one that *she* could lean on.

I hate that she let go of her social life for me—not that I asked her to—but I'm also embarrassed to admit that I hardly noticed it happening. She used to have so many friends I couldn't keep them all straight.

I guess I liked having her all to myself, which sounds so self-absorbed and needy. But she's right about how I latched on to Josh, then her, then back to Josh. Like I'm not made of substantial enough stuff to stay upright without some outside support.

I don't think she has any idea how much I idolized her as a child. How much I *still* do. She'll never understand what it's like to be the little sister, always in her shadow, watching her every move.

I want to tell her all of this—to walk across the hall, sit on her bed, and apologize in the hopes that everything will go back to the way it was—but something stops me. Because I'm not the only one at fault here. If Libby refuses to admit that what she did was wrong, that interfering in my relationship with Josh was inappropriate and cruel, then we can't move forward.

So instead, I'm avoiding her. I've heard her muffled voice through the walls as she talks with various friends about meeting for brunch at McGee's, drinks at Benchmark, and dinner at Topo Gigio. I assume she's starting to regain the social life she sacrificed.

Good for her.

My plan is to spend the weekend either out running or holed up in my bedroom, reading the manuscript for Serena and Preeti's book and working on the PR plan. I'm glad I never told Libby about the project. It seems only fair; she kept a much bigger secret from me for five whole years.

ON SATURDAY, I wake up and go for a long run, then take the hottest shower I can stand, trying not to think about Josh. Unfortunately, I end up crying, holding my hands over my mouth to muffle my sobs.

By the time I come out of the bathroom, Libby has left the apartment without a word or even a note. It feels like a deliberate jab; she knows how I feel about safety, that someone should always know where you are and when you expect to be home.

But I'm determined to stay busy, so I pull out my laptop and sit on my bed and work. At first, it's strange not having anyone to bounce ideas off, but pretty soon I settle into a groove. My creativity is expanding like a hot-air balloon, rising higher and higher.

When I glance at my calendar for the upcoming week, I realize that Lou is due for another check-in. Uh-oh. My earlier idea—to convince her that I've completed the spirit of the challenge—isn't likely to work anymore since I have no idea what is going to happen with Josh.

But I'll need to tell Lou *something*, and I haven't been on a date in weeks. So after I eat lunch, I download the One+One app and sign in. While I swipe, I turn on a documentary about a serial killer who used Tinder to find his victims; probably not the best choice, given my current situation, but it's always good to be prepared for the worst-case scenario.

When my phone dings with an alert, I jump. But it's not from One+One—it's a DM on Instagram from a handle I've never seen before: @FromJoshToHannah.

Confused, I open the message.

I know we were going to give ourselves a chance to think, but I want to share what I'm doing here, so I created this account.

Internet will be spotty out on the water, so I'll upload pictures and videos when I can. I'm not sure when you'll see them, or if any of them will even come through. I hope they do.

No matter what happens between us, Hannah, I want you to know that you're important to me. And that will never change.

I click over to the feed. Josh has posted pictures of the ship he'll be embarking on, with a caption describing how they get the vessel ready and load the scientific instruments. In every picture, he looks relaxed, totally in his element. I'm happy for him—but it's such a contrast to the loneliness I'm drowning in. He's living his best life, and I'm missing him so much I can't take a full breath.

I appreciate his attempt at communication; this didn't happen when he went to Australia. But as I click through the pictures again (Josh smiling at the port, Josh smiling on the ship's deck, Josh smiling next to a fancy microscope), I wonder what, exactly, he's trying to tell me.

Confused and heartsick, I close out of the post.

TO MY RELIEF, when I wake up the next morning, I see that Libby came home—her keys are hanging on the hook—but her bedroom door is closed. The sight makes my throat clench. I hate this. I hate the tension. I had stress dreams all last night, and I'm desperate to put this fight behind us.

So even though she hasn't apologized, I decide to bring back her favorite sugar-free vanilla latte after my run. It's a splurge—we should be making coffee at home—but it's an olive branch, an excuse to start a conversation.

When I return, her room is empty aside from her cat, who's curled up on her pillow, smirking at me. A pit of dread forms in my stomach. She just needs space, I tell myself.

But she's had three days of space now. There's no sign of this ending. And the longer it goes, the lonelier I feel.

It hits me all over again, how lucky I was to have her by my side after Josh dumped me back in college. But then again, Libby was partially to blame for that.

A surge of righteous indignation rises inside me, and I choke down the latte out of pure spite. Then I spend the day working on Serena and Preeti's PR plan and swiping through One+One on my breaks. Every time I consider swiping right, though, my chest tightens. It's more than the anxiety of meeting someone new; I'm too stuck on Josh, checking his Instagram constantly, disappointed when there isn't an update.

Finally, as I'm drifting off to sleep, my phone chimes: @FromJoshToHannah has a new post. This time he's shared underwater pictures of the reef, a selfie in his wet suit and scuba gear, and a video of a dozen teenagers saying "Hi, Hannah," with varying degrees of enthusiasm.

After that, I read the caption:

Today was a good day. These kids are freaking smart, Han, and so excited to learn. They're exhausting, too, and they use slang that makes me feel like I'm about fifty-three years old. But overall it's been awesome.

Oh, and here's something cool—two members of our crew brought their significant others along. Sanchez brought his girlfriend; she's a novelist and she uses these excursions to write. And Louisa brought her wife; she comes every year to get a break from the kids. This would be unheard-of on an academic research vessel, but the aquarium allows every excursion up to three "stowaways." They have to pay for their food and lodging, and they have to pitch in with the chores as part of the crew, but it's been fun having them around.

All this to say that I keep wishing you were here.

The screen blurs as my eyes fill with tears. I wish I was there, too, but that's the problem: it doesn't matter how much we wish for something if it just won't work.

I think back to our conversation about *Sliding Doors*, the idea that we were destined to end up together no matter what. What if it's the opposite? What if we're meant to go our separate ways, and this is just the universe setting things in order? Like Libby says about second-chance romances: the issue that drove Josh and me apart the first time hasn't magically resolved.

I can't explain all this, so I write a quick comment (Looks beautiful! Thanks for sharing), and turn off my phone.

The crocheted meerkat Josh gave me is sitting on my nightstand, and I grab it and hold it close to my chest, like I'm a child with a security blanket. Like if I'm holding on to this, I can somehow hold on to him.

Forty-Five

LIBBY

THIS WHOLE SUMMER, I'VE BEEN GIVING HANNAH CREDIT for all the progress I've made. Sure, we've both done the work, but she was the one who got me out there, who motivated me and kept me going. I honestly didn't think I could do it without her.

But I have. Every single day this week.

While I don't think I'll ever be the kind of person who finds working out "fun," I do love the thrill of doing something I wasn't able to do before. Take the jungle gym at the playground by our house. I can deadhang for almost two minutes now—a far cry from the three seconds I started out at. And even though I hate doing the steps by the river, I did them after work yesterday, not complaining once.

Of course, I didn't have anyone to complain to . . .

Not talking to Hannah this week has made me realize that maybe we don't need each other as much as I thought we did. But I do miss her.

I look up to see my sister on her side of the office we share.

She's hard at work—on what, I have no idea. The only active project we have at the moment is a press release for MySole.

Hannah smiles, and I'm both relieved to see her happy and instantly curious. I consider emailing or texting to ask what's going on, since it wouldn't *technically* be talking, but I don't want to be the one to break this silent treatment first. Plus, she might take my innocent curiosity as a ploy to swoop in and control her like an evil stepsister, minus the step part.

"Sisters!" Great Scott says. We both look up as he strikes a pose in our doorway. "What time do you want Hot Noah from MySole to come in tomorrow?"

"Did you look at our calendars?" I ask.

"Did I look at your calendars," Scott says with his typical flair. "Of course I did—but Hannah is only open from two to three, and you're booked from two to four."

I open my calendar. Suji and I are supposed to grab coffee with two friends of hers from grad school who are thinking about opening their own public relations firm. It's a meeting I could easily shift, but I'm not going to surrender so easily. Not without finding out what has Hannah's schedule so packed.

"Why don't you ask my sister to move her meeting?" I say, trying to ignore the look of indignation on Hannah's face.

"Ask *my* sister to change *her* meeting," Hannah says. "Her schedule isn't the only one that matters around here."

"Actually, Scott, it would be great if you could tell my sister—"

"Enough!" Scott yells, clearly exasperated. "My skin can't take this toxic work environment. If you bitches make me break out, I will never forgive you. I don't know what happened, but whatever it is, you need to talk about it like adults instead of acting like two ten-year-old girls fighting over a My Little Pony. Grow the hell up!"

With that, he turns and walks out of the office, leaving Hannah and me speechless. I'm about to say something about Scott having his panties in a bunch, but then I remember we're not talking. The crack in my heart deepens. I hate being mad at my sister even more than I hate her being mad at me.

I'm about to surrender victory and break the silence when Hannah's phone buzzes. She looks down and smiles again. This time, her happiness seems like a personal attack.

I look back at the browser window on my computer with the event-planning certification program Suji sent me. During our coffee break yesterday, I told her about some of the epic theme parties I used to throw.

"That's what you should be doing," she said when I finished. "Whenever you talk about planning events, your whole face lights up. I've never seen you get that excited about a press release."

It's true; I love creating experiences and moments that bring people together, but I never considered doing it professionally. I was born to be in PR. At least that's what I always believed.

I click through the sign-up button, surprised to see that the six-week certification course is only two hundred dollars. Not a bad investment—and if by some miracle we end up saving the business, it could open a whole new revenue stream.

If this was last week, I'd ask Hannah to do a cost-risk analysis, but in this new sisterless world, I'm going to have to get comfortable taking risks on my own.

"Ahem."

Scott is back. Hannah and I both snap, "What?!" in disgruntled harmony.

"You have a visitor," he says, and in walks Lou.

Hannah's face crumples, and I gulp. Lou's wearing her signature pink, but instead of her usual smile, there's a frown on her face, as if she can read the tension in the room.

"Ladies," Lou says, her voice tinged with disappointment and concern. She doesn't bother looking back at Scott as she says, "Give us a minute."

My stomach sinks as Lou closes the door. I feel like I just got called into the principal's office.

"I know we're not supposed to meet until Thursday, but I was in the neighborhood and thought I'd drop in to see how y'all were doing." Lou pauses, and her silence carries the weight of disapproval.

I feel Hannah's eyes on me, but I can't bring myself to look at her. Instead, I stay laser focused on Lou, giving her a smile I hope doesn't appear as false as it is.

"It's so good to see you," I say.

"Yes, so good," Hannah echoes.

"Everything is going great," I say, wondering if I should be giving Hannah the opportunity to take the lead here. "We've been busy, but we—"

"Cut the crap," Lou says. "Be real with me here."

Lou looks from Hannah to me and back again, but my sister and I stay quiet. As much as I want to tell Lou everything, I remind myself that she is not the imaginary friend I've been writing to in my journal—she's the leader of a massive self-help empire who has the power to save or shutter our business.

"I'm not leaving until someone tells me what's really going on," Lou says. "I've got all day."

Hannah's biting her cuticles, and I'm torn between wanting to shake my sister and give her a hug.

"I know this is uncomfortable," Lou says, "but if you've learned anything in the last few months, it's that you need to lean into the discomfort."

She's right about that—this whole summer has been nothing but putting myself in uncomfortable situations, both physically and emotionally.

"Libby," Lou says, looking at me. I bite my lip to keep my mouth shut. "Hannah."

My sister's eyes dart between me and Lou. If she's trying to tell me something, I can't understand what. But it looks like she's about to break. *Dammit.* I know it's proving everything she said right, but there's too much on the line. I need to control this narrative.

"Fine," I say. "I'll tell you."

Hannah exhales in relief, and I feel like a good big sister again.

"Hannah and I had an argument the other day," I admit. "We've been keeping secrets from each other, and it seems we both want different things."

"Secrets?" Hannah says, whirling around to glare at me. "There's a difference between me not communicating about how I'm feeling stifled at work, and *you* manipulating my relationship and getting my boyfriend to dump me! If *you* can't see the difference, then there's nothing else to talk about, Libby."

She's fuming as she folds her arms, but I catch tears in her eyes.

"When did this happen?" Lou asks Hannah.

"Five years ago," Hannah says, her voice wobbling. "But I just found out last week."

Lou looks at me, her expression more curious than judgmental. "Why did you tell Hannah's boyfriend to break up with her?"

"Because—" I sputter. "Because I didn't want that asshole to hurt her anymore."

Lou turns to Hannah. "And, Hannah, why didn't you tell Libby your feelings about work?"

Hannah swallows, then whispers, "Because she loves this company and I didn't want to hurt her."

"Ah, so you tried to keep each other's comfort zones comfortable, not wanting the other to be hurt," Lou says, nodding. "But tell me, my sweet girls. What ended up happening?"

Hannah and I are silent, but we both know what she's getting at: we hurt each other anyway.

"When I walked into this office three months ago, do you know what I saw?" Lou says. "I saw two sisters so in tune with each other it was like they were two halves of the same whole. I was a little worried, to be honest. It's not a healthy way to live, and it's not an effective way to run a business. But do you know what I see today?"

She pauses. I want to reach out and link my pinky finger with Hannah's, but I'm not sure how that would be received.

"I see two women who are blossoming as individuals for the first time," Lou says approvingly. "And I see two sisters who are trying to love each other the best way they know how."

My eyes fill with tears, and I glance over at Hannah. I hope she knows that even if it was misguided, I did it because I love her. Because watching her suffer is worse than any other pain I can imagine.

And it hits me—that this is exactly where I went wrong. I care so much about my sister that I was willing to risk anything to keep her from being hurt. Willing to go behind her back. To undermine her autonomy. To lie to her, for years.

I risked our relationship, in the name of protecting her.

"In my experience," Lou goes on, "this is a journey we all have to go on in our lives, as we grow out of the roles we've always played and come into our own. But I have to admit, I'm worried. Can you finish these challenges in the right spirit?"

I take a deep breath, determined to stay strong, to be brave. "I don't want you to worry, Lou. We're committed to seeing this challenge through. The last thing we want to do is disappoint anyone. Not you, and not . . ."

My eyes well with tears. I can't bring myself to say my grandmother's name. I think back to all our post-therapy Italian dinners, how I promised I'd protect Hannah and be a good example for her.

"Your grandmother?" Lou says.

I look down, unable to meet Lou's eyes. Next to me, Hannah sniffles.

"I don't know if anything I can say will help," Lou says, her voice gentler, "but I'd like to share some words with you both. Words that have been like a North Star since I was young."

She reaches into her bag to pull out a tattered envelope.

"I haven't told you much about myself," she says.

This gets my attention. The haziness of Lou's past is part of her mystique. It's like she didn't exist until she came bursting on the scene with her TED talk.

"You know that Lou is short for Louise," she says.

"Not Loser," Hannah says, and I fight a smile.

"But you may not know my last name is Horwitz."

Goose bumps run up and down my arms. It's a last name

I'm very familiar with—a name that has always been linked to our grandmother's earliest success.

"As in Horwitz Hotels?" I ask.

Lou nods. "My father was Abe Horwitz, one of the Freedman Group's first clients. As a little girl, I was in awe of your grandmother. I wanted to grow up to be just like her."

My eyes sting with fresh tears as I nod, missing GiGi fiercely.

"She gave me this card for my bat mitzvah," Lou says, setting it on my desk. "Her words were a gift to me then, and I hope they can be a gift to you both now."

And with that, she walks out of the room, leaving my sister and me speechless.

Forty-Six

HANNAH

LIBBY THRUSTS THE ENVELOPE TOWARD ME. "YOU OPEN IT."

Hands shaking, I do. Inside is a greeting card, yellowed and softened with age. *Mazel Tov on Your Bat Mitzvah*, it reads on the front.

Intrigued, I open the card. And when I see what's inside, my eyes flood with tears.

"What is it?" Libby says.

Wordlessly, I show her.

"GiGi's handwriting," she whispers.

My mind fills with an image of a twelve-year-old Lou in a fancy pink dress at her bat mitzvah party, and a younger version of GiGi there to support her.

Together, Libby and I read the words written more than forty years ago.

Dear LuLu,

Mazel Tov on your special day! You have a bright future ahead of you. As you follow your path toward woman—

hood, you will see many footsteps from those who have gone before you. I encourage you to use those footsteps as a guide, but I also want to caution you not to follow them too closely.

As the great writer Joseph Campbell said, "If you can see your path laid out in front of you step by step, you know it's not your path. Your own path you make with every step you take."

Someday, you will come to a point where there are no footsteps ahead of you, and you may find yourself faltering. But in that moment, you will know that you are truly creating your own destiny.

Remember that the best legacy is a life well lived, a path well chosen.

With love,
Ruth Freedman

"I miss her so much," Libby whispers.

I nod, silently agreeing. I miss her wisdom, her grace, her total lack of tolerance for bullshit. GiGi forged her own path, proving the naysayers wrong, creating a thriving business at a time when women weren't thought of as leaders.

The words on this card weren't written for us, but they feel like ours all the same.

"Maybe we've been too focused on continuing GiGi's legacy," I say quietly.

Libby's eyebrows shoot up. "What do you mean?"

"Maybe we need to find our own paths"—I point to the card—"instead of following hers."

"But GiGi made a real difference in this world, and she entrusted her company to us. I hate the thought of letting it fall apart because we don't have what it takes."

I hate that, too. And yet, something else is forming in my mind, shifting from thoughts into words.

"I don't think GiGi would've wanted her gift to be a burden," I say. "Maybe her legacy isn't the company—maybe it's everything she taught us. About working hard, taking risks, being compassionate. Maybe . . ." I pause. "Maybe her legacy is us."

Libby nods, and as we sit in silence, my mind drifts to the work I've been doing for Serena and Preeti, how I've been using the skills GiGi taught me—and some I've learned on my own, too.

"Have I ever told you about the podcast *Murder on the Mind*?" I ask.

"Maybe? I'm sorry, sometimes I—"

"Tune it out, I know," I say, lightening my voice so she knows I'm teasing. "The hosts of the podcast have a book coming out, and I pitched myself to them."

Libby's eyes widen. "Wow. That's—"

"Not how we work, I know, but—"

"I was going to say impressive," Libby says, giving a small smile. "Tell me about it."

Relieved, I pull over my laptop to show her what I've been working on.

"It's really good," Libby says when I finish. "I just wish you would have included me. And I wish you would've told me everything you've been feeling about work."

The hurt in her voice pricks at my heart. "I should have," I say. "Instead I let all my frustrations bubble out at the worst moment, and I'm sorry. I do love working with you. But sometimes, you can be a little . . ."

"Bossy? Overbearing?" she says, wincing.

"I was going to say assertive. But here's the thing: I let you take on that role. I let you take care of me, ever since we were little. That wasn't fair to you."

My sister waves her hand, like that's not a big deal. "But I'm *supposed* to take care of you. If I don't . . ."

Libby hesitates, and I expect her to say, *If I don't, then who will?* Instead, she says, "Then who am I?"

My heart constricts. Until this moment, I don't think I fully understood how deeply she feels this responsibility. The pressure to look out for me, even now. I've taken it for granted that she'll always be there.

"Maybe," I say slowly, "instead of being big sister and little sister, we can just be . . . sisters."

It's a subtle change, but Libby seems to understand what I mean, because she gives a tentative smile. "It might take me a while to unlearn some habits—"

"Same."

"But I like the idea."

Silence descends between us again. We're both treading carefully, navigating through years spent in our comfortable roles as sisters and business partners.

I take a deep breath, then bring up the elephant in the room: "What does all this mean for the Freedman Group?"

"Well, I've been thinking," Libby says, staring up at the ceiling. "We've been working so hard to keep it running that we haven't actually discussed if we *should*."

I sit bolt upright. This is the last thing I expected Libby to say. "Wait—what?"

She shrugs. "I never gave myself the chance to consider any other career. And don't get me wrong, I've loved so much of this job, but lately, I've wondered if I started working here because it was expected. And because it was scary to decide what *I* wanted to do. I could just follow in GiGi's footsteps."

I had no idea my sister felt this way, too. She's always seemed like she knew exactly where she was going in life.

"Maybe we should consider a different direction," I say, motioning to the card from GiGi to Lou. "We can create a new path together."

Libby faces me, her eyes solemn. "Or maybe separately."

A rush of fear steals my breath away. Yes, I want more freedom to explore my creative side, to step out of my narrow role in our partnership. But doing it *all* on my own? That's terrifying.

"What Lou said about the roles we've been playing as sisters," Libby continues. "I worry that if we keep working together, we'll continue to fall back into them."

I nod carefully, thinking about how easy it is for me to let my sister take the lead, to lean on her, to stay quiet and not speak up.

"I don't know," I say. "That's a huge decision."

"We don't have to decide today," Libby says, "but let's start talking about options. *All* our options."

"What about our challenges?" I ask, shifting subjects. Does Libby want to abandon those, too? "I'm supposed to do six more dates."

"Do you want to go on them?" Libby asks.

"No. If Josh and I don't work out . . ." A sharp pain strikes

400

my heart. "Well. I'll figure out what to do from that point on. But right now, I don't want to date anyone else."

"Then you should stop," Libby says firmly. It's surprising to hear her say those words. My sister, who always finishes what she starts.

"What about you? We don't have to do the Down & Dirty if you're not feeling good about it."

"I want to do the race. I don't care about proving anything to Lou—but I want to prove to myself that I can finish it."

I reach over and link my pinky with hers, my heart glowing with pride. "Then I'll be right by your side."

CRUSH YOUR COMFORT ZONE

THE ULTIMATE CHALLENGE COMPANION JOURNAL

WEEK 12

As you near the end of this challenge, reflect on what you've learned. These twelve weeks are only the first step on a path of lifelong growth. Make a plan for the future. Now what?

Hannah, 8/21

I have no idea. I don't know what's going to happen with Josh. I don't know what's going to happen with the Freedman Group. It feels like everything is burning down around me—like the fire that destroyed Chicago all those years ago.

GiGi had a fascination with that part of our city's history. Not the fire itself, but the lesson it represented in rebuilding after a setback. Coming back stronger and better than before. But how do I do that if I can't even see a way forward? If I have no path to follow, no blueprints?

And I know, I know, I KNOW: that's the point. Growth is scary. Change is uncomfortable. I guess I'm just going to have to trust the process.

I'm going to have to take some steps into the unknown.

CRUSH YOUR COMFORT ZONE

THE ULTIMATE CHALLENGE COMPANION JOURNAL

Libby, August 21

Hey, Lou.

I promise this isn't a cop-out, but I think I have to be comfortable with not having an exact plan. I've spent my whole life following the steps GiGi laid out for me.

She always used to say that the business would be ours one day, but the other day, I realized that's only part of what she said.

The whole quote, the words she said to Hannah and me so many times was, "If you and your sister want the business, it will all be yours one day."

My memory skipped past that crucial first part: IF we want it.

Forty-Seven

LIBBY

THE DOWN & DIRTY IS THIS WEEKEND, BUT INSTEAD OF AMP-
ing up, our training has actually slowed down. Hannah says
we've done the work, now we have to make sure our bodies
are rested and have the energy we'll need to finish the race.

Even thinking the word "race" sends my anxiety through
the roof. But I'm not going to stress about something that's
three days away. That's a Future Libby problem—as is the question about what will happen with our company. We're not
sure if Lou will want to hire us, or if there will even be an "us"
to hire. But Hannah and I have agreed to get through the
Down & Dirty together before we make any final decisions.

Current Libby picks up her phone and sends a text to
Hannah.

Libby: Want to walk home tonight?

My sister pops her head into the office we used to share.
She's moved into an empty office down the hall; we decided
that some space could be good for us both.

"You don't have to text," she says. "I'm literally three feet away."

I shrug. "I'm saving my steps for the lake path. It's a beautiful day."

Hannah smiles, and I wonder if she's thinking of the first time we walked home together, how she practically had to drag me every step. Now it's one of my favorite ways to unwind after work.

"Let's do it," she says. "Leave in five?"

Before I can answer, she's back in her office, changing into her sneakers. Things between us have gotten better since our "Come to Jesus" chat with Lou. (Or whatever the Jewish version of that would be. Come to Moses?)

We may not know what will happen to the Freedman Group—and yes, that uncertainty is scary—but we know what will happen to the Freedman sisters. We'll both be okay—on our own, and together.

TWENTY MINUTES LATER, Hannah and I are walking up the ramp toward the lake path. It's still warm, but the breeze off the lake carries a slight chill. A reminder that summer is winding down, and fall is waiting in the wings.

When we reach the top of the ramp, Michigan Avenue is to our left, all bustling and metropolitan, and Lake Michigan is on our right, wild and spacious. I inhale the cool lake air, appreciating how far I've come this summer.

Those early days of training seem like another lifetime. I was so hard on my body back then, focusing only on its flaws and imperfections instead of appreciating everything it allows me to do and experience. My body is my vehicle through life, and I want to take care of it—but also enjoy it.

I still have a ways to go on the whole self-love journey—a lifetime of negative thoughts and perceptions won't go away overnight—but I'm on the right path.

And to prove how much I've grown, I walk headfirst into the next topic of conversation. Something I wasn't ready to address the other day, but I am now.

"I need to apologize," I say, "for getting overly involved in your relationship with Josh all those years ago. I had no right to butt in like that. Just because I didn't mean to hurt you doesn't excuse the fact that I did."

Hannah turns and looks at me like she's seeing me for the first time. And maybe she is—this new and improved sister who understands and respects boundaries.

"I appreciate that," she says after a beat. "But I do believe that Josh and I needed to end—back then, I mean."

"Yeah?" My eyebrows arch in surprise.

"If we'd stayed together, we never would've had the chance to grow as individuals. Kind of like what Lou said about you and me."

"And now?" I ask gently. "Do you think you'll stay together?"

If they don't, my sister will be crushed, and that will crush me. But I'm not so sure anymore that Josh is the villain I've made him out to be for all these years. He's just a human being, like everyone else, stumbling his way through life.

"I don't know what's going to happen," Hannah says. "And I'm not sure I'm ready to talk about that with you."

Ouch. I glance away so she doesn't see how much her words sting.

"Only because I need to figure it out for myself," she says.

"But I'm so scared that if I lose him, I'll fall apart again. And I'll never be able to put myself back together."

Her voice falters on the last word, and I reach for my sister's hand, squeezing it.

"You won't break without him," I tell her. "The situation is different, and you're a different person now. Yes, you had a hard time back in college, but look at you now—Josh has been gone for weeks, and you haven't fallen apart once!"

Hannah scoffs. "You haven't heard me crying in the shower?"

"Feeling your feelings isn't the same as falling apart," I say—which sounds like it could be a Lou-ism.

"I've definitely been feeling them," she says, sighing. "Speaking of guys," Hannah says, "have you heard from Adam lately?"

"That would be a big, fat no."

Hannah hesitates, but then her words come tumbling out. "I know we literally just talked about boundaries, but after all the buttinskying you've done to my relationship, I feel like I deserve a turn. And I think you should give Adam another chance."

"No way," I cut in. "It's over."

"Libby," Hannah groans. "He really liked you."

"Liked," I say. "As in past tense."

"Feelings that deep don't just change after one little miscommunication."

"One big lie, you mean."

Hannah shrugs. "I wish you could—"

"Before you say you wish I could see myself the way you do, let me stop you. This has nothing to do with whether or not I think I deserve someone as wonderful as Adam. It has to do with the fact that I broke his trust. And you can't build a relationship if you don't have the foundation of trust."

"I was just going to say that I wish you could talk to him and explain where you were coming from. Have coffee or something."

I wish it were that easy.

Hannah bumps my shoulder with hers as we keep walking, our pace picking up naturally. It feels good to be out here with all the other active people and not feel like an outsider.

"Want to run for ninety?" I ask, figuring we can push ourselves a tiny bit without risking our rested body state.

Hannah grins. "I thought you'd never ask."

Forty-Eight

HANNAH

THE DAY BEFORE THE DOWN & DIRTY, I SLEEP LATER THAN I have in months. Maybe years. And it is *glorious*. Waking up to full sunlight streaming in my curtains, stretching out in bed like a starfish.

But then the anxiety hits me. Not so much about the race—although I'm not looking forward to scaling the fifteen-foot Ladder of Doom, balancing on slack lines, and swinging on monkey bars over mud pits—and not even because after the event, Libby and I will decide what to do with our company.

I'm nervous about seeing Josh. Scared to face the conversation we need to have. Scared to see where we land in the fallout.

He's posted on the Instagram account he created for me nearly every day, sharing pictures and videos of the reef, his research, the kids, and his team. I appreciate that he's making an effort to stay connected despite the distance.

But the posts are a daily reminder of how passionate he is about his career, and I can't silence the nagging sense that this will always be his priority. That even if I compromise for us—which I would; that's what makes a partnership—he won't do the same for me.

It's not that I want Josh to give up his dream for me. I just wish his dream *was* me.

It's a silly, romantic wish. Not something I'd expect from myself. But I suppose, deep down inside, even a crime junkie like me wants a happy ending.

There's a new post from Josh today—which surprises me, because he's flying home. It's just a video, no caption, and he must have taken it last night and uploaded it later. He's in almost total darkness, the light from his phone casting deep shadows around his eyes and mouth.

"Hey, Banana," he says. His voice is muffled, but it's still the voice I love, dark chocolate with a hint of gravel. "We're heading home tomorrow, and I can't sleep. I keep thinking about you, about my mom, and the future and . . ."

He runs a hand over his face and my heart tugs when I see the exhaustion lining his features. I wonder if he's been drinking; Josh after a few drinks becomes silly and fun, but Josh after lot of drinks turns contemplative and maudlin.

"Sanchez smuggled on some rum he bought at port," he says, answering that question, "and we drank it after the kids went to bed and . . . it was a bad idea. Tomorrow's gonna suck."

He sounds defeated—so unlike himself—and I stiffen with worry.

"I can't figure out how to make it work between us," he continues. "I want to convince you to come with me wherever I end up, but if you do, I worry you'll end up resenting me, and if I stay in Chicago for you, then I'll resent you. I don't want to do that to each other. So, who gets priority? Me or you? My career or yours? My dreams or yours? I don't know. I don't know. I'm so fucking sorry, Hannah. But I can't see how to make this work—"

The video ends abruptly, and I'm left holding my phone in my hands, a hollow sensation spreading through my chest.

I bite my lip and let the pain wash over me. This is what I've been anticipating. But a blow still hurts even when you're expecting it.

I'm not going to break without him, I remind myself. But right now, it sure feels like it.

AN HOUR LATER, I'm finally pulling myself out of bed when a text pings on my phone.

Great Scott: So this happened

He's sent a picture of his foot, propped up on a lime-green pillow.

Hannah: What's wrong?

Great Scott: Blister

Squinting, I zoom in on the picture. I can barely make out a red spot on his big toe. I've run entire marathons with far worse injuries. Still, I try to be sympathetic.

Hannah: Ouch. Put some moleskin on it and you'll be ok.

Great Scott: No can do. Can't put any weight on it without severe pain. Probably a brewing infection, tbh.

I roll my eyes. I'm about to type a less-than-sympathetic reply when Libby bursts into my bedroom, phone in hand, hair sticking up all over like a bird's nest.

"Did you see this? Freaking Great Scott." She groans and flops down on my bed. "At the literal last minute, too!"

"We'll figure it out—"

"How? We can't compete with only three people!"

It's true—the obstacles are designed for teams of four. Two pairs, to be specific.

We could back out. Relief washes over me—we could stay home tomorrow and watch movies all day. I could put off having to talk with Josh.

But then I turn my head and look at my sister, inches away on my pillow. I take in her freckles, the curl of her eyelashes, the scar on her forehead from a fall she took on her bike when she was six.

The view takes me back to all the nights I crawled into bed with her when I was scared of a spooky noise or worried about Mom and Dad fighting. Next to her, I could relax and sleep, secure in the knowledge that my sister was there.

And now she's looking to me with worry in her eyes.

"I'll find someone," I tell her.

Her eyebrows lift. "Who?"

"I'll ask my old running group, like I initially planned. Someone will be happy to join us." I try to sound more confident than I feel. "All you have to do is show up. I've got this."

Libby tenses, like she isn't sure if she can really let go, let me handle it. But then she exhales slowly, and I can feel the stress draining from her.

"Thank you," she says. "Want an omelet? I'm thinking avocado-spinach-feta."

"Sounds great," I tell her, surprised by her response. This is one of the few times in my life that I've been able to take care of her. It feels good, like the scales have shifted toward a balance.

As Libby heads to the kitchen, I pull out my phone to text my now disbanded running group. But then I pause as another idea hits me. It could be reckless—or smart. Should I do it?

The answer comes in the form of a memory. Back when Libby and I first started working for GiGi full-time, we watched in awe as she made a risky decision with a huge new client. Before we all went home that night, Libby asked her, *How do you know if something is worth taking a chance on?*

And GiGi responded: *Simple. If the potential payoff is greater than the potential loss.*

That's my answer.

I swipe to the One+One app. Time to find the fourth member of our team.

Forty-Nine

LIBBY

THE SUN ISN'T EVEN UP YET WHEN HANNAH AND I STEP OUT of our Uber at the northwest corner of Grant Park for the Down & Dirty check-in. The city skyline looms overhead, and the open field is swarming with participants, race officials, and spectators. I shiver and rub the goose bumps on my arms, realizing that we're only going to feel colder when we're covered in water and mud.

The starting line is in the distance, followed by a grassy field that leads to the first obstacle: a twelve-foot wall. Which we have to climb. Vertically.

"Isn't this amazing?" Hannah asks. I look over, shocked to see her grinning. "There's nothing like the energy before a race starts."

"Yeah," I say, my voice shaky. "Amazing."

At check-in, they give us a packet with a microchipped wristband to keep track of our time, a blue headband with our race number on it (I'm 393; Hannah is 394), and some other goodies, including a coupon for a free drink at the finish line. Which I'll definitely need.

I'm fastening the bracelet around Hannah's wrist when I see her shoulders stiffen. I look up and see the object of her desire and destruction walking toward us. Anger flares in my chest, and I have to hold myself back from screaming at Josh or clawing his eyes out. I promised Hannah I wouldn't butt in, and I'm trying *really* hard not to.

Instead, I stand a little closer to Hannah, shoulder to shoulder, and fold my arms.

"Good morning," Josh says, giving an awkward wave. "How are you?"

"Fine," Hannah whispers. Then she turns and heads in the opposite direction, toward the starting line. Josh watches her go, the saddest expression I've ever seen on his face.

It's his own damn fault. But I'm not going to waste my breath telling him that. Instead, I turn and follow my sister. We've got a race to win, or at least finish.

WE HAVE TO wait forty minutes for our heat's starting time, and the tension between Josh and Hannah still hasn't dissipated. It would bother me more if I wasn't so focused on my own raging nervousness. I don't want to make a fool of myself. Or let the team down. Or make them all do burpees. Well, I wouldn't mind making Josh do them. But not Hannah, or . . .

"You found a fourth for our team, right?" I ask my sister. I've been so distracted with everything else, I forgot to ask.

"Yeah," she says, turning to scan the crowd. "Oh—there he is."

He? I expected a woman from her running group.

I turn, and for a brief moment, I think I might be imagining things.

"Adam?" I don't say his name as much as I breathe it.

He's making his way through the throng of bodies, and when he catches my eyes, he waves.

I whirl on my sister. "You called *Adam*?"

She gives a guilty little shrug. "I figured he'd be a good addition to the team."

Of course he would. He's strong and athletic and so positive it's contagious—but she shouldn't have sprung this on me with literally no warning!

But there's no time to protest or argue; a race official has picked up a loudspeaker to call us all to attention.

Adam slides in next to me, and I sneak a glance at him. He's in a T-shirt and gym shorts, and his hair is a little wild, like he just rolled out of bed.

"I can't believe you're here," I say.

He shrugs. "I thought it sounded fun."

And that's all the conversation we have time for, because the gun fires, a cheer rises from the crowd, and the entire mass of people in our fleet starts moving forward.

"Here we go," Hannah says.

I think I'm going to throw up.

TWO OBSTACLES INTO the course, the shock has worn off and I might even be having fun. The crowd's energy is infectious, everyone cheering one another on—even people on other teams—and the participants are all sizes and ages. That's what surprises me the most; I thought I would stick out like a sore thumb, but it turns out, I blend right in.

But then it's time for the Ladder of Doom—a fifteen-foot ladder with huge spaces between the rungs, so you have to work with your team to get on, and then to get over. Josh goes first. His ridiculously long arms and legs make it easy for him to get to the top. Hannah's next, with Josh helping to pull her up as I boost her from below.

Then it's just me and Adam and a hundred other people standing there. It might take a whole gaggle of them to boost me up on the first rung, but Adam looks ready for the challenge. He squats and cradles his hands together, waiting for me to step in. God, I hope I don't break him.

"I've got you," Adam says, and I take his word for it.

One second, my foot is awkwardly in his hands, and the next I'm flying, feeling light as a feather as I reach the first rung. Somehow, I keep going, to the second and the third and on and on until I'm up at the top—reaching down with Josh to help Adam.

After that, we run to the water crossing—fifty yards of water, crossed while floating on our backs with a wire cage two feet above our noses. The water is frigid, and my teeth are chattering by the time we get halfway through. I keep waiting for the claustrophobia to set in, but with Adam next to me and Hannah behind me, we all make it without a problem.

As we run to the next obstacle, all of us dripping wet and shivering, Adam keeps pace next to me. I steal a glance as he wipes a lock of wet hair off his forehead, leaving behind a muddy handprint.

"You good?" he asks.

"I actually think I am," I tell him, even though I'm freezing and my thighs are raw from chafing together.

Adam and I are almost to the next obstacle—the spear throw—and we slow down to wait our turn. I sneak a glance behind me and see Josh and Hannah about twenty yards back in the crowd. Hannah's eyes are glassy, her skin pale, like she's barely holding herself together. Josh is about three feet behind her, looking so miserable I almost feel bad for him.

Almost.

"What's their story?" Adam asks, motioning toward them.

"That's the ex-boyfriend who came back into Hannah's life, just to ruin it again," I say, my voice bitter. "He's a huge reason I wanted to find someone better for Hannah on the app."

I stop, realizing I accidentally broached the subject that's been hanging between us all morning.

Adam winces. "Oh."

We both take a step forward as the line moves. This obstacle is a tough one, as evidenced by all the people who have failed and are now doing burpees around us. You have to throw the spear thirty yards, into one of the hay bales that are used as targets. Hannah said it was one of the most difficult challenges, requiring strength, accuracy, and coordination.

It's also the only one we haven't trained much for, given there aren't many places with targets hanging around. And I'm pretty sure it's illegal to throw a spear in the state of Illinois. We told ourselves we'd do our best but, if worst came to worst, we'd do our thirty burpees and move on.

But now that I'm in front of all these people, I wish we'd tried harder to prepare. I'm so nervous that I find myself stupidly saying to Adam, "Are you disappointed you never got to go out with Hannah after chatting with her?"

Adam blinks at me, confused. "I wasn't chatting with Hannah, though."

"Well, yeah, but you never got to meet the woman you swiped right on."

He looks genuinely surprised. "I'm not attracted to a picture, Libby. I'm attracted to a person when I feel a connection with them." Then he leans in close and says in my ear, "And if I didn't make it clear that I'm very, *very* attracted to you, then I was doing something really wrong that night in my apartment."

Heat sparks through me as I flash back. No, he couldn't fake that response. But still: it's one thing to want me in private. In public? I'm not sure about that.

"You're up," he says, clapping me on the shoulder.

I step forward, and a race official hands me a spear. It's heavier than I anticipated, smooth and cool in my hand. I heft it to my shoulder with a grunt and squint across the field to the hay bales, which look way too small.

Butterflies take flight in my stomach. Everyone around me is watching. Judging. Probably thinking that there's no way I can do this.

I'm scared. But I'm not going to let that stop me.

Gritting my teeth, I take a step forward and launch that spear with every ounce of my strength. As soon as it leaves my hand I squeeze my eyes shut; I'm afraid to look, terrified to see the spear hit the ground yards before the hay bales, like so many others.

A cheer rises, and my eyes pop open. My spear is stuck in one of the bales, the end swinging in the breeze.

A man next to me whistles. "Damn."

"Nice job," a woman says, patting me on the arm.

"Amazing!" Adam says, and I spin around to face him.

He gives me a high five, then, to my surprise, pulls me in for a hug. We're frozen in time, and I want to stay there, wrapped in his arms forever. But an official blows a whistle, and I reluctantly pull away to see him grinning down at me.

"I can't believe I did that!" I say, still shocked.

"She probably threw javelin in high school or something," someone mutters behind me.

"Or college," someone else says.

I nearly laugh out loud; these people seriously think I was an athlete?

"That was a ten out of ten," Adam says. Then he leans closer and says in my ear, "And really fucking hot."

Fifty

HANNAH

I'VE RUN SEVEN HALF-MARATHONS AND THREE FULLS IN MY life, along with countless shorter races. I've pushed myself to the limit, gone up hills and down, run through leg cramps and side aches. I know my body, and I know how to get through the toughest parts of a race.

But this has been the hardest experience of my life.

Being around Josh is acutely painful, especially after that last video. I know what's coming, and I'm sick about it.

Libby's voice echoes in my mind: *You won't break without him.* I want to believe her, I do, but every time I look at Josh, I feel like my heart is being wrenched out. I'm avoiding eye contact, avoiding physical contact except when absolutely necessary— like when we scaled the Ladder of Doom, I had to put my foot in his hands so he could boost me over, but I didn't steady myself on his shoulders. I can't handle touching him, knowing that it could be the last time.

Josh has stubbornly stuck next to me, even though I've hardly acknowledged him. Now we're at the barbed-wire crawl, where there's only three feet of space between the wire and the ground—which is more like a muddy bog after hundreds of people have crawled through. Libby and Adam are up ahead, nearly done, and Josh is just ahead of me, crawling with surprising grace.

I'm going as fast as I can, but the ground is cold and slippery, and when my hands slide out from under me, I fall flat on my stomach with a grunt. It feels very symbolic of where I am right now, emotionally—stuck in the muck, unable to move forward.

Two other participants squeeze past, barely giving me a backward glance. I can't just lie here as Josh gets farther and farther ahead, so I force myself back up to my hands and knees. Mud and crushed grass squelch between my fingers; the air smells dank and swampy. I start to crawl, but something tugs on the back of my shirt.

Shit. I'm snagged on the barbed wire. I twist around to try to pull myself loose, which sends another barb scraping down my neck.

"Ow," I hiss.

"You okay?" Josh calls from up ahead.

My face heats with frustration. "I'm fine. Keep going—I'll catch up."

I spit out a mouthful of dirt as I contemplate my options: my best bet is to wiggle backward out of my shirt and finish the rest of the race in my sports bra.

But as I start scooting backward, trying to lift my shirt over my head, something tugs my scalp, hard, like a hot poker lancing the skin.

"Dammit," I whisper as I realize what I've done. My hair is caught in a barb.

Panic ricochets through me—but then I look up and realize

that Josh is crawling back toward me. Even with his face streaked with mud, he somehow manages to look ridiculously hot. The Down & Dirty ought to use him as a model for their ads.

"Are you stuck?" he asks.

"No, just taking a rest in the middle of a freezing mud bog." I sound petty and frustrated, but my scalp hurts and my back hurts and my fingers feel like frozen fish sticks.

When Josh reaches me, he sucks air through his teeth. "Oh shit, you really are stuck. And bleeding, too. Let me see if I can get you out."

He wiggles around until he's behind me, the mud sloshing as he moves. I can't see what he's doing, but I feel a sharp tug on my scalp and yelp, "Ouch!"

"Sorry, sorry," he says. There's more tugging of the wires stuck in my scalp and shirt; I grit my teeth to keep from crying out again. "Your hair is like a rat's nest on here. I think we should ask one of the race officials to cut you out."

"No!" I shout, reaching behind me to swat at him. If we get any help at all, we fail the obstacle.

"It's just thirty burpees, Han. I'll do them with you."

"It's not the burpees!" I say. "I don't want to fail—"

"Most people fail at least one obstacle—"

"I don't want to lose, okay?" I shout, and my eyes fill with tears. I don't want to lose *him*.

He scoots around until he's next to me, and I wipe my eyes quickly with my hand, then look at him. My breath catches; he's so close it hurts. I can see each individual eyelash ringing his deep blue eyes. I can see dirt embedded in the creases in his forehead, water droplets caught in the dark stubble around his lips. Every tiny detail of my favorite face on the planet.

"The point isn't to win, remember?" he says gently. "The

point is to do it together, as a team. To help each other cross the finish line."

"Is it?" I say, smacking the soggy ground in frustration. "Please, explain it to me. Is that the point, Josh? To do it together?"

His eyes narrow in confusion. "Yes . . ."

"Then why won't you choose me?" The words are out before I can stop them, desperate and pleading.

"Hannah . . ."

"No, no, I get it," I say quickly. "Our lives are going in different directions. I shouldn't have said that."

Josh hesitates, his lips parting like he's wrestling with his next words. Like he doesn't want to hurt me, even though he knows he must.

I can't handle the sadness in his eyes, so I squeeze mine shut. My mind drifts back to our conversation on the Ferris wheel, when he told me what he wished he'd said the first time he left. And I remember my words back to him. *You're the most important person to me in the entire world. And I want you to be happy. Even if that means you need to leave.*

It's still true. And I can walk this path; I can go on without him. I'm not going to break.

"The whole time I was gone . . ." he says eventually. His voice is low, right next to my ear, a quiet hum that makes my heart ache with longing. "I thought about you. About us. Hannah, can you look at me?"

I shake my head, my eyes still shut. My chin wobbles and I hope he doesn't notice.

He sighs, and his breath tickles my cheek. "I've been trying to figure this out. Going around in circles, looking at it from every angle. But it's hard—I can't ask you to choose me, as much as I want to. And I can't choose you, either."

My heart stops; this is it. We're over. I swallow, trying to keep my voice from shaking. "I understand—"

"That's why I'm choosing us."

I look up sharply, but the barb tugs my hair again, making me wince. My eyes blur with tears. I blink to clear them, needing to see Josh's face. Needing to understand what he's saying.

His face comes into focus: dirt streaking his skin, hair wet with water and sweat. Lips curving in the softest, warmest smile.

"I realized," he says, "that I've been thinking of this as a choice between what's best for you and what's best for me, like we're on opposite ends of a tug-of-war. But I made that mistake before, and I refuse to do it again. I want to be on the same side. I want to choose us, over and over again, for the rest of our lives."

"But—but what does that mean for your career? For mine? Where will we end up?"

"I don't know yet. But we can figure it out together. Because this, right here"—he motions between us—"is the *most* important relationship of my life. There's nowhere I'd rather be than down in the mud with you, trying to figure out a way forward."

My eyes fill with tears again. There's nowhere else I'd rather be, either.

"I love you, Hannah Freedman," he says. "Please love me back."

A laugh bubbles out of me, incredulous joy. As if I could do anything else. "Josh. I've loved you since we were thirteen years old. You're as much a part of me as my own heart."

His face breaks into a smile and he leans in to kiss me. It starts as a chaste peck, but even that brief touch sparks a hunger inside me. My hair is still tethered to the wire, so I reach a hand up to cup his jaw, pull him closer and deeper until our tongues meet.

"You taste like dirt," I whisper.

He chuckles against my mouth. "So do you."

"And I just got mud on your face," I say, motioning. "Sorry about that."

He swipes some mud in his hand and dabs it on my nose. "There. We're even."

We stay there grinning at each other on our hands and knees until I speak.

"So . . . I'm still stuck." I motion above me, and the movement makes my scalp tug again.

"Can I try one last time?" he asks.

I nod, and he flips over so he's on his back next to me. He's patient and careful, untangling my hair strand by strand, as gently as he can.

"Most of it is out," he says after a while, "but there's some I can't get. Want me to see if the official has scissors?"

"No." I close my eyes and quickly bring my hand up to my scalp, holding my hair tight as I yank my head away from the barb. The spot on my scalp burns like a hot poker again, but I'm free.

"Badass," Josh says, sounding impressed. "Shit, that scratch on your neck is wicked. Sure you're okay?"

I turn to see the remains of my hair still left on the barb; more than I thought. "Yeah. Help me slip out of my shirt?"

He does; it's awkward, backing up in the mud as Josh lifts my shirt over my shoulders and reminds me to keep my head down so I don't get my hair stuck again, but soon I'm free, collapsing into the mud with nothing but my sports bra and shorts on.

We crawl forward under the wires until we reach the end, then stagger to our feet. My body is stiff and sore from being in one position for so long, but it feels amazing to be upright again. When I glance over at Josh, he's looking at me with a goofy grin on his face.

"What?" I say, touching my hair self-consciously. I'm sure I'm a mess.

"I just really, really love you."

I take his hand, smiling. "I love *us*."

"I love us, too. So much." He pulls me in for another quick kiss. "Ready?"

I nod, looking at the grassy stretch in front of me, the next obstacle a few hundred yards ahead. "Let's finish this."

Fifty-One

LIBBY

I HATE THIS WITH EVERY FIBER OF MY BEING.

It was stupid of me to be so cocky during the first part of the race—I may have started out strong, but I'm fading. Fast. The mud crawl was much harder than I thought it would be. It should have been easy (hell, even babies crawl!), but the mud was so slippery, and the barbed wire was *really* sharp. There's a reason they use that shit on fences to keep people out.

To add insult to injury, as soon as we made it through, we had to do the partner carry. Listening to Adam huffing and puffing away as he carried me on his back for fifty yards is no doubt going to be a future emotional wound. But we made it.

Then we did the monkey bars, followed by the sandbag carry up a steep hill, where I slipped and fell flat on my stomach and my sandbag rolled to the bottom of the hill so I had to do it all over again.

Now my muscles are heavy with exhaustion. Everything hurts and I probably look like a swamp monster, but I'm too tired to care.

Adam and I are heading toward an obstacle I've been dreading since Hannah first told me about it: the Stair Master. A giant wooden staircase with five stairs that are each three feet tall, it's even more evil than its namesake at the gym. I could have probably made it up with some help at the beginning of the race, but now? It's going to be torture.

I stop beside Adam at the base of the stairs. He doesn't look the least bit tired—in fact, he looks exhilarated. Like he's having the best day of his life.

"How are you feeling?" he asks.

"Not great," I say, channeling Great Scott.

Adam nods sympathetically. "We're getting close, though. Have you seen Hannah and Josh? We're supposed to cross the finish line as a team."

I glance behind and see them—running perfectly in sync, right next to each other. And they're smiling.

Worry flickers inside me, then fades away. I don't have the energy to be concerned. And even if I did, there's nothing I can do about it now. It'll have to be another problem for tomorrow.

I turn back to the Stair Master, staring up at it. Adam's already made it to the top, and he's bounding back down the other side. He circles back around to where I'm standing, paralyzed by fear. "Be careful up there," he says. "The mud makes it pretty slippery."

"I don't know if I can do this," I tell him.

"Of course you can," he says. "Do you want me to go again with you?"

I shake my head. "No, go ahead. I'll meet you on the other side."

He must understand that I need to do this alone, because he doesn't push me. But before he jogs off, he says, "Remember to shake the lead out."

I close my eyes and roll my shoulders, clearing the cobwebs from my mind. I shake away my doubts and fears and insecurities, until it's just me. I am David, the steps are Goliath, and if I remember the story correctly, I've got a fighting chance.

Taking a deep breath, I imagine the crisp air filling my lungs and, somehow, inflating my confidence. Trying is the hardest part, I remind myself.

Here goes everything.

I bend my knees, open my eyes, and channel all of my energy into this one moment. My feet are off the ground, the wind is blowing in my hair, the tips of my toes brush the edge of the stair and I realize too late that I didn't jump high or far enough.

I come down hard on my knees and hands, and a woman next to me gasps.

"You okay, honey?" she says.

I'm not sure I am; my hands are stinging, and when I look down at them, they're covered in scrapes and starting to bleed. "Shit," I whisper.

"Just try again," the woman says. "It's okay to fall as long as you get back up."

It's such a simple phrase, but it reminds me of something GiGi might have said, and I turn back to the stairs and take the leap. This time, I make it all the way to the top, then all the way to the bottom.

Success!

"Nice!" Hannah says, running up to me.

Josh is with her, and they're holding hands. Alarmed, I glare at Josh, but he meets my gaze straight on, confident and calm, with a hint of a challenge in his eyes. Like he's daring me to try to get between him and Hannah.

I blink, startled, and take a step back.

Hannah can explain it all to me later. Right now, my job—as her sister—is to trust her.

AFTER HANNAH AND Josh do the Stair Master, all we have to do is run the last half mile to the finish line. After everything we've done, it should be easy. But it's not.

I feel like my body is made of stone. My shoes are squishing with mud, and I can feel a blister forming on the bottom of my foot. My clothes are stiff with partially dried mud, and strands of frizzy hair keep flying in my face.

Luckily, everyone around me looks just as wrecked. We're all running together—Hannah and Josh ahead, still holding hands, then Adam, then me. I'm trying hard to keep up, but gravity keeps sucking me down. I want to cry, and then die, and then cry again.

Hannah glances back, her forehead furrowed with concern. "Libs? You okay?"

Adam looks back, too, and I flush with embarrassment. He said he wanted to get to know the real Libby, and he's getting an eyeful now. We're only two hundred yards from the finish, but I'm not sure I can make it even that far.

Just when it feels like my legs might collapse beneath me, Hannah drops Josh's hand and runs back to me. She scoops her arm under me so she's bearing my weight.

I try to shrug her away—I don't want her to have to carry her big sister, but she's insistent.

"Lean on me," she says. "We'll do it together."

And so we go, one painful step in front of the other, half hobbling, half jogging. Tears are running down my face and everything is so blurry that I hardly notice the finish line until we're there, crossing it.

Cameras are flashing; people are cheering. Hannah lets go of me and I'm about to stumble to the ground when I feel strong arms around me and realize it's Adam.

Before I can react, he pulls me in for a kiss. Not just any kiss—this is a *kiss*. Worthy of a full paragraph in a romance novel, passionate and soul consuming. I lose myself in the moment until I hear something around us—laughter?

Are people laughing at me? But no, I realize as Adam releases me, they're clapping and cheering. I glance over at Hannah, who's beaming at me, tears in her eyes.

Main-character energy, she mouths, and I feel it. I truly feel it.

Then she runs up and hugs me. "I'm so proud of you," she whispers. "I'm so proud of us."

"Me, too," I say, squeezing her back. For more reasons than just finishing this race.

We've accomplished so much this summer—although not what we expected when we started out. Our business may never make a comeback, but we have, growing as individuals and as sisters. We may not be able to see the path ahead, but like GiGi said, that just means we're forging our own. Creating our own legacy, step by step.

Just like she did.

One Year Later

To: Hannah@HannahFreedmanCommunications.com;
Libby@FreedmanEvents.com
From: Lou@CrushYourComfortZone.com
Subject: Your Anniversary

My dear girls,

This isn't something I usually do—as you know, I designed my challenge for twelve weeks, not twelve months. But you sisters are . . . well, special. And not just because I knew your grandmother.

I'll admit that I wasn't thrilled when you told me you didn't want to work with me on my public relations campaign. Still, I respect y'all for that decision. It would've been so much easier to take the job—but instead, you each chose a new path.

Cheers to you both, and thanks for being my guinea pigs. I hope you learned a thing or two from my little program. Either way I'm proud. And your grandmother would be, too.

—Lou

Epilogue

HANNAH

THE VIEW OF CHICAGO FROM THIRTY-FIVE STORIES OFF THE ground is stunning, especially on a June evening at sunset. I'm sitting in the back of the rooftop venue, watching as Libby says goodbye to the final guests from tonight's event. This was a joint effort, the first time the Freedman sisters have "worked" together since we dissolved the Freedman Group about nine months ago.

It's pushed us way outside of our comfort zones—but it's been worth it.

"Tonight was everything we could have imagined," Preeti says, coming up and giving me a hug.

"Thank you so much for recommending Libby," Serena adds.

"My pleasure," I say, beaming at them. My very first clients, now bestselling authors. "Congratulations—now go enjoy some well-deserved time off!"

Their book released two weeks ago, and I coordinated their media appearances and tour, culminating with this special event here in Chicago. Libby planned an epic, fifty-player

Murder Mystery Dinner, with each guest assigned a different role to play in a fictional case: detective, victim, accomplice, murderer, medical examiner, suspects, and more.

It was fascinating and twisted and morbid—perfect for a bunch of true crime junkies.

Serena and Preeti say goodbye and head out, pausing to thank Libby. She looks gorgeous tonight, wearing a dress that accentuates her curves and her cleavage, her hair and makeup perfectly done. Not to mention, she carries herself like a total boss. If I thought she was good at PR, it's nothing compared to how she's blossomed at the helm of Freedman Events—allowing herself full rein to be creative, to listen to and collaborate with her clients, creating an experience they'll never forget.

The past ten months haven't been easy, though. Dissolving our partnership was more challenging—and more painful—than we could have anticipated. We spent hours having difficult discussions that sometimes got heated or even tearful as we navigated our new dynamic and boundaries. But eventually, through lots of conversation and compromise, we figured out our new paths moving forward.

Selling the company (and all our office furniture) gave us each enough of a nest egg to set out on our own—a teeny, tiny, hummingbird-size nest egg. Just enough cushion to feel comfortable taking some risks. I started my own boutique PR agency for books, focusing on nonfiction and memoirs. I'm a one-woman show, which pushes me outside my comfort zone every day, but it also makes use of my strengths, and I can do it all from the comfort of my own home. Libby, on the other hand, has a gorgeous office space in Old Town with three full-time and five part-time employees (Great Scott was the first one she hired).

My thoughts are interrupted by the feeling of a familiar arm wrapping around my waist.

"You're looking especially beautiful tonight, future wife," Josh says in my ear.

I smile and lean against him. "Same to you, future husband."

As Libby predicted, I *am* engaged this summer, though not to the person she originally hoped. She's warmed up to Josh, though, seeing how he treats me. The wedding will happen this fall; we want Josh's mother to be able to participate before it's too late. It'll be a simple ceremony and an intimate reception—Libby will plan it, of course—followed by a honeymoon to Australia, with Josh finally showing me all the places he loved during his time there.

"I'm really proud of you," Josh says, nodding to Serena and Preeti as they leave. "Both you and Libby."

"Thanks," I say, and give him a kiss.

I'm also proud of me and Josh, for choosing each other, day after day. He still loves working at the aquarium, but he's also exploring positions at a few universities. With my new career, I can work from anywhere, but Josh hasn't taken that for granted. We're both full participants in all discussions of our future.

I glance over to see Adam sitting at a table in the corner, stroking his beard absently and watching Libby with a proud smile on his face. They took things slow at first, rebuilding trust while getting to know each other without any secrets between them. But it didn't take long before they were head over heels for each other. She moved into his apartment last month.

And I know something Libby doesn't: Adam has enlisted

me to help plan an epic proposal in a few months, one that blows every romance novel out of the water. It'll be way over-the-top and totally swoonworthy, just as Libby would like it.

AN HOUR LATER, the venue is clean and everyone else has left; it's just the four of us—Adam and Libby, Josh and me—sitting at a table overlooking the lake, sharing a bottle of champagne before calling it a night.

"I'd like to make a toast," Adam says, raising his glass. "To my talented, smart, beautiful girlfriend, Libby, for planning this amazing event."

"To Libby!" I say, raising my glass and smiling at my sister, who's blushing with pride. "You outdid yourself."

"And to Hannah," Libby cuts in, "for getting me this gig, plus coordinating an incredible book tour for the authors we celebrated tonight."

"Hear, hear," Josh adds, smiling at me. "And to both Libby and Hannah for each taking a big risk this year."

"For crushing our comfort zones," I say.

"And ending up with our crushes!" Libby adds.

Everyone laughs, clinks glasses, and drinks.

"It's hard to believe that it's been a year since we started Lou's program," I say, and Libby nods.

"Was it worth it?" Adam asks us. "Even though you didn't end up with her as a client?"

Libby pretends to ponder that. "Well, it led to us meeting, so I think it was worth it!" He pulls her in for a quick kiss, and then she continues. "But yes, I do think it was helpful. I proved to myself that I can do hard things, and I ended the challenge with a new appreciation for my body and the things it can do."

Adam's eyebrows waggle in a dance, like he's thinking of my sister's body (which is a little icky for me as her sister, even though it's sweet).

"What about you, Banana?" Josh asks me.

I tilt my head, thinking. "Well, my challenge—"

"Which you didn't actually finish," Libby interjects.

I swat at her. "I *know*, I know. But going on those dates did give me more confidence with meeting and interacting with new people, which has helped in my new career."

"Which you are rocking," Libby adds, and Josh agrees with a wholehearted "Absolutely."

Lou's program was just the opening act, that first nudge out of our comfort zones, and it's going to be an ongoing process to keep moving forward. Libby and I are walking our own paths, so every day is a mixture of scary and exciting, but that's life: complicated and messy, beautiful and thrilling.

GiGi used to tell us about the Great Chicago Fire, how the city rebuilt afterward—not just reproducing what was there before, but starting fresh, planning for the future. There's a refusal to be knocked down that's inherent to this city, a willingness to be flexible, to create new opportunities.

Kind of like us. The Freedman Group is gone, but we've used the foundation GiGi gave us to rebuild better than before. To create a life that matches our unique visions, that lets us achieve our individual goals.

To create our own legacy, just like GiGi did.

My eyes prick with tears, which I quickly blink away. My sister must notice, because she reaches her hand across the table and links her pinky with mine as we gaze over the city we both love.

Acknowledgments

First of all, we'd like to thank you, dear reader, for coming on this journey with Libby and Hannah. Right from the beginning of our first discussions about these characters, they've been so close to our hearts—which made writing them easy in some ways but challenging in others. It can be tricky to write about something that you, as the author, are also facing. We knew we'd have to force both sisters to confront their deepest insecurities around body image and mental health, but we didn't want to write a story *centered* on those issues—instead, we wanted to portray them as important aspects of our complicated, messy, beautiful characters. In doing that, we hoped to normalize living with chronic mental illness (with the help of medications and/or therapy) and to portray a plus-size woman who is exercising not to lose weight, but to feel more powerful and confident. We understand that no two people have the same experience with these issues, but we tried to be as authentic as possible, incorporating our own personal experiences and those of our family and friends.

We said this the last time, but it's still true—it really does take a village to bring a book to life! We are so grateful for all the people in ours, starting with our incredible agents, Joanna MacKenzie and Amy Berkower, for always being a phone call or an email away. Thank you to Cindy Hwang for welcoming us into the Berkley family, and to Kerry Donovan for bringing us into our next chapter.

We owe a huge debt of gratitude to Genevieve Gagne-Hawes for being our first reader, before the book was even finished. Your feedback helped make this book what it is, and saved us a lot of time in future revisions!

Writing is not a solo sport, and we are grateful to belong to so many supportive writing communities. A special shout-out to Robin Facer, who suggested making Josh a coral reef researcher (and took our author photo!), and to Mary Chase, who came up with the name "Down & Dirty," plus the whole Ink Tank crew, who helped us brainstorm some very important details of the plot! We're also thankful for the amazing women of the Berkletes, the Women's Fiction Writers Association (where we met!), the Every Damn Day Writers, the 2022 Debuts, and the Eggplant Beach Writers.

Thank you to Amy Gerhartz for the insider information on the Tough Mudder, to Colleen McTaggart for answering a few PR-related questions, to Dale Campbell for the support, and to Nate Godfrey for being our paparazzi in Chicago, showing us how high he can jump, and making our research trip so much more fun. (Also, thank you for putting Alison's table together, and watching the football game on mute so we could book-talk.)

We are grateful for the friendship and support of so many authors we admire, including but not limited to: Suzanne Park (who let us borrow the name Suji), Kathleen West, Lyn Liao Butler, Kimmery Martin, Lainey Cameron, Lisa Barr, Renée Rosen, Emily Henry, Christina Hobbs, Lauren Billings, Colleen Oakley, Nancy Johnson, Julie Carrick Dalton, Megan Collins, Kathleen Barber, Kristin Harmel, Patti Callahan Henry, Kristy Woodson Harvey, Amy Mason Doan, Tiffany Yates Martin, Orly Konig, Rochelle Weinstein, Laura Drake, Barbara Claypole White, Heather Webb, Danielle Jackson, Liz Fenton, Lisa Steinke, Camille Pagán, Ali Hazelwood, Zibby Owens, Emily Wibberley, and all of the @Friends_of_AliBradyBooks.

We'd like to thank the entire Berkley team: Claire Zion, Jeanne-Marie Hudson, Craig Burke, Angela Kim, Jessica Plummer, Daché Rogers, Mary Baker, Jennifer Lynes, Lindsey Tulloch, Ashley Tucker, Yahaira Lawrence, Eileen Chetti, and of course, Sarah Oberrender and Michael Crampton for working so hard to create the perfect cover! Thank you to Celeste Montano and the team at Writers House and to the team at Nelson Literary Agency. And many thanks to Kathleen Carter for helping to get more eyes on this book!

FROM ALISON

Bradeigh, Bradeigh, Bradeigh. Where do I begin . . . Thank you for marching forth with me, for steaming up my sex scenes, pushing me, inspiring me, and picking up the slack when I'm at the end of my rope. Your friendship and partnership mean the world to me, and there's no one else I'd rather write a book or drive four hours in the middle of the night with. I would be nothing without the support and encouragement of my friends and my family. The family I was born into: my mom, Kathy Hammer; my dad, Dr. Randy Hammer; and my little/big sister, Elizabeth Murray (my original NTNT partner in crime and baker of the RFGSCCs); my extended family (the Lewins, Bergers, Hammers, Blocks, and Kirbys). The family we've collected along the way: Nick Murray, Dylan Murray, Alex "Bear Bear" Murray, Louie Murray, and Carlene Jarrett. The friends who are the family I chose: My Girls, Meg McKeen, D.J. Johnson, Kristie Raymer, Julie Johnson, Krissie Callahan, #LibbyLove, Michelle Dash, Katie Ross, Mia Phifer, Jenna Leopold, Shana Freedman, Christina Williams, Robbie Manning, Beth Gosnell, Leah Conner, and Stephen Kellogg. Thanks to Pierrette Hazkial, Avi Pinchevsky, Lauren Lenart, and Kristin Zuccarini for your friendship and support. To the Rock Boat Family, the Rock by the Sea family, and the BoatCast podcast crew, thank you all for the never-ending support. And finally, to the Godfrey crew: thank you for letting me be an extended part of your family. I'm the luckiest.

FROM BRADEIGH

Alison, I couldn't be more grateful to be on this journey together. This book was a challenge for us in some ways, but we did it and I'm so proud of how it turned out. Nothing compares to the magic of creating a story with you—our two heads together are exponentially better than our two heads separately. I'm looking forward to many more novels, many more book tours, but hopefully no more grungy motel rooms with ONLY ONE BED. I'm lucky to have wonderful friends who celebrate every milestone with me, including my Murray Moms (Amanda Habel, Amy Rex, Erin Wiggins, Kellie Terry, Stephanie Higbee, and Suzanne James), as well as Susan Barton and Ashley Melgar. I'm grateful to the Women Physician Writers and Physician Mom Book Club for the support and inspiration (special shout-out to Lane Patten!). My Bookstagram community is so special, and while there are too many accounts to name, I hope you all know how much I adore you (especially my Bookish Ladies Club). I'm eternally grateful to my parents (Merrie and Jim Smithson) and siblings (Ellie and McLean) for always supporting my crazy dreams and schemes. I'm so lucky to have birthed four of the coolest humans on the planet; huge thanks to my children for understanding when Mom disappears into her writing room for hours on end. And to Nate: you're my everything. Thank you for being exactly who I need. Also: you know which parts of Josh's character are inspired by you!

And a little more from both of us: Last summer, we were lucky enough to be able to go on tour for our debut novel, *The Beach Trap*. It was a dream being able to meet so many readers and booksellers in person. Thanks to the stores that hosted us: Magers & Quinn in Minneapolis, the King's English in Salt Lake City, the Novel Neighbor in St. Louis, Volumes Bookstore in Chicago, Anderson's Bookshop in Naperville, Sundog Books in Seaside, the Ripped Bodice in LA, A Capella Books in Atlanta, M. Judson Booksellers in Greenville, and Litchfield Books on Pawleys Island. A special thanks to our friend Annissa Armstrong for the pastries for our long late-night drive!

We attended our first Book Bonanza event this year and can't wait for the one this summer! Thank you to Colleen Hoover for inviting us, and to Susan Rossman, Stephanie Spillane, and all the unicorns who make the magic happen. And to Kristin Prentiss Ott and everyone with the Savannah Book Festival, and Amy Danzer with Chicago Printers Row Lit Fest.

We would also like to thank the Bookstagrammers, Book-Tokkers, bloggers, and everyone on social media who put our book in front of potential readers. We're grateful for this entire community, especially the Bookish Ladies Club, Andrea Katz of Great Thoughts' Great Readers, Kristy Barrett of A

Novel Bee, Sue Peterson, Robin Kall of Reading With Robin, Jenna Paone and the team at A Mighty Blaze, Ashley Hasty, Ashley Spivey, Cindy Burnett of Thoughts from a Page, Courtney Marzilli with Books Are Chic, Lauren Margoline, the Good Book Fairy, and of course, Meg Walker and the Fab Four of Friends & Fiction.

An extra thank-you for any reader who picked up their copy of *The Beach Trap* or *The Comeback Summer* from an independent bookstore. Booksellers are the unsung heroes of the publishing industry, and we are grateful for all they do to bring authors and readers together. A special shout-out to Kimberly and Rebecca George, Mary Mollman, Loring Kemp, Laura Taylor, Stephanie Skees, Savannah Emory, Olivia Meletes-Morris, Wendy Meletes, Dallas Strawn, Annie Metcalf, Laura White, Laney Blanchard, Ann Holman, Calvin Crosby and Rob Eckman, Maxwell Gregory, Pamela Klinger-Horn, Ginny Wehrli-Hemmeter, June Wilcox, Teresa Lynch, and Mary Webber O'Malley.

And last but certainly not least: our readers. Thank you for picking up a copy of our book. None of this would be possible without you. We love hearing from you—so find us online at alibradybooks.net and on Instagram @AliBradyBooks.

Here's to crushing your comfort zones!

—Alison & Bradeigh
aka Ali Brady

THE

Comeback SUMMER

Ali Brady

READERS GUIDE

Questions for Discussion

1. Lou's Crush Your Comfort Zone program is all about pushing boundaries and getting out of your comfort zone. What challenge do you think Lou would give you? Would you ever do a challenge like that?

2. As the older sister, Libby feels a lot of responsibility for Hannah, and Hannah doesn't want to disappoint her big sister. Where in your family's birth order do you fall, and does it have an impact on your life and your relationships?

3. The book takes place in Chicago—what role does the city and its history play in the story?

4. Libby hates second-chance love stories because she thinks that whatever ended the relationship the first time has not changed or gone away. Do you think Hannah and Josh have resolved their issues? Will their relationship stand the test of time?

5. What do you think about Adam's reaction when he found out what Libby did, posing as Hannah? Would you be able to forgive someone who did that to you?

6. Hannah likes to prepare for the worst; Libby wants to hope for the best. Which sister are you more like? How does that impact the way you interact with the world?

7. How did Libby's relationship with her body change over the course of the book? What lessons did she learn?

8. Josh is reluctant to tell Hannah about his ADHD and Hannah rarely talks about her anxiety because they both worry people might judge them. How do you think we can continue to normalize medication and therapy for these types of issues?

9. What do you think GiGi would think of where Libby and Hannah ended up? Would she be disappointed or proud?

10. Last but not least, is Mr. Darcy a devil or a delight?

CONTINUE READING FOR A SPECIAL PREVIEW
OF THE NEXT NOVEL BY ALI BRADY

Camp People

FROM BERKLEY!

Jessie

WHEN I TOOK THE JOB AS CAMP DIRECTOR AT CAMP CHICKA-
wah, the first thing that surprised me was all the work that
goes on during the off-season. Even though I'd been a counselor for four summers, and a camper for twelve summers before that, I sort of assumed that it all shut down after everyone
left, like a carnival when it's over. But it soon became apparent
that the off-season was just as busy as the summer, albeit in
different ways.

The prior camp directors, Nathaniel and Lola, compared
it to theater: the summer is our eight-week run and the rest of
the year is all the work leading up to it—sets, costumes, rehearsal. Without the months of preparation, the entire per-
formance will fail.

Usually, I love this time. It's rejuvenating and relaxing, sen-
sible and systematic. But this year, with the property up for
sale and the last summer at Camp Chickawah looming ahead,
I'm having trouble keeping my spirits up.

"You okay, boss?" Dot asks as we walk across the big lawn
in the center of camp.

My assistant camp director has seemed concerned about me lately, and I don't want her to be. She has enough to worry about on her own—just like me, she'll have to find a new job after the camp closes.

So I force a smile and say, "Just a little tired. After we finish here, let's head back to the office. You check the boys' cabins, I'll do the girls'?"

"You got it," she says, tromping off toward the north end of camp.

Today's our last day on the property for the season, our last chance to make sure everything is winterized. Soon camp will be covered in a blanket of snow that won't melt until April. We'll spend the winter in town, sprucing up our website and social media presence, hiring counselors and staff, before opening to enrollment in February. Then it's a whirlwind of processing registration until we return to the camp in April to start prepping for summer. The *last* summer, I remind myself.

Stuffing my hands in my pockets, I head down the path that leads to the girls' area. My boots crunch through fallen leaves; they're dry and brittle, just like my mood. It's chilly today, a damp cold that seeps into your bones, but that's preferable to the icy dread in my stomach. Every time we check something off the list of tasks, it's a reminder that this is the last time we'll do it. The last time our handyman, Mr. Billy, will repair the old wooden shingles on the Arts & Crafts cabin, the last time Dot will inspect the watercraft for damage, the last time I'll count how many bows and arrows survived the season and how many I'll need to order for next year.

The first girls' cabin comes into view, with the others nestled in the pine trees behind it. They're all more than a hundred years old, each with a big front porch leading into a large main room with a peaked roof. During the summer, the porch railings are covered with drying towels and bathing suits, but today they're empty and barren. I wonder if the next owner of this land will save any of these buildings or if they'll just bulldoze everything, oblivious to the fact that a century of memories are contained in these cabins. The thought of all of that being erased makes me physically sick.

I climb the steps to the first cabin, open the door, and walk inside. The light is dim—we've pulled the shades on all the windows—and the air smells like pine and sap. My boots echo on the wood floor as I walk between the rows of bunk beds, six on each side. Stripped bare like this, they remind me of skeletons. I might be feeling a little melodramatic, though. *Focus*, I remind myself, and pull out my final inspection sheet.

Briskly, I check the beds, the mattresses, the blinds, crossing them off the list. Then I move from cabin to cabin, trying to avoid the onslaught of memories in each one. Cabin Two, where I stayed as a nervous eight-year-old. Cabin Four, which I pranked as a feisty twelve-year-old by putting sand in their sleeping bags. Cabin Six, where I was assigned for my first summer as an enthusiastic new counselor.

And Cabin Eight: my home each summer from ages nine through sixteen.

A strange feeling runs through me, a shimmering sort of déjà vu, when I reach the bunk I always shared with Hillary Goldstein. So many nights spent whispering as everyone fell asleep, sharing our secret crushes or plotting our next prank. I preferred the top bunk and Hillary liked the bottom because she could use her extra blankets to create a sort of canopy for herself. Standing on tiptoe, I push the top mattress to the side and there it is, carved into a wood slat: *Hillary and Jessie* BFFAEAE. Best friends forever and ever and ever.

Hillary was horrified when she saw what I'd done, certain that our counselor would find out and we'd be punished with toilet cleaning duty for a month. But our counselor never said a word, and I thought I'd outsmarted her; later, when I became a counselor myself, I learned the art of benign neglect— knowing when to allow campers to safely test limits, and when to intervene.

A wistfulness comes over me, almost like homesickness, which makes sense because camp felt like my home. As a child of divorced parents, I grew up moving from my mom's house to my dad's every week, so camp was the first time in my life I'd spent eight weeks sleeping in the same bed, hanging out with the same people, following the same schedule. My camp family felt more stable than my real family.

Especially Hillary. Every summer we'd be inseparable, and during the rest of the year we'd send letters or emails and eventually text messages when we got our own phones. Even though we lived hundreds of miles apart—she in Chicago and me in Minneapolis—we managed to have a few visits here and there. Those were fun, but nothing compared to returning to camp each summer. That first big hug. Running to claim our bunk together. Knowing that we had eight entire weeks stretching out in front of us.

It's strange to realize that Hillary has an entirely separate, adult life now. I still think of her as that round-faced girl with the sparkling brown eyes who'd always go along with my schemes—including our plan to become camp counselors together after our first year at college.

Of course, that didn't happen. She took an internship with her dad, who's the CEO of some big, fancy company. It was crushing at the time, but I learned an important lesson: camp friends aren't forever friends. Camp life isn't real life. For most people, it's somewhere they go for a break from reality, an escape from the real world. Whereas for me? It's my entire world.

My eyes fill with tears and I brush them away with the back of my hand. Quickly, I finish my checklist and head out of the musty cabin into the cool afternoon air.

Still, that sense of homesickness follows me. All my camp friends, all the counselors I've worked with over the years, have moved on while I've stayed here. I've always told myself that that was okay because I'm doing something important, something that's made a difference in the lives of hundreds of children. But once all this is gone and erased, will anything I've done here matter?

WHEN I GET to the office, Dot is already there, staring at her ancient PC with a scowl on her face. The director's office is cozy and quaint, filled with handmade wood furniture that dates back to the original camp.

It's also the only place on property that has internet, and my phone buzzes in my pocket as my alerts come in. I pull it out to see texts from my parents. Mom has sent an update on the kitchen remodel she and my stepdad, Mitch, are working on: The cabinets are finally in! Don't they look beautiful? They moved to California after my younger half siblings Milo and Colin graduated from high school. Dad has sent a picture of him and my stepmom, Amanda, with my twin half sisters after their high school basketball game: 72 to 47! They both played great.

I tap out a quick text to each of them and promise I'll Face-Time later tonight. I'm feeling too gloomy to chat now. My parents are good about keeping in touch, but sometimes it's just a reminder that I don't fully fit in either of their families. The only place I've ever fit is camp, and it's not going to be here much longer.

"What're you working on?" I ask Dot while hanging up my coat, hat, and scarf.

"Budget," Dot says. Her brow is furrowed with worry. "Money's gonna be tight this year."

"At least we won't have to worry about keeping a slush fund for unexpected expenses at the end of the summer, right?"

She harrumphs. "Got an email from Jack Valentine this morning. They've accepted an offer on the property and they're officially under contract."

My body stiffens. I knew this was coming—Jack and Mary, children of the prior camp owners, never loved this place like their parents did—but it still hurts to hear the words.

"Oh," I say, trying to keep my voice neutral.

"Those two little rat bastards," Dot says gruffly.

I stifle a bitter laugh, thinking of Jack's beady black eyes. They are rather ratlike. "Well, it's thanks to Mary that the closing of the sale is being delayed until the fall, so I'm not sure she should be included in that."

"She allows her rat bastard brother to walk all over her, which makes her a rat bastard enabler, which is just as bad." Dot clicks her fingers on the keyboard, punctuating each word. "Nathaniel and Lola must be rolling in their graves knowing that their children are throwing this place away. But Jack was never a camp person, not ever."

My eyebrows shoot up, hearing the ultimate insult from

Dot. In her mind, you're either a camp person . . . or not. And if you're not? You're worse than pond scum.

Continuing with this conversation will only make me sadder, so I walk over to the huge bulletin board on the far wall This is where Nathaniel and Lola stuck letters and cards they received from campers over the years, and I've kept up the tradition. Maybe I'm just torturing myself, but I want to see something positive right now. Something to prove that what we've done here matters.

I love all the drawings sent from campers of their favorite places—like a crayon rendering of Cabin Eleven signed, in blocky letters, *RYAN AGE 9* and a pencil sketch of the big tree near the archery area with *to Nathaniel and Lola from Kat S* written in careful cursive. There are graduation announcements and even a few wedding invitations from people who met their future spouse at camp, either as campers or as counselors. And most of all, dozens upon dozens of handwritten thank-you notes from former campers, now adults.

Camp Chickawah will always be my favorite place in the world, one reads. Another one says, *Thank you for making my childhood so magical.* Another: *All my most important life lessons were learned at camp.*

Card after card expresses gratitude and appreciation, which I expected. But there's something else, too, something I've never noticed before: yearning. An intense longing to return.

I wish I could come back to camp. I know that's impossible, but the place meant so much to me.

I wish I could capture the magic of camp as an adult.

If I could have one wish, it would be to experience just one day of camp again.

And a spark begins to form in my mind.

I TELL MY idea to Dot over lunch. We're sitting in the dining hall, which is a big empty cavern right now with all the tables and benches stacked against the wall. Mr. Billy has joined us for a meal of spaghetti with canned marinara sauce and microwaved frozen green beans—the last food we have in the kitchen.

"An adult summer camp?" Dot says, mulling it over.

"Exactly!" I nod, too quickly, and force myself to slow down; there's no way I can do this without her buy-in.

"I don't know, sounds complicated. What do we know about entertaining adults?"

"We don't have to entertain them," I say. "They just want to reexperience camp."

"Like?"

"Everything! Swimming in the lake, campfire songs, all of it. We could do the nostalgic activities everyone loves: the canoe parade, the camp musical, color wars."

"We'd have to have better food," Dot says, twirling spaghetti around her fork. "Like, with an actual chef. Adults aren't going to go for sloppy joes and soggy French toast."

"True."

"And booze," she adds. "Adults would want to drink, and that would get expensive."

This is a good point, and I take a bite of green beans as I ponder this. Our finances are already tight.

"But we wouldn't need counselors," I say. "That would save a ton of money—not to mention all the time spent hiring and training."

"Definitely would cut down on staff," Dot says, nodding.

"Mr. Billy, do you have any thoughts?" I ask.

He looks up from his plate of spaghetti and gives a grunt and a brisk nod, which I take as supportive.

"Adults wouldn't be able to come to camp all summer, though," Dot says to me. "They have jobs and responsibilities, kids of their own."

"Yeah. But we don't have to do a full eight-week session. Adults could come for a week, right?"

Dot nods. "I'd assume so."

"Mr. Billy, what do you think?" I say, turning to him. "Weekly sessions of adult camp with gourmet meals and booze included."

He takes a big bite of spaghetti, chews it, and swallows, then finally says, "Might work."

Two words out of Mr. Billy? That's a good sign. I look over at Dot, who raises her eyebrows like she's impressed.

For the first time since getting the news that the camp is being sold, I feel a glimmer of optimism. The thought of trudging through one last summer of kids' camp felt depressing, but doing something different, something nostalgic for former campers? It would be like a reunion. That is, if we could pull it off. Maybe no one would want to come.

"I don't even know where to start with this," I say.

Dot shrugs. "I guess the first thing is to see if anyone's interested in coming. Test the waters."

"Do you still have contact information for former campers?"

"Some of 'em," Dot says. "But I could work on gathering the rest. You know a lot of those campers set up Facebook groups to keep in touch. It'd be easy to ask for email addresses from everyone."

I look out over the empty dining hall and imagine what it

could look like filled with adults instead of kids. Not just any adults, though—a big, boisterous group of former campers who understand the magic of this place, who know all the songs and remember the traditions. It would be truly epic. For the first time in weeks, a genuine smile spreads across my face.

"If you start working on that," I say to Dot, "then I'll start drafting an email to send."

If we have to say goodbye to Camp Chickawah, this feels like the perfect way.

To: CampChickawahCampers ListServe
From: JPederson@CampChickawah.com
Subject: One last summer

Hello, former campers and friends!
Jessie here with some good news, and some sad news.

I'll start with the sad news—because like Nurse Penny always said, *You gotta rip off the Band-Aid and get back on the horse!* (In hindsight, I'm pretty sure she was mixing up two different sayings, but she meant well, and we all survived!)

Anyway, the sad news is that Jack and Mary Valentine have made the difficult decision to sell the Camp Chickawah property, which means this summer will be our very last.

But now for the good news—at least, the potential good news. As the current camp director, I'm thinking of trying something different this summer, and inviting past campers to spend a week at an adults-only camp.

Think of it as a walk down memory lane, a chance to say goodbye to a place that was so special in our lives. Or just a fun way to unplug from everyday life and get back to basics for a week. As Nathaniel used to say: the campfires may burn out, but the memories last forever.

Right now, I'm just gauging interest, so if this sounds like something you'd be interested in, please let me know.

Hope to see some of you at camp this summer!

Jessie Pederson
Director, Camp Chickawah

Photo by Robin Facer

Ali Brady is the pen name of writing BFFs Alison Hammer and Bradeigh Godfrey. Their debut novel, *The Beach Trap*, was featured in multiple "best of summer" lists, including the *Washington Post*, the *Wall Street Journal*, *Parade*, and Katie Couric Media. *The Comeback Summer* is their second book together. Alison lives in Chicago, where she works as an SVP creative director for an advertising agency. She has no kids, pets, or plants, but she does have two solo books, *You and Me and Us* and *Little Pieces of Me*. Bradeigh lives in Utah with her husband, four children, and dog. She works as a doctor and is the author of the psychological thrillers *Imposter* and *The Followers*.

CONNECT ONLINE

AliBradyBooks
AliBradyBooks
AliBradyBooks